CUT TO:
BAKER STREET

BY

NICKO VAUGHAN

Paperback ISBN 978-1-78705-384-7
ePub ISBN 978-1-78705-385-4
PDF ISBN 978-1-78705-386-1

Published by MX Publishing
335 Princess Park Manor, Royal Drive,
London, N11 3GX
www.mxpublishing

WELCOME

I hope this handy little guide to the on-screen adventures of Sherlock Holmes and Doctor Watson will provide you with a useful reference to the many film, television and Internet depictions of the Great Detective and his Boswell.

This book explores films from the early silent actors, such as Georges Tréville and Eille Norwood who graced the silver screen in the 1900s, to the contemporary television capers of Benedict Cumberbatch, who helped entice a younger audience over to the Holmes stories.

Inside you will find a wide-ranging collection of adaptations which have helped bring Holmes and Watson to life. Although some of these may be familiar to many Sherlock fans, I hope that there are also some new and interesting adventures within the pages of this book.

Written by Nicko Vaughan

Illustrations by Georgia Grace Weston

Additional illustrations provided by the artists at Dreamstime.com

ACKNOWLEDGEMENTS

With thanks to all of the Sherlock Holmes fans who have kept me sane, and fed me information. For Glenn, who continues to make me tea and for Sarah and her bionic eyes. With eternal thanks to mum and dad who do more than a book acknowledgment has space for.

Index

The Adventure of the Mazarin Stone
Television - 1951 (UK)

Writer: Anthony Cope
Director: Alan Bromly
Sherlock Holmes: Andrew Osborn
Doctor Watson: Philip King

Little is written about this BBC television adaptation which was broadcast as part of the "For the Children" portion of the BBC schedule which showed programmes targeted at school children. No footage has survived, but the narrative was faithful to the Conan Doyle original with Sherlock Holmes inviting a suspected jewel thief into 221b Baker Street in order to confirm the location of the stolen Mazarin Stone. In this story he once again utilises a wax figure of himself, as he did in *The Empty House,* (although this one is fashioned by Tavernier, and not Monsieur Oscar Meunier, of Grenoble) to fool murderous thieves into revealing that they are holding the precious stone. He does this by introducing the seated wax figure to the suspect, Count Negretto Sylvius, and then swapping himself for the dummy as the Count and his accomplice, Sam Merton, believe he is in the bedroom playing his violin. Having swapped places with the dummy, Holmes is able to overhear their conversation and discover that the Count has the stone in his pocket.

Trivia: This was the only time that Andrew Osborn and Philip King would play Holmes and Watson.

The Adventure of Sherlock Holmes' Smarter brother
Film - 1975 (USA)

Writer: Gene Wilder
Director: Gene Wilder
Sherlock Holmes: Douglas Wilmer
Doctor Watson: Thorley Walters

This high-energy comedy was Gene Wilder's directorial debut and has him playing the character Sigerson Holmes (a name some Sherlockians would associate more with Sherlock Holmes's father), the younger brother of Sherlock.

Jealous and bitter about his brother's fame and convinced he is a better detective, Sigerson takes the case of the stolen documents which have been swiped from Foreign Secretary Lord Redcliff's safe. Jenny Hill, a music hall singer, arrives at the apartment of Sigerson claiming she is being blackmailed by Eduardo Gambetti. After two attempts are made on her life, Hill becomes too frightened to continue with the investigation but Sigerson seduces her into giving him more information. She reveals that she had stolen the documents from Redcliff's safe and that he is her father, however, upon meeting Sigerson, Redcliff claims that Hill is not his daughter, but his fiancée. Gambetti makes a deal to sell Moriarty the stolen documents and offers to exchange them for money during one of his performances, but Sigerson arrives and he and Moriarty duel with swords as Moriarty mocks him for not being as good as his brother, Sherlock. As Sigerson is defeated, he hands over the document to Moriarty (who later falls from a ledge into the Thames) but the documents are a fake and the real ones are left to be found by Sherlock Holmes. Later, Hill confesses that she couldn't marry Redcliff and vows to stay with Sigerson.

Connection: The actor playing Sherlock Holmes, Douglas Wilmer, played Holmes previously in the 1964 television series *Sherlock Holmes* and again in 1964 in an episode of the television series *Detective*.

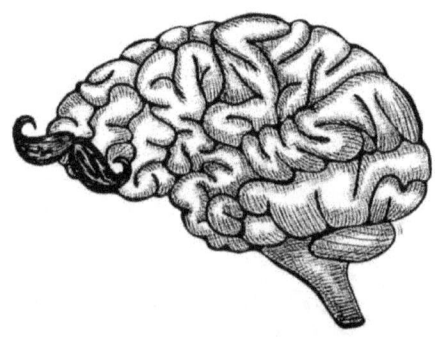

The Adventure of Sherlock Holmes'
Smarter brother

The Adventures of Jamie Watson and Sherlock Holmes
Internet - 2014-2016 (USA)

Writers: Shannen Michaelsen, Sara-Renee Weatherby & Colleen Marie Siler
Directors: Shannen Michaelsen, Cassy Ledger, Christie Valentin-Bati & Sara-Renee Weatherby
Sherlock Holmes: Shannen Michaelsen
Doctor Watson: Sara-Renee Weatherby

A low-budget web series broadcast on YouTube from 2014, made by the short-lived production company Remarkable Singular Curious Productions. This contemporary version of Holmes and Watson is not only gender flipped (both lead characters are played by women) but also has characters identifying as bisexual, asexual and aromantic. Set at SAC University, the web series evolved from Vlog pieces to camera to slightly longer, more intricate episodes of case-solving with their roots based in the original Conan Doyle works.

Interview: From their Indiegogo funding site the creators wrote, "Our Watson is bisexual and our Holmes is asexual, and we know that having two queer characters in starring roles (especially two characters that explicitly identify as two less recognized sexual identities) is a big deal."
A full episode list can be found in the "Television Episodes" chapter of this book

Adventures of Sherlock Holmes AKA Held for Ransom
Film - 1905 (USA)

Writer: Theodore A. Liebler Jr.
Director: J. Stuart Blackton
Sherlock Holmes: Gilbert M. Anderson
Doctor Watson: H. Kyrle Bellew

This 9-minute silent film (725 feet) is regarded as the first real attempts to film one of Conan Doyle's original stories and the only time Gilbert M. Anderson would play Sherlock Holmes. Later he would become the first star of Western/cowboy movies under the moniker Bronco Billy. Made by Vitagraph Studios, the story is very loosely based on The Sign of Four. A gang of criminals kidnaps a millionaire's daughter and signs their ransom note as "The Sign of Four." The father, in a blind panic, finds Sherlock Holmes and begs for him to help find his precious daughter. Holmes meets with the gang under the guise of handing over the money and the gang attempts to attack Holmes. However, he escapes and manages to free the daughter. Holmes and Watson return to Baker Street with the girl and reunite her with a very happy father.

Review: This more active and frenetic early film version of Holmes was commented on by Robert Pohle in Liberty Magazine where he wrote, "Deprived of his voice in those early silent films, Holmes was also transformed from an intellectual, armchair detective into a more kinetic action figure — almost a sort of cowboy-in-deerstalker."

The Adventures of Sherlock Holmes
Film - 1921 (UK)

Writer: William J. Elliott
Director: Maurice Elvey
Sherlock Holmes: Eille Norwood
Doctor Watson: Hubert Willis

This is the first batch of 15 silent Sherlock Holmes titles, made by Stoll Picture Productions in the UK, starring Eille Norwood and Hubert Willis as the iconic detective duo. Not much is written about a large portion of these films as many titles are unavailable due to non-viewable formats or poor quality. Willis played alongside Norwood for the majority of the Sherlock Holmes films with the exception of The Sign of Four in 1923 when the role was played by Arthur M. Cullin.

The Dying Detective
Released: April 1921

The Devil's Foot
Released: April 1921

A Case of Identity
Released: April 1921

The Yellow Face
Released: April 1921

The Red-Headed League
Released: April 1921

The Resident Patient
Released: April 1921

A Scandal in Bohemia
Released: April 1921

The Man with the Twisted Lip
Released: April 1921

The Beryl Coronet
Released: April 1921

The Noble Bachelor
Released: April 1921

The Copper Beeches
Released: April 1921

The Empty House
Released: April 1921

The Tiger of San Pedro
Released: April 1921

The Priory School
Released: April 1921

The Solitary Cyclist
Released: April 1921

Trivia: Norwood threw himself into the role and enjoyed disguising himself on set. His taxi driver disguise was so convincing, for example, that he was almost thrown off the movie set by the managing director for being an interloper.

The Adventures of Sherlock Holmes
Film - 1939 (USA)

Writers: Edwin Blum, William Absalom Drake
& William Gillette
Director: Alfred L. Werker
Sherlock Homes: Basil Rathbone
Doctor Watson: Nigel Bruce

Released under the title Sherlock Holmes in the UK, this film is loosely based on William Gillette's play of the same name – although very little of the original plot survives within the movie.

The film starts with Moriarty having just been acquitted of murder due to lack of evidence and he and Holmes swap barbs and insults as Holmes remarks that he would like to see Moriarty's brain pickled in a jar at the London Medical Society. Back at Baker Street they are visited by Ann Brandon who explains that her brother has received a drawing of a man with a bird (albatross) hanging around his neck and that her father also received the same before he was murdered. As Holmes and Watson hurry to find her brother, they discover he has already been brutally murdered. After deducing that Ann might be the next victim, Holmes disguises himself as an entertainer and attends her garden party. During the party he hears Ann's cries for help in a park and rushes to her side, capturing the attacker. The man, Gabriel Mateo, claims to be seeking revenge, with the help of Moriarty, after a dispute over a mine in South America saw his father murdered by Ann's father. At the mention of Moriarty's name Holmes deduces that the case is nothing but a distraction and he realises that his real plan is to steal the Crown Jewels. At the Tower of London Holmes intercepts Moriarty and the pair fight resulting in the Professor falling into the Thames, presumed dead.

Trivia: This was the final film to be produced by Twentieth Century Fox as well as being the last of the series to be set in Victorian England.

The Adventures of Sherlock Holmes
Television - 1984 – 1985 (UK)

Writers: Various
Directors: Various
Sherlock Holmes: Jeremy Brett
Doctor Watson: David Burke

The collective name given to the first two series of Granada Television's adaptations of the Conan Doyle stories, broadcast on ITV. The iconic Jeremy Brett's Holmes alongside the original casting of David Burke as Watson, played out the Victorian detective duo in some of Doyle's classic adventures, sticking as closely as possible to the original narrative. However, there are some marked differences, for example, the ending of *The Red-Headed League* included a scene of with a disgruntled Moriarty (Eric Porter) as a lead into the episode, *The Final Problem*.

Trivia: As well as trying to stay faithful to the narrative, the show also took the time to match scenes to the original Sidney Paget drawings from The Strand magazine which is the reason why this is one of the few adaptations to not have Holmes continually dressed in a deerstalker and Inverness coat. A full episode list can be found in the "Television Episodes" chapter of this book

The Adventures of Sherlock Howser: Doogie Howser M.D
Television - 1993 (USA)

Writers: David E. Kelley, Steven Bochco & Elaine Aronson
Director: Paul Robert Newman
Sherlock Holmes: Neil Patrick Harris
Doctor Watson: Max Casella

Episode 16, season 4 of the hit television series *Doogie Howser M.D* (broadcast January 20th 1993 on the ABC network), a show about a genius child who works as a doctor in the ER, sees the young Doogie Howser trying to examine his broken heart.
Doogie and Nurse Faber settle down to watch an old Basil Rathbone Sherlock Holmes movie as they snuggle on the sofa. When he offers her a pair Springsteen tickets she turns him down because she has a date that night. Dejected inwardly but reassuring her that he understands their relationship is very "casual," he says goodnight and goes back to the movie alone.

Doogie then puts himself into a Rathbone-era Sherlock Holmes mystery and tries to use Holmes's logic to figure out the parameters of his romantic entanglement. This black and white fantasy footage is spliced into the normal episode as Doogie Howser tries to figure out where he stands with Nurse Faber and if he wants their relationship to be more exclusive. Most of the episode concerns Doogie asking various friends and work

colleagues about relationships and love with the black and white Holmes narrative sparsely used.

Trivia: Although original in its narrative, this episode of Doogie Howser M.D does use lines from Conan Doyle's original stories as well as footage from the 1939 Rathbone and Bruce film *The Adventures of Sherlock Holmes*.

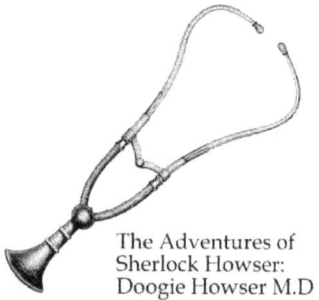

The Adventures of
Sherlock Howser:
Doogie Howser M.D

The Adventures of OG Sherlock Kush
Animation - 2015 - 2016 (USA)

Writer: Joseph Carnegie
Director: Ben Jones
Sherlock Kush: Peter Serafinowicz
Doctor Watson: Rich Fulcher

This low budget web series, which was produced by ADHD studios, also aired on the digital channel FXX in 2015, but the characters were first introduced in October 2014 during an episode of the show *Lucas Bros. Moving Co.* These short animations involve Holmes and Watson attempting to solve crimes but their progress is continually hampered by Sherlock's taste for marijuana.

Connection: Actor Peter Serafinowicz had briefly played Sherlock Holmes in a sketch from episode one of his BBC2 comedy series *The Peter Serafinowicz Show* which aired on October 4th 2007 alongside Alex Lowe playing Watson.

A full episode list can be found in the "Television Episodes" chapter of this book

The Adventures of Steel Rod Holmes
Film - 1977 (USA)

Writers: Todd Jacobsen & Scott Allen Nollen
Director: Scott Allen Nollen
Sherlock Holmes: Scott Allen Nollen
Doctor Watson: Troy Jacobsen

This 4-minute short, filmed in Iowa, centres around Sherlock Holmes and his son, Steel "Rod" Holmes who, along with Doctor Watson, try to bring to justice a notorious serial killer. Writer and actor Scott Allen Nollen also wrote and starred in another Sherlock Holmes short a year later called "Sherlock Holmes and Moriarty's Secret Weapon."

Trivia: Between 1976 and 2018 Scott Allen Nolen directed 60 films and music videos.

Arsène Lupin contra Sherlock Holmes
(Arsène Lupin against Sherlock Holmes)
Film - 1910-1911 (Germany)

Writer: Uncredited
Director: Viggo Larsen
Sherlock Holmes: Viggo Larsen
Doctor Watson: N/A

A collection of five silent movies produced by Deutsche Vitaskop GmbH Productions which pits Sherlock Holmes against Arsène Lupin, a gentleman thief and master of disguise. The character was created by the French writer Maurice Leblanc who serialized his adventures in the magazine Je sais tout. The titles of the silent movies released under the Lupin contra Sherlock Holmes banner are:

Der Alte Sekretar AKA The Old Secretary, also known as "Arsène Lupin", released August 20th, 1910 - 1133 feet

Der Blaue Diamant AKA The Blue Diamond, released September 17th, 1910 - 1415 feet

Die Falschen Rembrandts AKA The Fake Rembrandts, also known as "The Two Rembrandts," released October 7th, 1910 - 968 feet

Die Flucht AKA The Escape, released December 24th, 1910 - 1122 feet

Arsène Lupin's Ende AKA The End of Arsène Lupin, released March 4th, 1911 (although some believe the date to be April 22nd) - 880 feet.

Trivia: Although famed amongst Sherlock Holmes fans for his work depicting the great detective, Larsen also appeared in 140 films and directed 235 during his career.

Baker Street
Internet – 2015 (Canada)

Writers: Hannah Drew & Karen Slater
Director: MK Morris
Sherlock Holmes: Hannah Drew
Doctor Watson: Karen Slater

This short-run web series, which ran on YouTube, mixes live-action narrative with vlogs and pieces to camera by Jane Watson. The web episodes focus on Watson, a medical school dropout who has come back to her home town of Toronto, and her new flat mate Sherlock Holmes who is messy, highly intelligent and likes to solve mysteries. As well as swapping the genders of the main characters (Holmes and Watson are both female) the writing leans heavily towards the BBC show *Sherlock* rather than the original Conan Doyle Canon, even featuring slightly altered lines from the original Gattis and Moffat scripts.

Trivia: Although a second season was written, it was never made. One of the reasons given was that some members of the cast joined an actor's union which prevented, or greatly inhibited, their ability to work with team members who were not unionised. The scripts were, however, released online.

A full episode list can be found in the "Television Episodes" chapter of this book

The Baker Street Boys
Television - 1983 (UK)

Writers: Richard Carpenter & Anthony Read
Directors: Marilyn Fox, Michael Kerrigan
Sherlock Holmes: Roger Ostime
Doctor Watson: Hubert Rees

The Baker Street Boys was a BBC television production which followed the adventures of The Baker Street Irregulars. The Irregulars are featured in the Conan Doyle stories and were the eyes and ears of Sherlock Holmes all over London (this would become The Homeless Network in the BBC adaptation *Sherlock*). Set in Victorian London, the gang – Beaver, Queenie, Rosie, Shiner, Sparrow and Wiggins - help Sherlock Holmes (who appears sparingly in the episodes) solve mysteries and crimes as well as taking on cases of their own.

Connection: Writer Anthony Read had been a script editor and writer on the 1965 Sherlock Holmes series and was a long-time fan of the Irregulars, so much so that he continued to write fiction books about their adventures long after the series ended.

A full episode list can be found in the "Television Episodes" chapter of this book

Bartitsu: The Lost Martial Art of Sherlock Holmes
Documentary - 2011 (USA)

Writer: Tony Woolf
Directors: Paolo Paparella & Tony Woolf
Sherlock Holmes: N/A
Doctor Watson: N/A

A feature length documentary following Tony Woolf as he travels to locations around the world, including the Reichenbach Falls, researching the history, and surprising modern revival, of the Victorian martial art Bartitsu. With Sherlock Holmes as its focus, Woolf interviews martial arts historians, writers and Baritsu experts about the lost art and its association with Sherlock Holmes and *The Empty House* story.

Trivia: Although it is assumed that Conan Doyle was referring to the self-defence art

form of Bartitsu he actually spelled it incorrectly as Baritsu.

Bartitsu: The Lost Martial Art
of Sherlock Holmes

The Beryl Coronet
Film - 1912 (UK/France)

Writer: Uncredited
Director: Georges Tréville
Sherlock Holmes: Georges Tréville
Doctor Watson: Mr Moyse

The silent story stays, somewhat, faithful to the Doyle original with the famous Beryl Coronet being held as collateral for a loan. Here though, it is the fiancé of the banker's daughter who is accused of taking the coronet as he grapples it from the thieves who have broken in to steal it. With only a piece of torn cloth as a clue, Sherlock Holmes and Doctor Watson unravel the mystery which could prove the undoing of Professor Moriarty.

Trivia: Unfortunately this two reel silent film is considered to be one of the 'lost' films of Georges Tréville's Sherlock Holmes

BraveStarr: Sherlock Holmes in the 23rd Century
Animation - 1988 (USA)

Writer: Bob Forward
Director: Tom Tataranowicz
Sherlock Homes: Pat Fraley
Doctor Watson: Peter Cullen

This two-part episode of the animated television series *BraveStarr* was broadcast on February 8th & 9th in 1998 on a first-run broadcast syndication (although it was distributed by NBC). *BraveStarr* was a cartoon western set in space in the 23rd century on a desert planet called New Texas. In the episode *Sherlock Holmes in the 23rd Century*, Holmes lands in the year 2249 due to a time warp transportation device at the Reichenbach Falls. He is taken to the hospital where he is treated by Dr. Wt'sn of Harley Str. Hospital. There is even an appearance from a woman who is a direct descendent of Mycroft Holmes. Along with *BraveStarr*, the gang gets straight to work in trying to solve the disappearance of an alien boy called Fleeder. It transpires that Professor Moriarty has also survived the Reichenbach Falls and plans to use the alien boy's hypnotic singing talents to take over the Earth.

Quote:
<u>Sherlock Holmes:</u> This century is certainly confusing. This confounded scanner pipe, for instance. I simply cannot get it to function. Why can't I have my old one?

<u>Dr. Wt'sn:</u> Tobacco's been outlawed, old boy. It was dangerous.

<u>Sherlock Holmes:</u> Well, I was aware of that. I see this century has more sense than mine.

Call me Sherlock
Internet - 2015-2016 (USA)

Writers: Joshua Starnes & Phil Malone
Director: Joshua Starnes
Sherlock Holmes: Travis Ammons
Doctor Watson: Tom Long

This very low-budget and short-lived web series by Purple Fly productions follows a man who believes he is Sherlock Holmes attempting to solve mysterious crimes with his "Watson." This contemporary Holmes, complete with shoulder length hair, has an interesting and amusing animated title sequence where he introduces the characters of Lestrade and Watson, both of whom reiterate the fact that those are not their names and that nobody calls him Sherlock.

Trivia: Travis Ammons is said to have originated this reincarnation of Holmes from a short film version of Sherlock Holmes in 2004. Although no trace of this film can be found.

A full episode list can be found in the "Television Episodes" chapter of this book

The Case of Marcel Duchamp
Documentary - 1984 (UK)

Writer: Uncredited
Director: David Rowan
Sherlock Holmes: Guy Rolfe
Doctor Watson: Raymond Francis

A drama documentary in which Sherlock Holmes, along with Doctor Watson, comes out of retirement to investigate the artist Marcel Duchamp. Under investigation, specifically, is his piece *The Bride Stripped Bare by Her Bachelors, Even (The Large Glass)*. As they both feed information into a computer called TOBY the pair tries to analyse the meanings behind the piece as well as looking into art movements such as Surrealism, Dadaism and Cubism. Although this isn't your usual Holmes and Watson adventure, it's an interesting and playful marriage of education, entertainment, sleuthing and art.

Trivia: The computer name TOBY is thought to be a reference to the dog from *The Sign of Four* whom Holmes describes as a, "queer mongrel, with a most amazing power of scent. I would rather have Toby's help than that of the whole detective force of London."

The Copper Beeches
Film - 1912 (UK/France)

Writer: Arthur Conan Doyle
Director: Adrien Caillard
Sherlock Holmes: Georges Tréville
Doctor Watson: N/A

Mr. Rucastle becomes furious when his daughter, Alice, announces her engagement to William Johnson. Knowing that this will mean the loss of his late wife's estate as it transfers to Alice and her new husband, Mr. Rucastle locks her in an outbuilding which is guarded by a vicious dog. Mr. Rucastle then offers a young Violet Hunter a job with a wage of two hundred pounds a year to be governess for his family, but she becomes uncomfortable when he demands that she cut her hair and wear Alice's dresses. When Violet hears the sound of moaning coming from the outbuilding and is threatened by Mr. Rucastle, she hurries to Sherlock Holmes for help. Violet explains that she suspects she is being asked to impersonate whoever is being held captive in the outbuilding. Later, thinking that Violet is Alice, Johnson rushes to her but is followed by Mr. Rucastle carrying a shotgun and intent on killing him. Luckily, Holmes arrives in time to intercept the murder and he marches Rucastle to the outbuilding where he is forced to release Alice. There is no Doctor Watson in this version of the story and the ending has been changed so that it is Sherlock Holmes who frees the daughter instead of her having escaped by the time he arrives at the scene.

History: This movie is hailed by some as the first "legal" portrayal of Sherlock Holmes on screen as Conan Doyle officially signed the rights to use his works over to the French production company Éclair.

The Case-Book of Sherlock Holmes
Television - 1991 – 1993 (UK)

Writers: Various
Directors: Various
Sherlock Holmes: Jeremy Brett
Doctor Watson: Edward Hardwicke

The third set of Granada-made Sherlock Holmes adaptations for ITV starring Jeremy Brett as Holmes and Edward Hardwicke as Watson. This series also included three feature length episodes, *The Master Blackmailer*, *The Last Vampyre* and *The Eligible Bachelor*. During this series Jeremy Brett's health problems became more visible including his weight gain from his medication and the laboured breathing due to his smoking and heart problems. However, his performances are still ranked as one of the favourites among fans of Holmes and Watson. In his obituary in the New York Times it was written, "Mr. Brett was regarded as the quintessential Holmes."

Quote:
Sherlock Holmes: The world is big enough for us. No ghosts need apply. – The Last Vampyre

A full episode list can be found in the "Television Episodes" chapter of this book

The Copper Beeches

The Case of the Screaming Bishop
Animation - 1944 (USA)

Writer: John McLeish
Director: Howard Swift
Sherlock Holmes: John McLeish (uncredited)
Doctor Watson: Harry E. Lang (uncredited)

This 7-minute black-and-white animation was produced by Screen Gems for Columbia pictures and is a parody staring Hairlock Combs and his trusty side kick Doctor

Gotsum. One of the dinosaur skeletons has gone missing from the "Museum of Unnatural History" and so Combs and Gotsum – who live at 223 Baker Street – are called in to investigate. Cunningly disguising themselves as a horse, they sneak into the museum, reconstruct the crime scene by making a giant dinosaur skeleton out of scrap wood. It is only after Gotsum's "conductor of light" moment that Combs realises the culprit and apprehends the criminal.

Trivia: Writer and actor John McLeish was part of the writing team for Disney's 1940 film *Fantasia*.

The Case of Sherlock Holmes
Documentary - 1987 (UK)

Writers: David Pearson & Brian Thompson
Director: David Pearson
Sherlock Holmes: Various
Doctor Watson: Various

This is a documentary which aired on BBC 2 on December 10th, 1987, as part of the *Forty Minutes* programme. The special was made to celebrate 100 years of Holmes and has Tim Piggot-Smith using archival footage, as well as interviews with Sherlockians, historians and writers, to explore the culture of the Sherlock Holmes fandom. During the documentary Piggot-Smith adopts a dreamlike, Sherlock Holmes-style narration as the viewer is shown festivals and rituals from both sides of the Atlantic. These include a Sherlock Holmes pub in Liverpool holding a Sherlock Holmes look-a-like competition, a young fan who is keen to demonstrate inconsistencies in Doyle's writing via Mrs Hudson's tea-making abilities, and a group of people who celebrate the death of Moriarty each year by visiting a town of the same name and singing, ""Happy Unbirthday, You Bastard" at the ground.

Connection: Tim Piggot-Smith played Doctor Watson opposite John Wood as Holmes for 471 performances of the William Gillette play *Sherlock Holmes* on Broadway from December 1974–January 1976.He also played Sherlock Holmes in the BBC Radio adaptation of *The Valley of Fear* in 1986.

The Case of the Whitechapel
Vampire
Film - 2002 (Canada)

Writer: Rodney Gibbons
Director: Rodney Gibbons
Sherlock Holmes: Matt Frewer
Doctor Watson: Kenneth Welsh

The title of this film might suggest some connection to the Conan Doyle story *The Adventure of the Sussex Vampire* but the narrative of this Canadian made-for-TV movie is an original one.
Set in Victorian London, Holmes and Watson are called to Whitechapel to investigate a spate of murders which the locals believe to be the work of a vampire from Guyana. The monks and nuns of the Hermitage of St Justinian find one of their monks dead in the abbey church and all indicators point to it being the work of this vampire. It is explained to Holmes and Watson that years earlier Brother Marstoke, head of the Hermitage, worked in a mission in Guyana where there was an outbreak of rabies. Thinking this was the work of the local bats, Marstoke wiped them out. Later two monks were found dead with bite marks in their necks and a scrawled message on a wall from a vampire demon warning of revenge. Typically, it is Watson who is swayed by the tales of the supernatural but Holmes remains steadfast in his pursuit to find a more logical explanation for the killings. Holmes cunningly disguises himself as a monk to investigate a monastery in order to solve the crime which, as it turns out, has more to do with revenge than anything paranormal. Even so, Holmes visits a psychic called Madame Karasky who tells him that he will be saved by the church. Shortly afterwards Holmes is pushed in front of a moving carriage by the supposed vampire and is saved by a pedestrian who, later, turns out to be named Reginald Church. After further investigation at the monastery, Holmes uncovers the truth, that Brother Abel is responsible for the murders. Abel wanted revenge on the monks from the Guyana mission who ignored his pleas about the bats and, as a result, became deathly ill.

Interview: When asked by the AVClub about his portrayal of Sherlock Holmes, Frewer said, "I based my interpretation on my father-in-law, who is this brilliant eye surgeon, and he doesn't talk to you so much as lecture you."

The Case of the Whitechapel Vampire

The Consulting Detective Mystery: Father Dowling Investigates
Television - 1991 (USA)

Writers: Dean Hargrove & Gerry Conway
Director: Sharron Miller
Sherlock Holmes: Rupert Frazer
Doctor Watson: N/A

This episode was broadcast as part of the television show *Father Dowling Investigates* on the ABC network in America, a show where a priest solves murders with a nun as his sidekick. In this episode a murderer runs from the crime scene without the object which he so desperately killed for, a candlestick which holds a secret paper. The murder alongside the appearance of a strange man in the parish has Father Dowling frustrated at being unable to solve the mystery. Later a man appears in his home, sitting in a chair and smoking a pipe. He introduces himself to Father Dowling as Mr Sherlock Holmes (Rupert Frazer). However, it appears that he is merely a projection of his own love of Holmes which he utilises to crack the case. Dowling and imaginary Holmes work together until the killer is brought to justice.

Connection: Father Dowling actor Tom Bolsey also played the recurring part of Sheriff Amos Tupper in the American television show *Murder, She Wrote*. The pilot episode of that show was called, *The Murder of Sherlock Holmes* where another "fake" Holmes was featured.

The Crucifer of Blood
Television - 1991 (USA)

Writers: Paul Giovanni, Fraser C. Heston
Director: Fraser C. Heston
Sherlock Holmes: Charlton Heston
Doctor Watson: Richard Johnson

This television movie, in which Charlton Heston plays Sherlock Holmes, was broadcast on the TNT network in America on November 4th, 1991. The story is based on the Paul Giovanni play of the same name, which in turn, is very loosely based on Conan Doyle's *The Sign of Four* and *The Man with the Twisted Lip*.

The film starts back in India with Jonathan Small falling into possession of a treasure chest during the Indian Mutiny at the Red Fort of Agra. When Colonel Alistair Cross and Captain Neville St. Claire discover the treasure they kill in order to keep it. Even though they believe that it is cursed, the three men swear a blood oath to share their spoils of war.

As thirty years have now passed, St. Claire's daughter, Irene, comes to Baker Street to enlist Holmes and Watson to help her father who has become addicted to opium as he begins to feel haunted by the curse of the treasure and the death of his wife. When they visit St. Claire at his home, they discover him terrified, and he explains that he sold his share of the cursed treasure to Colonel Cross in return for a small pension but he still fears that the curse is upon him. A small time later, during a stormy night, Cross dies under suspicious circumstances (believed to have been poisoned) after receiving a letter containing a cross-shaped mark in blood. With St. Claire clearly paralysed with fear and with Cross now dead, Holmes deduces that it can only be Small who is committing the murders. Sensing that St. Claire is in danger, Holmes follows him to an opium den where he disguises himself as the owner, Fu Tching. However, this does not prevent St. Claire from succumbing to the fate of Cross and he is also found to have been poisoned by a dart from a blow pipe. Holmes and Watson now understand that they are not only hunting Small but also his manservant, Tonga, who is believed to have been carrying out the poisonings. Irene becomes drugged and, under the influence, mistakes Doctor Watson for her father and confesses her love for the Doctor. When Irene becomes more lucid, Watson confesses his love for her and the pair share a passionate kiss. Holmes, Lestrade and Watson head to the wharf as Holmes tells them that Small will certainly be in a row boat trying to make his escape with the stolen treasure. The trio find Small and his sidekick aboard a boat and attempt to halt their passage. When Tonga attempts to kill him with a poisoned, dart Holmes shoots him dead.

Small throws the treasure overboard but it is rescued by Lestrade and as Small lays dying Holmes questions him about the open window and the messages on the other murder victims, but Small knows nothing about it. Back in Baker Street, Watson attempts to open up the treasure chest and is confronted by Irene, dressed in a low cut, bright red gown who orders him to spill the treasure all over the floor. Irene confesses to be the person behind the murders in order to claim her rightful treasure and she shoots Watson, dead. When Holmes enters the room he seems unconcerned by Watson's death and explains to Irene that he already knew she had killed her father and so had loaded her gun with blanks. Watson is not dead, merely fainted, and Irene is cuffed and taken away by Lestrade.

Connection: The cast of the Los Angeles production of the play included Charlton Heston as Sherlock Holmes, and Jeremy Brett as Doctor Watson. Kiran Shah who appeared as Tonga also played the same role in the BBC version of The Sign of Four with Jeremy Brett as Holmes.

Deduce, You say
Animation - 1956 (USA)

Writer: Michael Maltese
Director: Chuck Jones
Sherlock Holmes: Mel Blanc
Doctor Watson: Mel Blanc

This Looney Tunes cartoon from Warner Brothers sees Daffy Duck assume the identity of "Dorlock Homes" with his trusty sidekick Porky Watkins. From his address of 221 7/16 Beeker Street, Dorlock and Watkins start their investigation into the mystery of the Shropshire Slasher, who has escaped from Dartmoor prison. Following the trail of clues they find him at a pub called *Henry the Eighth's Fifth* and attempt to apprehend him. After numerous examples of the Slasher proving to be too strong for Homes to apprehend, Watkins interjects and asks him, in a reasonable manner, to peacefully turn himself in to the police. At that moment, a flower seller enters the pub and Homes chastises her for selling without a licence, the Slasher then grabs Holmes by the neck and starts to shake him violently as the sweet, elderly flower seller is the Slasher's mother. As he puts Homes down he explains to his mother that he promised the nice man (Watkins) that he would give himself up and so they leave.

Quote:
Dorlock Holmes: Watkins, in a moment there'll be a knock at the door heralding the start of the case of the Shropshire Slasher. Answer it. My pants are caught on a nail.

The Diogenes Documentaries
Internet – 2014 - 2017 (UK)

Writer: Ross K. Foad & Howard Ostrom
Director: Howard Ostrom
Sherlock Holmes: Various
Doctor Watson: Various

This collection of short documentaries made by Ross K. Foad, for the internet, covers a wide variety of topics and subject matters connected to Sherlock Holmes. Most of the content is adapted from essays by Ostrom, although there is input from other writers and sources later on in the series. Ostrom is widely regarded as one of the leading authorities and experts on the history of Sherlock Holmes through the media. He has also written numerous essay series on a variety of subjects within the Sherlock Holmes world.

Trivia: Howard Ostrom keeps a record of every person who has portrayed Sherlock Holmes, including Holmes imagery in print and online. There are almost 5,000 names on the list, so far, which also includes myself.

A full episode list can be found in the "Television Episodes" chapter of this book

The Diogenes Documentaries

The Double-Barrelled Detective Story
Film - 1965 (USA)

Writers: Adolfas Mekas, Mark Twain
Director: Adolfas Mekas
Sherlock Holmes: Jerome Raphael
Doctor Watson: N/A

Adapted from a short story of the same name by Mark Twain, this is a satirical comedy about a carpetbagger who marries a wealthy plantation owner's daughter in order to disgrace him. After a terrible marriage, he abandons her as she gives birth to a son, Archie, who is found to have a heightened sense of smell much like a human bloodhound. When he is old enough, he is sent away to seek out his father and destroy his reputation. Later, the nephew of Sherlock Holmes is found to have murdered his boss and so Holmes, who is visiting America at the time, sets outs to deduce and

investigate until he pinpoints the guilty party. However, his conclusions are proved to be utterly wrong by Archie and his sense of smell.

Quote:
Fetlock Jones: Uncle Sherlock... Anybody that knows him the way I do knows he can't detect a crime except where he plans it all out beforehand and arranges the clues and hires some fellow to commit it according to instructions

Dr Watson and the Dark Water Hall Mystery
Television - 1974 (UK)

Writer: Kingsley Amis
Director: James Cellan Jones
Sherlock Holmes: N/A
Doctor Watson: Edward Fox

This made for television feature for the BBC, broadcast on December 27th, 1974, focuses on the crime-solving prowess of Doctor Watson with Sherlock Holmes being absent throughout. Holmes is away on a rest cure at a manor house in the Cotswolds with Reginald Musgrave when Lady Emily Farfax calls at Baker Street. Her husband, Sir Henry, is in danger of being murdered by a poacher. With Holmes unable to return, Watson travels to Darkwater Hall to investigate the case himself. As well as meeting Sir Henry's twin brother Miles, he also spies the suspected poacher, Black Jack, and finds that a man called Captain Bradshaw is in love with Lady Farfax. When a rifle goes missing and it transpires that Sir Henry has been shot, Watson puts together his case and goes about bringing the suspect to justice.

Connection: Edward Fox also stared alongside Charlton Heston's Holmes and Richard Johnson's Watson as Alistair Ross in the 1991 TV *movie The Crucifier of Blood*.

Dressed to Kill AKA Sherlock Holmes and the Secret Code
Film - 1946 (USA)

Writer: Leonard Lee, Frank Gruber
Director: Roy William Neill
Sherlock Holmes: Basil Rathbone
Doctor Watson: Nigel Bruce

This film was released in the UK under the title *Sherlock Holmes and the Secret Code* as well as under the alternative title *Sherlock Holmes is Dressed to Kill* in the USA.

Holmes is visited by Julian Emery, a friend of Watson, to inform them of a robbery at his flat. He was knocked unconscious and so the details of his attack are not clear. He tells Holmes that the only thing missing from his expensive collection of music boxes is a cheap music box which he had purchased that day, from an auction. Holmes and Watson find out that the box is one of three and that the thief is willing to kill anybody who stands in their way of collecting them all. Holmes becomes convinced that the music boxes are hiding a very valuable object. Using the tunes from the music boxes to deduce the location of the artifact, and spurred on when he finds that 221b Baker Street has been ransacked, Holmes and Watson set their sights on retrieving it before the criminal. The plot shares some similarities with Conan Doyle's *The Six Napoleons* and also uses the trick of starting a fire to reveal the location of a hidden object as used in plot of *A Scandal in Bohemia*.

Trivia: This was the 14th and last film to feature Basil Rathbone as Sherlock Holmes and Nigel Bruce as his Doctor Watson.

Droske 519 AKA Cab Number 519
Film - 1909 (DENMARK)

Writer: Viggo Larsen
Director: Viggo Larsen
Sherlock Holmes: Viggo Larsen
Doctor Watson: N/A

Released as *Cab number 519* in the USA, this film is the story of a young man who comes into a large inheritance. His jealous friend, along with an accomplice, plans to kidnap and then impersonate the young man in order to steal his money. Once he is drugged, the young man is placed onto a ship and held against his will in one of the cabins. Luckily Sherlock Holmes recorded the number of the cab where the young man was drugged and sets about finding him. After incapacitating the cab driver, he takes the cabin next door to the victim aboard the ship and intervenes just as the poor man is about to be thrown overboard. Now they must get to the impersonator before he takes the money and runs.

Review: A write up in the popular periodical *The Moving Picture World* the film states that the film is, "...a very melodramatic story, very skillfully worked out, which we think will be popular with all classes of audience. The picture is full of excitement from start to finish."

Das dunkle Schloß
Film - 1915 (Germany)

Writer: Uncredited
Director: Willy Zehn
Sherlock Holmes: Eugen Burg
Doctor Watson: Uncredited

This title was also released as *The Hound of the Baskervilles: The Dark Castle,* and is a silent movie of 7 reels. The story starts with the death of Colonel Warringer who is found murdered with a picture of Else Schmidt, who happens to be the bride of detective Braun. The butler confirms to the police that she was the last person to have visited the Colonel. Now a murder suspect, it is up to Braun to solve the crime and absolve poor Else of any wrongdoing. But can he trust the statement of the servant?

The detective in the movie had to be changed from Sherlock Holmes to detective Braun as *The Dark Castle* (originally to be the third part of the film series called *The Dog of Baskerville*) became caught up in a legal dispute. Litigation with Julius Greenbaum and his new production *The Scary Room* meant that the defeated production company, Projektions-AG Union (PAGU), was no longer allowed to use the title. The villain, Stapleton, is the only reference left which ties the film to the Baskerville narrative.

History: Eugen Burg was one of the earliest Sherlock Holmes impersonators. His film career, however, was stopped when he was disqualified by the Nazi Party and sent to a concentration camp after attempting to flee Germany. Sadly he died in the Theresienstadt camp on November 15th, 1944, at the age of 73.

Elementary
Television – 2012 – Present (USA)

Writers: Various
Directors: Various
Sherlock Holmes: Jonny Lee Miller
Doctor Watson: Lucy Liu

This contemporary American, take on the adventures of the Sherlock Holmes character sees a change in gender for John Watson, who becomes Joan Watson, and for Professor James Moriarty who, becomes Jamie Moriarty. Running for more than 140 episodes, and counting, the show continues to portray a very different Holmes and Watson dynamic as they solve crimes in New York rather than London. Although criticised by some and loved by others for its startling departure from the Canon, the show includes a variety of nods to die-hard Sherlockians to demonstrate its affection for the original. A recurring character named Detective Bell was created in reference to Conan Doyle's professor at medical school, Joseph Bell, who was the inspiration for Sherlock Holmes. Throughout the show, the creators also make reference to Holmes's study of bees, foreshadowing *His Final Bow*. The episode list is up to date at time of writing. (The writers recently announced that the show's upcoming seventh season will be its last.)

Quote:
Doctor Watson: Your hobby is conspiracy theories?

Sherlock Holmes: No, of course not. Conspiracy theories are pure sophistry. Large groups of people cannot keep secrets. My hobby is conspiracy theorists. I adore them as one would a barmy uncle or a pet that can't stop walking into walls.

A full episode list can be found in the "Television Episodes" chapter of this book.

Elementary, Dear Data. Star Trek: The Next Generation
Television - 1991 (USA)

Writer: Brian Alan Lane
Director: Rob Bowman
Sherlock Holmes: Brent Spiner
Doctor Watson: LeVar Burton

Aired as part of the sci-fi *Star Trek* spin-off *The Next Generation,* this episode has the chief engineer, Geordi La Forge, and Data (artificial intelligence and synthetic life force) playing through an immersive Sherlock Holmes story recreation on the ship's Holodeck. Frustrated at the ease with which Data, dressed as Holmes, solves the crimes due to his knowledge of the Doyle Canon, Dr. Pulaski challenges him to solve a new mystery generated by the computer. She is then kidnapped by Moriarty and becomes the crime they need to solve.

Moriarty soon learns that he is part of a computer simulation and begins to become sentient in order to try to control the USS Enterprise. Captain Pickard is informed and reasons with Moriarty that, at this time, he cannot live outside of the simulation. However, he will save the programme and convert him into a permanent form when technology has advanced enough for them to do so. The character Moriarty also appeared again in 1993 in the episode *Ship in a Bottle* when anomalies are reported within the Sherlock Holmes Holodeck programs, and he takes control of the Enterprise.

Connection: The episode contains references to a variety of original stories, including A *Scandal in Bohemia, The Red-Headed League, The Speckled Band, The Valley of Fear* and *The Bruce-Partington Plans.*

Elementary, Dear Data. Star Trek: The Next Generation

Elementary, My Dear Pan. Peter Pan and the Pirates
Animation - 1991 (USA/Japan)

Writers: Chris Hubbell, Sam Graham & Jim Carlson
Director: Uncredited
Sherlock Holmes: Jason Marsden
Doctor Watson: Jack Lynch

This episode of the American/Japanese collaboration children's television series, which ran on the Fox Kids network between 1990–1991, follows the adventures of Peter Pan in Neverland. This episode opens with the story *The Red-Headed League* being read to the Lost Boys by Wendy and is interrupted when Peter Pan reveals he has never heard of the detective.

Doubting Holmes's superior abilities at first, the story is switched to The Hound of the Baskervilles which is re-enacted by Peter and his friend John. Coming back to reality with a bump, Peter discovers that his pan pipes are missing and so he and John become Holmes and Watson to solve the mystery. A mystery which leads them aboard Captain Hook's pirate ship. Captured and buried up to their necks in sand they call upon the mermaids to rescue them and reward them with Captain Hook's stolen treasure. After the big adventure Peter Pan reveals that his pan pipes were not stolen after all, he had simply forgotten that he let his friend Hard-To-Hit borrow them the day before.

Quote:
Peter Pan: Quickly, there is no time to waste. The game is a shoe!

Elementary, My Dear Simon. Alvin and the Chipmunks
Animation - 1988 (USA)

Writer: Roger Merwin
Director: Don Spencer
Sherlock Holmes: Ross Bagdasarian Jr.
Doctor Watson: Janice Karman

This special episode of the television show *Alvin and the Chipmunks* (1983-1990) titled *The Chipmunks Go to the Movies* was broadcast on the NBC network in America. Simon plays the role of Sherlock whilst his brother Theodore plays Watson. Instead of Lestrade there is Inspector Seville of Scotland Yard (Dave) and together they investigate a series of baffling burglaries. As the case unfolds it is discovered that Moriarty (Alvin) is behind the thefts which he is using to build a Matter Transfer Machine in order to try to steal the Crown Jewels, all of the gold in The Bank of England and all the priceless art in the museums. Moriarty succeeds in his evil scheme; however, Holmes recognises a pattern in his locations and is hot on his trail to stop him before he escapes with the loot. Disguised as his carriage driver, Holmes confronts Moriarty and locks him safely away. The episode has very few nods to the original Canon and focuses, instead, on the H.G. Wells book The Time Machine.

Quote:
Sherlock Seville: No, Watson. I need you.

Watson: No you don't.

Sherlock Seville: Yes, I do...If you don't come up with the wrong answers, how can I come up with the right ones?

Elementary, My Dear Watson: An Interview with Edward Hardwicke
Documentary - 2003 (UK/USA)

Writer: David Stuart Davies
Director: Carl Daft
Sherlock Holmes: Jeremy Brett
Doctor Watson: Edward Hardwicke

This 18-minute documentary was made by the Blue Underground and was an accompaniment to the Granada television

Sherlock Holmes release on DVD. The documentary intersperses clips from a variety of episodes with Hardwicke talking about his experiences. In his interviews he talks in some depth about taking over the role of Watson from previous actor, and friend, David Burke. During the interview, Burke reveals that the series producer, Michael Cox, made sure that Brett and Hardwicke filmed at least two episodes together before attempting to film *The Empty House* in order for the chemistry to develop between the two actors and for Hardwicke's confidence to grow in playing Watson.

Interview: Hardwicke reveals that his favourite episode was *The Priory School,* directed by John Madden, saying, "It was a little film...when I saw it, I was very impressed by the way John Madden had put it together."

Elementary, My Dear Watson - The Strange Case of the Dead Solicitors: Comedy Playhouse Television - 1973 (UK)

Writer: N.F. Simpson
Director: Harold Snoad
Sherlock Holmes: John Cleese
Doctor Watson: Willie Rushton

This wonderfully odd Holmes and Watson pastiche was broadcast as part of the Comedy Playhouse, a long running BBC anthology series of self-contained comedy productions from 1961-1975.

Five identical solicitors are found in identical positions with identical daggers in their backs. Waylaid on their way to solve the mystery of Lady Cynthia's grudge-ridden rattlesnake, Holmes and Watson arrive at the solicitor's office to find that one has been stolen. Possibly, posits Holmes, to be used on an episode of *Call My Bluff* as a mystery object of the week. The pair push their chosen dead solicitor from London to Manchester where the episode of Call My Bluff is already underway and the corpse is identified as a travelling showman's hoopla stall, a practical garden gnome, and dead solicitor, prized in Imperial China as a conversation piece. A pigeon from Fu Manchu sends a message for Holmes and Watson to rush to Lady Cynthia to continue the investigation into the murderous rattlesnake. A brief story involving Moriarty as Mother Goose unfolds and goes nowhere (later it is revealed that they just needed to add more content to make up time) and throughout the show the police desk sergeant has to deal with crank calls from Jack the Ripper. After they have the criminals in their sights Holmes and Watson give chase around an airfield before saving the day once again. An absurdist, post-modern take on a Sherlock Holmes story that makes no apology for its lack of solid narrative and revels in the comic abilities of its performers.

Connection: As well as John Cleese, who played Holmes in the film *The Strange Case of the End of Civilization as We Know It* (1977), other cast members have connections to Sherlock Holmes. Josephine Tewson also played the part of a nun in the Pete and Dud version of *Hound of the Baskervilles* (1978) and appeared as Miss Hoskins in *The End of Civilization as We Know It.* Norman Bird appeared an episode of *Sherlock Holmes and Doctor Watson – A Motive for Murder* (1980) as well as the 1973 television series *The Rivals of Sherlock Holmes.* And finally, Dawn Addams appeared in the 1955 American series of *The Adventures of Sherlock Holmes* in the episode *The Case of the Careless Suffragette.*

Elementary, My Dear What-Not. T.Bag and the Pearls of Wisdom Television - 1990 (UK)

Writers: Lee Pressman & Grant Cathro
Director: Leon Thau
Sherlock Holmes: Georgina Hale
Doctor Watson: John Hasler

The third episode of the T-bag series of children's television shows which ran from 1985–1992 on the ITV network's CITV (Children's ITV). The series was about the eponymous witch T-Bag and her assistant T-Shirt with each season adopting a different title from the last.

Season Eight, The Pearls of Wisdom, includes the episode *Elementary, My Dear What-Not*. After watching The Hound of the Baskervilles, T-Bag becomes Shirley Holmes and T-shirt becomes Dr. Whatsit to help solve their mystery. Together they must track down a dog, Willoughby, belonging to Lady Ruffles as he has been kidnapped. Willoughby has one of the precious pearls in his collar and so when the dog is returned to the police, Constable Clodd hatches a plan to hide the dog until the reward money increases. So it is up to Holmes and Whatsit to unravel the reprehensible mess.

Trivia: All of the episodes of season eight were put together as a single, two hour, VHS release. However, *Elementary, My Dear What-not*, did not make the final cut.

Elementary My Dear Winston.
The Real Ghostbusters
Animation - 1989 (USA)

Writers: Dan Aykroyd, Richard Mueller & Harold Ramis
Director: Will Meugniot
Sherlock Holmes: Maurice LaMarche
Doctor Watson: Frank Welker

The Real Ghostbusters was a spin off cartoon which ran from 1986-1991 on the ABC network in the USA. It featured characters from the original Ghostbusters movies, as well as a recurring role for Slimer, as they continued their adventures, busting ghosts in Manhattan. In *Elementary My Dear Winston*, New York is under attack from the evil Professor Moriarty and his sidekick, the Hound of the Baskervilles. When Sherlock Holmes and Doctor Watson turn up as ghostly apparitions driving through Ghostbusters HQ they are mistaken for mischief-causing spectres. Watson is taken by the Hound and Holmes is captured and held in a trap. Winston recognises the detective as Sherlock Holmes, however, and Egon puts forward the theory that these fictional characters are alive due to the faith the public has in them. Holmes and Winston chase after Moriarty who is trying to steal the evil energy from objects in order to make himself real. The most evil energy, however, can be found at the Ghostbuster's

containment unit and so he plans to release every evil spirit held inside it. After a brief fight, Watson is released in time to see Holmes and Moriarty fall together into the containment unit. Being ever the man's sidekick, Watson jumps in after and the unit is safely locked up. The episode is peppered with facts about Sherlock Holmes and references from the original stories.

Trivia: Sherlock's explanation for knowing the names of each of the Ghostbusters is that he could read the name tags on their outfits. However, apart from the name tag on Spengler's jumpsuit, none of the other Ghostbusters are sporting name tags and even Spengler's vanishes after the scene.

Elementary My Dear Winston:
The Real Ghostbusters

Elementary, My Dear Turtle.
Teenage Mutant Ninja Turtles
Animation - 1992 (USA)

Writers: Dennis O'Flaherty & Bruno-René Huchez
Director: Bruno-René Huchez
Sherlock Holmes: Peter Renaday
Doctor Watson: Pat Fraley

The cartoon Teenage Mutant Ninja Turtles (AKA Teenage Mutant Hero Turtles in the UK) ran from 1987-1996 and aired on the CBS network in the USA.

In the episode, Elementary, *My Dear Turtle*, the TMNT are in London and whilst exploring an atomic clock are sent back in time where they try to stop Moriarty from stealing the timepiece. Mistaking Holmes and Watson as criminals, they attack them, putting Holmes out of action with a badly sprained ankle. It is revealed that Moriarty is traveling through time and collecting artifacts with which he will construct a time machine in order to go back and rule the world. With Holmes out of action, the four turtles pursue Moriarty into a different timeline where he is Emperor of the World. Stuck in a dystopian future, they solicit the help of the new timeline's April but fall straight into the arms of Moriarty and his henchmen, who are waiting for the turtles in his lair. After a brief tussle, the atomic clock is captured and the turtles return to their own timeline where Moriarty has one more attempt at stealing the clock before he vanishes into thin air.

Trivia: The episode references the 1948 Basil Rathbone and Nigel Bruce movie *The Spider Woman* (which Michelangelo calls a "primo flick") as well as narrative nods to *The Golden Pinz-Nez* and *The Empty House.*

Elementary, My Dear Turtle:
Teenage Mutant Ninja Turtles

Elementary My Dear Viewer Documentary - 2007 (UK)

Writer: Uncredited
Director: Richard Denton
Sherlock Holmes: Various
Doctor Watson: Various

A documentary made from the ITV network in the UK about the history of Sherlock Holmes and his lasting appeal. Presented and narrated by Richard E. Grant (somebody who is no stranger to appearing in Holmes adaptations) this documentary is more of a personal journey of Grant's to learn more about "the greatest detective who ever lived. Except, of course, he never lived." The documentary looks at the history of the character as well as the author and splices clips from popular television and film adaptations with interviews from people such as Kim Newman, Edward Hardwicke, P.D James and Sir Anthony Richards from the Sherlock Holmes Society. As well as the actors who played Holmes, Grant also delves into the forensic element of his investigations commenting on how Doyle wrote about techniques which were still experimental at the time.

Trivia: The documentary includes a touching tribute to the actor Jeremy Brett who played Sherlock Holmes in the Granada Television Series for ten years.

Elementary, My Dear Worty. Worzel Gummidge Down under Television - 1989 (UK)

Writers: Willis Hall, Fran Walsh & Keith Waterhouse
Director: Graham McLean
Sherlock Holmes: Jon Pertwee
Doctor Watson: Ian Mune

Broadcast as part of the *Worzel Gummidge Down Under* series, these stories are set in New Zealand (or Zwe Nealand as Gummidge calls it) as Worzel follows Aunt Sally overseas because she has been bought by a museum owner there. After it appears that somebody has stolen the Golden Turnip, Worzel is determined to find the perpetrator and so he pops on his "investigating head" and immediately adopts the persona of Sherlock Holmes. Helped by his version of John Watson (Worty Yam) the pair follow clues in order to find their culprit, a tall, broad, limping scarecrow with bad teeth.

Their efforts, however, are hampered by Mickey and Manu, two children who are determined to scupper Sherlock's chances of solving the case. Although a program for children, Jon Pertwee pulls no punches in his Holmes characterisation and uses words and language more suited to Holmes than to a young audience, "he stubbed his toe and let out a loud explicative."

Connection: Jon Pertwee's son, Sean Pertwee, also has connections to Sherlock Holmes as he plays the role of inspector Lestrade in the American television show *Elementary*.

Elementary Steele: Remington Steele
Television - 1984 (USA)

Writer: Michael Gleason
Director: Seymour Robbie
Sherlock Holmes: Peter Evans
Doctor Watson: William Griffis

Shown as part of the television series *Remington Steele*, starring Pierce Brosnan as a private investigator, the program was broadcast on the NBC network in America and ran from 1982-1987. In this episode it appears at first that Holmes and Watson may be the villains as they are caught breaking into the apartment of Rocky Sullivan who manages to escape but is committed to a mental health ward in hospital after she tells her story to the police. Once she manages to convince Steele that she is not crazy, he confronts Holmes and Watson who are actually role-playing as part of a game for amateur detectives who are paid $500 to pursue small or fake cases. Murder, intrigue and a $50,000 blackmail scheme are eventually uncovered by the gang of amateur sleuths. Although the episode references the films *The Big Sleep* (1946) and *Death Race 2000* (1975) there are no further references to Doyle's Sherlock Holmes.

Quote:
Sherlock Holmes: For five hundred dollars we get to impersonate our favourite fictional detective...We've got a fun group on this trip. There's Mr. Moto, Miss Marple [and] Philip Marlowe.

Epic Rap Battles of History: Batman vs. Sherlock Holmes
Internet - 2012 (USA)

Writers: NicePeter, EpicLLOYD, Dante Cimadamore, Zach Sherwin & Mike Betette
Director: Dave McCary
Sherlock Holmes: Zach Sherwin
Doctor Watson: Kyle Mooney

Epic Rap Battles of History is a web series which was created by Lloyd Ahlquist and Peter Shukoff in 2010 that continues to preserve its popularity with over 14 million YouTube subscribers. The premise of the show is to pit two opposing figures against each other in a battle of wits to construct a rap which denigrates their opponent with the audience deciding the winner. In 2012 Sherlock Holmes entered into a battle with Batman, once again bringing into question who should wear the "greatest detective" moniker.

Quotes: The video, which is under three minutes, saw both sides giving as good as they got with Batman exclaiming, "Nobody likes you! Not your brother, not your partner, not Scotland Yard. You'll die alone with no friends except that needle in your arm." But not to be outdone, Sherlock Holmes counters with quips such as, "I believe your parents' homicide is why you mask your face. You're shamed and traumatized and haunted by the vast disgrace of watching like a passive waste as momma died and daddy was dispatched with haste."

Der Erdstrommotor
(The Earthquake Motor)
Film - 1917 (Germany)

Writer: Paul Rosenhayn
Director: Karl Heinz Wolff
Sherlock Holmes: Hugo Flink
Doctor Watson: Not credited

This German silent movie, which also went by the name *Der geheimnisvolle Hut (The Mysterious Hat)* was the first of a run of Sherlock Holmes adaptations starring Hugo Flink. This silent movie of 5 reels was produced by director Karl Heinz Wolff's production company Kowo. Not much is known about this very early adaptation of Sherlock Holmes but it is part of a series of movies with Flink playing Holmes in three others: 1917 - *Die Kasette (The Mysterious Casket);* 1917 - *Der Schlangenring (The Snake Ring)* and 1918 - *Die Indiesche (The Indian Spider).*

History: Hugo Flink was a prolific actor and started acting at the age of six. He was trained at Vienna Burgthater and was one of the first actors to play Holmes on screen.

Fu er mo si yu zhong guo nu xia

(Sherlock Holmes and the Chinese heroine AKA Sherlock Holmes in China)
Film - 1994 (China)

> **Writers:** Zhanghe Ke, Changfu Li & Fengkui Wang
> **Director:** Yunzhou Liu & Chi Wang
> **Sherlock Holmes:** Fan Ai Li
> **Doctor Watson:** Zhongquan Xu

Featuring a Holmes wearing what appears to be a top and tails, puffing on a comically large pipe and using his violin as a martial arts weapon whilst flying round the tree tops, *Fu er mo si yu zhong guo nu xia* is not your run-of-the-mill Sherlock Holmes adaptation. Holmes and Watson find themselves in 19th century China where they are in deep water. Holmes may be a master of disguise normally, but his startling blue eyes give him away, as well as his aversion to the local food, and his cover is blown. Sherlock Holmes is in China to help fight a war against a band of evil opium traders and to defeat the head of the gang, a martial arts master, and thus put an end to his tyranny. The film is confusingly slapstick and uses broad comedy to tell the story of Holmes against the opium traders; however, there are many wonderful fight sequences to admire within the magical realism of the narrative. Sherlock even uses his famed boxing skills but eschews his Bartitsu training in favour of "Violin-fu" to defeat his enemy.

Trivia: Not only was this the only time that actor Fan Ai Li was to play Sherlock Holmes

on screen, it was the only film the actor ever appeared in.

Fu er mo si yu zhong guo nu xia

Den Gra Dame

(The Grey Lady)
Film - 1909 (Denmark)

> **Writer:** Viggo Larsen
> **Director:** Viggo Larsen
> **Sherlock Holmes:** Viggo Larsen
> **Doctor Watson:** Holger-Madsen

Film number six in the Sherlock Holmes series of films made by the Nordisk Film Company this silent movie runs at 14 minutes. Holmes and Watson are called to the manor house of Lord Beresford as people keep dying under mysterious circumstances and a ghostly apparition seems to be the cause. The legend of the Grey Lady warns that anybody within the grounds of the mansion who so much as peeks at the lady dressed in grey will die. Being a man of practicality and logic, Holmes suspects a more earth-bound reason for the horrific deaths and sets about, with Watson, to question the inhabitants and find the perpetrator.

Review: A write up in *The Moving Picture World* stated, "..we found our unemotional selves being carried away by the excitement of the story. And later when we told a small boy of nine what we had seen, he clapped his hands and said, 'Oh, I wish I could see that picture.'"

Die Graue Dame
(The Grey Lady)
Film - 1937 (Germany)

Writers: Erich Engels, Hans Heuer
& Müller-Puzika
Director: Erich Engels
Sherlock Holmes: Hermann Speelmans
Doctor Watson: N/A

Also known as *Sherlock Holmes: The Grey Lady* and based on the play written by Müller-Puzika, this film follows detective Jimmy Ward who has infiltrated a criminal gang to bring them down from the inside. However, it is revealed later that Jimmy Ward is non-other than Sherlock Holmes working undercover. The film has been criticised by some Holmes fans because the character played by Hermann Speelmans is so far removed from the Sherlock Holmes that they are familiar with. He possesses few of the quick deduction skills and looks more like a film noir private eye than a consulting detective. For this reason the film is seen as more of a "cash in" on the Holmes name rather than a true representation of the detective.

Trivia: In this adaptation the detective owns a large, black poodle who sleeps on his bed.

Give Me a Hand - Something's Afoot: The Fonz and the Happy Days Gang
Animation - 1981 (USA)

Writers: Tom Swale & Duane Poole
Directors: George Gordon, Carl Urbano
& Rudy Zamora
Sherlock Holmes: Not credited
Doctor Watson: N/A

A sci-fi style animated spin off from the popular American sit com *Happy Days*, *The Fonz and the Happy Days Gang* is a cartoon adventure where The Fonz and friends become trapped in a time travelling machine and stop off at various points in history as they try to make it back to 1957. The show ran on the American network ABC from 1980-1982 and was voiced by the original *Happy Days* cast. In this episode, the gang lands in England in the year 1899 where a young woman is being chased by the evil Moriarty. The woman was on her way to ask Holmes to help solve the mystery of her missing father who worked in the Tower of London, and who had been acting strangely before he vanished. Moriarty plans to steal the Crown Jewels and use them in his deadly machine of destruction to bring the world to its knees. It's up to Fonz and the gang to dismantle the machine before Moriarty gets a chance to use it.

Quote:
Richie Cunningham: We've gotta hurry. If Fonzie is right, Professor Moriarty may attempt to steal the Crown Jewels at any moment.

Goluboy karbunkul
(The Blue Carbuncle)
Television - 1980 (Russia)

Writer: Anatoli Delendik
Director: Nikolai Lukyanov
Sherlock Holmes: Algimantas Masiulis
Doctor Watson: Ernst Romanov

This adaptation of *The Blue Carbuncle* for Soviet television was produced by the Belarusfilm Studio and opens with a charmingly simple cut-out animation which narrates the history of the blue carbuncle. The programme then launches into a musical number as a group of men prepare the streets for Christmas with paper decorations and greenery. With its rather saucy humour (and half naked ladies), musical numbers, strange Eastern references, slapstick comedy and random musical numbers, this isn't a faithful adaptation of Doyle's original tale. However, the crux of the story still remains with Holmes and Watson trying to track down the criminal who has tried to use a goose to steal the blue carbuncle gem. This adaptation has a more than happy Christmas ending.

Trivia: Although Sherlock Holmes is seen wearing a number of hats throughout the film – including a top hat and a fez – he is never seen in his trademark deerstalker.

Goluboy karbunkul

The Great Mouse Detective.
Film - 1986 (USA)

Writers: Peter Young, Vance Gerry, Steve Hulett, Ron Clements, John Musker, Bruce Morris, Matthew O'Callaghan, Burny Mattinson, David Michener & Mel Shaw
Directors: Ron Clements, Burny Mattinson, David Michener & John Musker
Sherlock Holmes: Barrie Ingham
Doctor Watson: Val Bettin

This charming Disney adaptation of the Eve Titus book series Basil of Baker Street, which depicts a mouse who emulates Sherlock Holmes, is still well-loved by adults and children alike. After a little girl, Olivia, hears her father being kidnapped, she seeks out the help of Basil of Baker Street to help find him. Aiding Basil is Doctor David Q. Dawson (the mouse version of Dr. Watson). Together, the pair, along with Basil, uncover a dastardly plot by Professor Ratigan (Moriarty). He plots to force Olivia's toymaker father to create a clock work robot of Queen Victoria which he will use to control all of England. Once Basil foils his plans, he must run and fight for his life against the evil Ratigan who now wants him dead. Basil of Baker street was named after the Sherlock Holmes actor, Basil Rathbone, who also appears in the film.

Trivia: Holmes and Watson appear in shadow during the film, speaking a few lines from the story *The Red-Headed League*, "It is introspective, and I want to introspect." Basil Rathbone's actual voice was used for

this, but Nigel Bruce isn't playing Watson. This is reasoned to be because the audio clip is taken from the 1966 Caedmon Records recording of *The Red-Headed League* narrated by Rathbone, rather than being taken from a Rathbone and Bruce film.

Hands of a Murderer AKA Sherlock Holmes and the Prince of Crime
Television - 1990 (UK/USA)

Writer: Charles Edward Pogue
Director: Stuart Orme
Sherlock Holmes: Edward Woodward
Doctor Watson: John Hillerman

This TV movie was made in association with Yorkshire television and broadcast on the CBS network in America. In a puff of smoke the troublesome Professor Moriarty manages to escape the gallows and is, once again, loose on the streets of London. Mycroft Holmes comes to his brother to find who has been leaking government secrets, but Holmes is not interested until he discovers that Moriarty is the cause of it. It appears that a hypnotising, seductive woman has managed to put a young government official under her spell and, unbeknownst to him, is stealing information. When Moriarty becomes frustrated at a piece of cryptic information which he is unable to solve, the only answer is to kidnap Mycroft to get some answers.

Connection: The film contains some references to the original Sherlock Holmes Canon with an issue of The Strand arriving at 221b Baker Street which contains Watson's account of *The Adventure of the Engineer's Thumb*.

Herlock
Internet - 2015 (USA)

Writer: Lee Eric Shackleford
Director: David E. Duncan
Sherlock Holmes: Gia Mora
Doctor Watson: Alana Jordan

Originally this was a web series, in four parts, based on the Conan Doyle story *Silver Blaze* but is also available as a single 46-minute film. Set in contemporary America this series takes core ideas from the original

Canon and twists them. The main roles are played by female actors, Alana Jordan plays Jonny Watts who is an aspiring veterinary surgeon (an interesting take on John Watson, a surgeon and veterain) who also writes mystery stories in her spare time. When researching horse sabotage online, Jonny notices the same person cropping up at races where these horses were harmed, leading her to believe that the mystery person is the criminal. However, it turns out the woman is the detective, Sheridan Hume, and Jonny starts becoming obsessed with her, to the detriment of her relationship and her studies. After briefly talking online about an unsolved murder, Hume decides to make Watts her assistant and together they attempt to catch the criminal gamblers who are fixing races through sabotage. Unlike other Holmes and Watson inspired narratives, these two characters interact through computer video chat and it is only in the very last scene that they actually meet.

Quote:
Sheridan Hume: I do not work for the police. In general they work for me, although they are rarely aware of this fact.

Det Hemmelige Dokument
(The Secret Document)
Film - 1908 (Denmark)

Writer: Viggo Larsen
Director: Viggo Larsen
Sherlock Holmes: Einar Zangenberg
Doctor Watson: N/A

This silent, one-reel movie, produced by the Nordisk Film Company has traces of the Conan Doyle story *The Adventure of the Second Stain*. A state document has been stolen and a letter of blackmail has been sent to the Chief of Intelligence offering the document back in exchange for £5,000. Sherlock Holmes is brought in to help solve the case but there is more than just the document to play for as Holmes is taken and chained to a large pipe in a gas chamber. He will have to use his deductive skills and boxing prowess to overpower his captors and return the document to its rightful place.

Trivia: The film was also released under quite a few titles:-

- Sherlock III
- Sherlock Holmes i Gaskjeldfren (Sherlock Holmes in the gas fire)
- Sherlock Holmes in the Gas Cellar (UK)
- Sherlock Holmes III: The Detective's Adventures in the Gas Cellar (USA)
- The Theft of the State Document (USA)

Holmes University
Internet - 2013 – 2016 (USA)

Writer: Scott Achord
Director: Scott Achord
Sherlock Holmes: Ben Lord & Justin Maldonado
Doctor Watson: Chris Rodriguez

A web series, made by Meteor Fist Films, follows the friendship and adventures of Holmes and Watson as they become roommates in college.   There were four episodes made and broadcast on YouTube with the part of Sherlock Holmes changing from Ben Lord to Justin Maldonado for episodes 3 and 4.

Trivia: Ben Lord had left the film in pre-production due, partly, to scheduling conflicts but also due to on-set tensions.

A full episode list can be found in the "Television Episodes" chapter of this book.

Holmes & Watson
Film - 2018 (USA)

Writer: Etan Cohen
Director: Etan Cohen
Sherlock Holmes: Will Ferrell
Doctor Watson: John C. Reilly

This comedy pastiche of Sherlock Holmes and John Watson has its tongue firmly placed into its cheek with both characters batting below average in intelligence. Professor Moriarty sends a note to Sherlock Holmes, a birthday gift of a great case which will challenge his wits. He now has four days in which to find and stop Moriarty from destroying London and killing Queen Victoria. His motive is to re-write history and only Holmes and Watson can stop him.   This slapstick comedy is more in the vein of Ferrell and Reilly's previous films such as *Stepbrothers* and *Talladega Nights,* however, there are some references not only to the Canon, but also other adaptations. The Baker Street Irregulars make an appearance as does a female doctor who is called upon to help conduct an autopsy (much like Molly Hooper in *Sherlock*). The gross comedy, factual errors (Queen Victoria visits the Titanic, for example, which set sail eleven years after her death) and slapstick nature of the film didn't garner favourable reviews with Terry Staunton of The Radio Times writing that the film was, "A sad and embarrassing stain on the CVs of everyone involved."

Connection: Will Ferrell has played Sherlock Holmes once before. He played opposite Darrell Hammond as Watson in a *Saturday Night Live* sketch in 2001 where he performed as Robert Goulet playing the part of Sherlock Holmes.

Hotelrottern
(The Hotel Rats AKA The Hotel Thieves)
Film - 1911 (Denmark)

Writer: Not credited
Director: Not credited
Sherlock Holmes: Einar Zangenberg
Doctor Watson: N/A

This one-reel silent movie was another release by the Norkdisk Film Company although the writer and director are unknown. The victim of a theft at his hotel room comes to Sherlock Holmes for help. Unfortunately for Holmes, he is recognised by the criminals when he takes up a room in the hotel and they attempt to suffocate him by blocking the vents in his chimney. Ironically he is saved as burglars break into his room by smashing through the window. He pursues the criminals and is attacked and thrown from a moving train. There is a shoot-out on the rooftops before he traces the thieves to Switzerland. Once there he faces off with his arch enemy who, during a fight and a struggle, falls over a precipice in a nod to the death of Moriarty at Reichenbach Falls.

Review: In January 1911 *The Moving Picture World* praised this movie whilst offering a slight to its predecessors. *"Sherlock Holmes is engaged to run down the criminals, and the adventures that befall him are much more numerous and serious than is usually the case with this detective."*

Der Hund von Baskerville
(The Dog of Baskerville)
Film - 1914 (Germany)

Writers: Richard Oswald, Julius Philipp & Robert Liebmann
Directors: Rudolf Meiner, Richard Oswald & Willy Zeyn
Sherlock Holmes: Alwin Neuß
Doctor Watson: N/A

This hour-long silent movie was the first in a series of six Baskerville Hound movies made by Vitascope. The film stays, somewhat, faithful to the original book with Holmes being called to help Lord Henry who is being dogged by the evil Stapleton. In this adaptation there is no John Watson and Lord Henry is engaged to be married to Laura Lyons. The series was not without its problems, a film called *The Dark Castle* was meant to be the third in the Baskerville series but due to a legal dispute involving the unions, the film was released separately without Holmes as the detective. The Eerie/Creepy room was released as film number three instead.

History: The last two films, even though produced in 1916, became the subject of a censorship ban due to World War I. German authorities were not happy with the portrayal of an English gentleman as the hero and as such, the films were not released until 1920.

Titles in the Series:

Der Hund von Baskerville: Das einsame Haus
(The Lonely House/ The Isolated House) - **1914**

Stapleton manages to escape the night before he is due to be executed for his terrible crimes. He kidnaps Lord Henry and

Laura Lyons and keeps them in an ingenious house which can be lowered into a lake. When Holmes finds and rescues the couple, Stapleton attempts to murder them by shattering a window and letting in the lake water. As Holmes completes his rescue it seems that Stapleton may not have been so lucky.

Der Hund von Baskerville: Das unheimliche Zimmer

(*The Eerie Room/The Creepy Room*) -1916

Having managed to escape a watery grave, Stapleton returns to torment Lord Henry and Laura Lyons and seek vengeance on Sherlock Holmes. A sophisticated battle ensues resulting in one man being eliminated.

Der Hund von Baskerville: Die Sage vom Hund von Baskerville

(The Legend of the Hound of Baskerville) - **1915**

Set back in the 16th century, a lust-filled knight sets his sights on the pure Countess Baskerville. When he is rejected, he returns to forcibly take the Countess. When the count, the ancestor of Sherlock Holmes, finds out he vanquishes the villain.

Der Hund von Baskerville: Dr. Macdonald's Sanatorium

(The Sanatorium of Dr. Macdonald) **1920**

Virtually no information exists on the narrative of this film which is stored at the Gosfilmofond film archive / Filmmuseum München film archive. According to the character list the film does feature Stapleton, Laura Lyons and Sir Henry Baskerville.

Der Hund von Baskerville: Das Haus ohne Fenster

(The House without Windows)
 1920

The new nobleman of Baskerville finds more than he bargained for as it transpires that a curse threatens him and his family. Sherlock Holmes is sent for to investigate.

Der Hund von Baskerville

Der Hund von Baskerville Film - 1937 (Germany)

Writer: Carla von Stackelberg
Director: Karel Lamac
Sherlock Holmes: Bruno Güttner
Doctor Watson: Fritz Odemar

Another Hound adaptation from Germany, this time by the Ondra-Lamac-Film company. Starting with Lord Baskerville murdering his wife and the man with whom she has been having an affair. The curse is placed upon Baskerville and it is said that the sounds of dogs howling and a woman screaming can be heard over the desolate moors. The familiar story of the Baskervilles is allowed to unfold, meaning that Holmes and Watson do not appear in the first 30 minutes of the film. Much the same as the novel, more time is given to Dr. Watson in this version as he and Lord Baskerville carry the bulk of the story. More is made of the escaped convict narrative and the hound itself hardly gets any film time.

History: The film has fallen into infamy, not for the beautiful cinematography or the chemistry between Guttner and Odemar, but because this was one of only two films found in the bunker of Adolf Hitler when the Allies infiltrated it in 1945.

The Hound of the Baskervilles Film - 1931 (UK)

Writer: Edgar Wallace
Director: Gareth Gundrey
Sherlock Holmes: Robert Rendel
Doctor Watson: Frederick Lloyd

The film stays, mostly faithful to the original story with Sherlock Holmes coming to the aide of Sir Henry Baskerville who is being threatened by the family curse and a monstrous hound. With a budget of £25,000 this adaptation was the first version of The Hound of the Baskervilles to be made into a talking picture. For many years, however, it was thought that only the visuals existed and the film remained silent.

When the soundtrack was, eventually, discovered a crude restoration of the film was made and donated to the British Film Institute by the Rank Corporation. Those Sherlockians who have seen the film have been less than enthusiastic about Robert Rendel's performance and the film's poor production values.

Review: *Picturegoer* magazine in the UK wrote, "...this picture fails to do justice to Conan Doyle's thrilling Sherlock Holmes story."

The Hound of the Baskervilles Film - 1939 (USA)

Writer: Ernest Pascal
Director: Sidney Lanfield
Sherlock Holmes: Basil Rathbone
Doctor Watson: Nigel Bruce

This is certainly one of the more popular cinematic remakes of Doyle's novel, and also the first film where the iconic Basil Rathbone and Nigel Bruce play the roles for which they will forever be remembered (although *The Adventures of Sherlock Holmes* was also produced in the same year). The film stays faithful to the original narrative with Watson being sent on whilst Holmes stays in London, joining him later to help solve the case of this mysterious and murderous hound, The hound, a Great Dane, was referred to as Chief but its real name was Blitzen.

The studio thought that the name sounded "too German" and changed it. Although the film was made at the time of the Hays Code (a list of cinematic rules of propriety and censorship) it does make some reference to Holmes's drug habit with the last line of the film being, "Oh Watson, the needle." In the original story, it is discovered that Miss Stapleton is the wife of the villain John Stapleton and not his sister. But this narrative is not part of this adaptation.

Trivia: Fox was, at that time, unsure of how successful the films or the actors would become which is why the top billing on the original release went to Richard Greene who played Sir Henry Baskerville.

Hound of the Baskervilles Film - 1959 (UK)

Writer: Peter Bryan
Director: Terence Fisher
Sherlock Holmes: Peter Cushing
Doctor Watson: André Morell

This was the first Sherlock Holmes film to be made in colour and brought together two of Hammer Horror's most well-known actors, Peter Cushing and Christopher Lee. In a move away from Dracula and Frankenstein flicks into the world of Conan Doyle, they made their own interpretation of the story. There were plans to make more Sherlock Holmes movies but the Hammer Horror audiences wanted more monsters, so the idea was dropped.

There are many deviations from the original film including Sir Henry being attacked by a tarantula, Watson falling into quicksand, mentions made of diabolical satanic rituals, John Stapleton's wife/sister becomes his daughter, and Sir Henry suffers a slight heart attack at the mere sound of the hound. The daughter, Celia Stapleton, is a cold-blooded killer, luring Sir Henry to the moors and revealing her intentions of letting the hound kill him. But when her plan is interrupted by Holmes and Watson, she attempts to kill Watson. The hound is shot and, wounded, it attacks and mauls John Stapleton to death before Holmes kills it. The hound is nothing more than a Great Dane wearing a hideous mask and, in this version, it is Celia who runs off into the mire and sinks to her death.

Trivia: During filming they couldn't get the hound, Colonel, to attack Christopher Lee, no matter how many times they goaded it. At the point where Lee gave up, the dog suddenly lunged and bit into his arm.

The Hound of the Baskervilles
Television - 1972 (USA)

Writer: Robert E. Thompson
Director: Barry Crane
Sherlock Holmes: Stewart Granger
Doctor Watson: Bernard Fox

This TV movie is the first American made colour adaptation of the novel and was shown on the ABC network. It was supposedly part of a proposed series of TV movies which would feature a variety of literary detectives. However, the ratings and the reviews for *The Hound of the Baskervilles* were none too favourable.

Due to the bad reviews and audience feedback The series never came to fruition. Although the adaptation sticks mostly to the original narrative, the biggest complaint by viewers was the distractingly bad sets, with the moor studio sets and crude blue screen seemingly the worst offenders. This is regarded as one to watch for Sherlock Holmes completest and fans of "so bad it's good" movies.

Review: This proved to be another Holmes adaptation which fell victim to some bad press, with the LA Times writing that the film was, "laborious, talky, often poorly staged and it suffers intermittently with show-and-tell direction."

The Hound of the Baskervilles

The Hound of the Baskervilles
Film - 1978 (UK)

Writers: Peter Cook, Dudley Moore
& Paul Morrissey
Director: Paul Morrissey
Sherlock Holmes: Peter Cook
Doctor Watson: Dudley Moore

This absurdist and comical take on the Baskerville story is far removed from the actual novel with only a few characters and narrative strands surviving. Whist their comedy sketches played well for laughs, this adaptation was not well-received by Sherlock Holmes' fans, Pete and Dud fans or fans of cinema. The Washington Post wrote that it was "one for the dogs," actor Terry Thomas (who plays Dr. Mortimer) is quoted as saying, "there was no magic...it was bad," and the movie maintains a 0% rating on the film review aggregation website Rotten Tomatoes.

Too tired to bother with the Baskerville case, Holmes gives it to Watson whom Dudley Moore plays with a very strong Welsh accent. Peter Cook, it should be noted, gives Sherlock Holmes a strong, stereotypical Jewish accent which is something else that audiences found confusing. Sherlock's mother is a psychic who shams old ladies for money. Ms. Stapleton tries to seduce Watson and is frequently possessed by spirits. Sir Henry and John Watson are treated like prisoners at Baskerville Hall; there is a recurring urinating Chihuahua; the escaped convict is friends with the Stapleton family who invite Watson and Sir Henry to dinner only to have Mrs Stapleton cover them in blue vomit during a possession. As they leave, the daughter follows intending to murder Sir Henry and Watson only to fall into a quagmire and the hound turns out to be nothing more than a dog with a loud bark. The dog, as it turns out, is the heir to the family fortune and is actually the target rather than the perpetrator.

Connection: Comedy writing and performing duo "Pete and Dud" first played the iconic detective and doctor in a sketch for the television show *Goodbye Again* in 1968 for the British network ITV.

The Hound of the Baskervilles Television - 1982 (UK)

Writer: Alexander Baron
Director: Peter Duguid
Sherlock Holmes: Tom Baker
Doctor Watson: Terence Rigby

This four part BBC drama was broadcast during the Sunday Classics era of period drama and literary adaptations. The story is faithful to the original with only a few story strands being removed for time constraints. The relationship between Mr. Franklin and his daughter Laura is almost non-existent and the ending has been changed so that after a lacklustre attempt to rescue Stapleton from the mire, he is witnessed sinking to his demise. This was Tom Baker's first television role since playing Doctor Who and in the episode *The Talons of Weng-Chiang* his doctor is dressed in the Sherlock Holmes outfit of deerstalker, coat and pipe. As in most productions, the dog was the most troublesome part with it forming a strong attachment to the actor Nicholas Woodeson who was playing Sir Henry Baskerville. This being the case, the dog refused to attack him and the crew went so far as to try sewing sausages into the lapels of Woodeson's jackets in an attempt to lure the dog to jump up.

Interview: Tom Baker has often been criticised for his portrayal of Holmes but he is also not above criticizing his own performance. In a Radio 4 interview from 2009 he stated, "I wasn't very good at playing Sherlock Holmes, the BBC apologised for my performance in it."

The Hound of the Baskervilles Television - 1983 (UK/USA)

Writer: Charles Edward Pogue
Director: Douglas Hickox
Sherlock Holmes: Ian Richardson
Doctor Watson: Donald Churchill

This creation of American producer Sy Weintraub and British producer Otto Plaschkes was broadcast on the HBO network and shown in the UK under the title *Sir Arthur Conan Doyle's The Hound of the Baskervilles.* This adaptation stays fairly close to the original story with only a few minor differences. The farm girl at the start of the legendary tale does not die of fear after running for her life, instead the horse she rides falls into the Grimpen Mire and as she drags herself out she is attacked by Lord Baskerville. The character of Laura Lyons does not make it out of the story unscathed but she does acquire Brian Blessed as an estranged husband. During the film Blessed's character, Geoffrey Lyons, demonstrates his impressive strength which is a reference to Dr Grimesby Roylott's poker bending skills in Doyle's *The Adventure of The Speckled Band*. This is also another adaptation where Holmes tries to save Stapleton from the grip of the mire, but fails.

Trivia: There were plans to make a series of Sherlock Holmes television movies, however, shortly after production it was announced that Granada Television had been given the go-ahead to film the Jeremy Brett adaptations. After a court case which found in Weintraub's favour, he decided to simply abandon his plans to make any further episodes.

The Hound of the Baskervilles Television - 2000 (Canada)

Writer: Joe Wiesenfeld
Director: Rodney Gibbons
Sherlock Holmes: Matt Frewer
Doctor Watson: Kenneth Welsh

This is the first of four Sherlock Holmes stories to star Matt Frewer in the title role. Although the narrative never strays far from the original Doyle story, the film is often criticised due to the performance of Frewer. With Watson remaining the focus of the investigation, one critic wondered if Frewer's rubber faced over-acting was a ploy to make the most of his time on screen, "...he didn't just go over the top, but took a running jump over the top with a boost from a springboard!" The film has also been criticised due to the diminished on screen appearances of the hound as well as for its lack of authenticity in its location.

Trivia: In 2001 the film's costume designer won a Gemini Award (the Canadian equivalent of an Emmy Award) for Best Costume Design.

The Hound of the Baskervilles
Television - 2002 (UK)

Writer: Allan Cubitt
Director: David Attwood
Sherlock Holmes: Richard Roxburgh
Doctor Watson: Ian Hart

Another BBC adaptation, this time in conjunction with Tiger Aspect production company. The film made quite a few changes to the original story as well as showing a graphic scene of Holmes shooting up heroin recreationally and during a case rather than to stave away the boredom of having no puzzle to occupy his mind, as in the original. Here it is Stapleton who is the anthropologist rather than Dr. Mortimer and here Mortimer's wife is a psychic who performs séances. The escaped convict, Selden, attacks Lord Baskerville in this version and Mrs Stapleton is murdered by her husband. The narrative strand of Mr. Frankland and his daughter Laura Lyons has also been removed. Amongst a few other minor changes the backstory takes a detour with Hugo Baskerville no longer obsessing and kidnapping a farm girl whom he chases after only to have her escape and die at the spectre of the monstrous hound. In this film, Hugo beats his wife in a fit of jealous rage and chases her out onto the moor where he murders her but is then murdered himself by her protective dog the ghost of which is said to now haunt the family.

Connection: The cast is full of familiar Sherlock Holmes faces with Ian Hart reprising his role of Watson in the 2004 film *Sherlock Holmes and the case of the Silk Stocking*, Richard Roxburgh played Holmes's nemesis, Moriarty, in the 2003 movie *The League of Extraordinary Gentleman* and Richard E Grant who has played Mycroft in the 2002 TV movie *Sherlock: A Case of Evil* and Sherlock Holmes in the 1992 BBC drama *The Other Side.*

The Hound of London
Film - 1993
(Luxemburg/Canada)

Writers: Craig Bowlsby & Craig Bowlsby
Directors: Gil Letourneau & Peter Reynolds-Long
Sherlock Holmes: Patrick Macnee
Doctor Watson: John Scott-Paget

Based on the stage play by Craig Bowlsby the film sees Inspector Lestrade needing the help of Sherlock Holmes to investigate a murder at The Strand Theatre which happens to include "The Woman," Irene Adler, as a murder suspect. A host of characters involve themselves in comedic slapstick which did not ingratiate the film to its viewers, and most of the action happens on the theatre stage with suspects being brought in and taken away one by one to be questioned by Holmes and Watson. Whilst deducing that the actor Lance Sterling planned to swap the blanks in the stage gun for real ones in an attempt to murder the King of Bohemia (who is bound to want to see Irene Adler perform), Lestrade is knocked unconscious and his gun is stolen by lead actor Rex London. He removes his stage make up to reveal that he is, in fact, Moriarty who intends to start up his criminal empire once Bohemia is plunged into chaos following the death of the king. After a game of verbal chess, played out by Watson at the chess board, the scores are settled in a dashing sword fight.

Review: The production has been criticised for its poor production values and Macnee's performance was described by writer Alan Bates as, "a truly dreadful Holmes, wheezing out every line while resembling nothing less than an unshelled tortoise poured into a monkey suit."

The House of Fear
Film - 1945 (USA)

Writer: Roy Chanslor
Director: Roy William Neill
Sherlock Holmes: Basil Rathbone
Doctor Watson: Nigel Bruce

Number ten in the Rathbone/Bruce series of films and the only film where Sherlock

Holmes uses Doctor John H. Watson's full name and title.

Very loosely based on Conan Doyle's *The Adventure of the Five Orange Pips* (to the point where only the actual pips signifying death remain), Sherlock Holmes is asked to help investigate when two members of the exclusive Good Comrades Club die under suspicious circumstances. Both men have received envelopes containing nothing but dried orange pips which correlate to the number of members left in the club.

It is revealed that a large insurance policy has been taken out by each member which cites the other members as beneficiaries of the policy. As the murders continue, each member suspects the others of trying to kill the others in order to cash in the policies. Holmes solves the mystery when Watson goes missing; he has been kidnaped by the club members who are all alive and well. In a major plot twist it is revealed that the members all faked their deaths in order to frame the last man standing, Bruce Alistair, and collect his insurance pay-out.

Quote:
Sherlock Holmes: This is a most unique case. Instead of too few we have too many clues and too many suspects. The main pattern of the puzzle seems to be forming, but the pieces don't fit in.

The House of Fear

How Sherlock Changed the World
Documentary - 2013 (USA)

Writer: Not credited
Director: Paul Bernays
Sherlock Holmes: Edward Cartwright
Doctor Watson: Geraint Hill

A documentary, which was broadcast on the PBS network in America, explores the relationship between Sherlock Holmes and real-life crime investigations and forensic sciences. The program mixes dramatic re-enactments of Holmes and Watson collecting data at crime scenes with interviews from historians, Sherlockians and forensic scientists to explore how Holmes solved crimes through seemingly inconsequential details. This two-part television documentary covers such areas as toxicology, ballistics, fingerprints and handwriting samples as tools for crime-solving and talks to the real-life scientists and detectives who were inspired by Holmes.

Trivia: As mentioned in the program, Sherlock Holmes is the only fictional character ever to be honoured by the Royal Chemistry Society. In 2002 he received a Fellowship and a silver medal was struck in his name.

Incident at Victoria Falls
Television - 1992 (UK, Belgium, Italy & Luxembourg)

Writers: Gerry O'Hara & Bob Shayne
Director: Bill Corcoran
Sherlock Holmes: Christopher Lee
Doctor Watson: Patrick Macnee

Also known as Sherlock Holmes and the *Incident at Victoria Falls* and *Sherlock Holmes: The Star of Africa* this is Christopher Lee's last outing playing Holmes on screen. Sherlock Holmes is all set to retire and move to Sussex to keep and study bees, when he receives a message from his brother via King Edward VIII. Holmes and Watson must now travel to South Africa to retrieve a precious diamond named The Star of Africa and bring it safely to the UK. Once there the jewel is stolen and a dead body is left at the scene of the crime. Whilst investigating the crime Holmes interacts with various famous people including Theodore Roosevelt and Lillie Langtry. The plot bears some similarity to the Basil Rathbone movie *Terror by Night* (1946) where Holmes and Watson oversee the security of the diamond the Star of Rhodesia. Other references include death by blow pipe as in *The Sign of Four* which was coated with the poison extracted from the devil's foot root, the same poison used by Tregennis and Sterndale in *The Adventure of the Devil's Foot.*

Quote:

Sherlock Holmes: Watson, I think you should perform a post-mortem on this woman.

Doctor Watson: Good God, Holmes, she was ripped apart by crocodiles.

It's a Mystery, Charlie Brown
Animation - 1974 (USA)

Writers: Charles M. Schulz, Joseph A. Bailey,
Jerry Juhl, Jeff Moss, Norman Stiles,
Jon Stone & Ray Sipherd
Director: Phil Roman
Sherlock Holmes: Snoopy
Doctor Watson: Woodstock

An animated television special from the creators of Charlie Brown which was broadcast on the CBS network. Woodstock's nest has vanished and so he turns to his friend Snoopy to help him find it. Assuming the dress and persona of Sherlock Holmes and Watson, they search high and low until they come across a set of footprints which lead away from Woodstock's tree. These lead to a school where the nest is being displayed in a glass case. The nest is retrieved but Charlie Brown's sister, Sally, complains that the nest for her class project has been stolen. Insisting that the nest belongs to her and not Woodstock they end up in a make-shift courtroom presided over by Lucy who rules that the nest does, indeed, belong to Woodstock. Although distraught at having no project for school, Snoopy volunteers to recreate the experiment with Pavlov's dog and Sally ends up with an A.

Trivia: This is the first special which Bill Melendez did not direct - although it is claimed that he provided the "voices" for Snoopy and Woodstock.

In Search of...Sherlock Holmes
Television – 1978 (USA)

Writer: J.Francis Hitching
Director: J.Francis Hitching
Sherlock Holmes: Various
Doctor Watson: Various

Presented by Leonard Nimoy. *In Search of* was a television series which ran in syndication in America from 1977–1982 and was devoted to unexplained phenomena, mysteries and interesting historical events. It covered subjects such as Pyramid Secrets, Bermuda Triangle Pirates, The Lost Colony of Roanoke and The Loch Ness Monster. In this episode, broadcast on December 21st,1978, the program dedicated its time to solving the mystery of Sherlock Holmes and asking the question, did he actually exist? Mixing clips of classic on-screen portrayals of Sherlock Holmes with biographical elements of Sir Arthur Conan Doyle, including looking at Professor Joseph Bell, the show "investigates" how much of Doyle's real life experiences can be found in his stories. Unfortunately the show opens with Nimoy quoting lines from literature, starting with Shakespeare's, "To be or not to be..." followed by the Dickens line, "It was the best of times, it was the worst of times" and ending it with "Elementary, my dear Watson. Elementary," which he attributes to Sherlock Holmes. However, as all Sherlockians know, Holmes never said that line which brings into question the credibility of the show, even more so when it is declared at the end that, yes, Sherlock Holmes "in a very real way" did exist.

Connection: In the movie *Star Trek VI: The Undiscovered Country*, Leonard Nimoy's character Spock quotes Sherlock Holmes with the line, "An ancestor of mine maintained that if you eliminate the impossible, whatever remains, however unlikely, must be the truth."

The Interior Motive
Film - 1976 (USA)

Writers: Richard Smith, David Benjamin, Stephen Jordan, Willard Whitson, Greg Wombel, Guy Mendes, Marsha Cooper Hellard, Tim Tassie & George Rasmussen
Director: George Rasmussen
Sherlock Holmes: Leonard Nimoy
Doctor Watson: Burt Blackwell

Forming part of an educational series of programs under the title *The Universe & I Presents...*, this 20-minute film was made by Kentucky Educational Television and then broadcast on a closed TV circuit only to schools in Kentucky. Holmes finds a globe at the foot of his front door with a strange note attached. "My secret within you must seek out, but spare my skin or break my heart". Holmes is intrigued by the riddle which is nothing but the rules to the game of finding out what is inside the globe without breaking it. Watson is keen for him to solve the puzzle but even keener that he solve it before their guests arrive that evening. Holmes then conducts a number of experiments on the globe, noting its weight, temperature, vibrations and sound. A handy compass continues to point north each time it is near the globe which leads Holmes to his conclusion which he says he shall announce to Watson and the Royal Society when they arrive later. He deduces the location of the core, its material and its temperature noting that "Every good detective, at heart, is a scientist and every good scientist, a detective."

Connection: Even though the programme was used as a tool to engage children in scientific techniques, some thought had gone into adding some Holmes references to the interior of 221b. As well as the more obvious pipe rack and violin, the makers included the Persian slipper by the fireplace, as well as a wax head in reference to *The Adventure of the Empty House* and *The Adventure of the Mazarin Stone*.

In the Footsteps of Sherlock Holmes
Documentary - 1968 (UK)

Writer: British Pathé
Director: British Pathé
Sherlock Holmes: Various
Doctor Watson: Various

Broadcast as part of the *Pathé Pictorial: Picturing this Colourful World* series of news reels, this wonderfully iconic narration depicts members of the Sherlock Holmes Society of London dressed in Holmes attire and arriving in Switzerland. The six-minute film shows members dressed as Sherlock Holmes chasing Moriarty across the country, Holmes and Moriarty's fateful fight at the Reichenbach Falls and the unveiling of a memorial at the foot of the falls. The film also shows members of the society socialising and researching each location where Holmes, Watson and Moriarty may have visited. Not just for completests, this is a lovely look back at Holmes and Watson as well as a historic document of Sherlockians and their dedication to Doyle's iconic character.

History: The Sherlock Holmes Society of London was formed on Tuesday 20 January 1951 and was a resurrection, of sorts, of the 1930s society which included the crime writer Dorothy L Sayers.

In the Footsteps of
Sherlock Holmes

In the Footsteps of Sherlock Holmes
Documentary - 1996 (USA)

Writer: Monica M. Cushman
Director: David McKenzie
Sherlock Holmes: Various
Doctor Watson: Various

Made by Associated Television International this television documentary has now found its home in the DVD market. Hosted by Patrick Macnee, no stranger to Sherlock Holmes, this documentary travels around the city of London where many of the crimes and murders that Holmes investigated were committed. The documentary is split between Macnee taking viewers to the various locations where Sherlock Holmes and John Watson lived and spent time, and extracts from a variety of rare and not-so-rare performances of Holmes and Watson on screen. As well as touring the living quarters of 221b Baker Street, viewers can also put themselves at the locations of some of the most exciting pursuits in which Holmes and Watson were embroiled.

Trivia: Patrick Macnee starred in six television adaptations of Sherlock Holmes (including an episode of 80s action favourite Magnum P.I) but he was not always on the right side of the law. His obituary in *The Telegraph* reads, "His corruption began when he was introduced to whisky by the Roman Catholic Archbishop of Cardiff, who had escaped into the garden with a bottle when brought in to consecrate Evelyn's private chapel. Macnee was then expelled from Eton for running a pornography and bookmaking empire."

The Loss of a Personal Friend
Television - 1987 (UK)

Writer: N.G. Bristow
Director: N.G. Bristow
Sherlock Holmes: Peter Harding
Doctor Watson: Ian Price

This obscure, 14-minute pastiche which focuses mostly on John Watson and his grief after losing his most intimate friend, Sherlock Holmes, is one of the darker forays into the Holmes and Watson relationship. Opening with Watson at the Reichenbach Falls, who cries out in anguish at the murderous event which he is too late to stop. A lone gunshot then rings out in the darkness. Taking up the narrative from *The Empty House*, Watson knocks into an old bookseller, but in a different narrative turn, he notices the old man is carrying the cigarette case which belonged to Holmes. When Watson sees Holmes, just as he does in the story, he faints. Sitting comfortably at 221b Baker Street, Holmes recounts how he escaped the clutches of Moriarty and that he felt he could not inform his friend of his survival in case he were indiscreet and let slip he was not dead.

Holmes must leave and continue his search for his would-be assassin and, naturally, Watson gets his gun to protect Holmes. However, it would appear that Watson has been talking to a figment of his imagination as the viewer is shown the figure of the bookseller, dead with a bullet wound in his head sitting in Holmes's chair in Baker Street. This is a rare find, a downbeat glimpse into the mind of a man driven mad with grief and despair but a refreshing change to see an on-screen Watson who isn't just the patsy for Holmes.

Trivia: This Holmes adaptation is so obscure that the majority of the information about the broadcast comes from the 2012 book *Sherlock Holmes on Screen* by Alan Barnes.

Lelícek ve sluzbách Sherlocka Holmesa
(Lelicek in the Services of Sherlock Holmes)
Film - 1932 (Czechoslovakia)

Writer: Václav Wasserman & Hugo Vavris
Director: Karel Lamac
Sherlock Holmes: Martin Fric
Doctor Watson: NA

This short film from Czechoslovakia, promoted as a comedy, has Holmes being asked by Fernando XXIII to find him a body double as he fears he will be assassinated. Holmes finds František Lelíček an almost identical looking man to Fernando (played by the same actor Vlasta Burian) and he quickly takes his place. The Queen refuses to run from possible assassinators and so stays and finds herself embroiled in a love affair with lookalike Lelíček. Whilst planning another assassination attempt, the villainous terrorists overpower Holmes and lock him in a basement. They plan to attempt the assassination, releasing the "hell machine" which is to be launched after a new state anthem is played. Luckily Holmes escapes in time to thwart the attempt and saves the lives of Lelíček and the Queen. Sadly the king, Fernando, dies whist in hiding and so the Queen and Lelíček decide to continue with their façade.

Trivia: The film is based on the book *František Lelíček v službách Sherlocka Holmesa* (Frantisek Lelicek in the service of Sherlock Holmes) by Hugo Vavrečka under the pseudonym Hugo Vavris.

Lost in Limehouse
Film - 1933 (USA)

Writer: Otto Brower
Director: Harrington Reynolds & Walter Weems
Sherlock Holmes: Olaf Hytten
Doctor Watson: Charles McNaughton

Also known as *Lady Esmeralda's Predicament,* this early parody features the characters Sheerluck Jones and Hotson who must come to the rescue of Lady Esmeralda. The daughter of the Duke of Dunkwell, Esmeralda has been kidnaped by Sir Marmaduke Rakes and is being held in a Chinese den of caricatured gangsters in Limehouse. The pair disguise themselves as Chinese gentlemen and go undercover hoping to avoid detection; however, Holmes keeps sneezing due to having a cold and one of the criminals mistakes it for a coded sign that they are mighty warriors. After rescuing her from a literal powder keg, she is captured once again by Marmaduke but this time he is confronted by Esmeralda's fiancé, Harold Heartright, and a bizzare "fight" breaks out between the two with Marmaduke being repeatedly punched down a set of

stairs. Having overpowered Marmaduke, Harold frees Esmeralda just in time to have the entire street blow up around them. This quirky social satire is full of oddities and is more like an episode of *The Goon Show*, but its comments on social standing and the class system are still relevant today.

Quote:
Sheerluck Jones: There's a body on the floor.

Harold Heartright: How can you tell?

Sheerluck Jones: I'm standing on it.

Les Dalton Contre Sherlock Holmes. Les Nouvelles Aventures de Lucky Luke (*Lucky Luke vs. Sherlock Holmes: The New Adventures of Lucky Luke*)
Animation - 2001 (France/Canada)

Writer: Yves Coulon
Director: Olivier Jean Marie
Sherlock Holmes: Eric Legrand
Doctor Watson: N/A

This episode was broadcast as part of *The New Adventures of Lucky Luke* animation on the France 3 network in France and the Télé-Québec network in Canada. The series is about the cowboy Lucky Luke and his horse Jolly Jumper and ran from 2001–2003. Here, Queen Victoria visits President Grant in the White House and, over dinner, states that Sherlock Holmes is the greatest detective in the world. To counter this, the butler reminds Grant that America has Lucky Luke the cowboy, a man so quick that he can out draw his own shadow. The two then wager on who can catch the Daltons first (a gang who are continually brought back to prison by Lucky Luke after they keep escaping). Luke discovers Sherlock Holmes in a forest; he has been assaulted by criminals and is precariously hanging by his neck from a tree. Luke rescues Holmes and they discover that they are both on a quest to recapture the Daltons. Their investigation takes them to a bar where Holmes becomes embroiled in a fight and wins a large amount of money in a poker game; however, he is picked up by a very angry Queen Victoria who is determined to win her bet, but before he can resume his investigation their carriage is ambushed. The Daltons take the kidnaped Queen Victoria and Holmes and hide them in a cave behind a waterfall, an obvious reference to the famous Reichenbach Falls. It is now up to Lucky Luke to follow the clues and find the villainous gang. Although Luke does rescue Holmes and the Queen, and puts the Daltons back in prison, Luke is not happy that the escape was a set up in order to win a bet. The episode ends with Lucky Luke punching President Grant in the eye and walking out in disgust.

Trivia: In this adaptation, Queen Victoria refers to Holmes as *Sir* Sherlock Holmes even though Watson made reference in *The Adventure of the Three Garridebs* that Sherlock Holmes, "…refused a knighthood for services which may perhaps some day be described."

The Man Who Disappeared
Television - 1951 (UK)

Writers: Not credited
Directors: Richard M. Grey
Sherlock Holmes: John Longden
Doctor Watson: Campbell Singer

The plot is based on the original Doyle story *The Man with the Twisted Lip* and it was released under the original title as an alternative in the UK. Although Conan Doyle is the only credited "writer" of the film, the plot differs significantly from the original story. Mr. Neville St. Clair is visited by a mysterious woman during a party and then vanishes. Mrs. St. Clair then employs the services of Sherlock Holmes and John Watson (who was at the party and saw the mysterious woman) to help find her husband. Rather than Neville St. Clair using his theatrical make-up and performance skills to beg for money as an income, as in the original version, here he is being blackmailed into disguising himself as a beggar to work as a dope peddler for the drug dealer Luzatto. Luzatto has managed to convince St. Clair that he murdered the husband of Doreen (the mysterious woman at the party) whilst awakening from a "drugs sleep." In this version it is Doreen who sends the ring to assure Mrs. St. Clair that her husband is safe and Mr. St. Clair is not arrested for

murder, but held captive by the criminal gang. Holmes and Watson follow the clues, free Mr. St Clair and vanquish the criminal gang.

Trivia: Originally intended to be part of a series of Sherlock Holmes adaptations, this pilot failed to make an impression with the networks and so the series never materialised.

The Man who Disappeared

Der Mann, der Sherlock Holmes war
(*The Man Who Was Sherlock Holmes*)
Film - 1937 (Germany)

Writers: Robert A. Stemmle & Karl Hartl
Directors: Karl Hartl
Sherlock Holmes: Hans Albers
Doctor Watson: Heinz Rühmann

This film was also released in the USA under the title *Zwei Lustige Abenteurer* (Two Merry Adventurers) and follows two confidence tricksters who pose as Sherlock Holmes and John Watson in order to gain a free train ride. They also take this opportunity to become a little friendly with two orphan sisters who are travelling to receive a large inheritance. When a group of criminals hear that "Holmes and Watson" are on board they flee and the pair maintain their false identities and start investigating. They then manage to talk their way into a free room at an expensive hotel under the guise of needing it for their investigation. Once they get fully into the role of the detective duo, they manage to track down and capture a gang of counterfeiters and also manage to recover a priceless stamp collection. However, in calling the police, the pair are arrested for impersonating Holmes and Watson. Luckily the tricksters are found not guilty and live happily ever after with the two sisters from the train. The film was made in the same year that the production company, Universum Film (UFA), fell under German state control and is often commented on due to the lack of any *heavy* propaganda. It has been noted that the film may have been an attempt by the state to demonstrate that Germany could produce a quality detective movie which was able to hold its own with the best American films of the same genre.

History: Alongside *The Hound of the Baskervilles* (1937), this film was the other title found in the bunker of Adolf Hitler when the Allies captured it in 1945.

The Many Faces of Sherlock Holmes
Documentary - 1985 (USA)

Writers: Ray Atherton, Michael Avery & Bob Greenberg
Directors: Michael Muscal
Sherlock Holmes: Various
Doctor Watson: Various

Christopher Lee hosts this archival footage documentary focusing on the many adaptations of Sherlock Holmes from, the original writings of Conan Doyle to the actors who have played him on the big and small screen. From a mocked up 221b Baker Street – as well as a little outside location work – Lee presents a dynasty of Holmes and Watson as portrayed by many actors between 1900 and 1985. The documentary also includes interviews with Sherlockians and academics.

Trivia: Hard to believe, but this well-loved actor struggled in his early years to get film roles because, at 6' 5", he was markedly talker than the majority of leading actors.

The Mary Morstan Mysteries
Internet - 2012 – 2015 (USA)

Writer: Ross K. Foad
Directors: Ross K. Foad
Sherlock Holmes: Ross K. Foad
Doctor Watson: Mike Archer

This Internet based web series is a companion piece to the web series *No Place Like Holmes*, created by Ross. K. Foad. In the three years of production, nine episodes were made, all of which were set in the 1800s and focused on the adventures of Dr. John Watson's wife. Stories included Mary Morstan becoming embroiled in the suffragette movement, a blackmail case involving Charles Augustus Milverton, an alter ego called Horace Moustachio and an investigation into The Moriarty Club after they release a strength enhancement serum to the black market. Although low budget and amateur in its execution, it is an interesting addition to the Holmes narrative web.

Trivia: Actor Andy Wolf was cast as the character Eduardo Estaban and asked a Spanish friend to record herself speaking his lines in order to make his accent more believable. He also learned the famous *Monty Python and the Holy Grail* line, "Your mother was a hamster and your father smelled of elderberries" in Spanish to use during the show.

A full episode list can be found in the "Television Episodes" chapter of this book

The Masks of Death. 1984
Television - (UK)

Writers: Anthony Hinds & N.J. Crisp
Directors: Roy Ward Baker
Sherlock Holmes: Peter Cushing
Doctor Watson: John Mills

Notable for being Peter Cushing's final television appearance before his death on August 11, 1994; this is a story from the "retired Holmes" genre of stories. Inspector MacDonald of Scotland Yard approaches an almost retired Sherlock Holmes to help solve a baffling spate of murders in London's East End. The only thing connecting the victims is the same terrified expression on their faces. As Holmes and Watson investigate this intriguing case, another even more interesting case turns up at the door of 221b Baker Street. The Home Secretary brings Graf Udo von Felseck, a man who is visiting England on a secret mission to accompany a very wealthy and important companion, to visit Holmes as his wealthy travelling partner has been kidnapped. Unless Holmes can track him down, war between Britain and Germany will become imminent. As the elderly Holmes and Watson begin their investigation into this new case (whilst also escaping an attempt on Holmes' life) they happen across the path of Irene Adler and indulge in a little nostalgia. During his investigation, Holmes discovers a plot that will destroy Britain should there be a war, it becomes apparent that the kidnapping and Felseck are part of a bigger plan to bring Britain to her knees.

Trivia: As well as being the final performance of Peter Cushing, this was also to be the last film performance of Anne Baxter who played the part of Irene Adler. There were plans to make a follow-up TV movie called *The Abbot's Cry,* but this proved unworkable as insurers would not cover the elderly Peter Cushing for filming.

Meitantei Holmes
(*Sherlock Hound)*
Television - 1984-85
(Italy/Japan)

Head writers: Marco Pagot, Mayumi Shimazaki
& Keishi Yamazaki
Series directors: Kyôsuke Mikuriya & Hayao Miyazaki
Sherlock Holmes: Taichirô Hirokawa
Doctor Watson: Lewis Arquette

This animated series was a joint project between Japan's *Tokyo Movie Shinsha* and the Italian public broadcasting corporation *RAI*. Taking the Disney route of anthropomorphic animals, Sherlock Hound (who is actually a fox) solves crimes with Dr. Watson as they battle their nemesis Professor Moriarty (who is a wolf). Many of

the episodes were based on the Conan Doyle original stories and appear with amended titles such as *The Four Signatures, The Crown of Mazalin, The Disappearance of the Splendid Royal Horse* and *The Missing Bride Affair*. The production was suspended in 1981 due to issues with the Conan Doyle estate and the long delay meant that a new director, Kyôsuke Mikuriya, had to be brought in as the original director, Hayao Miyazaki, had moved on to other projects. Although in the English dubbed version of the cartoon, Holmes was called Sherlock Hound by the rest of the characters, in the original version his name continued to be Sherlock Holmes.

Trivia: The original director, Miyazaki, wanted to write Mrs. Hudson in as the real genius of the show, but the studio overruled it.

A full episode list can be found in the "Television Episodes" chapter of this book

The Memoirs of Sherlock Holmes
Television - 1994 (UK)

Writers: Various
Directors: Various
Sherlock Holmes: Jeremy Brett
Doctor Watson: Edward Hardwicke

The last in the run of Granada-made Sherlock Holmes series and the last time Holmes was to be played by Jeremy Brett who died on the 12th of September 1995. His ill health was also evident in the production of these last six episodes, with episode 5, *The Mazarin Stone*, featuring Brett only briefly. Here Watson teams up with Mycroft Holmes in order to solve the mystery. The episode was also a combination of two Conan Doyle stories, *The Mazarin Stone* and *The Three Garridebs*.

Trivia: In the episode *The Golden Pince-Nez* actor Mycroft Holmes (Charles Gray) became Sherlock's partner instead of Doctor Watson Because Edward Hardwicke was busy filming the movie *Shadowlands* (1993).

A full episode list can be found in the "Television Episodes" chapter of this book

The Memoirs of Sherlock Holmes:
The Adventure of the Golden Pince-Nez

Milliontestamentet
(*The Stone Legacy*)
Film - 1911 (Denmark)

Writer: Not credited
Director: August Blom
Sherlock Holmes: Alwin Neuss
Doctor Watson: N/A

Also released under the title *Den stjaalne millionobligation* (The Stolen Million Bond) this one-reel, silent movie is presumed to be lost. A wealthy Count makes a will in which his wife stands to inherit a large fortune. A master criminal, by the name of Dr. Mors, plans to steal the will and so fashions a wax impression of the safe keyhole and gives the newly made key to his accomplice who is posing as the Count's nurse. When the will is found to be missing, Sherlock Holmes is brought in to investigate and, suspecting he may be a target, throws his followers off the scent by sending a look-a-like out in his place.

The countess is kidnapped by Mors who sends a note saying he will kill the Countess at midnight if his demands are not met. After breaking into Holmes's chambers Mors reminds Holmes that he cannot be harmed as the Countess will be murdered if he does not return to where she is being held. Mors brings Holmes back to the cottage where the Countess is bound and sets a trap to kill Holmes. The attempt fails and Holmes is able to rescue the Countess and imprison Dr. Mors.

Review: The film received a small write up in the Independent section of *The Moving Picture World* on May 6th, 1911, writing that the film had, "...much merit and interest" and "The photography is good and the acting is quite in keeping with the subject."

The Missing Rembrandt
Film - 1932 (UK)

Writers: H. Fowler Mear & Cyril Twyford
Director: Leslie S. Hiscott
Sherlock Holmes: Arthur Wontner
Doctor Watson: Ian Fleming

Considered to be a lost film, the plot is loosely based on *The Adventure of Charles Augustus Milverton* but in this story he is a master art forger. Sherlock Holmes is brought in to find a missing Rembrandt painting which is believed to have been stolen by a drug-addicted and bitter artist working for the arch-scoundrel, the Baron von Guntermann. There is also another matter involving a blackmail case and the Baron's secretary. A variety of disguises later and a raid on an opium den in Limehouse leads Holmes to unravel the Baron's dastardly plan. Holmes manages to recover the painting and release the secretary from the blackmailer's grip.

Review: A write up in The New York Times stated that, "The Sherlock Holmes of Arthur Wontner is the same ascetic-looking unraveler of mysterious crime" and that the film brought back, "a number of screen actors who by this time seem to be perfectly at home in their parts."

Miss Sherlock
Film - 1908 (USA)

Writer: Not credited
Director: Edwin S. Porter
Sherlock Holmes: Florence Turner
Doctor Watson: N/A

This American silent movie, produced by *Edison Manufacturing Co. / Edison Films*, depicts a broker's daughter, Nell, who has two men fighting for her hand in marriage. Nell favours Jack, which angers the other pursuer, Jim. In order to besmirch the name of the other suitor, Jim plans to frame Jack, but Nell disguises herself as a boy in order to spy on Jim and prevent him from framing Jack. Jim robs the safe and plants damning evidence in Jack's coat in order to remove him from Nell's life. But Nell witnesses the crime and places the documents in Jim's coat instead. When the police are called and find nothing in Jack's coat, Nell suggests they search Jim's pockets where the evidence is found and he is arrested. Nell is praised for her Sherlockian detective skills and is given a blessing by her father for Jack and Nell to marry.

Review: A short write up in *The Moving Picture World* from December 12th , 1908 stated that, "*The photography and acting are good and the film works smoothly.*"

Miss Sherlock
Television - 2018 (Japan)

Writers: Jun'ichi Mori, Nobuaki Kotani, Amane Marumo, Yôsuke Masaike & Mami Oikawa
Directors: F Yûsuke Taki, Jun'ichi Mori, Takashi Matsuo
Sherlock Holmes: Yûko Takeuchi
Doctor Watson: Shihori Kanjiya

This television series, primarily set in contemporary Tokyo, has a female Sherlock Holmes and Dr. Watson and is a co-production between *HBO Asia* and *Hulu Japan*. Sara "Sherlock" Shelly Futaba solves crimes with her flatmate Wato Tachibana, a doctor who has not long returned from volunteering in Syria. Although there is a variety of mysteries and murders to solve, the focus for Sherlock is the secret organization, Stella Maris, who are believed to be behind a number of crimes being committed. There are some changes to other familiar faces; Mrs. Hudson now becomes landlady Kimi Hatano and Mycroft Holmes becomes Kento Futaba, who is the Prime Minister's Secretary.

Trivia: In the series Sherlock plays the cello instead of the violin and the actor Takeuchi spent two and a half months learning to play Bach's Cello Suite No. 1 in G so she could play it during the show.

A full episode list can be found in the "Television Episodes" chapter of this book

Mr. Holmes
Film - 2015 (UK/USA)

Writers: Mitch Cullin & Jeffrey Hatcher
Director: Bill Condon
Sherlock Holmes: Ian McKellen
Doctor Watson: Colin Starkey

A film of multiple story strands that involve flashbacks to past cases as well as travels abroad, this film focuses on a long-retired Sherlock Holmes, now in his early nineties and living in Sussex. He becomes dogged by a 30-year-old case involving a man who needed to know why his wife, Ann Kelmot, had become distant. As Holmes follows the client's wife, he observes her purchasing poisons, cashing cheques and seeming as though she is planning to murder her husband. He deduces, however, that the poison is for herself and she is not paying for an assassin but for grave stones for her miscarried children. As Holmes offers comfort, she offers herself and her companionship to him, but he refuses, telling her to go back to her husband. Although she pours away the poison in front of him, she later kills herself by stepping in front of a train. This fact is what spurred Holmes into retirement and a spiralling depression. The film also takes Holmes to Japan as his health deteriorates; he goes there in search of a product made from prickly ash to help with the onset of dementia.

In Japan he meets Tamiki Umezaki who tells him that Holmes once advised his father to stay in the UK. Holmes, however, has to explain that he never met the man's father, and he probably just wanted to start a new life. Back in Sussex and with his health declining he becomes more reliant on his housekeeper and her son, with whom he forms a special bond as they tend to his apiary. But when the child is found unconscious and covered in stings, his mother becomes angry and tries to burn down the apiary until Holmes explains the stings were from wasps when the child tried to remove a wasp's nest. He confesses that he is full of regret at turning down the opportunity for family and companionship with Ann Kelmot and so Holmes offers to leave his entire estate to his housekeeper and her son after his death if they stay with him.

Trivia: In order to make his performance believable, Sir Ian McKellen took a course in beekeeping with The London Honey Company prior to filming.

Connection: Sherlock Holmes fans will also recognise the actor playing Holmes on screen in the cinema scene, as Nicholas Rowe, who had previously starred in the film *Young Sherlock Holmes* (1985).

Mr. Holmes

Mr. Magoo's Sherlock Holmes: The Famous Adventures of Mr. Magoo
Animation - 1964 (USA)

Writer: True Boardman
Director: Abe Levitow
Sherlock Holmes: Paul Frees
Doctor Watson: Jim Backus

This Sherlock Holmes themed episode was part of the cartoon series *The Famous Adventures of Mr. Magoo* and was broadcast on the NBC network in America. Instead of taking up the lead role of Sherlock Holmes, Mr. Magoo becomes his assistant, Dr. Watson, in order to help solve a mysterious crime. Helen Parkham, a woman who is being followed and has just been run down by a stranger, seeks the help of Sherlock Holmes. She has fallen in love with a ship's officer, Joseph, who has given her a necklace made from a large gold nugget which he brought back from South Africa. Since she came into its possession, she feels as though she has been followed and that her rooms are constantly being searched. Holmes takes

the case and informs Watson that the box in which the necklace was housed was from London, not South Africa, and that the nugget is being used to conceal a precious diamond, the star of Bengal. After stealing the diamond, the criminals send Holmes a letter asking for £2,000 in exchange for the gem. The case takes them to the Marylebone Wax Museum (there could possibly have been rights issues with using the name Madame Tussauds) as the exchange takes place. But the case is not over yet. The diamond which was taken by the crooks was a fake and the real diamond has been hidden inside a wax work. As the wax works are destroyed, the stolen diamond is found and returned to its rightful place, a sacred temple in the Punjab. Holmes then buys Ms. Parkham a diamond necklace with the reward money. For a comedy cartoon, this episode is surprisingly gripping and not that far removed from a live action Sherlock Holmes adaptation.

Connection: The cartoon contains a few nods to some original stories: The smashing of the figures to find the treasure can be found in *The Adventure of the Six Napoleons* and the chasing of stolen treasure is a feature of *The Sign of Four*.

Murder on the Bluebell Line: QED
Documentary - 1987 (UK)

Writer: John Lynch
Director: John Lynch
Sherlock Holmes: Hugh Fraser
Doctor Watson: Ronald Fraser

This episode was part of *QED*, a popular science and general interest documentary series shown at prime time on BBC1 in the UK. This dramatized documentary focuses on the fascinating discovery of The Piltdown Man back in 1912. A collection of bone fragments thought to have been the fossilised remains of a previously unknown early human, were discovered and widely publicised as a possible "missing link" which led to a long scientific investigation in order to determine their legitimacy. It wasn't until 1953 that the bones were confirmed as fake, being a jawbone with orangutan's teeth combined with a human skull. The more interesting part of the Piltdown Man forgery, and the reason for the Holmes and Watson dramatization, is that Conan Doyle was, for a long time, considered to be one of the suspects in perpetrating the hoax. This was due to his home being close to the discovery spot, that he played golf in Piltdown, was a collector of fossils and also wrote about a fossil hoax in his book *The Lost World*. As the detective duo takes a train ride they discuss and analyse the fraud using the same analytical deducing skills as they would if it were one of their cases. In fact they reference many of their cases together whilst Dr. Watson explains the investigation that led to the fraud being exposed. The episode comes to a close at the location in which the fragments were found and Holmes states that he blames British values and British science for taking too long to figure out that the bones were fake. He argues that the scientists were too enraptured with the idea of fame and recognition to carry out their job properly. This disgust at the non-scientific behaviour of the science community leads Holmes to note, *"Our faith in science was dealt a mortal blow, here at the end of the Bluebell Line, that was the real crime of Piltdown Man."* Holmes even casts suspicion on Professor J. T. Hewitt's confession of being the Piltdown hoaxer.

Trivia: In August 2016, Sir Arthur Conan Doyle was exonerated of any suspicion of being involved in the hoax with the blame being directed towards Charles Dawson.

Murder on the Bluebell Line: QED

The Musgrave Ritual
Film - 1912 (France/UK)

Writer: Arthur Conan Doyle
Director: Georges Tréville
Sherlock Holmes: Georges Tréville
Doctor Watson: Mr. Moyse

Released in France under the title *Le tresor des Musgraves.* This 18-minute silent film plot sticks as close to the original Conan Doyle story as a short film will allow, with the butler and maid planning to carry out a robbery based on a mysterious ritual which is handed down to each new member of the household. In this version, however, it is greed rather than revenge which drives the maid to take the treasure and seal the butler in the vaults of the great house. Holmes tries to solve the mystery by calling in the staff and presenting a piece of parchment containing the ritual. He then confronts the woman who gives herself away by showing signs of recognition and fear. She is forced to confess to her crime by Holmes, a crime which has led her, almost, to madness.

Trivia: The film credits Mr. Moyse as playing Doctor Watson but he doesn't feature in the film at all.

My Dear Uncle Sherlock: ABC
Weekend Specials
Television - 1977 (USA)

Writers: Judson Philips & Manya Starr
Director: Arthur H. Nadel
Sherlock Holmes: Royal Dano
Doctor Watson: Robbie Rist

This was broadcast as part of the *ABC Weekend Special*, a Saturday morning anthology of 30-minute films made for children for the ABC Network in America. Young Joey Trimble enjoys spending time with his Uncle Joe, playing Doctor Watson to his Sherlock Holmes. His uncle is keen to impart the Sherlockian idea that circumstance and motive can be misleading, and that he should always trust facts and data. When Joey deduces there is a problem with Mrs. Leggett, the old recluse who lives nearby, because her dog is no longer barking in the yard, it is discovered that her house has been burgled and the elderly woman is in a bad way. The drunken, penniless nephew, Bill Leggett, is suspected of the crime but insists he is innocent. Fuelled by a need to solve the mystery like his hero, Holmes, Joey goes missing and is suspected of being with Dave Taylor, the man the police discover was fired by Mrs Leggett and who still holds a grudge. Whilst Joey and Dave look for Mrs. Leggett's missing dog, Joey becomes suspicious and deduces that it was Dave who was responsible for the break-in. The problem is that he is now stranded in the middle of nowhere with the criminal. Escaping his clutches and leaving him at the bottom of a mountain, Joey runs back to town to tell his uncle "Sherlock" all about the true criminal which allows Bill to walk out a free man.

Quote:
Uncle 'Sherlock' George: You look for the most incriminating, unique piece of evidence. Deduce the truth from that. Circumstance and motive, they can be very confusing. It's evidence that hangs a man.

My Dear Watson: Alfred Hitchcock Presents... Television - 1989 (USA)

Writer: Susan Woollen
Director: Jorge Montesi
Sherlock Holmes: Brian Bedford
Doctor Watson: Patrick Monckton

This episode is part of the iconic *Alfred Hitchcock Presents* anthology of stories which was originally broadcast on the *CBS* and then *NBC* networks in America. Inspector Lestrade has just been released from a sanatorium, having been sent mad by the constant public humiliation of Holmes solving his cases for him, and Sherlock Holmes has just arrived back from a trip abroad. All seems to be going smoothly until Watson gets himself kidnapped. Sherlock is on the case but Lestrade wants to help in order to redeem himself for his past failings. During the investigation, a subterfuge backfires leading to Holmes becoming, seemingly, responsible for the death of his

brother Mycroft. This sends him into a deep, drug-fuelled depression but a letter from Watson, declaring his faith and his love for Sherlock, awakens an enthusiasm within Holmes and spurs him into action once more. Finding Watson, however, is only part of the problem as it is revealed that Lestrade is behind the kidnaping, wanting to prove that he could, indeed, outsmart Sherlock Holmes. But in a twist, and double bluff, Lestrade is actually the evil Moriarty in disguise.

As Watson, Moriarty and Holmes battle wits and spout deductions, the air in the tower where they stand becomes more toxic and so Holmes must fight Moriarty to escape. A swordfight ensues and Holmes and Watson escape as Holmes runs Moriarty through with his blade. Holmes knew of Moriarty's plans all along and, much to the relief of Watson, Mycroft Holmes was also part of the scheme and is alive and well. Holmes and Watson then return to 221b Baker Street to prepare for the return of the Napoleon of Crime.

Quote:
Sherlock Holmes: I have lost whatever skill I once possessed. My total incompetence has caused my best friend's abduction and the death of my brother.

My Dear Watson: Alfred Hitchcock Presents...

The Mystery of Boscombe Vale
Film - 1912 (France/UK)

Writer: Arthur Conan Doyle
Director: Georges Tréville
Sherlock Holmes: Georges Tréville
Doctor Watson: Mr. Moyse

This two-reel silent movie was also released as *Le mystère de Val Boscombe* and treads a very similar path to the Conan Doyle original story *The Boscombe Valley Mystery,* with only a few differences.

The body of McCarthy is found dead, presumably killed by his son with whom he had quarrelled a short time previously. Whilst the authorities are focused on the son, Sherlock Holmes begins his investigation to uncover the truth. It is revealed that, in the past, McCarthy and a man named James Turner knew each other from prospecting for gold in Australia. During a dry spell, the workers threatened to mutiny over poor results when a group of rich prospectors passed by and were set upon and robbed by Turner and his gang. McCarthy, however, flees the scene to safety with his young daughter. Years later a poor McCarthy finds that Turner is now a rich farmer and in order to keep silent over his past, and so not to ruin his reputation, Turner offers McCarthy money in exchange for silence. Jack McCarthy later falls for the daughter of Turner, Alice, but when he asks for her hand in marriage, her father refuses. Enraged, McCarthy threatens to expose Turner if he does not consent to the marriage. Turner bribes McCarthy once again but this is witnessed by Jack who demands an explanation. This is the cause of the argument heard by the passers-by. Whilst the police still believe that Jack murdered his father, Holmes finds a piece of evidence which points to Turner and once pressed by Sherlock Holmes, he confesses the murder, takes a gun and shoots himself. Jack and Alice, however, are married and live happily ever after.

Review: There is scant information about this film but a small piece from *The Moving Picture World* writes, "By marvellous deduction and phenomenal precaution and intuition, Sherlock Holmes unravelled the startling mystery and fastened the guilt upon the real perpetrator of the crime."

Nápady ctenáre detektivek
(*Ideas for Detective-Story Readers*)
Film - 1966 (Czechoslovakia)

Writer: Josef Skvorecký
Director: Václav Táborsky
Sherlock Holmes: Frantisek Husák
Doctor Watson: Jirí Bruder

This idiosyncratic 26-minute short from Czechoslovakia squeezes a lot of murderous plot points and strange twists into a small run time. Whilst Doctor Watson visits the château of a rich family, he is shown into the library by the butler. The room is filled with a vast, rare and valuable collection of detective stories which the family holds in high esteem. The owner of the collection, Sir Arthur, is silent and fears he will be the subject of a murderous plot as the heirs to the fortune and châteaux are killed off one by one. His brothers have been killed by an axe and another stabbed with scissors. It appears that the murderer is killing in alphabetical order and with no pattern to be found to link the murders to each other (this includes poisoned candles, a spider bite, a cat with poisoned claws and, strangely, poisoned toothpaste). Sherlock Holmes is called in to investigate and discovers other murder victims along with the bodies of Sir Arthur's daughters. Unable to take the consequences of his murderous actions, Sir Arthur kills himself by taking a bath in a tub full of acid. With every member of the family now dead, the estate is left to the butler, James, and also to Doctor Watson. But in another strange twist, both men feel so possessive over the book collection and house that neither is willing to share and so they both reach for their guns and shoot. As both men are now dead there is no longer any victim or killer to investigate and so Sherlock Holmes simply goes home.

History: Writer Josef Skvorecký was a popular and much respected author. In 1982 he was nominated for a Nobel Prize for Literature; in 1992 he was inducted into the Order of Canada, and in 1996 was made a chevalier of the Ordre des Arts et des Lettres.

No Place like Holmes
Internet - 2010 - (USA)

Writer: Ross K. Foad
Director: Ross K. Foad
Sherlock Holmes: Ross K. Foad
Doctor Watson: Mike Archer

This on-going web series creates contemporary storylines which juxtapose with the original characters of Conan Doyle. The series starts with the episode *Moving Forward* where Holmes and Watson are investigating the Hound of the Baskervilles once more. Instead of a demonic hound, however, they are confronted by a demonic Sir Henry Baskerville who freezes them in time and throws them forward from 1895 to 2010. The rest of the episodes in the first series see Holmes and Watson coming to terms with modern life, finding a new home and setting up their detective consulting business again. The stories have a "fish-out-of-water" style narrative while the character of Holmes remains staunchly in 1895.

Trivia: The show also created a spin off show *The Mary Morstan Mysteries* which are not set in modern day.

A full episode list can be found in the "Television Episodes" chapter of this book

On the Scent of the Baskerville Hound
Documentary - 1989 (UK)

Writer: Not Credited
Director: Tim Watson
Sherlock Holmes: N/A
Doctor Watson: N/A

This short television documentary, broadcast on the Television South West network in the UK, presents the history and narrative of the popular Conan Doyle classic, *The Hound of the Baskervilles*. The programme features filmed interviews with Sherlockians and historians as well as taking the viewer to the various locations in Dartmoor where the story is set. The documentary is also

noteworthy as it features an interview with Sir Arthur Conan Doyle's daughter, Dame Jean Conan Doyle, as well as an interview with Richard Lancelyn Green, a well-respected writer, who was once considered the world's foremost Sherlockian scholar. Although the documentary may not throw any new light upon the topic for true Sherlock Holmes fans, the locations and narrative lend another layer of interest to those who are fans of the story.

History: It is reputed that in 1901, whilst staying in the Old Duchy Hotel in Princetown, that Conan Doyle wrote several chapters of his novel *The Hound of the Baskervilles*. The hotel was turned into a Prison Officer's mess in 1941 before becoming a visitors' centre in 1993 with its own Conan Doyle exhibition.

The Other Side
Television - 1992 (UK)

Writer: David Ashton
Director: Gareth Davies
Sherlock Holmes: Richard E. Grant
Doctor Watson: N/A

Broadcast as part of the TV series *Encounters,* this was made by the BBC and broadcast on BBC2. The drama starts with Arthur Conan Doyle visiting the home of a medium who becomes agitated as she brings out the ghost of Sherlock Holmes. Doyle balks at the sight before him stating that this cannot be the ghost of Sherlock Holmes as Sherlock Holmes was never alive. Undeterred, Holmes claims that thought is material and that he has come to put Doyle on trial in *The Case of the Three Betrayals,* where Doyle is accused of having a hand in the death and betrayal of three people. First a ghostly apparition of his father appears in the mirror causing Doyle some distress. Holmes accuses him of betraying his love and loyalty by putting his father into an asylum and leaving him to rot and die. Doyle denies this stating that his mother put his father in the asylum due to his violent mood swings and deep depressive state. The second ghost is that of his first wife Louisa. Doyle is accused of neglecting her while she was dying of tuberculosis in favour of spending time with the woman who would become his second wife. He, again, denies a betrayal saying that he cared for his wife and did not touch Jean Leckie until Louisa had died. The third betrayal is towards Holmes himself, accusing Doyle of denying him glory and killing him at the Reichenbach Falls. Most of all he is angry at Doyle for turning his back on solid, reasoned argument in favour of spiritualists and psychic phenomena. As Doyle attempts to leave, Holmes begs him to acknowledge him as his creation and, most of all, his child. When Doyle refuses, Holmes picks up a sword in an attempt to attack him, but is foiled when Conan Doyle punches him in the face and knocks him out.

It is only then that it is revealed the ghost is actually the brother of the psychic, a man who is being driven mad with worry that he will turn out to be just like his violent father whom he murdered in order to save his sister. When the brother awakes, Doyle, instead of punishing him, takes a sword and knights him as *"Sir Sherlock Holmes, my child, my creation, my reality."* Conan Doyle leaves with the promise that Sherlock Holmes is now safe in the hands of the brother.

Quote:
Arthur Conan Doyle: Please grasp this remark with your cerebral tentacles. The doll and its maker are never identical.

The Other Side

O tlustém pradedeckovi
(*The Fat Prey*)
Film - 1970 (Czechoslovakia)

Writers: Josef Capek & Kveta Kursová
Director: Pavel Kraus
Sherlock Holmes: Jirí Holý
Doctor Watson: N/A

This is another quirky Sherlock Holmes pastiche from Czechoslovakia. This story tells the tale of an elderly man who wanders into a strange pub during a storm. The bar is full of odd-looking characters dressed in a variety of costumes, and each sings and dances his way around the tables. The old man soon realises that these are crooks and finds himself held at their mercy as they mock him (they make him wear a small chalk board sign saying *"Nikdo"* meaning *"Nobody"*) whilst singing, dancing and quaffing ale. Just as he thinks all hope is lost, Sherlock Holmes enters the pub and instead of his companion, Doctor Watson, he has brought another two Sherlocks, both of whom are dressed in the deerstalker and Inverness cape, whilst he wears a top hat. Spurred on by the Sherlocks, the elderly man finds the confidence to thwart the robbers who sing and dance to ask for mercy. Criminals dealt with, Sherlock Holmes, the elderly man and his dog settle down to eat some dinner.

History: The film is based on a short story by Josef Capek who was also a painter, playwrite and poet. Because most of his work was critical of Adolf Hitler, he was arrested during the German invasion of Czechoslovakia in 1939 and detained in Bergen-Belsen concentration camp where he died in internment in 1945.

The Pearl of Death
Film - 1944 (USA)

Writer: Bertram Millhauser
Director: Roy William Neill
Sherlock Holmes: Basil Rathbone
Doctor Watson: Nigel Bruce

Loosely based on the original story *The Adventure of the Six Napoleons* (the motive and the thief differ from the original), the story starts with the cursed Borgia Pearl on display at the British Museum. Whilst Holmes explains how easily the pearl could be stolen the cunning Giles Conover does just that. Although he is arrested, the pearl is not in his possession and so he is let go. Unbeknownst to them Conover had hastily pushed the pearl into one of the half-dried busts of Napoleon in a factory whilst he was running from the authorities. As well as the missing pearl mystery, Holmes's attention is caught by a seemingly unconnected murder of an elderly colonel who has been found dead amongst a litter of broken china. Holmes recognises the style of murder (a broken back) as the work of The Hoxton Creeper who is also known to work closely with Conover. After three murders, all involving smashed china, and an attempt on his own life, Holmes deduces that there must be a link between the murders and the busts of Napoleon and so he tracks down the seller. It seems that it is not only Holmes and Watson who are on the trail of the last bust, but also Conover and The Creeper. When Conover arrives at the address of the final bust he is greeted, instead, by Holmes who talks The Creeper into believing that Conover has no scruples and will, eventually, double-cross him. After a struggle, The Creeper murders Conover leaving Holmes with no choice but to kill The Creeper. When the police arrive Holmes smashes the bust and hands the pearl over.

Connection: One of the nicest nods to the original Canon comes when Sherlock Holmes tells Watson that if he is wrong about the hiding place of the Borgia Pearl he shall, *"retire to Sussex and keep bees."* Of course, this is exactly what Holmes does when he retires.

Pipe Dream Continues: An Irregular Look at Sherlock Holmes in Minnesota
Documentary – 1998 (USA)

Writer: Rolf J. Canton
Director: Rolf J. Canton
Sherlock Holmes: James D. Wallace
Doctor Watson: Terry O'Sullivan

This documentary was a VHS cassette made by a sub-section of the Sherlockian society *The Baker Street Irregulars of New York* called the *Norwegian Explorers of Minnesota* and commemorates their 50th anniversary. The cassette also comes with a book titled *The Moriarty Principle – An Irregular Look at Sherlock Holmes* by Rolf J. Canton. This drama/documentary contains interviews with a variety of members and co-founders of the Sherlock Holmes Society. There are also some dramatic reconstructions of conversations between Holmes and Watson who are preparing to visit Minneapolis for the anniversary conference. As well as Holmes and Watson, there are comments from characters such as Irene Adler, Professor Moriarty, Mycroft Holmes and a woman called Violet who preens at having been featured in three original stories (Violet Hunter in *The Copper Beeches,* Violet de Merville in *The Illustrious Client* and Violet Smith in *The Solitary Cyclist*). The tape also shows a dramatization of Moriarty confronting Holmes about the Reichenbach Falls. This is an interesting film which documents not only the historical aspect of Holmes and Watson, but also one of its longest-serving societies.

Quote:
Rolf J. Canton: ...the need for Sherlock Holmes is now greater than ever. Just read the newspapers and you'll agree. A murder here and a robbery there; a vandalism here and a mugging there. Yes, Sherlock Holmes, stay awhile longer with us, will you?

Priklyucheniya Sherloka Khomsa i doktora Vatsona (*The Adventures of Sherlock Holmes and Dr Watson*)
Television – 1980 (Russia)

Writer: Vladimir Valutskiy
Director: Igor Maslennikov
Sherlock Holmes: Vasiliy Livanov
Doctor Watson: Vitali Solomin

The second mini-series of Holmes stories from Russia with Vasiliy Livanov playing Holmes and Vitali Solomin playing Watson. Created by *Lenfilm* during the time of the

Soviet Union, these period Holmes adventures are based on the Conan Doyle originals *The Adventure of Charles Augustus Milverton, The Final Problem* and *The Adventure of the Empty House.* Rather than leave viewers waiting for Holmes to announce his survival from the Reichenbach Falls for the start of a new season, as many other television adaptations have done, the producers made the return of Holmes their finale with their take on *The Empty House.* Rather than being three separate stories, the producers have intertwined the narratives to form a large, overarching story which feeds into all three episodes.

History: In 1988 the Holmes actor Vasili Livanov was given with the title People's Artist of Russia. From 1988-1992 he was also the Artistic Director of Moscow Experimental Theatre and in 2017 was awarded with a Golden Eagle Award for his contribution to Russian Cinema.

A full episode list can be found in the "Television Episodes" chapter of this book

Private Life of Sherlock Holmes
Film - 1970 (USA)

Writers : Billy Wilder & I.A.L. Diamond
Director: Billy Wilder
Sherlock Holmes: Robert Stephens
Doctor Watson: Colin Blakely

Famously, this long and complicated film contains two separate stories. Starting with a dusty old box containing the possessions of Holmes and a manuscript of Watson's, it is revealed that the story it contained was so controversial that it had to remain under lock and key. Going back fifty years, Holmes gripes at Watson due to a black mood and apathy. After refusing a case involving the disappearance of *"six acrobatic midgets,"* Watson suggests attending the Russian ballet as they have been sent a couple of rather expensive tickets. After being invited backstage, Watson (ever the one for the ladies) keeps the dancers company whilst Holmes is taken to the dressing room of Madame Petrova, the lead dancer. She proposes to Holmes that they have sex in order for her to conceive a child with beauty and brains and, for this, she will give him a

Stradivarius violin. He refuses and lies to spare her feelings, telling her that he and Watson are embroiled in a homosexual affair. Watson becomes angry at Holmes, worried that this false rumour may affect his love life and they both retire to their rooms. Later, a cab driver comes to Baker Street with a half-drowned woman whom he has rescued from the River Thames. She was clutching a card with the address of 221b Baker Street. Staying with Holmes and Watson she awakes, naked, and confuses Holmes for her husband, Emil.

As she beckons him to her bed, Holmes notes the numbers on her hand and puts her back to bed. When they awake, Holmes is nowhere to be found but he returns later with the woman's luggage having recognised the numbers as check luggage numbers from Victoria Station. The woman is distraught and needs to find her missing engineer husband and begs Holmes and Watson to help her. The investigation begins but Mycroft Holmes warns him to drop the case as it involves the British Government. The detective ignores his brother's threats and heads up to Scotland to a graveyard where the gravedigger tells him of a father and two sons who drowned at Loch Ness.

The gravedigger says that he blames the famous Loch Ness Monster for the crime. But when the grave is visited by four little people (not children as he first thought) Holmes digs up the grave to find the body of man and two dead canaries. Watson tells Holmes that he is also sure that he saw the "monster at the lake." The confusing mystery is solved when Mycroft explains the monster is actually a secret submarine and the little people are sailors which the government has employed because they take up less space and air. Mrs. Valladon is also not a grieving wife, but a German spy named Ilse Hoffmanstal who has been sent to steal the plans for the submarine. Queen Victoria inspects the submarine but orders it to be destroyed, claiming it too unsportsmanlike in war. The film ends, later, with Holmes finding out that Hoffmanstal has been captured and killed, sending him, once more, into a black mood.

Trivia: Originally Peter O'Toole was going to play Sherlock Holmes with Peter Sellers playing Dr. Watson. Other possible names attached to the film were Charlton Heston and Rex Harrison for the role of Sherlock Holmes and Richard Attenborough for the role of Watson.

Private Life of Sherlock Holmes

Pursuit to Algiers
Film - 1945 (USA)

Writer: Leonard Lee
Director: Roy William Neill
Sherlock Holmes: Basil Rathbone
Doctor Watson: Nigel Bruce

The twelfth film to feature Rathbone and Bruce as Holmes and Watson, this film borrows from the original stories of *The Adventure of the Red Circle* and, in part, *The Adventure of the Norwood Builder*. Just as the detective duo is about to leave for a fishing trip to Scotland, they get a coded message at a fish and chip shop that leads to a meeting with the Prime Minster of Rovinia. He needs Holmes to escort Prince Nikolas home as his father has been assassinated so the heir has to get back safely. After issues with the airplane, a smaller plane, which can only hold Holmes and the Prince, is chartered and Watson takes the trip via ship. It is on the ship where he learns that the plane has crashed in the Pyrenees, leaving no survivors. Luckily Holmes and the Prince are also, secretly, on board the ship which is also full of suspects (including a knife-thrower, a mysterious steward, two archaeologists behaving strangely, and an armed British dowager) and so the Prince poses as Waston's nephew. Eventually the plan to kidnap the prince is successful and he is taken when the boat docks in Algiers. But Holmes reveals that the boy playing Watson's nephew was a decoy; the real prince is safe and has been posing as a steward.

Trivia: The film includes some references to the *untold cases* of Holmes and Watson. One of these is *The Giant Rat of Sumatra*, an untold case which is mentioned in *The Adventure of the Sussex Vampire*. The film also includes some events from *The Adventure of the Red Circle* and the S.S. Friesland which features in *The Adventure of the Norwood Builder*

Raffles Flugt Fra Faengslet
(Raffles Escape From Faengsle**)**
Film - 1908 (Denmark)

Writer: Viggo Larsen
Director: Viggo Larsen
Sherlock Holmes: Viggo Larsen
Doctor Watson: N/A

This silent movie, made by the *Nordisk Film Co,* takes a little from the original story *The Empty House,* as this also uses the dummy decoy to avoid being shot from across the street. Having been sent to prison for stealing a diamond necklace, Raffles (the gentleman thief) escapes and is determined to get revenge on Sherlock Holmes. Enlisting the help of a young female criminal, Raffles lures Sherlock Holmes to a dilapidated house and, disguised as an old lady, attacks him and throws him through a concealed entrance into the sewer. Proving that a sewer is no match for his skills, Holmes escapes and returns safely to Baker Street. Furious, Raffles takes up residency in the house across the street from Holmes with the intention of shooting him. Again, Holmes is one step ahead and has placed a dummy in the window and when Billy the house boy is given the signal, he throws open the blind to reveal the dummy. Raffles takes his shot but is shocked when he turns to find Sherlock Holmes standing next to him. As he tries to escape, he is caught by the police and restrained.

Review: A glowing review from *The Moving Picture World* of February 27th 1909 writes: "If you have seen "Sherlock Holmes I," you know that for excellence of photography, the Great Northern Film Company cannot be excelled, you know that the acting is practically what you would expect to see at the famous "Comedie Francaise" of Paris, and you know that the manufacturers of this film pay the greatest attention to all the details and are unsurpassed in their staging. "Sherlock Holmes II" is as much a masterpiece as its predecessor, and "Sherlock Holmes III" promises to hold the same rank."

The Real Adventures of Sherlock Jones and Proctor Watson
Television - 1987 (USA)

Writer: Paul D. Marks
Director: Leo Eaton
Sherlock Holmes: Mark Ritts
Doctor Watson: Michael Costello

Shown on the PBS channel in America, this Sesame Street style show with puppets interacting with humans demonstrated how to solve problems while enjoying adventure. During the show, Sherlock Jones and his sidekick dog, Proctor Watson, are helped by Bryan and Teddy to crack mysteries such as the disappearance of exotic bird eggs from the zoo, the case of the vanishing neighbourhood dogs, trying to catch the school locker thief and Sherlock and Watson coming to the help of Bryan and Teddy who have been accused of selling pirated tapes. Very little is written about this show with episodes being increasingly difficult to find.

Trivia: Actress Mona Lee Fultz, played Mrs. Hudson, opposite her real life brother-in-law, Michael Costello, who played her husband.

A full episode list can be found in the "Television Episodes" chapter of this book

The Real Sherlock Holmes.
Documentary - 2012 (CANADA)

Writer: Gary Lang
Director: Gary Lang
Sherlock Holmes: Various
Doctor Watson: Various

This documentary which intermingled clips and interviews looks at how the famous detective has influenced a lot more than future police detectives and crime writers.

The fast-paced program interviews academics, writers and scientists about Holmes in popular culture, how Sherlock Holmes met Batman, how he influenced NASA with one of the representatives calling some of their work Holmes in the 21st century. Lt. Gen. Samuel Wilson, former director of the Defence Intelligence Agency, states that without Sherlock Holmes there would be no James Bond, calling him the patron saint of intelligence analysis. *The Sign of Four* is also held up as a book which all forensic scientists should read. It's an informative documentary, even though it deals in speculation and conjecture, placing Holmes at the centre of nearly every scientific and cultural development. Still, it is an entertaining look at how the greatest detective that never lived, changed the world.

Quote:
Scott Brown: You could go back and say that Holmes was the Model T of all modern science fiction, of mystery fiction [and] of genre fiction.

Return of Sherlock Holmes: Murdoch Mysteries
Television - 2013 (CANADA)

Writer: Carol Hay
Director: Gail Harvey
Sherlock Holmes: Andrew Gower
Doctor Watson: N/A

This is the second Sherlock Holmes appearance in an episode of this Canadian television program which aired on the City and CBS networks in Canada and is set in the late 1800s – early 1900s. In the first appearance *A Study in Sherlock* (which was aired seven months before this was broadcast) the show sets up the premise of David Kingsley, a man who considers himself to be Sherlock Holmes.

In *Return of Sherlock Holmes*, Murdoch becomes embroiled in an altercation where a man is being prevented from touching the body of a dead person at the Queen's Hotel. The person is "Sherlock Holmes" who insists he knows the identity of the body and has been hired to find a missing woman with red hair. After rejecting the cause of death as a drunken accident by finding and presenting the victim's Scottish Prohibition Society card, Holmes leaves to continue his investigation, the same case on which Murdoch is also working. Eventually, he is allowed to continue after Murdoch is advised that Kingsley's delusion is a coping mechanism for his father's death and calling him anything other than Holmes may cause him distress. Together they uncover a plot involving train wrecks, confidence tricksters and stolen identities. The nanny, it seems, had gone into hiding and is now seeking to protect the little boy who was in her care.

Quote:
Sherlock Holmes: She went into hiding. In plain sight, as it happens. At the tearoom. I should have seen through her disguise on our first visit.

The Return of Sherlock Holmes
Film - 1929 (USA)

Writers: Basil Dean & Garrett Fort
Director: Basil Dean
Sherlock Holmes: Clive Brook
Doctor Watson: H. Reeves-Smith

Made by Paramount Pictures and bringing in elements of two Conan Doyle stories, *The Dying Detective* and *His Last Bow*. Most of the action in the film is set on an ocean liner where Watson becomes concerned for his daughter's fiancé, a reformed criminal named Roger who used to work for Professor Moriarty. Whilst Holmes is attending the wedding of Roger to Mary, Roger's father is found murdered in his study. Holmes deduces that the killer has murdered his victim with a cigarette case which contains a needle dipped in poison that springs out to pierce the victim's skin when the case is opened. Roger vanishes and acting on some deductions, they all rush onto the ocean liner and head to America. Roger has been kidnapped and is also on the ocean liner but is soon to be departed as he is carrying with him papers which document Moriarty's criminal activity. Holmes begins to suspect the ship's doctor. After some sleuthing, a few disguises and a dinner invitation, Holmes finds himself sitting at the table with Moriarty who removes his disguise in order to face Holmes. Trapped and caught in Holmes's web, Moriarty takes the only course of action

he can, and kills himself in order to escape the consequences of his actions.

Trivia: This was the first Sherlock Holmes film to be made with sound (although a silent version was also produced to be played in cinemas not yet equipped for sound). It was also the first film to use a contemporary setting of Holmes and one of the first where the line, "Elementary, my dear Watson" is known to have been uttered. The film also gives John Watson a daughter, Mary.

Return of Sherlock Holmes
Television - 1986 -1988 (UK)

Writers: Various
Directors: Various
Sherlock Holmes: Jeremy Brett
Doctor Watson: Edward Hardwicke

This is the second collection of Sherlock Holmes stories to be produced by Granada Television and broadcast on the ITV network in the UK. Starting with *The Empty House,* the series also sees the actor Edward Hardwicke replace David Burke as Watson as Burke was tied up with other commitments and unable to film the series. This collection produced thirteen episodes over two years, of which two were feature length adaptations of the novels, *The Sign of Four* and *The Hound of the Baskervilles*.

Trivia: There was a noticeable height difference between Brett and Hardwicke and when he started filming the show, Hardwicke wore lifts in his shoes in order to reduce the difference. However, these were uncomfortable and disposed of early on in the filming.

A full episode list can be found in the "Television Episodes" chapter of this book.

The Return of Sherlock Holmes
Television - 1987 (USA)

Writers: Bob Shayne
Director: Kevin Connor
Sherlock Holmes: Michael Pennington
Doctor Watson: Margaret Colin

This quirky television movie which was shown on the CBS network in America starts with Jane Watson, a distant relative of John Watson, bringing Sherlock Holmes back to life after he has been cryogenically frozen for eighty years. Jane Watson, a private detective on the verge of financial ruin, comes back to England from America to sell her country estate which belonged to Doctor John Watson. After being given a set of instructions, Jane goes into the basement of the house and finds Holmes in a cryogenic pod and she soon brings him out of his frozen sleep. It would appear that Holmes was infected with the plague by Moriarty and frozen so he might find a cure in the future. Watson assists Holmes to a hospital where he is cured and then they fly back to America. As Sherlock Holmes tries to comprehend the modern world he is soon distracted with a case when they return to find Jane's office has been ransacked and a message has been left by a man called Small. Holmes and Watson find the FBI reluctant to release any information. Holmes discovers that Agent Morstan was part of an investigation into a hijacking and the disappearance of a large amount of counterfeit money. Although Small was responsible for the hijacking he was paid off by Morstan and the other three agents involved in the case who later quit the FBI and kept the money for themselves.

Trivia: The British actor John Wood flew to America, at his own expense, to audition for the role of Sherlock Holmes. Although Wood had previously played Holmes in the RSC production of William Gillette's play *Sherlock Holmes* the role was given to Michael Pennington.

Return of Sherlock Sooty. Sooty's Amazing Adventures
Television - 1997 (UK)

Writers: Jon Doyle
Director: Roger Stennett
Sherlock Holmes: N/A
Doctor Watson: N/A

This episode was shown as part of *Sooty's Amazing Adventures,* an animated spin-off of the puppet show featuring Sooty the bear (a silent hand puppet who communicates through various handlers) and broadcast on the ITV network in the UK. The premise of the show involves a trapdoor located on the main stage in the theatre where they live. Once opened it takes them to various places

and times for adventures. Here Sooty wants to travel to Victorian London to solve a case as Sherlock Sooty where he meets a new friend, Morris the Mouse.

Trivia: There is an on-going relationship with Sooty and Sherlock which dates back to 1956 and the episode *Sherlock Sooty* where he appeared alongside Harry Corbett. Sherlock Sooty has also featured in the episodes *Sleepwalking with Sooty* (1981) *Sherlock Sooty* (1984) *Sherlock Sooty Visits* (1995) and *Sherlock Sooty Rides again* (1998)

Return of Sherlock Sooty: Sooty's Amazing Adventures

Return of the World's Greatest Detective
Television - 1976 (USA)

Writers: Dean Hargrove & Roland Kibbee
Director: Dean Hargrove
Sherlock Holmes: Larry Hagman
Doctor Watson: Jenny O'Hara

This TV movie made by Universal and broadcast on the NBC network in America, sees LA cop, Sherman Holmes, suffer a head injury when his motorcycle falls on top of him whilst reading a Sherlock Holmes story. The resulting injury convinces him that he is the famous detective Sherlock Holmes and is now blessed with heightened observation and detective skills. Dressed in full regalia of deerstalker hat, Inverness coat and pipe he even adopts a (bad) British accent. He is assigned a social worker and psychiatrist Dr. Joan Watson (not unlike the meeting in the film *They Might be Giants*) who finds him a place to stay which is an apartment complex in Baker Street (LA) number 221b. Holmes must solve the mystery of a murdered embezzler who was under increasing levels of fear to reveal the location of a half million dollars. In addition, the city is being plagued by the detonation of smoke bombs.

Holmes deduces that he may have revealed the location in return for police amnesty and that whoever it was he confided in would be the murderer. A car wreck, some strange disguises and a basement filled with cardboard boxes of dirt all lead Holmes to the location of the stolen money and the murderer. Having dug a tunnel from the basement to the flower bed of a construction site for a new bank, the criminal's intention was to serve his time in prison and then retrieve the money. Holmes and Watson believe that the perpetrator must be laying low for fear of his own life. Their main suspect, Vince Cooley, is on trial for arson and Holmes tries to reason with him during the trial to confess to having taken the money and give them the name of the man to whom he gave the money. A smoke bomb is detonated as a mystery figure tries to kill Cooley. Luckily he is intercepted by Holmes who is hot on the trail of the killer. The killer turns out to be the judge who has hidden the money in the legal books in his office. A trifling matter of the smoke bomb attacker is cleared up almost instantly.   A water delivery man is stopped by Holmes whose deliveries coincide with the smoke bomb attacks. When his water bottle is opened, a smoke bomb is revealed.

Trivia: The film was intended to be a pilot for a series that would have been called *Alias Sherlock Holmes* but the network passed on making it a full series.

The Royal Scandal
Television - 2001 (Canada/USA)

Writer: Joe Wiesenfeld
Director: Rodney Gibbons
Sherlock Holmes: Matt Frewer
Doctor Watson: Kenneth Welsh

This is the third movie to feature Matt Frewer as Sherlock Holmes for broadcast on Canadian television. The legendary opera star Irene Adler plans to destroy the reputation of the future King of Bohemia by revealing their illicit affair.   She is blackmailing the prince with a photograph of the two of them in her bedroom which would jeopardise his marriage to the daughter of the King of Scandinavia. It would also be an embarrassment to the man who is to become the future Kaiser of the German Empire. Holmes, however, is already familiar with the work of Irene Adler and suspects that her intentions go beyond petty blackmail and so he digs a little deeper. Here Holmes is distracted and side-lined by apparently falling in love with Irene Adler, the result of which finds his investigation severely compromised. Once Sherlock's brother, Mycroft becomes involved with the case, asking one too many probing questions about the Prince, Holmes suspects that there is more to the case than an embarrassing photograph. He learns that the government has developed a new kind of submarine which will increase its superiority in the event of a war. It transpires that the Germans want the plans and have deployed a traitor who will sell these sensitive documents to them. Holmes has to navigate his way past his manipulative brother and the even more manipulative woman to solve this case.

Trivia: The narrative adapts features of the original stories *A Scandal in Bohemia* and *The Bruce-Partington Plans.*

Sangerindens Diamanter
(The Theft of the Diamonds)
Film -1909 (Denmark)

Writer: Viggo Larsen
Director: Viggo Larsen
Sherlock Holmes: Viggo Larsen
Doctor Watson: N/A

This silent movie tells the story of the despicable Alfred Farley who visits his uncle and has his eye caught by a rather expensive diamond necklace. Down on his luck, he asks his uncle if he can loan him some money and when he is refused, he attempts to steal the necklace. Defeated, Farley is kicked out of the house as his uncle takes the necklace to its intended owner, a gift for the singer Margaret Hayes.   After he gives her the necklace, the pair leave just before Farley enters, searching for the necklace but finding only an empty box. As Hayes enters, she is distraught at the break-in and immediately calls Sherlock Holmes. However, Farley attacks her before she can give her location and all Holmes can do is listen to her being attacked. Tracing the number to find the address, Holmes rushes to her apartment to find the woman unconscious. Noticing the rope at the window, Holmes climbs up in an attempt to catch him. A battle commences on the roof with Farley shooting at Holmes and his helpers but out of bullets and desperate, he falls and is captured. At the apartment of Miss Hayes he is identified, forced to give back the necklace and taken away into custody.

Review: In a short review for *The Moving Picture World* the writer states, "There is always a more than ordinary degree of interest attaching to a story of this sort, and in this instance the audience is not disappointed in the way it is worked out."

The Scarlet Claw
Film - 1944 (USA)

Writers: Edmund L. Hartmann, Roy William
Neill, Paul Gangelin
& Brenda Weisberg
Director: Roy William Neill
Sherlock Holmes: Basil Rathbone
Doctor Watson: Nigel Bruce

The eighth movie from Rathbone and Bruce is the only one of their films to have an additional voice over narration.

Sherlock Holmes receives a letter from Lady Penrose from Canada who fears for her life as it appears that a disturbing creature is terrorising the village where she lives. The legend tells of a monster who murdered the villagers of La Mort Rouge by ripping out their throats. It seems as though the phantom is back as residents start to see strange luminous shapes and several sheep are found with their throats torn out. When Holmes and Watson arrive to help, they find

they are too late, Lady Penrose has been found dead, with her throat cut. Whilst many believe it is the cursed monster, Holmes believes the cause to be human as he recognises Lady Penrose as the actress, Lillian Gentry. Gentry was at the centre of a murder investigation when an actor named Alistair Ramson killed another actor in a jealous rage over her affections. It was thought that Ramson was killed during a prison escape attempt but Homes deduces that he is alive and well. He explains that Ramson, being an actor, is a master of disguise and is, more than likely, still in the village, posing as a resident. La Mort Rouge is also home to Judge Brisson who sentenced Ramson so when he is also murdered (despite being warned by Holmes) he knows he is on to his man. Holmes learns of his next victim, a former prison guard who has gone into hiding. Not being able to kill his victim, Ramson kills his daughter instead. Disguising himself as the next target, Holmes confronts Ramson who, after a struggle, is killed by his own weapon, a garden weeder.

Quote:
<u>Sherlock Holmes:</u> Consider, Watson, the irony, the tragic irony, that we accepted the commission from the victim to find her murderer. For the first time...we've been retained by a corpse.

The Seven-Per-Cent Solution
Film - 1976 (USA)

Writer: Nicholas Meyer
Director: Herbert Ross
Sherlock Holmes: Nicol Williamson
Doctor Watson: Robert Duvall

This is an interesting take on the possible events that occurred between the two original Conan Doyle stories *The Final Problem* and *The Empty House* during the "Great Hiatus." Doctor Watson becomes increasingly worried about Sherlock Holmes and his cocaine habit. As Holmes talks with much fervour about his nemesis Moriarty, Watson locates the man who turns out to be the old math teacher of Sherlock and Mycroft. Believing Moriarty to be a harmless man, who is exasperated at the attentions of

Sherlock Holmes, Watson devises a plan to help his friend rid himself of his drug-fuelled delusions. He constructs a ruse to bring Holmes to Vienna where Watson has actually arranged a meeting with Sigmund Freud, a man who is sure he can cure Holmes of his addiction using psychology and hypnosis. Holmes is angry and suspicious of Freud and becomes a difficult patient, but during his stay another addicted patient, Lola Deveraux, goes missing. She is found in a river, appearing to have attempted suicide having relapsed and used cocaine once more. However, it is revealed that she was actually taken by a short man with a pockmarked face and held captive only just managing to escape.

As Watson, Freud and Holmes investigate it appears that they are being followed by the suspect, Lowenstein, who fits Deveraux's description. The suspect leads them into a trap and Holmes realises too late that it had all been a distraction so that the real criminal could recapture Lola Deveraux. Once Holmes has Lowenstein captured, it emerges that the man behind the crimes is Baron von Leinsdorf, who is known by Freud and who made anti-Semitic remarks to him and is seeking revenge for a lost "tennis match." Holmes and Watson take over a train heading to Istanbul and embroil themselves in sword fights onboard, a hectic chase and the daring rescue of Lola. Case solved, Holmes thanks Freud for curing him of his addiction but Freud wants one more session in order to find the root of Holmes' addiction. It is discovered that the root of his addiction and his need to become a detective stems from witnessing his father killing his mother because of an infidelity. The identity of the lover is revealed to be Moriarty.

Connection: The part of Mycroft Holmes was originally offered to Orsen Wells but was eventually played by Charles Gray. Gray also played Mycroft Holmes in the Granada ITV series of Sherlock Holmes alongside Jeremy Brett.

The Seven-Per-Cent Solution

The Shackles of Sherlock. Documentary -2007 (UK)

Writer: Nicholas Meyer
Director: Paul Griffin
Sherlock Holmes: N/A
Doctor Watson: David Burke

A documentary made by ITV and shown on the ITV3 network in the UK, it is presented by David Burke who sits in a variety of plush Victorian rooms and recounts the history of the relationship between Conan Doyle and Sherlock Holmes. Cutting between Burke's informative pieces to camera and interviews with Sherlockians, historians and lovers of Doyle, the documentary looks at many of Doyle's other achievements which have gone largely unrecognised.

The documentary touches on his cricketing success with the MCC, his enthusiastic involvement in spiritualism, his time and training as a doctor and how he wanted to kill off Sherlock Holmes so he could be remembered as the writer of great historical fiction. Using Conan Doyle's personal correspondences (with permission from the Conan Doyle estate) which are held at The British Library, the documentary highlights the effect Sherlock Holmes had on him as he took over his life, the pressure, the frustration he felt towards Sherlock Holmes and why he felt shackled to the character.

Quote:
David Burke: More than seventy five years after his death, he remains in the shaddow of his greatest creation, Sherlock Holmes.

Sherlock
Computer game -1984 (UK)

Writer: Philip Mitchell
Director: Philip Mitchell
Sherlock Holmes: N/A
Doctor Watson: N/A

Created for the ZX Spectrum and the Commodore 64, Sherlock was a text adventure game (a game where commands are typed into the computer rather than controlling a character with a controller) developed by Beam Software.

The premise of the game is that Sherlock Holmes comes to work with Doctor Watson who is already investigating crimes for the police in the role of a coroner. There has been a double murder in the town of Leatherhead and Dr. Watson needs Holmes (the player) to investigate. There is also an appearance from Inspector Lestrade and Moriarty (who appears to be a heroin dealer). The text descriptions are accompanied by crude graphics but give the player a sense of where they are and what they are doing.

Quote:
Game Text: You can see a bloodstained sofa. On the bloodstained sofa there is a body. Watson enters. You examine the body. You see the body of a woman who was shot in the head. The face is now mutilated beyond recognition.

Sherlock
Television 2010 – (UK)

Writer: Various
Director: Various
Sherlock Holmes: Benedict Cumberbatch
Doctor Watson: Martin Freeman

Produced by the BBC and broadcast on the BBC1 network in the UK, this modern day retelling of Sherlock Holmes has proved to be an almost instant international hit. The show incorporates original narratives that contain elements of Conan Doyle's stories with references to the books throughout. Its global popularity has made household names of Benedict Cumberbatch and Martin Freeman as well as bringing a new generation of fans to Doyle's work.

Trivia: In the first episode of Season Four, *The Six Thatcher's*, John Watson is heard to say to Sherlock, ""A *jellyfish*? *You can't arrest a jelly fish*!" This is a reference to the Conan Doyle story *The Adventure of the Lion's Mane* where a deadly jellyfish is found to be responsible for a man's death.

A full episode list can be found in the "Television Episodes" chapter of this book.

Sherlock: "The Lion's Mane"

Sherlock Blue's Clues:
CollegeHumor Originals
Internet - 2012 (USA)

Writer: Jenny Jaffe
Director: Matthew Pollock
Sherlock Holmes: Thomas Middleditch
Doctor Watson: N/A

This short three minute parody of the Children's show *Blue's Clues* – a live action in animation children's show where the presenter solves puzzles with an animated dog – was made as part of The College Humour channel online.

Blue the dog is unhappy and so we must find three clues to figure out why, but there is no need as Sherlock (BBC's Sherlock rather than "Sherlock Holmes") bursts onto the scene to solve the problem. Whilst disparaging the peppy host and the "insufferable imbeciles" who are the children calling out for clues, Sherlock deduces that Blue's ball has been popped recently. Sherlock tries to subdue the host by telling him about his parents who died of a heroin overdose for which he blames himself. Holmes then deduces that Blue is a genetic government experiment and was sent to Indonesia to go into hiding.

Connection: The short has many references to the television show *Sherlock* and even created its own *Blue's Clues* style animation of the opening titles.

Sherlock Chuckle: Chuckle Vision
Television - 2004 (UK)

Writer: Rory Clark
Director: Martin Hughes
Sherlock Holmes: Paul Chuckle
Doctor Watson: Barry Chuckle

This episode was part of the long running children's televisions series *Chuckle Vision,* made and broadcast by the BBC television network in the UK. The show ran from 1987 to 2009 and followed the misadventures of brothers Barry and Paul Chuckle.

In *Sherlock Chuckle*, the brothers are at a party for the Great Detective when there is a break-in down in the pantry. The only clue is a strange noise heard by one of the guests. The room is locked with the only way in being a small opening too narrow for a person to climb through. Finding a fishing lure and licence the pair go to find Sergeant Potts, but it is his day off and he has gone fishing. Sherlock Chuckle immediately suspects him. Whilst at a sweet shop, Dr. Barry figures out that the strange sound heard at the party during the robbery is a device used to pick jars off high shelves.

Whilst investigating the brothers are put in prison; luckily, Dr. Barry has taken the jar-picking device and uses it to take the keys from outside their cell. The pair break into a jewellery store and call Potts to report a robbery, but the thief is not Potts but policeman Harris who is arrested and put behind bars.

Trivia: Instead of his trademark violin, Sherlock Chuckle likes to think through his cases whilst playing a tuba.

Sherlock Doo: The New Scooby-Doo Mysteries
Animation - 1984 (USA)

Writer: John Semper, Cynthia Friedlob & Glenn Leopold
Directors: Oscar Dufau, Rudy Zamora & Ray Patterson
Sherlock Holmes: Not Credited
Doctor Watson: N/A

Sherlock Doo is an episode of the short lived spin off of the Scooby-Doo brand *The New Scooby-Doo Mysteries,* which ran for only two seasons and was shown on the ABC network in America.

Based on the original Doyle story *The Blue Carbuncle*, the Scooby Gang travels to London where Mystery Solvers Magazine is having its first crime-fighters competition. The event is happening at 221b Baker Street and on the way there, the ghost of Sherlock Holmes appears offering to lead the way. Pitting themselves against the other detectives the gang has to solve the mystery of the Blue Carbuncle which, here, was Sherlock Holmes's last unsolved case. The gang is followed by Iggy and Ziggy Moriarty (who intend to cheat by tailing them instead of solving the crime themselves) but the ghost of Holmes appears once more to frighten them away. Scooby and Shaggy follow the ghost who tells them he knows the location of the carbuncle, however, instead he breaks open a cabinet and steals some security system blueprints. The gang are then arrested for the theft but escape to find out who the ghost of Sherlock Holmes really is. After searching Buckingham Palace it is discovered that the ghost was really Stapleton, the contest supervisor, who used the blueprints in order to pull off a grand jewellery theft.

Quote:
Shaggy: Excuse me, old chap. Can you tell us the way to 221b Baker Street?

Sherlock Holmes: Just follow me, Gents. It's one of my favourite haunts.

Shaggy: ZOINKS! It's the ghost of Sherlock Holmes.

Sherlock Gnomes.
Animation -2018 (US/USA)

Writer: Ben Zazove
Director: John Stevenson
Sherlock Holmes: Johnny Depp
Doctor Watson: Chiwetel Ejiofor

A sequel to the film Gnomeo & Juliet (2011) this brings back the eponymous characters for yet another CGI adventure.

Sherlock Gnomes is the protector of all of the garden gnomes in London and when gnomes suddenly start going missing, Gnomes and Watson are on the case. After finding a card with the letter M on it, Gnomes believes that the evil Professor Moriarty is behind the disappearance. Meanwhile, Gnomeo is trying his best to woo Juliet and so he breaks into a florist to steal her favourite flower. After triggering the alarm he is saved by Juliet and when they return to the garden they discover that all of the gnomes have vanished. Gnomeo and Juliet meet Gnomes and Watson whilst they are investigating and join the hunt to find their friends. It seems that Moriarty has left a treasure trove of clues for them to follow, one of which leads them to the National History Museum where they split up. Juliet follows Holmes and Gnomeo goes with Watson but they are chased by a gargoyle and Gnomeo is captured. During the chase Watson is seen by Gnomes and Juliet to fall from the high building to his probable death. At the gargoyle's lair, Gnomeo discovers the lost gnomes are unaware of the plan to have

them all smashed. Gnomeo plans and executes his escape whilst Gnomes and Juliet follow the rest of the clues to The Tower of London, a place where he and Watson solved their first case. In an unexpected twist, Gnomes does not find Moriarty but Watson, who is alive and well. He tells Gnomes that the card was not an M but a W and he just wanted to prove that he was just as clever as Holmes and not just his dogsbody. However, when the gargoyles show up they also reveal that they were never planning to work with Watson and he, along with Juliet and Gnomeo are thrown into a box on a ship. Moriarty plans to trap all of the gnomes under Tower Bridge so they will be crushed when the bridge raises to let their ship pass under it. This means that Sherlock Gnomes will be responsible for the destruction of every gnome in London. In order to save the gnomes, Watson and Gnomes reconcile and as Gnomeo and his helpers stop the bridge from opening, Gnomes goes after Moriarty once more. After an exciting battle on top of London Bridge both Moriarty and Gnomes fall towards the river, but Gnomes is saved by Watson who offers his cane to grab on to, leaving Moriarty to be carried away in the Thames. Harmony is returned to the garden and Gnomes and Watson are friends once more.

Trivia: When Watson and Juliet are locked into a cargo crate the company name emblazoned on the side is "Moffat and Gatiss." This is tribute to Mark Gatiss and Steven Moffat, creators of the BBC show *Sherlock*.

Sherlock Goof: Goof Troop
Animation - 1992 (USA)

Writer: Stephen Levi
Directors: Robert Taylor& Karen Peterson
Sherlock Holmes: Bill Farmer
Doctor Watson: Frank Welker

This cartoon series, featuring Disney's Goofy raising his son in Spoonerville whilst trying to outwit the odious neighbour, Pete, ran for 79 episodes on the Disney and ABC network in America.

In this episode Max is trying to catch a rat in order to make it his pet. His father, Goofy, interrupts him with the family album to tell him about his famous great, great, great uncle Sherlock Goof, the greatest rat-catcher of all time. The story recounts Sherlock Goof's first day as a rat-catcher at the house of Sir Reginald. Meanwhile the house is broken into by a less-than-smart criminal who, with instructions from Professor Inferiority, locates and steals the key to the Tower of London. But after he falls into the trap meant for the rat, Sherlock Goof gets a reputation for being a brilliant detective and is given the job of protecting the Crown Jewels.

Sherlock Goof seeks out Dr. John Watson, who lives at 221b Baker Street, for a copy of his book *How to be a Detective*. However, he still manages to be captured by Professor Inferiority and only escapes thanks, once more, to the help of the rat he's been trying to catch. With the Crown Jewels safely in his pocket, his only task is to catch the criminal. The chase ends at a waterfall (of course) where Inferiority drifts away down the water whilst Goof and Sparky the rat are saved by Doctor Watson who has been following them. Sherlock Goof goes on to invent a fool-proof mouse trap and Goofy passes the heirloom to his son.

Quote:
Goofy: Watch it, that could really smart.

Pete: Stand still and I'll make you a genius.

Sherlock Holmes
Film – 1916 (USA)

Writers: H.S. Sheldon & William Gillette
Director: Arthur Berthelet
Sherlock Holmes: William Gillette
Doctor Watson: Edward Fielding

This seven-reel silent film is the only preserved record of Gillette's performance as Holmes. Thought to be lost, the print was discovered in 2014 at the Cinémathèque Française in Paris. The film, based on Gillette's play, has a small connection to

Doyle's *A Scandal in Bohemia* and *The Adventure of Charles Augustus Milverton*, with its themes of royalty and blackmail but that's where the similarities with Holmes end.

A young woman, Alice Faulkners, had a sister who had a love affair with a member of the royal family. During this time the prince wrote passionate love letters and, on her death bed, these letters were given to her sister for safe keeping. Knowing these letters exist and the possible scandal they could cause, the prince's assistant Count von Stalburg and the British officer Sir Edward Palmer are tasked with negotiating their return. Unfortunately they are not the only ones who know of the letters, the husband and wife criminal team, 'The Larrabees,' also realise the value of the letters. The pair keep Alice at their house and try tricking her into revealing where the letters are with a view to blackmailing the prince. Having failed in their task Stalburg and Palmer request the help of Sherlock Holmes who finds Alice and, after making sure the Larabees have not harmed her, manages to find out the location of the letters. Alice escapes the clutches of the Larabees but falls straight into the clutches of Moriarty's henchmen. Luckily, Holmes comes to the rescue and not only persuades her to give the letters back to the prince but also gives her his heart.

History: William Gillette sent a telegram to Conan Doyle asking, "May I marry Holmes?" to which Conan Doyle replied "You may marry him, murder him, or do anything you like to him."

Sherlock Holmes

Sherlock Holmes AKA Moriarty
Film – 1922 (USA)

Writers: Earle Browne, Marion Fairfax & William Gillette
Director: Albert Parker
Sherlock Holmes: John Barrymore
Doctor Watson: Roland Young

This nine-reel silent movie, thought to be lost, started its restoration in 1970 when a print was discovered but cut out of order and incomplete. Prince Alexis is accused of stealing athletic funds at the university and so he turns to his friend, Watson, who recommends he ask for help from fellow classmate Sherlock Holmes. Holmes accepts the case and suspects Forman Wells of committing the crime. When he confesses, Holmes then learns about the criminal mastermind Moriarty. The prince learns that he is now to be the crown prince and, as such, must not marry his intended, Rose Faulkner. When Rose hears this news, she commits suicide.

Years later, once Holmes is established as a great detective, he learns that Moriarty is trying to locate the love letters of Rose Faulkner and Prince Alexis in order to blackmail the prince. Rose's sister, Alice, has the love letters and intends to publish them to avenge her wronged sister. She now works as a secretary, after the position was secretly created by Moriarty. Disguised as a butler, Holmes works in the same household and eventually gets Alice to reveal where she has hidden the letters. Holmes uses the letters as bait for Moriarty and, along with Alice, is brought to his "gas chamber" to be murdered but they manage to escape.

Hell bent on revenge, Moriarty sends all that he has to try and kill Holmes but the Great Detective is always one step ahead of him, at one point arranging a car accident as a distraction. With most of his network captured, Moriarty disguises himself as a cab driver in an attempt to catch Holmes but he is handcuffed and taken away leaving Holmes to plan his honeymoon with Alice.

Trivia: Director Albert Parker and Holmes actor John Barrymore apparently visited some of the roughest places in New York in order to cast convincing looking criminals and gang members.

Sherlock Holmes
Film – 1932 (USA)

Writers: William Gillette & Bertram Millhauser
Director: William K. Howard
Sherlock Holmes: Clive Brook
Doctor Watson: Reginald Owen

As in the previous *Sherlock Holmes* films, this is also based on William Gillette's play but doesn't stick so rigidly to the original text.

Professor Moriarty is sentenced to death as a consequence of being the catalyst for murder and vows that the three people who led to his confinement will die, including Sherlock Holmes. Holmes plans his retirement and marriage to the lovely Alice Faulkner but his designs of living on a farm and selling eggs are disrupted when he hears of Moriarty's jail break. The professor has also left behind a note on the wall of his cell which reads, "Tell Sherlock Holmes I'm OUT!" Now a free man, Moriarty puts his dastardly plan into action and the judge, Erskine, who convicted him is found hanged in his home behind a secret sliding panel. Moriarty then calls for the help of some internationally renowned criminals and Holmes believes that Moriarty will send one of them, Adetti, to his home.

Ready for him, Holmes arms himself and shoots Adetti when he enters only to find it is actually Detective Gore-King with whom Holmes has often fought. It is revealed that Gore-King came to Holmes after receiving a fake summons and Holmes is arrested. Not only does Sherlock Holmes now face disgrace and public shame, he is also sentenced to the death penalty. Moriarty uses Holmes's incarceration to rob the Faulkner bank, informing Falkner that he has kidnaped his daughter, Alice to ensure his silence. Holmes, disguised as an elderly lady, disrupts the theft with Gore-King who only staged his death in order to catch

Moriarty. Homes pursues Moriarty, rescues Alice and marries her with Gore-King as best man as Watson is taking care of his mother in law.

History: The film was recorded using Movietone technology which meant that the sound was recorded onto the actual film, which was fortuitous as the audio disks for this film had been lost.

Sherlock Holmes: The Case of the Christmas Pudding

Sherlock Holmes
Television: 1954 – 1955 (USA)

Writers: Various
Director: Various
Sherlock Holmes: Ronald Howard
Doctor Watson: Howard Marion-Crawford

This television show ran between October 18, 1954–October 17, 1955 on a first-run syndication basis in America. Although some episodes were based on the original Conan Doyle stories such as a simplified version of *The Red-Headed League* and *The Case of the French Interpreter* (a paired down version of *The Greek Interpreter*) most of the episodes were original stories. Produced in Paris the series remained the only American television adaptation serial of Sherlock Holmes to be broadcast in America until 2012 when the show *Elementary* was first aired.   It is thought that Howard Marion-Crawford was determined to play Doctor Watson as a competent and intelligent companion to Holmes as a conscious break from the famous, bumbling Watson of Nigel Bruce.

Review: The adaptation garnered positive reviews from both audience and critics, with the trade paper Variety writing that the show was successful because it avoided the "customary clichés that seem inevitable in any treatment of the Conan Doyle stories."

A full episode list can be found in the "Television Episodes" chapter of this book.

Sherlock Holmes
Television – 1964 – 1968 (UK)

Writers: Various
Director: Various
Sherlock Holmes: Douglas Wilmer & Peter Cushing
Doctor Watson: Nigel Stock

This BBC-produced television version of Conan Doyle's original stories spanned two series which saw two actors playing the lead role of Sherlock Holmes. The BBC secured the rights to adapt any five Sherlock Holmes stories from the Doyle estate with an option for a further eight with *The Hound of the Baskervilles* excluded from the deal because the Hammer Films' rights to the title didn't expire until 1965. Series One had Douglas Wilmer playing Holmes alongside Nigel Stock's Watson between 1964-1965 and in series two, 1968, Peter Cushing replaced him but Stock remained as Watson for the rest of the series.   Cushing had already played Holmes in the Hammer Horror version of *Hound of the Baskervilles* in 1959 and he would reprise that story later on in this series.   It is rumoured that the reason Douglas Wilmer refused to return for a second series was because he was told that the rehearsal schedule would be cut. He had already complained about the quality of the script-writing, stating that he would sometimes stay up until the early hours of the morning, rewriting them himself. The first series was shot in black and white but the second was one of the earliest BBC shows to be shot in colour.

History: The productions were criticised by Peter Cushing who struggled with the scheduling stating, "Whenever I see some of those stories they upset me terribly, because it wasn't Peter Cushing doing his best as Sherlock Holmes – it was Peter Cushing looking relieved that he had remembered what to say and said it."

A full episode list can be found in the "Television Episodes" chapter of this book.

Sherlock Holmes
Television – 1968 (Italy)

Writer: Edoardo Anton
Director: Guglielmo Morandi
Sherlock Holmes: Nando Gazzolo
Doctor Watson: Gianni Bonagura

This Italian mini-series consisted of just two Adventures which were split into three episodes, *The Valley of Fear* and *The Last of the Baskervilles*. The programmes followed the original stories rather faithfully and due to their length and being split into three parts, very little of the original novels had to be cut.

The Valley of Fear
Episode broadcast dates: October 25th, 1968, November 1st,1968 & November 8th, 1968

The Last of the Baskervilles
Episode broadcast dates: November 15th, 1968, November 22nd, 1968 & November 29th, 1968

History: The broadcast had a very shaky debut, with only a few hours until the first episode was to be aired on October 11th, 1968, the Conan Doyle estate questioned their contract with the network *Radiotelevisione Italiana* and the show was pulled from the scheduling. After more negotiations, the first episode aired nearly two weeks later on October 25th.

Sherlock Holmes
Film – 2009 (USA)

Writers: Michael Robert Johnson, Anthony Peckham, Simon Kinberg, Lionel Wigram & Michael Robert Johnson
Director: Guy Ritchie
Sherlock Holmes: Robert Downey Jr.
Doctor Watson: Jude Law

This reboot of Sherlock Holmes by director Guy Richie was the first Holmes movie to be released in American cinemas since the 1988 comedy *Without a Clue*.
Lord Henry Blackwood has been involved in ritual murders and so Sherlock Holmes and Doctor Watson have been engaged to bring him down. Whilst in prison, having been sentenced to death, Blackwood warns of three further deaths and is then hanged. Irene Adler wants Holmes to help find a missing man, Luke Reordan. However, when Holmes follows her in disguise, he discovers that she is taking orders from a mysterious man.

With Blackwood's tomb destroyed it is revealed that he is alive and will now lead the diabolical cult. After studying the cult's rituals Holmes works out a pattern of recent murders and that the target of the final murders will be the members of Parliament. Holmes, Watson, and Adler take to the sewers where Blackwood's men are guarding a device designed to release cyanide gas into the chambers of Parliament and kill all but those who have been given the antidote. His plans destroyed, Blackwood flees and is chased by Holmes to the top of Tower Bridge. The pair fight on the bridge, which is still under construction, and Blackwood falls and is hanged by a chain. Irene Adler confides to Holmes that her employer is Professor Moriarty and Holmes looks forward to more run-ins with the man who is his intellectual equal.

Connection: The film is full of references to the original Canon with many lines of dialogue from Conan Doyle's stories popping up including the well-loved line, "My mind rebels at stagnation. Give me problems, give me work," from *The Sign of Four*.

Sherlock Holmes: Wherever He Goes the Mistery Follows the Pipe
Film 2011 (USA)

Writer: David Wallace
Director: George Anton
Sherlock Holmes: Kevin Glaser
Doctor Watson: Charles Simon

Set in contemporary America, this ultra-low-budget project offers the viewer an adaptation of the Basil Rathbone story *The Woman in Green* (1945).

Inspector Gregson and the police commissioner are baffled by a string of murders where young woman are killed and then their right forefinger removed. While at the morgue, Holmes (who wears a flat cap rather than a deerstalker) ponders that he needs to find a motive which links them all together. Fenwick awakes in a hotel room unable to recall the night before. He visits the woman he picked up at a bar, who happens to be a hypnotist, to see if he can recall anything. During his visit Professor Moriarty calls on them and hands Fenwick his wallet saying that he witnessed him killing a woman and chopping off her finger. Moriarty then blackmails Fenwick in return for his silence. At his home, Holmes is visited by Miss Fenwick, who is worried about her father. She hands Holmes a bag which she saw her father bury in the garden at night, inside the bag is a severed finger. They rush to her house but when they arrive, Fenwick is dead.

Moriarty warns Holmes not to take up the finger murder case and later a sniper shoots Holmes through his window. Luckily, it was just the bust of Julius Caesar in a hat, and Holmes deduces that the murderer has been hypnotised. Moriarty and Lydia are hypnotising victims and then blackmailing them with the evidence of their killing. Holmes meets Lydia at the Mesme Club (a club for all the top hypnotists) and she takes him home in order to hypnotise him. Moriarty gets him to write a note which states that he is unable to solve the finger case and is, therefore, going to commit suicide. Holmes is given a glass of poison to drink and he starts to convulse just as Watson and Gregson

burst in. The hypnosis and the poisoning were fake, Holmes had convinced Lydia to cooperate with him in order to convict Moriarty.

Trivia: It is still unclear if the misspelling of the title word Mystery as "Mistery" is intentional or accidental.

Sherlock Holmes: Wherever he Goes the Mistery Follows the Pipe

sHERlock Holmes
Internet – 2016 (USA)

Writers: Lisa Bunker, Charmaine L. Clark, Helen Davies & Kate Tracy
Directors: Kate Tracy & Helen Davies
Sherlock Holmes: Helen Davies
Doctor Watson: Lisa Bunker

sHERlock Holmes is a Web Series which puts a LGBTQIA positive spin on Sherlock Holmes and the other characters created by Conan Doyle. The genders of the characters have been swapped, Sherlock Holmes keeps the same name and is portrayed as asexual, and John Watson becomes Johanna Watson. The show is set in Portland in 1995 instead of 1895 with Sherlock and Watson solving crimes but taking none of the credit. The show received funding from a Kickstarter campaign but only managed to make four episodes, all of which were released simultaneously on April 2nd, 2016.

Interview: Creators Tracy and Davies stated in an interview that their intentions were to modernise the original stories but keep the character of Sherlock Holmes intact, "Sherlock Holmes will be still written as Sherlock Holmes. I wanted to utilize Holmes for the moody, but observant instigator of justice he is."

A full episode list can be found in the "Television Episodes" chapter of this book.

Sherlock Holmes in the 22nd Century
Animation – 1991 – 2001 (USA/UK)

Writers: Various
Directors: Robert Brousseau & Scott Heming
Sherlock Holmes: Jason Gray-Stanford
Doctor Watson: John Payne

This animated series ran for two seasons on the Fox Kids network in America and put a futuristic twist on the original Conan Doyle stories. Each episode was a reworking of an original story and was the brainchild of Sandy Ross who came up with the idea whilst on a skiing holiday. The animation is set in London in the 22nd century and follows Beth Lestrade, a descendent of the original Inspector Lestrade. Beth discovers that Moriarty has been cloned from cells taken from his corpse which had been buried in a cave in Switzerland and, knowing she needs the superior brain of Sherlock Holmes to combat him, she goes to revive him.

In the basement of Scotland Yard the body of Holmes has been preserved in honey, and so Beth sets about rejuvenating him out of his suspended animation in order to help her take down Moriarty. Although 221b Baker Street is now a preserved museum, when Holmes comes back to live he moves into his old address once more. Lestrade also has a police droid and as it reads through the old journals of Watson, it morphs into the character, calls himself Watson and assists Holmes as the real Watson once did.

Trivia: The original pilot for the show was actually the Holmes-centric two part episode of *Bravestarr: Sherlock Holmes In The 23rd Century.*

A full episode list can be found in the "Television Episodes" chapter of this book.

Sherlock Holmes in the 22nd Century

Sherlock Holmes Another Bow
Computer game – 1984 (UK)

Writer: Peter A. Golden
Directors: N/A
Sherlock Holmes: N/A
Doctor Watson: N/A

This text adventure Sherlock Holmes game, issued for the PC by Bantam Software. Much like *Sherlock*, which was released in the same year, *Another Bow* puts the player in the role of Sherlock Holmes as they type in their instructions to look for clues. This adventure is set aboard the S.S. Destiny where a murder has been committed and it is up to you to catch the culprit with Watson at your side. The text game screens are also accompanied by graphics of the locations and characters which continue to look impressive today, considering the limitations of the software.

History: The game was first made for the Commodore 64 but then released a year later for gaming on the PC and Apple Mac.

Sherlock Holmes: The Awakened
Computer game - 2006 (Ukraine/Ireland)

Writer: Jalil Amr
Director: Jalil Amr
Sherlock Holmes: Rick Simmonds
Doctor Watson: David Riley

The third in a series of adventure games by Frogwares, this PC adventure game contains an original storyline where Holmes and Watson investigate mysterious crimes which may be linked to the mythology of Cthulhu. The game is played via the "point and click" method which lets the player explore the 3D world of Holmes. Holmes learns that a young servant boy has vanished. He believes the boy to be kidnaped, and he has two suspects in his sights. Whilst looking for clues down at the docks, Holmes learns of other mysterious kidnappings and his investigation uncovers a sacrificial altar containing the body of drugged victim. With his only lead being a box from the "Black Edelweiss Institute," Holmes and Watson leave for Switzerland. Holmes attempts to break into the mental asylum run by Doctor Gygax but is captured and locked into a cell.

At the asylum he finds that Dr. Gygax has not only been experimenting on his patients but is a member of a cult whose followers are waiting for the "One" to return. Holmes is also shocked to see Moriarty is one of his patients and uses him as a distraction as he flees the asylum. Holmes and Watson fly to New Orleans to continue their investigation. Here a man and his servant have gone missing. Watson finds and treats the servant boy who is too traumatised to speak, but writes down a code on a chalkboard. After saving his employer from cult sacrifice, Holmes and Watson take a mysterious book back to London with them and learn about the mythical sea god who can be summoned by sacrificing people from different parts of the world. The code given to them by the servant boy leads them to a lighthouse in Scotland where the cult is trying to summon Cthulhu, but Holmes interrupts them. The leader, Lord Rochester, mistakes the storm for the coming of Cthulhu and jumps to his death into the sea below.

Trivia: Throughout the game the front page of The Strand magazine reads, "Francis X. Bushman & Beverly Bayne in *The Great Secret*" which is referencing the 1917 film directed by prolific film director Christy Cabanne.

Sherlock Holmes Baffled
Film - 1900 (USA)

Writer: Arthur Marvin
Director: Arthur Marvin
Sherlock Holmes: Uncredited
Doctor Watson: N/A

This is the earliest known appearance of Sherlock Holmes on film and was made to be shown in Mutoscope machines in amusement arcades. The short film, just over thirty seconds, sees Sherlock Holmes entering his living room to find that he has been burgled. When he confronts the burglar he is astonished to find that he vanishes into thin air. After reaching for a cigar the burglar reappears and Holmes tries to grab his possessions and takes a pistol from the pocket of his dressing gown. When Holmes fires the gun the criminal vanishes once more and appears behind him before disappearing again. Pleased that he has managed to retrieve his stolen property, Holmes is astounded when the bag vanishes from his hand and appears in the arms of the burglar who is now making his escape through the window. The film ends with Sherlock Holmes looking, as the title suggests, baffled.

History: The large metal Mutoscope machines worked on the same principle as a flip book. When the operator turned a handle it set the rolodex-style cards flipping past the screen to create movement.

Sherlock Holmes and the Baker Street Irregulars
Television - 2007 (UK)

Writers: Richard Kurti & Bev Doyle
Director: Julian Kemp
Sherlock Holmes: Jonathan Pryce
Doctor Watson: Bill Paterson

This one-off television drama, which focuses on Sherlock Holmes' gang of street children whom he employs to help him solve cases, was produced and broadcast on the BBC network in the UK.

The drama starts when the leader of the Baker Street Irregular gang, Jack, goes missing. Naturally they turn to Sherlock Holmes, however, he is busy investigating the murder of a police officer and, instead, asks them to travel to Chinatown in order to find out some information. Jack is believed to have drowned in the Thames and his sister begins to turn against Holmes and encourages the Irregulars to do the same, claiming that he doesn't really care for them, only what they can do for him. However, when Holmes is arrested for murder and confined to house arrest, the Irregulars find that they both need each other's help. In order for Holmes to figure out what happened to Jack, they need to help Holmes solve the murder case and clear his name. The Irregulars run all over London picking up clues for Holmes, coming face to face with Irene Adler, who is no longer the clever and witty woman Holmes admires but, it seems, a cold-hearted killer. After being sent to the dockside to search for more clues, Adler's next plan is foiled by the gang and they manage to set free their members. This then leads to a chase through the London sewers before Alder is caught. The Irregulars are commended on their bravery and Holmes is commended for his cunning and intelligence in figuring out that Irene Adler's motive was to exact revenge upon him and ruin his reputation.

Quote:

Doctor Watson: This afternoon, a librarian showed me something quite remarkable. A machine that cross-references cross-references. A sort of engine for searching.

Sherlock Holmes: I like the sound of this.

Sherlock Holmes and the
Baker Street Irregulars

Sherlock Holmes Baskerville Curse
Animation – 1983 (Australia)

Writer: Eddy Graham
Director: Alex Nicholas
Sherlock Holmes: Peter O'Toole
Doctor Watson: Earle Cross

Part of a series of four animated Sherlock Holmes stories made in Australia by Burbank Films, this production is a, mostly, faithful adaptation of the original *Hound of the Baskervilles* story.

As Sir Charles leaves his dinner with Mr. Mortimer in order to go walking on the moors he is suddenly attacked by a glowing and snarling hound. Despite the lead-up to the attack, the verdict of death by heart attack is attributed to his death. Mortimer seeks the help of Sherlock Holmes, bringing with him a written account of the Curse of the Baskervilles; he wants Holmes to prove that Sir Charles' death was not by natural causes and protect the new Lord Henry Baskerville. From here the animated show follows the well-worn path of the Baskerville story, Watson's meeting with the Stapletons, Lord Baskerville's attachment to Miss Stapleton, Barrymore helping his brother-in-law who has escaped from prison, Watson finding Holmes's hideout on the moor and the eventual demise of Stapleton and the Hound are all there in some detailed animation. The story does change slightly, with Sir Henry Baskerville fainting as the hound leaps on him rather than being bitten.

History: The other three animated titles created by Burbank Films and starring Peter O'Toole also remain faithful to the original text and are animated with the same style and detail:

Sherlock Holmes and The Sign of Four (1983)

Sherlock Holmes and A Study in Scarlet (1984)

Sherlock Holmes and The Valley of Fear (1984)

Sherlock Holmes en Caracas
(Sherlock Holmes in Caracas)
Film - 1991 (Venezuela)

Writer: Juan Fresan
Director: Juan Fresan
Sherlock Holmes: Juan Manuel Montesinos
Doctor Watson: Gilbert Dacournan

This film is a bit of a curiosity in that it was never actually released on DVD or in theatres and was shown only as part of the Cartagena Film Festival in 2009. A comical and satirical representation of Holmes rather than a straight pastiche, Holmes travels through Caracas on his way to seek out an old friend who is married to a former beauty queen, Miss Venezuela. After a run-in with a pagan governess he begins to investigate the strange goings on in the village and uncovers a pagan cult which is headed by Miss Venezuela, a woman who happens to be a blood-sucking vampire. Watson is there to record the case via camcorder as well as pen and paper, and the duo rushes in to break up the cult, destroy the vampire queen and save the children from her demonic clutches.

Review: Paul Lenti, of Variety Magazine, who managed to see and review the film wrote, "This curiosity owes more to the Firesign Theater's *'Giant Rat of Sumatra'* and Monty Python than to Arthur Conan Doyle."

Sherlock Holmes and the Case of the Silk Stocking
Television – 2004 (UK)

Writer: Allan Cubitt
Director: Simon Cellan Jones
Sherlock Holmes: Rupert Everett
Doctor Watson: Ian Hart

This BBC-produced television movie was broadcast on BBC one, part of the BBC network, in the UK. This story is set in 1903 and Watson comes to an almost fully retired Holmes for help on a mysterious case. Young women are being murdered and the bodies of all the victims have silk stockings lodged in their throats. Holmes takes up the case and deduces almost immediately that

they are looking for a killer who has a foot fetish. Watson's fiancée is an American psychologist who informs Holmes of the many theories of sexual kinks which could be connected to the crime. Holmes talks to a young girl who survived an attack by the serial killer, she was set free because she has an unattractive clubbed foot, and tricks her into meeting the suspected murderer. When she identifies him as the man who took her, he is arrested, but unfortunately his fingerprints do not match those found at the crime scene. Holmes then sets a trap for the killer using a woman dressed in a Grecian-Roman costume, revealing her feet in sandals. After she has danced at an event for the King she walks home and is attacked and drugged but Holmes intercepts the attacker and she goes home to her father. The young woman is taken from her home and Holmes puts forth the idea that the killer has a twin. When the police capture one twin and order him to take them to his brother, he escapes, but Holmes tracks him down just in time to see the young woman being choked by a silk stocking tied around her neck. Watson cuts her free and gives her the kiss of life and Holmes gets the killer twins to confess their crimes. The film has a bit of a sad ending with Holmes being left alone as Watson leaves to get married.

Trivia: The makers were hoping to bring back Richard Roxburgh to play Sherlock Holmes and continue his role from *The Hound of the Baskervilles (2002)* but he was unavailable and so Rupert Everett was cast. Ian Hart, however, came back to reprise the role of Dr. Watson.

Sherlock Holmes: The Case of the Silver Earring
Computer game - 2004 (Ukraine/Ireland)

Writer: Jalil Amr.
Director: Sergey Geraschenko
Sherlock Holmes: Guy Harris
Doctor Watson: David Riley

The second in the *Sherlock Holmes* series of adventure games developed by Frogwares for PC gaming, this game allows the player to investigate and solve a murder as both Sherlock Holmes and Doctor Watson. The player must investigate a murder at the Sherringford Hall mansion during a party to honour Lavinia Bromsby, daughter of a wealthy industrialist. In the middle of a speech given by the host Sir Melvyn, he is shot by an unseen guest; luckily, Holmes and Watson are at the party and so begin their investigation. The evidence puts Lavinia in the cross-hairs of suspicion, especially when Holmes finds Lavinia's passport, train and boat tickets from Geneva to London and a gun in her bag. Holmes, however, believes there is more to the crime than a simple act of revenge or hatred. The player walks through each room collecting clues and interviewing suspects which create a very complicated history of Sir Bromsby's estate and family. Eventually it is revealed that the nephew of Sir Melvyn has secretly travelled to the estate and planned to murder him and claim the inheritance.

Trivia: In a nod to the creator of Holmes, most of the gameplay takes place at Sherringford Hall and, as most Sherlockians are aware, Sherringford Hope and Ormond Sacker were the names which Conan Doyle had originally chose for Holmes and Watson.

Sherlock Holmes: The Case of
the Silver Earring

Sherlock Holmes: Consulting Detective
Computer game – 1991 (USA)

Writer: Laurie Rose Bauman
Director: Ken Tarolla
Sherlock Holmes: Peter Farley
Doctor Watson: Warren Green

This video game made by ICOM Simulations for the PC is based on a tabletop game-book hybrid of the same name.

As either Holmes or Watson you are tasked with solving three mysteries, *The Mummy's Curse,* in which the death of three men is being blamed on an ancient curse. *The Mystified Murderess,* in which a woman has been convicted of the murder of her boyfriend but is suffering from temporary amnesia and can't remember anything about the night of the murder and, *The Tin Soldier,* where a retired general has been murdered which uncovers a tumultuous past and a suspect with a motive to kill. At the start of each case a live action "film" is shown which sees Holmes and Watson in their living room in Baker Street meeting their new client and learning about the case before they attempt to solve it.

Trivia: During the game you can also ask for help from either the Baker Street Irregulars, the gang of street children who often help Holmes with his cases, or the Baker Street Regulars, a collection of well-connected gentlemen who can help with official documents and reports.

Sherlock Holmes: Consulting Detective Vol. II
Computer game – 1992 (USA)

Writer: Laurie Rose Bauman
Director: Ken Tarolla
Sherlock Holmes: Peter Farley
Doctor Watson: Warren Green

With the, somewhat, enthusiastic response to *Sherlock Holmes: Consulting Detective*, a sequel was released in 1992 with the same actors playing Holmes and Watson and the same mix of live-action and game play.

This time the player is asked to solve the case of *The Two Lions,* in which Holmes receives a mysterious note on his door which leads him and Watson to investigate the death of two lions from a travelling circus. Next is *The Pilfered Paintings,* which presents the mysterious circumstances surrounding a pair of paintings which have been stolen from the National Gallery just days before their unveiling at an art show, and the final crime, *The Murdered Munitions Magnate*, where a wealthy gun factory owner is murdered in an alley outside his office. Scotland Yard believes it was a robbery but Holmes learns of a secret government project which links the magnate's company to the murder.

Review: The game garnered a mixed reception but, despite its slow pace and short gameplay, the gaming magazine Computer Gaming World wrote that it would "provide several captivating hours of armchair investigation."

Sherlock Holmes Contre Conan Doyle
(Sherlock Holmes Against Conan Doyle)
Documentary – 2017 (France)

Writer: Michel Le Bris
Director: Emmanuelle Nobécourt
Sherlock Holmes: Various
Doctor Watson: Various

The documentary narrates the story of the birth of Sherlock Holmes and Conan Doyle's uncomfortable relationship with him as well as celebrating the 130-year anniversary of *A Study in Scarlet* being published. The documentary uses clips from a variety of television shows and films, from William Gillett to Benedict Cumberbatch, as well as shows which have been influenced by Holmes, such as *House*. The narration is intercut with interviews from Holmes historians, program makers and Sherlockians such as Roger Johnson, officer of The Sherlock Holmes Society of London; and the writer, Anthony Horowitz. The documentary also looks at the relationship between the audience and Holmes as being manipulated through the eyes of John Watson. As well as analysing the troubled relationship between Holmes and Doyle it also celebrates the relationship between Holmes and Watson.

Trivia: This episode was part of the *We Are Legend* mini-series which studied three characters who grew bigger than their

authors, – Dracula, Tarzan and Sherlock Holmes – was shown on the French television network, France 5.

Sherlock Holmes Crimes and Punishments
Computer game – 2014 (Ukraine/Ireland)

Writer: Unreal Engine
Director: Unreal Engine
Sherlock Holmes: Kerry Shale
Doctor Watson: Nick Brimble

The seventh adventure mystery game in the Sherlock Holmes series to developed by Frogwares and released to play on PC, XBox and the PlayStation.

It differs slightly from other games in that you are placed in London in the years 1894 and 1895 and that you are tasked with, not only, finding the right culprit but making a moral choice of absolving or punishing them. There is a narrative arc running through the entire game which focuses on finding a group of terrorists called the "Merry Men" who are attempting to overthrow the government because they want to destroy the people's debt (much like Fight Club). There are also six separate cases to solve, some of which are adaptations of the original Conan Doyle classics. In *The Fate of Black Peter*, Holmes investigates the murder of Peter Carey who is a bad-tempered drunkard found impaled with a harpoon. In *The Riddle on the Rails*, Holmes and Watson solve the puzzle of a train which has mysteriously disappeared from its tracks. This mystery strikes some similarity to Conan Doyle's *The Story of the Lost Special*, which appeared in *The Strand* in 1898. In *The Blood Bath*, Holmes investigates the death of a man in a ritual pose, in the locked steam room of the Roman Baths in London. While in *The Abbey Grange Affair*, Holmes is called to the scene of a murder where the violent-tempered Sir Eustace Brackenstall has allegedly been murdered by burglars who also tied up his wife and held her hostage. *The Kew Gardens Drama* is a case where Holmes is asked by an old friend to investigate the theft of some exotic plants at Kew Gardens, which quickly turns into a murder case. In *A Half Moon Walk*, the brother of Baker Street Irregular leader, Wiggins, has been charged with double murder and Wiggins comes to Holmes and Watson to clear his name. The game concludes with Holmes confronting the "Merry Men" who plead their case and state that their plan was for the greater good of the British people and here Holmes can choose to allow them to carry out their plan or to stop them.

Review: The game review site *PC Gamer* wrote a detailed review and concluded, "It doesn't have the inflated budget of Rockstar's game, but it makes up for its rough edges with quality detecting, compelling cases, beautiful world-building, and endearing gusto."

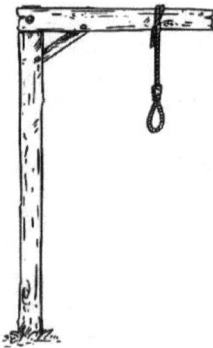

Sherlock Holmes Crimes and Punishments

Sherlock Holmes: The Devil's Daughter
Computer Game – 2016 (Ukraine/Ireland)

Writer: Luke Openshaw
Directors: Aurélie Ludot & Mark Estdale
Sherlock Holmes: Alex Jordan
Doctor Watson: Andrew Wincott

Much like the other Frogwares *Sherlock Holmes* games, this involves exploring crime scenes and examining clues over five separate mysteries where you play as Sherlock Holmes.

All five of the case are linked in some way, and during the game Holmes has to confront dark family secrets, both in the cases and in his personal life. The game also features Sherlock Holmes's daughter whom he adopted at the end of *The Testament of Sherlock Holmes* and is really the daughter of Professor Moriarty. The cases faced by Holmes in this adventure are *Prey Tell*, where Holmes is visited by a young boy who is distraught due to the disappearance of his father; *A Study in Green*, where Sherlock investigates a murder at a bowls tournament award ceremony; *Infamy*, where an actor asks to follow Sherlock Holmes in order to study him for a role but then vanishes; *Chain Reaction* when on his way home, Holmes witnesses the aftermath of an accident in which a large group of people died. Believing it was no accident, he starts his investigation in order to find the truth. Lastly, *Fever Dreams* is a more personal adventure, where Holmes's daughter is kidnaped and he must find her before it's too late.

Trivia: There was a featured episode of Outside Xbox – a web based show dedicated to Xbox Games – titled Let's Play: Sherlock Holmes: The Devil's Daughter –Victorian Urchin Simulator 2016. Here the actors who created the voices for the game were invited to play along and provide a live commentary.

Sherlock Holmes and Doctor Watson
Television – 1980 (Poland/UK)

Writers: Various
Directors: Various
Sherlock Holmes: Geoffrey Whitehead
Doctor Watson: Donald Pickering

This obscure and rarely seen television adaptation of the Sherlock Holmes stories has a past that could be said to be slightly more interesting than some of the episodes. The series was produced by Sheldon Reynolds who had previously produced the American television show *Sherlock Holmes* in the 1950s starring Ronald Howard as Holmes. In fact, many of the episodes from that television show were rehashed and produced for this series. Reynolds had brokered a deal with the state-run Polish

Television network to take over Poltel Studios and produce television shows on a low budget to be show in Poland and the United Kingdom. Each episode has a specific structure and always ends with Holmes and Watson back in the living room of 221b Baker Street sharing a joke about their case whilst obnoxious violin plucking plays over them. As the episodes were never broadcast, there is no broadcast date.

History: Twenty four episodes of *Sherlock Holmes and Doctor Watson* were filmed, but before they could be aired, the head of Polish television was arrested for corruption and the production master tapes and film were all confiscated. This meant that the show was never released in the UK and has since strayed, very occasionally, onto late night cable in the USA as well as low-budget and poor-quality DVD releases.

A full episode list can be found in the "Television Episodes" chapter of this book.

Sherlock Holmes Faces death
Film - 1943 (USA)

Writer: Bertram Millhauser
Director: Roy William Neill
Sherlock Holmes: Basil Rathbone
Doctor Watson: Nigel Bruce

The sixth film to feature the pairing of Rathbone and Bruce has a narrative that is very loosely based on the original Conan Doyle story, *The Adventure of the Musgrave Ritual.*

Here Doctor Watson is doing some volunteer work at Musgrave Hall tending to soldiers convalescing from shell shock. When a young lady, Sally Musgrave, falls for one of the recovering soldiers, Capt. Pat Vickery, her brothers quickly voice their disapproval. After one of the doctors, Dr Sexton, is attacked, Watson calls on his friend and colleague Sherlock Holmes. When Holmes arrives he finds that one of the Musgrave brothers, Geoffrey, has been murdered, and Lestrade is quick to blame Vickery for the murder. The next day the other brother, Philip, is also found murdered in the boot of

a car and suspicion now falls on Brunton, the butler, who had been dismissed after his behaviour was deemed inappropriate. Holmes and Watson, discover the "Musgrave Ritual" which is performed each time a new family head is appointed and start searching for clues connected to it. These lead to the pair uncovering a secret burial crypt beneath the hall where they find Brunton's murdered body. Later, Holmes breaks back into the crypt and waits for the murderer to show himself. When Dr. Sexton is confronted and confesses to murdering the brothers he attempts to shoot at Holmes but finds that his gun is full of blanks, Holmes had swapped the bullets beforehand. Holmes deduced that Sexton had discovered a document which showed the true value of Musgrave Hall and its land, meaning that it was worth millions of pounds. His plan being to kill the Musgrave brothers, implicate Vickery and allow Sally to inherit the fortune alone, possibly leaving her free to marry him. In the end Sally Musgrave destroys the document stating that she did not want to inherit wealth at the cost of other people's lives.

Trivia: It is rumoured that, because of his short stature, Milburn Stone who played Captain Vickery was never filmed below the waist during his scenes with Sally Musgrave, Hillary Brooke, because he was forced to stand on a box.

Sherlock Holmes Game of
Shadows
Film – 2011 (USA)

Writers: Michele Mulroney & Kieran Mulroney
Director: Guy Ritchie
Sherlock Holmes: Robert Downey Jr.
Doctor Watson: Jude Law

The sequel to the 2009 *film Sherlock Holmes,* this film takes some of the narrative of *The Final Problem* and a little from *The Empty House* at the conclusion.

After failing to deliver a bomb under the instruction of Moriarty, thanks to Holmes interjection, Irene Adler is deemed inadequate by Moriarty who murders her by poisoning her tea. Watson visits Holmes who discloses that he is currently working on connecting terrorist attacks to Professor Moriarty and the pair go out to a bachelor party. Whilst out, Holmes meets a fortune teller, Simza, who was the intended recipient of a letter Holmes took from Irene Adler, and prevents her death by overpowering her assassin. In order to protect them, Holmes disguises himself as John's fiancée, Mary, and stows away on a train which is taking them on their honeymoon. After pushing Mary off the train and into the water below, where Mycroft is waiting for her, Holmes explains the danger to Watson and together they fight off the attackers who have come to kill Mary and John.

In France they explain to Simza that her brother, Rene, has been working for Moriarty. Believing that Moriarty is planning to bomb the opera house, they quickly head over to stop it but Holmes realises, too late, that he has been tricked as a nearby hotel blows up, killing its occupants. Holmes discovers that Moriarty is using a variety of pseudonyms to buy up war profiteering companies in order to instigate a world war and make his fortune. At Moriarty's next target, a peace summit, Holmes and Moriarty play a game of mental chess on the balcony. Holmes then reveals to Moriarty that he has evidence which links him to a variety of crimes which is safe with Mary Morstan. Holmes then blows soot into the eyes of Moriarty to distract him, grabs him and throws them both off the balcony and into the Reichenbach Falls. After the funeral for Holmes, Watson receives a package containing a mobile breathing device and has a glimmer of hope that Holmes may be alive. Holmes, however, is hiding in plain sight, camouflaging himself as the living room chair.

Trivia: Doctor Watson's narration during Holmes's funeral was almost word for word what Conan Doyle wrote in the original story *The Final Problem.*

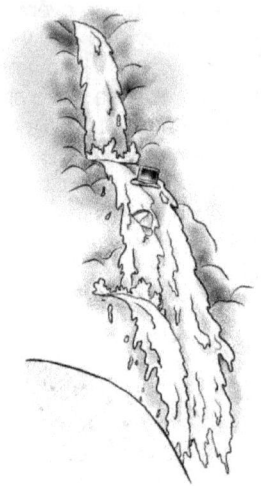

Sherlock Holmes Game of Shadows

Sherlock Holmes: The Great Detective
Documentary – 1995 (USA)

Writer: Peter Swain
Director: Peter Swain
Sherlock Holmes: Various
Doctor Watson: Various

This documentary about the life of Sherlock Holmes was shown as part of the *Biography* documentary series broadcast on the CBS, A&E, and the Biography Channel network in America.

Each episode explores the life of a person or character using clips and interview footage from a variety of experts. This episode explores the question: "What sort of man was Sherlock Holmes?" Headed by Anthony Howlett, at that time, President of the Sherlock Holmes Society of London, a dinner party is held for Doctor Watson who is being played once more by David Burke, famed for playing Watson to Jeremy Brett's Holmes in the Granada Series *The Adventures of Sherlock Holmes.* Each collection of narrated clips is preceded by an anecdote from Watson at the dinner table, who describes the private and public life of Holmes with his fellow guests. Watson also references examples from "cases" (the titles of Conan

Doyle's original stories) to further illustrate Holmes's methodology and personality.

Quote:
Doctor Watson: To Holmes it has all been quite elementary. My friends, his life was packed full of adventure and intrigue and it has been my pleasure to act as his Boswell.

Sherlock Holmes in the Great Murder Mystery
Film – 1908 (USA)

Writer: Uncredited
Director: Uncredited
Sherlock Holmes: Uncredited
Doctor Watson: Uncredited

The production details of this black and white silent movie have been lost and so the actors and director of this film remain unknown. The film starts with Jim and his girlfriend talking of marriage before he is called away. Meanwhile, at the shipyard, one of the containers which houses a large gorilla has broken and the animal has escaped. The crew of the ship chase the animal up the porch of the young woman which the animal attacks and kills. The ship's captain witnesses the attack but runs away in fear of losing his job. When the body is discovered, Jim is arrested for murder as he waits to board a train. At Baker Street, Watson tells Holmes of the murder in the newspaper and how the perpetrator is pleading innocence and Holmes agrees to look at the case.

After searching for clues at the young woman's home, Holmes begins to put his theories together. But after hearing of the escaped gorilla he pieces together a scenario where the animal may have murdered the woman. Holmes tries many leads before he discovers the right ship and chastises the captain for allowing the tragedy to continue. Just as Jim is about to be sentenced to death Sherlock Holmes rushes in with all the evidence needed to set him free.

Connection: This is a hybrid narrative of Sherlock Holmes and C. Auguste Dupin, as Edgar Allan Poe's story *The Murders in the*

Rue Morgue involves his detective finding an orangutan guilty of murder.

Sherlock Holmes und das Halsband des Todes
(Sherlock Holmes and the Deadly Necklace)
Film - 1962
(France, Germany, Italy)

Writer: Curt Siodmak
Director: Terence Fisher
Sherlock Holmes: Christopher Lee
Doctor Watson: Thorley Walters

This black and white Holmes adventure was a West German-French-Italian international co-production and so, as it was common in many German movies of the time, it was shot without recording sound in order for the film to be dubbed later in various languages.

The film starts with a necklace, believed to be cursed and worn by Cleopatra, stolen shortly after Professor Moriarty's trip to Egypt. Holmes puts a theory to Inspector Cooper that the necklace may be linked to Moriarty as well as a spate of murders, but Cooper dismisses the idea. During a visit to 221b, Inspector Jenkins starts to have a fit on the sofa and dies whilst, apparently, flailing his arms around in panic. After some deduction Holmes realises that the man was trying to mime out a location, The Hare and Eagle pub, which is a rough drinking hole down by the docks. Holmes and Watson take a trip to the pub and after listening in on a conversation between Moriarty and one of his accomplices, it is confirmed that Moriarty is involved in stealing the precious necklace. Disguised as a bookish academic, Holmes gains entry to Professor Moriarty's office and finds the necklace in a sarcophagus where Moriarty had stowed it. Taking the necklace Holmes finds Inspector Cooper and hands it to him for safe keeping until the piece is sold at auction. This time Holmes dresses as a thuggish seaman, and heads over to The Hare and Eagle once more. He manages to become part of Moriarty's gang which plans to steal the necklace. The gang, including Holmes, hides under the streets in a sewer and waits for the police van carrying the necklace to stop over a specific manhole. When it does, the gang emerges and steals the necklace once more. After a violent fight, Holmes takes the stolen property and outruns the rest of Moriarty's gang. At the auction, Inspector Cooper is apprehensive but is relieved when a package arrives containing the necklace and Professor Moriarty is arrested but not charged due to lack of evidence. Back home, Holmes and Watson learn that the spate of London murders have been attributed to a man named Jack the Ripper.

Trivia: Astonishingly Christopher Lee was not asked to dub his own performance and later said, in an interview, "What I found most unacceptable was the fact that, without my knowledge or permission, my voice was dubbed by another English actor. The results were disastrous."

Sherlock Holmes I Ludzie Jutra
(Sherlock Holmes and People of Tomorrow)
Film – 2014 (Poland)

Writer: Tomasz Gwincinski
Director: Tomasz Gwincinski
Sherlock Holmes: Tomasz Gwincinski
Doctor Watson: N/A

Although his name is in the title, Sherlock Holmes plays very little part in this artistic and avant-garde film from Poland. Promoted as a "metaphysical thriller," the film features four people sitting around a table playing a game. The rules of the game are never explained. Meanwhile there is the mystery of a decapitated head which has been marked with the name Anna W to be solved. As the "main character" Max tries to investigate the head it is taken from a strange figure in the woods and placed in Max's fridge. The head now wears the mask of Sherlock Holmes. Later, however, Holmes becomes more than just a head and can be seen sitting behind the players of the game. It is up to Sherlock to investigate the mystery of the human head which, ultimately, will be lost to the game.

Interview: In an interview actor Joanna Gwincinska stated, "The film itself is highly metaphorical and is not based on any book of Sir Conan Doyle...We are fans of Sherlock Holmes and that is why the director and the author of the script wanted Sherlock to be a part of it."

Sherlock Holmes I Ludzie Jutra

Sherlock Holmes Leading Lady
Television - 1991
(Belgium/ France/ Italy/ Luxembourg/ UK/ USA)

Writers: Bob Shayne & H.R.F. Keating
Director: Peter Sasdy
Sherlock Holmes: Christopher Lee
Doctor Watson: Patrick Macnee

This internationally produced television movie along with its sequel, *Incident at Victoria Falls*, was made under the banner of *Sherlock Holmes the Golden Years* and features stories involving an older, retired Holmes and Watson.

Set in 1910, Mycroft Holmes tells Sherlock of a remote-control bomb device stolen from Dr. Froelich in Vienna and instructs Holmes to go and investigate it, if not for himself, then for his country. Whilst in Vienna, Holmes meets Irene Alder and he learns that that her husband passed away leaving her to restart her career as an opera singer. In a clandestine conversation, Adler informs Holmes that the device he is looking for may be hidden somewhere in the opera house but she is not sure how or why she knows this information. Holmes then calls on Sigmund Freud to hypnotise Adler and when an anarchist called Oberstein learns of this, he becomes worried that she will divulge any information she has suppressed. Oberstein attempts to kill her but only succeeds in killing her maid. Holmes then travels all the way to Budapest with Freud in order to find and destroy the blueprints for the device but then hears that Irene Adler has been kidnaped.

Deducing the location of the anarchists' hideout Holmes rescues Adler and, when safe, asks Freud to hypnotise her once again. Under hypnosis, Adler revels that there is a plan to have Franz Joseph assassinated that night whilst she sings *Die Fledermaus* at the opera house. Adler also reveals her love for Holmes and says that she would give up everything to be his wife. Regardless of his feelings toward her, Holmes rejects her offer. At the opera house Watson finds the detonator and disposes of it whilst Holmes identifies the man who was about to use it. The perpetrator is Franz Hofferman, a sarcastic critic who, during a scuffle, falls from the rafters of the theatre and dies. Back at Baker Street Holmes confides that he is growing too old for adventure and may consider Irene Alder's offer to settle down after all.

Trivia: The film was also supposed to be part of an eight-hour mini-series under the same moniker but the eight one-hour episodes were, instead, turned into two three-hour films.

Sherlock: L'Enquête
(Sherlock: Behind the Scenes)
Documentary – 2014 (France)

Writers: Alain Carrazé & Romain Nigita
Directors: Alain Carrazé & Romain Nigita
Sherlock Holmes: Benedict Cumberbatch
Doctor Watson: Martin Freeman

This behind the scenes documentary about the BBC television production *Sherlock* was shown before the French broadcast of Season Three on the France 4 Network.

Through a variety of interviews with the writers Mark Gatiss and Stephen Moffat, as well as cast members Benedict Cumberbatch and Martin Freeman, the documentary shows behind-the-scenes footage of the cast and crew on location and in the studio and gives insights into the modernisation of Holmes and Watson for the adaptation.

As well as recapping the past narratives, the directors and writers discuss how the actors were chosen, why they work well together and reveal how some iconic shots were made using unexpected means and materials.

Connection: The documentary is narrated by Gilles Morvan who is the voice of Benedict Cumberbatch in the French dubbed version of *Sherlock.*

Sherlock Holmes' London: The Investigation
Documentary – 2011 (UK)

Writer: Mark Conroy
Director: Mark Conroy
Sherlock Holmes: N/A
Doctor Watson: N/A

This *Artsmagic* documentary distributed mostly online takes the viewer on a tour of real-life locations which feature in the original stories of Sir Arthur Conan Doyle. Presented by Mark Conroy it starts outside the Sherlock Holmes museum in Baker Street, and explains how the building might have stood during the times of Holmes and Watson. Conroy goes into great depth at all of the locations, not simply adopting a "show-and-tell" presentation of each London spot, but taking the time to give the viewer historical background and pertinent information on Sherlock Holmes, Conan Doyle and the history of London. It also stops at the pharmacy where Holmes would have fed his drug habit; Kendall Place, the location of *The Empty House*; Welbeck Street, where Holmes was nearly taken out by a two horse carriage in *The Final Problem;* as well as Simpson's on the Strand where Holmes and Watson would often dine. The journey ends at the Sherlock Holmes

Pub, which was formerly the Northumberland Hotel, where Henry Baskerville stayed, in *The Hound of the Baskervilles,* and lost the majority of his boots. The hotel was converted to a pub in 1957. Conroy takes the viewer around the iconic location's knick-knacks and *objets d'art*, all dedicated to Sherlock Holmes, and points out their significance. It's a documentary which doesn't rely on interviews and clips but on knowledge and history to widen the contextual understanding of Holmes.

Trivia: The actual location of The Sherlock Holmes Museum is not, as the door suggests, 221b Baker street but between 237 and 241 Baker Street.

Sherlock Holmes and Moriarty's Secret Weapon
Film - 1978 (USA)

Writer: Scott Allen Nollen
Director: Scott Allen Nollen
Sherlock Holmes: Jeff Nelson
Doctor Watson: Charles Kline

This amateur short film which has now found its way onto the internet was written and produced by a young Scott Allen Nollen who has continued to make short films as well as written a series of film history books. In this fifteen minute movie, Holmes and Watson are called to lend their help to a case where they must solve a coded picture puzzle. The solved puzzle will help them find the evil Professor Moriarty and stop him before he can sell his new secret weapon to the highest bidder amongst the enemies of the Britain.

Connection: The story is a loose adaptation of the film *Sherlock Holmes and the Secret Weapon*, which owes a debt to Conan Doyle's original story *The Adventure of the Dancing Men*

Sherlock Holmes: Mystery of the Mummy
Computer game - 2002
(Ireland/Ukraine)

Writer: Aurelie Ludot
Director: Aurelie Ludot
Sherlock Holmes: Uncredited
Doctor Watson: N/A

This adventure game by Frogwares was the first in a series of Sherlock Holmes games for the PC (and later the Nintendo DS) and is played from a first-person perspective as the player becomes Sherlock Holmes, searching a variety of locations for clues to solve the bigger puzzle.

As Holmes (Watson is currently on holiday), the player investigates a museum in order to solve the mystery of the vanishing Lord Montcalf who owns and lives at the museum. Lord Montcalf's daughter, Elisabeth, has called upon Holmes, her soon-to-be cousin, to help find her father. Scotland Yard believes that Lord Montcalf has committed suicide but Holmes believes otherwise. Whilst investigating Sherlock is attacked by a mummy, twice, in an attempt to scare him away from the museum and the more he investigates the more attempts are made on his life. When a mummy shoots a gun at Holmes he uncovers a clue which leads to the discovery that, at one point, Elisabeth was keen to follow in the footsteps of her father and become an archaeologist but her father refused her. As a possible motive for murder Holmes digs a little deeper and finds the motive may not be as simple as revenge. A group of statues dotted around the museum are being targeted and stolen and it is discovered that when these are grouped together they, supposedly, release a deadly curse. Holmes deduces that Elisabeth is working with Montcalf's cousin, Jonathan Parkey, who has already been arrested for a robbery at Lord Montcalf's museum, in a plot to kill her father and release the curse. Jonathan is killed in his attempt to steal from the museum due to Lord Montcalf setting up traps to kill anybody who tries to take his most treasured possessions. It comes to light that Lord Montcalf was being treated for madness, induced by a constant search for immortality. The result of this madness is Lord Montcalf creating another persona, the murderous mummy. As the mummy, Montcalf then made it his mission to kill his daughter as, not only had he not been murdered, or committed suicide, but he disguised himself as the butler and had been at the house all along. In a strange twist, it is revealed that the entire Montcalf family are a set of cultists and murderers who were all planning to kill each other, all disguised as the mummy.

Trivia: This was Frogwares' first official Sherlock Holmes game and the only game where the entirety of the action takes place indoors.

Sherlock Holmes: Mystery of the Mummy

Sherlock Holmes nevében
(In the Name of Sherlock Holmes)
Film – 2011 (Hungary)

Writer: Mark Kis-Szabo
Director: Zsolt Bernáth
Sherlock Holmes: Szénási Kristóf
Doctor Watson: Ungvár Ádám

Although not strictly a film about Sherlock Holmes but rather about the living embodiment of the great detective, this Hungarian film is set in a small town where strange things appear to be happening to the local children. Two boys who live in the town are big fans of Conan Doyle's Sherlock Holmes' books, even calling themselves Holmes and Watson. They make friends with a young girl named Ica after they start to notice strange occurrences and behaviours in the town. Although the adults around them are oblivious, the trio realizes the local children are vanishing only to return a few days later acting like brain-dead zombies.

Watson has already attempted to figure out the problem but he needs his Holmes if they are to save the children from these mysterious happenings. As they investigate further they become scared by the supernatural forces they stumble across, including an eye-witness who claims he saw a terrifying monster kidnap a little boy. In addition, the names of victims keep appearing at the school they attend. It is revealed that Ica's father had also been investigating similar inexplicable behaviour which had plagued the town years before. Then her father vanished. The trio learns that Ica's father had left behind a circus ticket and they take that as the next big clue for further investigation. The exploration of the circus reveals more secrets about the legend of the Dream-master, an apparition who steals the dreams of children. After they discover cases of neglect, abandonment and horrific childhood traumas, it is up to this mini Holmes and Watson to rid the town of the evil aura which is infiltrating their sleeping and living nightmares.

Review: A piece in the Hungarian Film site Filmtekercs writes, "The exciting story, superb post-production, exciting venues and dreams are fun for kids. We believe in the resourcefulness of children and we are cheering for them to succeed."

Sherlock Holmes in New York
Television – 1976 (USA)

Writer: Alvin Sapinsley
Director: Boris Sagal
Sherlock Holmes: Roger Moore
Doctor Watson: Patrick Macnee

Made by 20th Century Fox and broadcast on the NBC network in America, this made-for-TV Sherlock Holmes movie was cut by six minutes during its original broadcast to make room for two election adverts for Gerald Ford and Jimmy Carter.

Moriarty has fled to New York with nothing but evil on his mind and so Holmes and Watson seek him out with the assistance of Inspector Lafferty of the NYPD. During their investigation Holmes and Watson happen upon Irene Adler, no longer an opera singer but a very popular music-hall performer. Adler is distraught that Moriarty has kidnaped her son, Scott. Holmes reads a note from Moriarty stating that when he is contacted by the police to help solve their most recent crime he must refuse, and if he does not, the child will be killed. Holmes is indeed contacted by the NYPD in regards to a large theft at the gold exchange where an entire vault of gold bars has disappeared. Holmes does as Moriarty requests and does not take the case, instead he aims to find Scott and, once the threat of harm is removed, to find Moriarty.

Holmes deduces that Scott may not have been forcefully taken but rather tricked into thinking he was playing a game. Using this to his advantage he finds the boy, devises his own game and brings him home to safety. Holmes then investigates the vaults and the tunnels and whilst reading about the history of the exchange and, in particular, the lift, Holmes notices that rather than taking 45 seconds to reach the vaults the lift stops after only 42. It is quickly discovered that the gold has not been stolen at all, rather, Moriarty has built a second, fake vault, above the real one in order to steal the actual gold over time whilst the so-called robbery was being investigated. Before leaving for London, Adler tells Holmes that Scott may actually be his son and tells him that the boy has great observation skills and the ability to quickly solve puzzles. Holmes, however, still leaves for London but not before Adler gives him a picture of Scott to keep.

Trivia: Roger Moore revealed that he asked Oliver Reed if he would be interested in playing the role of Moriarty but Reed turned it down, allegedly, because Moore had been critical of Reed's acting in the past.

Sherlock Holmes Returns AKA 1994 Baker Street
Television – 1993 (USA)

Writer: Kenneth Johnson
Director: Kenneth Johnson
Sherlock Holmes: Anthony Higgins
Doctor Watson: N/A

This made-for-television movie was broadcast on the CBS network in America. A police officer is mauled by a wild tiger in a park and Dr. Amy Winslow tries in vain to save him at the ER. Later she tell his friend, Lieutenant Louis Ortega, that his mentor has died. Winslow is invited to visit Mrs. Hudson's house as a thank you for helping her husband, whilst looking for a bottle of wine she discovers a secret door and triggers a blackout. Mrs. Hudson spirals into a panic because, in her cellar, is a special chamber which holds the frozen body of Sherlock Holmes. After coming out of his cryogenic coma, Holmes has shaved and dressed and is keen to start solving the case which has been reported in the local paper with the headline "Murder by the Phantom Tiger." Although he is reluctant to work with the help of anybody, especially a woman, Holmes reluctantly agrees to stay with Dr Winslow who happens to live at 1994 Baker Street.

After getting used to his new surroundings, and having been thrown out by Winslow for his harsh deductions about her life, Holmes wanders around the park. During this time he hears about a woman being eaten by a tank of piranhas and connects it to the case of the Phantom Tiger. Holmes is also searching for leads as to the whereabouts of his personal papers and during this investigation discovers that Moriarty's descendent is now a priest, but that his cousin James Moriarty Booth is the head of a crime syndicate. Holmes takes a visit to police HQ where he overhears another odd crime about a man who has been killed by beetles. Holmes suspects a connection between Booth and the crime boss Enrique Pavon as all of the murders had some kind of "tiger" connection and Pavon's murdered brother was nicknamed Tony the Tiger. Holmes tells Winslow that Moriarty Booth has been committing the murders in retribution for the death of Pavon's brother in order to propose a working crime relationship with Pavon. When the pair arrives at the pier, they corner Pavon and Moriarty Booth in time for the police to arrive. It is revealed that Pavon's car boot is also full of cocaine. After the case is solved, Holmes moves in with Winslow, inviting Mrs. Hudson to stay as their housekeeper as well as starting his new detective business.

Trivia: The show was intended to be a pilot for a series of Holmes adaptations but it was not picked up by the network. Much like the premise in the animated show *Sherlock Holmes in the 22nd Century*, this episode has Holmes being awakened from a suspended animation chamber.

Sherlock Holmes and the Secret Weapon
Film - 1942 (USA)

Writers: Edward T. Lowe Jr, Scott Darling
& Edmund L. Hartmann
Director: Roy William Neill
Sherlock Holmes: Basil Rathbone
Doctor Watson: Nigel Bruce

Film number four to star the pairing of Rathbone and Bruce opens in a cafe in Switzerland where two men plot to abduct Dr. Franz Tobel, who has invented a new bomb sight. The men find their plans are scuppered when an old book seller, who is Sherlock Holmes in disguise, sends the two Nazi officers after a decoy whilst he escorts Tobel safely to London. Whilst at 221b Watson is tasked with keeping Tobel safe, however, when Watson falls asleep, Tobel sneaks out to meet his girlfriend, Charlotte, instructing her to give a coded message to Holmes should anything happen to him. Watson is attacked but is brought back to Baker Street by an intervening police officer. When Tobel's bomb sight testing is successful he agrees to make his invention for the RAF but insists on producing it himself so nobody else can have his invention plans. When Tobel goes missing again, Holmes manages to trace the number of his girlfriend and goes to visit her. She hands him the envelope containing the

coded message but inside is a note which reads, "We meet again, Mr. Holmes," which Holmes knows has come from Professor Moriarty. Holmes manages to figure out Tobel's coded messages which reveal the names and addresses of three out of the four scientists who are working on various parts of the bomb sight. The final code only seems to decipher into nonsense until Holmes works out that it is coded in mirror image. Moriarty works out the code at the same time and sends his thugs to the address to capture the scientist and the final package but, when he opens it, it contains a note which reads "We meet again, Professor." The captured scientist is really Holmes in disguise, and he has also daubed Moriarty's car with luminous paint which will lead Lestrade and Watson straight to his door. Moriarty tells Holmes that he is about to be killed and Holmes accuses him of being boring. Holmes says that if the roles were reversed, he would kill Moriarty by slowly draining his blood. Moriarty sets about trying to kill Holmes in the same way but the time it takes to set up allows Lestrade and Watson to arrive and rescue him. Moriarty escapes through a secret tunnel but Holmes had already anticipated this and opened up a trap door within, sending Moriarty plunging sixty feet into the sewer below him.

Connection: This adaption borrows from the original Conan Doyle story *The Adventure of the Dancing Men*. However, it's only really the idea of a stick figure code which survives this adaptation.

Sherlock Holmes Shadow Watchers
Film - 2011 (Canada)

Writer: Anthony D.P. Mann
Director: Anthony D.P. Mann
Sherlock Holmes: Anthony D.P. Mann
Doctor Watson: Terry Wade

This straight-to-DVD, ultra-low-budget Sherlock Holmes adventure is a film (which some might call a vanity project) by writer, director, producer and star of the film, Anthony D.P. Mann. Although the film references Conan Doyle's stories, the narrative is original.

The Daily Gazette of London reports on the sensational details of a particularly horrible murder and Scotland Yard calls for the help of Holmes and Watson.   Apart from the grizzly details of the murder which need to be solved, it is discovered that the article reporting the murder was written and published more than two hours before the crime took place. The writer of the article is then arrested for the murder of a Miss Sainsbury and he awaits trial in prison. Meanwhile Holmes, Watson and Lestrade investigate the scene of the murder, and Holmes deduces poor Miss Sainsbury was killed for sport. At a church, a nervous priest is approached by a mystery figure who instructs him to confront the prostitute Evelyn who knows too much because of his late-night meetings with her. When Evelyn becomes angry, both she and the priest are murdered. Holmes and Watson take a trip to St George's Cathedral to meet with Cardinal Alverston about the murdered priest but the cardinal seems more concerned about the scandal that will come from a priest having a relationship with a prostitute.   Later, the masked villains gather in front of Alverston, worried that Sherlock Holmes is close to identifying them. Alverston requests they pause their killing spree. Holmes then reveals himself as one the masked men and deduces that all the men were killed due to having a personal "darkness." Holmes is attacked by the Cardinal's associate who throttles him as the Cardinal poisons himself. Luckily Holmes is saved when Watson and Lestrade burst in and shoot the villain.

Trivia: Anthony D.P. Mann has also made low budget adaptations of *A Christmas Carol* (2015), *Terror of Dracula* (2012) and *Phantom of the Opera* (2014).

Sherlock Holmes Solves the Sign of Four - Film - 1913 (USA)

Writer: Lloyd Lonergan
Director: Lloyd Lonergan
Sherlock Holmes: Harry Benham
Doctor Watson: Charles Gunn

This two-reel silent movie made by the *Thanhouser Company* is the only recorded instance of Holmes being played by Harry Benham.

When retired British officer Major Sholto dies, his two sons search the house to find the treasure that they know their father brought back from India. Eventually, in the attic, behind a secret panel they find a brass box which contains a mass of jewels as well as a letter. This instructs them to share their treasure with   a woman called Mary Morstan.   Whilst the younger brother, Thaddeus, prepares to carry out his father's last wishes, his elder brother, Bartholomew, is vehemently opposed to the idea of sharing. Thaddeus writes to Mary Morstan, anonymously, explaining that she is being cheated and wants to meet. Miss Morstan takes the strange letter to Sherlock Holmes and Doctor Watson who accompany her to meet Thaddeus, and he explains about the treasure.   As they all reach the house, Bartholomew is found dead in his chair with a piece of paper on his chest which reads, "The Sign of the Four" and the treasure has vanished.

Holmes inspects the body and finds a poisonous thorn in its head. As he looks around he finds other clues which suggest a break-in, including a boot print next to the indentation of a wooden leg, two tiny foot imprints and a rope dangling from the roof to the ground.   Holmes quickly rushes to borrow a bloodhound who traces the intruders to a dockyard where Holmes is told that men answering the description have taken a boat down the river. Securing another boat, Holmes and Watson pursue the criminals but before they are captured the treasure is thrown overboard. The criminals are identified as Jonathan Small and Tonga who are both taken back to Baker Street where it is revealed that the treasure box is now empty and the two men are sent to jail for murder.

Review: In a copy of The Moving Picture World from March 8th, 1913 the reviewer writes that the film is, "An exceedingly interesting release of the detective order. " But comments that lead actor Harry Benham, "gives us a new kind of Sherlock Holmes, a younger and heavier built man than we usually see in the part."

Sherlock Holmes Solves the Sign of Four

Sherlock Holmes: The True Story Documentary - 2003 (Canada)

Writer: Michael Sheehan **Director:** John Crawford
Sherlock Holmes: Various
Doctor Watson: Various

Aired on the Discovery Channel network in America this Canadian documentary focuses on the work and research of Dr. Joseph Bell, lecturer at the medical school of the University of Edinburgh where Conan Doyle was his student.

Looking at his work within forensic science, the program visits his research and how the work and the man influenced Arthur Conan Doyle in creating the character of Sherlock Holmes. The documentary uses dramatic reconstructions of methods used by Bell in his field of work and how these have evolved into the methods used in today's scientific fields of study. The dramatic reconstructions are intercut with interviews from literary historians and heralded Sherlockians who look to answer the questions of how and why the detective became so real, how he influenced further scientific study in forensics and what part Bell himself played in the field of forensic medical science.

History: The show states that Joseph Bell aided the police with the Jack the Ripper case, although the extent of his actual involvement varies from source to source.

Sherlock Holmes Vs. Arsène Lupin AKA Sherlock Holmes: Nemesis
Computer game – 2007 (Ireland/ Ukraine)

Writer: Maurice Leblanc
Director: Jalil Amr
Sherlock Holmes: Rick Simmonds
Doctor Watson: David Riley

This is the fourth game by Frogwares in their *Sherlock Holmes* series and features Arsène Lupin.

The year is 1895 and Sherlock Holmes is discussing with Doctor Watson the news about the French cat burglar, Arsène Lupin, when a letter arrives. It is from Lupin himself challenging Holmes to defeat him by following clues to his next target. The player then follows these clues to each new location as well as becoming a number of characters, including Watson and Lestrade. The player must then prevent the theft of five priceless artefacts over the next five days, stored all over London in places such as the National Gallery, the British Museum, the Tower of London and Buckingham Palace.

If the player successfully completes the levels, he will come face to face with Lupin just as he is about to steal the crown jewels. Here Lupin congratulates Holmes on finding him and Holmes congratulates Lupin on his abilities and his cunning. This is not a story based as the other games as it requires more referencing, puzzle solving and clue finding than interacting with a story.

History: Arsène Lupin was a gentleman thief character created by French writer Maurice Leblanc. Lupin was frequently paired with Holmes in the early European Sherlock Holmes films.

Sherlock Holmes Vs. Jack the Ripper
Computer game - 2009 (Ireland/ Ukraine)

Writer: Uncredited
Director: Jalil AMr.
Sherlock Holmes: Rick Simmonds
Doctor Watson: David Riley

The fifth Microsoft game by Frogwares in their *Sherlock Holmes* series and this time the action takes place in Whitechapel, 1888, at the site of the famed Ripper murders.

In the East End of London the police are struggling to cope with the hysterical residents and the lack of clues in regards to a series of gruesome murders. As Holmes, you will need to go on a manhunt to find the murderer by interviewing suspects, collecting clues, and revealing the identity of the murderer. The focus of the game is on a community of Jewish immigrants where tens of thousands of people are crammed within terrible housing on dirty streets. After piecing together clues, Holmes deduces that the killer only targets prostitutes because he blames them for the misery in his own life caused by passing on the syphilis he contracted from sleeping with one of them to his wife and child. After a piece of bloodied apron is found in an alleyway near a murder, Holmes concludes that the killer must also be a butcher as butchers work at night and can walk around covered in blood, unnoticed, and carry knives. After more investigation, Holmes concludes that, as well as the prostitutes, the murderer is also out for revenge against those in the Jewish community who have wronged him and may get his revenge by serving up human organs to his customers. After Holmes, with the help of the Jewish community, captures the suspect, Jacob Levy, he sits in a room whilst the criminal re-enacts his crimes for him. Holmes decides to leave the man and not tell the police of his findings which angers Watson. Holmes reminds Watson that he doesn't serve justice, he serves truth. If they had delivered the man to the police and it was exposed that he forced his family and those of his faith to eat human flesh, there

would be anti-Semitic tensions and violence in London.

Trivia: With the exception of Sherlock Holmes and John Watson, all of the characters featured in this game are people who actually existed at the time of the Ripper Murders.

Sherlock Holmes and the Voice of Terror
Film – 1942 (USA)

Writers: Lynn Riggs, John Bright & Robert Hardy Andrews
Director: John Rawlins
Sherlock Holmes: Basil Rathbone
Doctor Watson: Nigel Bruce

The third film for the pairing of Rathbone and Bruce is where Holmes and Watson start their journey out of the Victorian 221b and into a more "contemporary" 1940s setting.

Holmes is asked to by Sir Evan Barham to stop the Nazis from infiltrating Britain and to seek out and destroy those who are already in the UK and who announce their activities over a broadcast by The Voice of Terror. After some investigation Holmes makes the discovery that the radio broadcasts are actually recordings made ahead of time. Using an oscilloscope he determines that these records are made in the UK but broadcast from Germany. After speaking to Kitty, the wife of a murdered British operative, Holmes and Watson take their investigation to the dock yard (followed by Sir Anthony Henry from the British Intelligence Council) where all three are captured by Nazi spies. The team calls for help from some East End locals and manages to escape; however, the leader, Meade, manages to get away on a speed boat.

Kitty is persuaded to play the role of a thief on the run and joins up with Meade on the coast. Holmes pursues Meade, with Kitty's help, and manages to capture Meade, with the help of some British troops, along with other German soldiers who are all hiding out in an abandoned church. Here Holmes reveals the real identity of The Voice of

Terror as Sir Evan Barham, an imposter in the ranks of the Intelligence Service. Holmes tells all present that the real Evan Barham was executed in a war camp but because he bore a resemblance to Heinrich Von Bock, a member of the German Secret Service, this was used as a way to infiltrate the UK government. In fact, Von Bock had been impersonating Barham for twenty-four years. He also notes that he knew from the start Sir Evan Barham was an imposter as the scar from his childhood was missing. When Holmes informs the spies that the German invasion force has been destroyed, Meade shoots and fatally wounds Kitty, but is then killed when he tries to escape.

Trivia: The film ends with dialogue taken from Conan Doyle's original story *His Last Bow*. "There's an east wind coming all the same. Such a wind as never blew on England yet. It will be cold and bitter, Watson" Although the original quote refers to the first World War rather than the second.

Sherlock Holmes in Washington
Film – 1943 (USA)

Writers: Lynn Riggs & Bertram Millhauser
Director: Roy William Neill
Sherlock Holmes: Basil Rathbone
Doctor Watson: Nigel Bruce

The fifth film for Rathbone and Bruce and an original story which is not based on any of the original Conan Doyle books. Holmes and Watson also do not appear in the film until much later in the story.

Secret Agent Alfred Pettibone is on his way to deliver secret war plan documents to America at the same time that a decoy is sent to put the enemy spies off the scent. Pettibone, travelling under the alias John Gregson, has reduced the document to a microfilm which he hides within a V for Victory match-book. Without her knowledge, Pettibone palms the match-book off onto a Washington debutante and fiancée of a Navy Lieutenant, Nancy Partridge. The matches end up in the possession of Richard Stanley who is actually a spy named Heinrich Hinkel. Soon after, Pettibone is kidnaped, tortured,

and murdered by Nazi agents. When asked to help with the case, Holmes reveals that he and Pettibone worked together on a variety of cases in the past and agrees to investigate. Holmes and Watson travel to America and work with the local Washington D.C. police to help solve the case. His investigation leads him to a small antiques shop, where he confronts Heinrich Hinkel and even goads Hinkle about the missing microfilm he wants so much, telling him that "the man who has it doesn't know he has it" and all the while, the match-book is in plain sight to all in the room. Holmes is then taken prisoner alongside Nancy who is interrogated as to the whereabouts of the microfilm, but as they are about to be murdered, the police arrive and save them. Holmes had told Watson to break in if he didn't return. In the scuffle, Hinkel gets away (with the matchbox) and so Holmes goes to Senator Henry Babcock's office. Whilst there he speaks about the importance of finding a letter which, he says, contains the microfilm underneath the stamp. Hinkel reveals himself and points his gun at Holmes to force him to hand over the letter, but the police arrive to take him away. Holmes then takes the matches, sets fire to the letter, revealing that the microfilm was in Hinkel's possession all along.

History: In 1959, the film was re-released and dubbed in Germany but, because of post-war sensitivity, the film removed all Nazi references and changed the story to gangsters trying to get hold of a secret medical formula.

Sherlock Jr.
Film - 1924 (USA)

Writers: Jean C. Havez, Joseph A. Mitchell & Clyde Bruckman
Director: Buster Keaton
Sherlock Holmes: Buster Keaton
Doctor Watson: N/A

This almost surrealist silent film was originally titled *The Misfit*. A cinema projectionist, who dreams of being a detective, falls in love with a beautiful woman but has little to no money in order to impress her. All he can afford to buy is a one dollar box of chocolates but to appear less stingy, he changes the price to four dollars. His rival for her affection, the "local Sheik" (also a man of little money) steals her father's watch and pawns it in order to buy a more expensive box of chocolates. Later, when the father realises his watch is missing, the Sheik takes his pawnbroker ticket and slips it into the projectionist's pocket. The projectionist offers to find the culprit but when the ticket is found in his possession, he is thrown out of the girl's home. Dejected, he returns to work and whilst showing a film about a theft of a necklace he falls asleep and begins to dream of himself as the detective, Sherlock Jr. In his dream the father calls Sherlock Jr. to help solve the case of the theft and, fearing that he will be exposed, the Sheik gets the butler to help him in his attempt to kill Sherlock Jr. by setting up a series of elaborate traps. When all this fails, they try to escape but Sherlock Jr. tracks them down; however, they are not alone and he is outnumbered by a large gang of thieves. During the fight Sherlock Jr. sees that the gang has kidnaped the girl and so fights his way with the help of his assistant, Gillette (named after William Gillette, the applauded Sherlock Holmes stage actor), through the gang to save her. As the projectionist wakes up he is met by the girl and her father who have visited the pawnbroker and realise that it was not he who stole and pawned the pocket watch. The film ends with the couple embracing.

History: This film was selected for preservation in the United States National Film Registry due to it being culturally, historically, and aesthetically significant.

Sherlock Jr.

Sherlok Kholms i doktor Vatson
(Sherlock Homles and Doctor Waston: The Acquaintance)
Television – 1979 (Russia)

Writers: Yuli Dunsky & Valeri Frid
Director: Igor Maslennikov
Sherlock Holmes: Vasiliy Livanov
Doctor Watson: Vitali Solomin

Forming part of a five-part television movie series, based on the original Conan Doyle stories and which aired between 1979 and 1986, this Soviet television series was split into eleven episodes. Broadcast under the heading of Sherlok Kholms i Doktor Vatson for the first "series" which was two stories combined under one narrative (each at just over an hour long), the program continued, later, under the title Priklyucheniya Sherloka Kholmsa i Doktora Vatsona (*The Adventures of Sherlock Holmes and Doctor Watson*). Although faithful to the books the television show has some originality to it with Doctor Watson spending much of the first episode trying to figure out what Holmes's occupation might be. For a while he is suspicious of him, thinking he may be a criminal mastermind.

Part 1:

Znakomstvo

Doctor Watson meets Sherlock Holmes and just as he is settling in, helps him solve the case of a young woman who is afraid of her stepfather and his hand in the mysterious murder of her sister.

Part 2

The Bloody Inscription

When a murder scene holds a message written in blood, Sherlock Holmes is called in to figure out the significance of the message as well as the ring which has been left behind.

Connection: The actor playing Helen and Julia Stoner, Mariya Solomina, was married to the show's Doctor Watson, Vitali Solomin.

Sherlock: Undercover Dog
Film - 1994 (USA)

Writer: Richard Harding Gardner
Director: Richard Harding Gardner
Sherlock Holmes: Huey the dog
Doctor Watson: N/A

This low-budget children's movie which sees Sherlock Holmes' skill and personality transferred into a talking dog was, unsurprisingly, panned by audiences and critics.

Billy comes to spend the summer with his father who is a toy designer and who is divorced from Billy's mother. While out, the pair finds an injured dog lying in the road and takes him to a local veterinarian. During the dog's stay, they both visit frequently and become friendly with the vet and her daughter Emma. When alone with Sherlock, Billy discovers that the dog can actually talk and he tells Billy that he needs his help to save his owner, a police detective who has been kidnaped by a gang of drug smugglers. The dog introduces himself as Sherlock Bones and reveals that only children who really believe in him and his powers can hear him talk. Meanwhile Billy's father, William, preoccupies himself with trying to find a company who will invest in his invention of a robotic underwater turtle called TURT which can be used as an educational toy to help young children learn to swim. After giving up trying to tell his father about Sherlock Bones, he and Sherlock go off hunting for clues. Sherlock picks up the scent of his owner, Mike, and follows it to a casino museum where Emma happens to work as a tour guide for children. They call the police but the crooks figure out they have been discovered and escape on a boat before they arrive. After Sherlock barks to get Emma's attention she reluctantly joins Billy and Sherlock in a row boat as they row out to the crook's yacht and find Mike tied up. Back on shore the police hand Sherlock Bones over to the captain of the drug-dealer's yacht as he has forged papers claiming to be Sherlock's

owner. After Emma and Billy convince William to help, they form a plan and use TURT in their rescue attempt. Billy steers TURT over to the yacht and causes the anchor to drop whilst William para-sails onboard knocking over the bodyguards as Emma and Billy find and untie Sherlock and Mike. Bones thanks Billy for his help and is happy that his town is now free from smugglers. The pair hugs before Sherlock has to leave.

Quote:
Billy: What's your name? I'm not going to help you if I don't know your name.

Sherlock: Sherlock

Billy: Sherlock what?

Sherlock: Sherlock Bones.

Billy: Sherlock Bones. That's neat.

Sherlock: Don't push it.

Sherlock Yack - Zoo-Détective
(Sherlock Yack: Zoo-Detective)
Animation – 2011 (France/ Germany/ South Korea)

Writers: RSébastien Thibaudeau, Sophie Decroisette, Frédéric Lenoir, Claude Scasso, Olivier Croset, François Deon, Jean-Rémi François, Bruno Merle, Bruno Regeste, Michel Amelin, Stéphane Melchior-Durand & Colonel Moutarde
Directors: Jérôme Mouscadet & Jeon Sung-ho
Sherlock Holmes: Martial Le Minoux
Doctor Watson: Céline Melloul

This animated television series for very young children is made up of 52 short 13-minute animated episodes and aired first on the TF1 network in France. The show, aimed at 5–8-year-olds, was adapted from a book of the same name, the only difference being that here the animal criminals all have a bad reputation to begin with. The action takes place at a zoo where detective Sherlock Yack and his assistant, Hermione, make it their job to seek out and stop criminals who are up to no good. This interactive children's show lets the audience, as well as the detectives, follow the clues of a crime and encourages the viewer to recap what Sherlock Yack and Hermione have found out about the criminal and the crime. The audience is then given a timer in which to deduce which of the three animals they believe is responsible for the crime, for example, *Who Broke the Kangaroo's hand? The Old Horse, the Gorilla or the Chihuahua?* At the end of each episode, the culprit is punished and Holmes and Hermione declare the case to be closed.

Quote:
<u>Sherlock Yack:</u> With great agility, and leaving claw marks on the trunk, you climbed the tree. You leaped into the void to steal my hat, but your aim was low and you hit me when you swung back.

A full episode list can be found in the "Television Episodes" chapter of this book.

Sign of Four
Television - 2001 (Canada)

Writer: Joe Wiesenfeld
Director: Rodney Gibbons
Sherlock Holmes: Matt Frewer
Doctor Watson: Kenneth Welsh

The second television movie out of four to star Matt Frewer as Sherlock Holmes with an adaptation of the Conan Doyle novel of the same name. Although the film stays faithful to the central narrative of the Doyle original there are a few significant differences.

The story still centres around Mary Morstan, the annual package of a precious pearl sent to her address and the note which leads her, Holmes and Watson to meet the Sholto brothers. This meeting, however, is at the Sholtos' home and Thaddeus Sholto is an eccentric novelist.

The discovery of Bartholomew's corpse sees Holmes push for Thaddeus to be arrested as

a suspect in order to get everybody out of the crime scene. In another departure from the original story, Holmes meets Professor Morgan, a chemist who identifies the poison which killed Bartholomew Sholto as being made from a compound found in a black widow spider. The Baker Street Irregulars are brought in to try to find the location of a boat where Holmes believes the killer to be hiding out. When Jonathan Small and Tonga are revealed (here Tonga is no longer the disfigured pygmy but an Asian man who has distinctive markings on his face) the game is on to catch and contain them. Instead of the river chase there is a police raid down the dock yard where a stand-off takes place between Inspector Jones, Holmes, Watson, the criminals and a small boy who has been taken hostage.

When Tonga blows his poisoned dart at the police, Watson comes to their assistance and administers the antidote which he has made. Holmes then gives chase and kills Tonga with his own blowpipe. Cornered and manic, Small then pricks himself with a poisoned dart and kills himself to avoid capture. The treasure chest is found but the treasure has been lost and later, at 221b, Holmes discovers that Miss Morstan (instead of marrying Watson) has left with Thaddeus Sholto to help the orphans of Agra.

Trivia: Holmes makes a reference to the murderous Dr Crippen, the alleged poisoner, during the show. However, the story is set in 1890 and Crippen was not convicted and hanged for murder until 1910.

Sign of Four: Sherlock Holmes' Greatest Case
Film - 1932 (UK)

Writer: W.P. Lipscomb
Director: Graham Cutts
Sherlock Holmes: Arthur Wontner
Doctor Watson: Ian Hunter

In a change of pace from the original story as well as the era - this is set in "contemporary" London (1930s) - this film takes some of its narrative from the original

Conan Doyle story whilst adding its own twists.

The film starts with Jonathan Small serving a prison sentence on the Andaman Islands. Desperate to escape, he makes a deal with Major Sholto and Captain Morstan to share his stolen treasure in return for them helping him escape. When Sholto and Morstan find the treasure in an Indian fortress they fight over who will take it all.

The resulting clash sees Sholto shoot and kill Morstan, taking the treasure back to England, leaving Small to rot in jail. Sholto, now a wealthy gentleman, goes mad after he reads that Small has escaped prison. Convinced that he will be murdered, he tells his sons, Bartholomew and Theodore about the stolen treasure and also Mary Morstan, the impoverished daughter of the murdered Captain Morstan. He tells them to send her a valuable necklace and split their inheritance three ways, but before he can reveal where the treasure is, he is murdered. Small and his tattooed Tonga go after Theodore, goading and threatening him until he reveals the identity of Mary, and then they threaten her. Mary turns to Sherlock Holmes and Doctor Watson for help but when they arrive at the Sholto house, they discover that Bartholomew has been murdered and the treasure has been taken.

Theodore is arrested but Holmes assures him he will find the murderous gang and clear his name. When Watson takes Mary with him on his part of the investigation the duo overpowers him and kidnaps Mary. Small's plan is to take the jewels and then flee the country with Tonga in a boat on the Thames. Their plans are scuppered when Holmes and Watson pursue them and the film climaxes in a fight at an abandoned warehouse where guns, fists and blowpipes are used to gain the advantage.

Trivia: The opening shot of the film shows the address of Holmes and Watson as 22A Baker Street rather than the famous 221b.

Sign of Four: Sherlock Holmes' Greatest Case

Silver Blaze AKA Murder at the Baskervilles
Film - 1936 (UK)

Writers: H. Fowler Mear & Arthur Macrae
Director: Thomas Bentley
Sherlock Holmes: Arthur Wontner
Doctor Watson: Ian Hunter

This adaptation brings in some elements of the original Conan Doyle story and a hint of Hound of the Baskervilles. It too is set in the 1930s rather than Victorian London. This would also be the last time Arthur Wontner would play Sherlock Holmes on screen.

Sherlock Holmes and Doctor Watson receive a letter from Sir Henry Baskerville inviting them both to his estate for a holiday. Inspector Lestrade is also staying in the area to oversee security for the Barchester Cup horse race. A bookie by the name of Miles Stanford is becoming desperate, having placed £150,000 worth of bets for the horse Silver Blaze to win when it was an unknown outsider. Now the favourite, he stands to lose all of his money, and more, if it wins. He calls for the help of Professor Moriarty and visits him in a secret office which has been created from a disused tube station in London.

Although it is not Moriarty's usual type of crime, he takes Stamford's money, rounds up his henchmen and heads towards Exeter. The horse Silver Blaze belongs to Colonel Ross, the local chief of police and on the morning of the race he is informed by Mrs.

Straker, the stable manager's wife, that the night watchmen is dead and that her husband and Silver Blaze are missing. A trip to the moor sees Holmes and Watson find the body of Mr. Straker who has died with a scalpel embedded in his side and, after following a trail, Silver Blaze is discovered in a nearby estate with black paint covering its distinctive white patch. Having pieced together the order of events, that the trainer poisoned the stable boy and took the horse to the moor to cripple it but stabbed himself when the horse bolted and lashed out, Holmes tells the Colonel to enter Silver Blaze in the race. Moriarty is, however, a step ahead and has one of his men shoot the jockey with an air-gun disguised as a film camera. Moriarty flees, but with Holmes on his tail, he has Watson kidnaped and brought to him. Moriarty interrogates Watson and then attempts to throw him down an abandoned lift shaft with a sheer drop of 80 feet. As Moriarty presses the button to open the door, Holmes and Lestrade appear, Holmes explaining that he has fixed the lift and is using it to his advantage.

Quote:
Sherlock Holmes: Elementary, my dear Watson. Elementary.

Silver Blaze: The Sunday Drama Television - 1977 (Canada/UK/USA)

Writer: Julian Bond
Director: John Davies
Sherlock Holmes: Christopher Plummer
Doctor Watson: Thorley Walters

This television produced adaptation was a British *Harlech Television* (ITV West and West Network) and OECA (publicly funded Canadian network) co-production which was made as part of the *Classics Dark and Dangerous* series of *Sunday Drama*. With a run time of only twenty-five minutes the production attempted to get as much of the original narrative from Conan Doyle's story but many fans believe the production suffers as a result.

The story stays faithful to the original with the missing Silver Blaze and the murder investigation leading to the conclusion that the horse was the murderer alongside the surprise ending of Silver Blaze turning up at the end in disguise. However, because the length is so short, most of the scenes fly by too quickly, needing to get all of the plot to squeeze into the thin run time.

Interview: Christopher Plummer hoped the adaptation would be successful enough to spawn a series and even told *Photoplay* magazine that he hoped it to be a part of "six of the best stories which have not been done before." It was 18 months after the interview that the show finally aired and, by that time, the idea of creating a television series had been dropped.

Sir Arthur Conan Doyle's Sherlock Holmes AKA Sherlock Holmes Film – 2010 (USA)

Writer: Paul Bales
Director: Rachel Lee Goldenberg
Sherlock Holmes: Ben Syder
Doctor Watson: Gareth David-Lloyd

Produced by The Asylum, who are probably known more for their *Sharknado* franchise, this 2010 straight-to-DVD adaptation is an original story and, perhaps, one of the strangest adaptations on film.

The film starts with an elderly Dr. John Watson, in his final hours, recounting a strange case to his nurse so it can be recorded before he dies. We are then taken back to May 1882 where a treasury ship is destroyed by what seems to be a giant octopus, killing nearly all on board. Holmes and Watson are called in by Lestrade to interview the survivor and investigate the shipwreck. Later, in Whitechapel, a young man looking to lose his virginity is killed by a dinosaur who has broken into a brothel. Holmes and Watson are obviously skeptical about the attack but during a walk in a forest, they are attacked by the same dinosaur.

After hiding out in a disused mill, Holmes picks up a bit of material that leads him to deduce that the monster is a fake and is the product of a criminal who is using fake monsters to collect parts, possibly to create another, even bigger monster. Further investigation leads them to a rubber factory where Holmes is sure the criminal is sourcing the material for the monster costumes. The shifty owner lets in Holmes, Watson and Lestrade, but Holmes senses danger and runs out with Watson as the factory explodes. After escaping a gas-filled room through a hatch in the floor they find themselves facing a large mechanical man. The mechanical monster is, in fact, Sherlock's brother, Thorpe. The female accomplice, Ivory, is also a lifelike mechanical robot. Thorpe explains that he built a mechanical suit so he could walk again after he became paralysed by a shot fired by Lestrade when they worked together.

His plan is to destroy London, assassinate Queen Victoria and force Lestrade to claim responsibility as punishment. Ivory carries the device which will detonate when she reaches Buckingham Palace, while Thorpe throws Lestrade into his flying machine, which is an enormous fire-breathing dragon, and escapes. Watson is sent to stop Ivory from reaching Buckingham Palace and Holmes follows in a giant steampunk hot air balloon. Watson manages to overpower Ivory and remove the detonation device and Holmes sends the dragon crashing down outside the palace. Thorpe tries to escape but is shot by Holmes before he can shoot Watson.

Back in the present, Watson dies as he comes to the end of his story and in the last scene his nurse visits his grave as Ivory visits the grave of Thorpe Holmes.

Quote:
Sherlock Holmes: My given name is Robert Sherlock Holmes. But who would ever remember a detective called Robert Holmes?

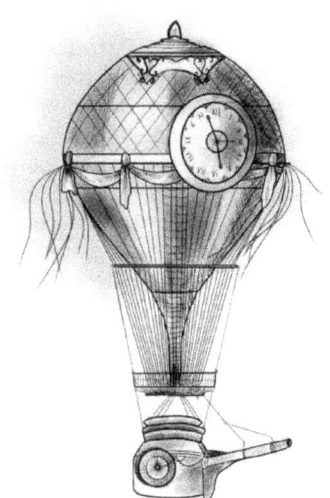

Sir Arthur Conan Doyle's Sherlock Holmes

Sir Arthur Conan Doyle's The Sign of Four
Television - 1983 (UK)

Writer: Charles Edward Pogue
Director: Desmond Davis
Sherlock Holmes: Ian Richardson
Doctor Watson: David Healy

Another of the British-made Holmes adaptations by Sy Weintraub and Otto Plaschkes, broadcast on the American television network HBO. The films stays, mostly, faithful to the central narrative of Doyle's original novel, but it does include some significant deviations.

At Pondicherry Lodge Major Sholto's last wish to his sons is that they split the stolen Agra treasure between themselves and Mary Morstan. Explaining to his sons, Thaddeus and Bartholomew, that in India, he and Captain Morstan stole the treasure to bring back to the UK, leaving behind the prisoner they agreed to help free. Back in England, Morstan came looking for Sholto for his share of the treasure but they fought and, during this fight, Morstan had a heart attack and died. Afraid, Sholto buried the body. After Major Sholto dies, the brothers find a piece of paper with "The Sign of Four" written on it and, after searching their home, finally locate the stolen treasure. Instead of a pearl, Thaddeus sends Mary Morstan the Great Mogul diamond much to the anger of his brother. He demands that Mary be brought to the lodge so they can split the treasure equally but as Thaddeus leaves, Bartholomew is killed by a poisonous dart. Mary Morstan arrives at Baker Street with the mysterious letter and package as well as a map with The Sign of Four written upon it. She explains the strange occurrences and Holmes and Watson come with her to meet Thaddeus. Once at Pondicherry Lodge they discover the body of Bartholomew along with another "Sign of Four" letter. The investigation leads to Mordecai Smith who owns the boat Aurora, and Holmes brings in the Irregulars to find it. The criminal, Jonathan Small and his native friend, Tonga, interrogate Thaddeus about the missing diamond; he lies and explains that his father sold it, but later when Watson and Mary arrive at the Lodge they find a dead servant and Thaddeus being killed by Small. Holmes gives chase through a fairground but they are lost in the crowd. Later the Irregulars inform Holmes that they have located the Aurora and so Holmes, Watson and the inspector give chase along the Thames.

Watson shoots Tonga and Holmes jumps ship to fight and capture Small. At 221b Small explains how Sholto and Morstan stole from him and claims to have thrown the treasure into the Thames. However, Holmes deduces that Small's wooden leg is too heavy and the treasure is revealed to be inside it. The inspector claims the treasure for the Queen but secretly Holmes still has the diamond which he gives to Mary.

Connection: Ian Richardson also played real life inspiration for Sherlock Holmes, Doctor Joseph Bell, in the short lived BBC television series *Murder Rooms: Mysteries of the Real Sherlock Holmes* (2000).

The Sleeping Cardinal AKA Sherlock Holmes' Fatal Hour Film – 1931 (UK)

Writer: Cyril Twyford
Director: Leslie S. Hiscott
Sherlock Holmes: Arthur Wontner
Doctor Watson: Ian Fleming

This first of five movies starring Arthur Wontner as Sherlock Holmes is not based on any one particular story it draws inspiration from both *The Final Problem* and *The Empty House.* Ronald and Kathleen Adair gamble at cards to support themselves after being left with nothing after the death of their guardian. Kathleen confronts her brother about cheating, threatening to shoot him if he's a cheat but she is interrupted by the butler.

Holmes is busy investigating a bank robbery, a curious case where no money was stolen but a paper bag was left. Holmes believes this to be the work of Moriarty. Meanwhile, Ronald is blindfolded and taken to a room where a mystery voice plays from behind a picture of a sleeping cardinal. He is told to take some items to Paris and if he does not comply he will be exposed as a card cheat and forced to kill himself because of the shame. Having created a reason for Watson and Mrs. Hudson to step out of 221b Baker Street, Moriarty, in disguise, calls on Holmes to tell him that his card is marked. When Watson returns, Holmes notices that he gets his boots made at the same place as the professor (J.J Godfrey) which is significant as the brown paper left at the bank robbery bears his name. At the shop, the mystery voice warns Sebastian Moran that Lestrade, Holmes and Watson, along with police, are on the way. As Holmes inspects the workshop he uncovers a printing press for counterfeit English bank notes and Godfrey is arrested along with his workforce. Holmes then finds a wire leading to the room above where they discover Watson tied up and gagged. Later, the butler finds Ronald dead, with a bullet wound to his head, collapsed in the middle of writing the note "The sleeping cardinal forced me to…".

Kathleen Adair is asked to accompany Lestrade to the police station to answer some questions but Holmes informs them that Adair was shot from outside the room through the window. Back at Baker Street, Holmes tells Watson about two incidents that happened earlier which nearly killed him and tells Watson that he needs to leave by taxi. In the shadows, a figure climbs the stair of a disused house and shoots the silhouette of Holmes through the window but he is immediately captured. Holmes reveals that he is unharmed, having employed Mrs. Hudson to move a statue which stands at the window in order to fool the would-be assassin. Moriarty is unmasked as the killer and he is taken and arrested for the murder of Ronald Adair.

History: The film was deemed lost having gone missing after being shown at a Sherlock Holmes Society reception. However, a print was discovered in an unnamed location somewhere in the United States and restored to a watchable condition.

The Speckled Band
Film – 1931 (UK)

Writer: W.P. Lipscomb
Director: Jack Raymond
Sherlock Holmes: Raymond Massey
Doctor Watson: Athole Stewart

This adaptation marked Raymond Massey's first film role and is one of the early Sherlock Holmes adaptations to be made with sound and set in the "contemporary" 1930s. The story remains faithful to the original but starts with Gypsies camping out on the grounds of the Rylott estate (instead of the original Roylott). Instead of Julia Stoner, the character is changed to Violet although her sister, Helen, remains the same. The film didn't garner a lot of critical acclaim with American journalist Vincent Starrett writing that Massey looked, "like almost any nice, young, brown-haired college boy, wrapped in a dormitory dressing gown, smoking a bulldog pipe."

Violet Stoner screams and collapses in the hallway of her home and her dying words to her sister are "the band, speckled." Later, Doctor Watson is at the Rylott estate as an inquest into the mysterious death of Helen begins. Rylott is eager to hear the outcome of the jury, pressing Doctor Watson for his opinion but he is reticent to give it. A year passes and Helen Stoner is now engaged to be married but the news seems to anger Mr. Rylott and he moves her into Violet's old room. Frightened she turns to Holmes and Watson for help, explaining how her sister was engaged before she mysteriously died. Apparently Violet heard strange music before her death and now Helen hears it too. As Helen is escorted out of the office, Rylott enters through another door and threatens Holmes to leave his family alone. Disguised as a workman Holmes and Watson investigate Rylott's room and discover a bowl of milk, a whip and a mirror. In Violet's room they also discover a bell rope which doesn't work and a ventilator which opens on the other side behind a painting in Rylott's room. That night, as Holmes and Watson keep their eye on Violet's room, snake charm music is heard to play as a snake slithers in through the ventilator. Quickly Holmes attacks it, sending it back to where it came from and it delivers a deadly bite to Rylott. Holmes then makes the servant, Ali, charm the snake so they can put it back into the safe. Later Watson returns from the wedding of Helen Stoner and Holmes offers his condolences rather than congratulates stating that not all men feel the need to marry.

Trivia: Instead of a cosy room at 221b Baker Street, here Sherlock Holmes works out of a large, official looking room with two offices and a staff of assistants and secretaries.

The Spider Woman
Film – 1943 (USA)

Writer: Bertram Millhauser
Director: Roy William Neill
Sherlock Holmes: Basil Rathbone
Doctor Watson: Nigel Bruce

The seventh film to star the paring of Rathbone and Bruce as Holmes and Watson. Holmes is tasked with investigating a number of strange apparent suicides – named 'The Pyjama Suicides' by the press – which he attributes to a female equivalent of Moriarty. During a fishing trip in Scotland, Holmes falls down a sheer drop over a waterfall. As a devastated Watson begins clearing out Holmes's belongings from 221b, a postman arrives with a package for Holmes to be signed for. Watson becomes more and more agitated with him as he speaks ill of Holmes and then punches the postman, knocking him to the ground. The postman then reveals himself to be Holmes and explains that he needed people to think he was dead so he could work undercover. Now disguised as Rajni Singh, he starts to investigate a variety of gambling clubs in London. He discovers that a woman named Adrea Spedding is seeking out men who have no money and persuading them to pawn their life insurance policies. Her accomplices then murder them using a deadly spider, the venom causing so much pain that the victims elect to kill themselves.

News of Holmes's resurrection is now widespread, and Spedding visits him with a child she says is her nephew, asking for his help in finding Singh, but on the way out throws a candy wrapper into the fire which billows out poisonous smoke. Holmes, however, smashes a window and saves himself and Watson from being overpowered by the fumes. The pair then make their way to Chipping Walton to visit arachnologist Matthew Ordway, as they suspect he is the man who is supplying the spiders. During their conversation Holmes realizes that the man is actually an impostor, but he manages to escape before Holmes can restrain him. The investigation is moved to a nearby fairground, where Holmes is captured by Spedding and her gang and, tied up and gagged, he is placed behind a moving target of Hitler in a shooting gallery. Coincidentally it is the same shooting gallery where Lestrade and Watson are shooting. The target passes by Watson a couple of times and by the time the shot is lined up the target has vanished and Holmes appears behind Adrea calling for Lestrade to round them up and arrest them all for murder.

Connection: Although the plot is original, there are many references to Conan Doyle

stories within it. The bust in the window comes from *The Empty House*. It features a deadly pygmy as in *The Sign of Four* and the igniting of poison from *The Adventure of the Devil's Foot*.

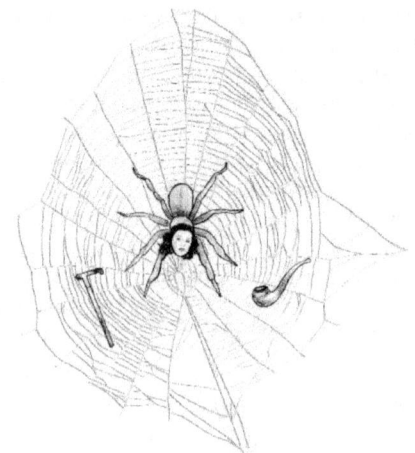

The Spider Woman

Standing room only: Sherlock Holmes – The Strange Case of Alice Faulkner
Television – 1981 (USA)

Writer: William Gillette
Director: Peter H. Hunt
Sherlock Holmes: Frank Langella
Doctor Watson: Richard Woods

This was broadcast as part of the series *Standing Room Only* which was an entertainment series featuring live concerts, plays and variety shows and ran from 1979-1986 on the HBO network in America.

The production stays true to the original narrative with Alice Faulkner, whose sister died of grief when she was abandoned by a prince to marry another woman, hell-bent on getting revenge for her sister by making public their scandalous letters. Alice is held prisoner by two swindlers (the Larabees) who want to use the letters for blackmail. The pair keep the letters in a safe but Alice manages to break into the safe box and hide them again. With the royal marriage fast approaching, the family of the prince employs Holmes to find the letters in order to avoid blackmail or scandal. After a visit from Holmes, the Larabees panic and are approached by Moriarty who instructs them to create fake letters which he then intends to use to take Holmes down. Having been lured to a sealed room which acts as a gas chamber, Holmes picks up the fake letters and manages to escape the murderous gang and takes Alice with him. When the criminals descend on Doctor Watson's office looking for Holmes, who is disguised as an old man in a wheelchair, it is Holmes who has them disposed of by the police. After calling for a cab and instructing the driver to help with his luggage, Holmes cuffs him and reveals his true identity, Moriarty. After tricking Alice into giving the letters over to the royal family, Holmes tries to convince Alice that his motives were inspired by his love of "the game"; however, the two realise that they are actually in love and the play ends with the possibility of a marriage proposal.

Trivia: The production featured a very young Christian Slater as Billy the boy in buttons and was the only time Frank Langella played Holmes on screen, but he did play him later in 1987 on stage in *Sherlock's Last Case* by Charles Marowitz.

The Stolen Papers
Film - 1912 (France/UK)

Writer: Arthur Conan Doyle
Director: Georges Tréville
Sherlock Holmes: Georges Tréville
Doctor Watson: Mr. Moyse

The sixth silent film to be made by Société Française des Films Éclair and starring Georges Treville, this movie is based on the original Conan Doyle story *The Adventure of the Naval Treaty*.

Whilst in the country with his fiancée, a young diplomat, Percy Phelps, is called back to London to copy some important documents. His soon to be brother-in-law, Harrison, comes with him as he needs to meet with his creditor and negotiate an extension on a loan, but this is refused. That evening, when Phelps steps out of his office, he comes back to find the document he was copying has been stolen. The theft sends him mad and he is ordered home to stay in the downstairs room usually occupied by Harrison. Sherlock Holmes is called to help investigate the missing documents and Phelps recalls waking from a nightmare and seeing a ghost in his room. When Holmes returns the following night, waiting by the window, he sees a shadow enter Phelps's room and watches as it opens a trap door and pulls something out of a hiding place. As the shadow passes the window, Holmes attacks it and, after a fight, takes the paper which turns out to be the stolen documents. In the struggle Holmes also takes the ring of the culprit which gives him all he needs to identify the criminal. The next morning Holmes reveals the documents to Phelps on a large dish, much to his relief. Holmes then takes Harrison aside and, as they shake hands, he returns his ring and says he will keep silent about the crime for the sake of his sister and Phelps but warns him to stay out of trouble.

History: Mr. Moyse is credited with playing Doctor Watson to George Tréville's Sherlock Holmes but whilst there is much written about Tréville, the identity of Moyse remains a mystery.

The Strange Case of the End of Civilization as We Know It
Television – 1977 (UK)

Writers: John Cleese, Jack Hobbs & Joseph McGrath
Director: Joseph McGrath
Sherlock Holmes: John Cleese
Doctor Watson: Arthur Lowe

This low-budget Sherlock Holmes spoof was made by London Weekend Television & Shearwater Films for the ITV network in the UK and centres around the grandson of Sherlock Holmes trying to outwit the last living descendent of Professor Moriarty.

Dr. Gropinger misplaces his diary whilst travelling on a private jet and quickly spins into a complete panic. When he lands, he addresses an audience of Arabs and accidentally offers a Jewish greeting. As a result, he is shot dead. Later the son of the American president receives a threat from Moriarty about his plan to take over the world and so the President sends one of his top men to London to work with their security agency in order to figure out how to defeat Moriarty who has given civilisation five days to live. Arthur Sherlock Holmes is contacted by the police commissioner after their "computer" suggests it to be the best course of action. At Baker Street Mrs. Hudson frantically cleans as the Commissioner of Police waits for his arrival. Holmes bursts through the door and starts attacking him only to have Mrs. Hudson slap them apart. When Watson arrives, the Commissioner outlines the case and Holmes accepts it insisting that the bungling Watson be included as, although he is stupid, he has a bionic nose and leg which makes him ideal for tracking. Unfortunately the Commissioner is stabbed in the back and killed (mostly due to Watson's buffoonery) before he can leave the building. At Scotland Yard, the members of the international commission are shot one by one.

Holmes suggests organising a convention to which they will invite all of the world's greatest detectives. The logic being that Moriarty wouldn't be able to resist killing all at once and so can be captured. In an opulent hotel the most famous fictional detectives gather and Watson appears to be going on a killing spree, murdering fictional detectives one at at time in a storage cupboard. It turns out that Moriarty has been killing the detectives disguised as Watson, and Holmes then tells a joke to the Watsons in order to determine which one is the real Watson but both fail to understand the joke. Holmes then asks the location of his engraved meerschaum pipe and deduces that the Watson who knows where it is, is the imposter because the real Watson is "so sodding dim, so consistently, relentlessly, almost magically half-witted." Moriarty is then revealed to be Mrs. Hudson (really Franceen Moriarty) and shoots Watson followed by Holmes.

Holmes then reveals that he told Watson to fill the gun with blanks, but then Watson confesses he forgot. As Holmes lays injured,

he gives Moriarty's wig to Watson and tells him to use his bionic nose and legs to track her down but he jumps too high and knocks himself out on the ceiling resulting in both Holmes and Watson dying.

Quote:
Arthur Sherlock Holmes: Get a crossword, Watson. There are several moments to lose.

A study in Terror
Film - 1965 (UK)

Writers: Donald Ford, Derek Ford & Jim O'Connolly
Director: James Hill
Sherlock Holmes: John Neville
Doctor Watson: Donald Houston

Filmed at Shepperton studios in London, this British Sherlock Holmes movie sees the detective hot on the trail of Jack the Ripper. After Watson reports two similar murders near Whitechapel, he and Holmes decide to investigate. After concluding that all of the victims are, and will continue to be, prostitutes, Holmes turns his attention to the seedier side of London. Later, Holmes is sent a medical supply of scalpels, which includes a missing glove, and finds himself at the home of Lord Carfax.

It is revealed that Carfax's son, Michael, a former medical student, has been missing for the past two years and after interviewing street missions, pimps and landlords, Holmes suspects that Michael may be the killer. Holmes also suspects Anthony Quayle, a police mortician who is hell-bent on ridding Whitechapel of debauchery and prostitution.

Trivia: The US poster for *A Study in Terror* features an artistic representation of Sherlock Holmes alongside Batman comic style stings of Biff! POW! And BANG! These graphics, as well as the tag line, "Here comes the original caped crusader," feed into the on-going Batman vs. Sherlock Holmes battle for the title of "world's greatest detective."

Terror by Night
Film - 1946 (USA)

Writer: Frank Gruber
Director: Roy William Neill
Sherlock Holmes: Basil Rathbone
Doctor Watson: Nigel Bruce

The is thirteenth film to star Rathbone and Bruce as Holmes and Watson and although the film is not based on a specific Conan Doyle story there are flavours of *The Adventure of the Empty House*, *The Disappearance of Lady Frances Carfax* and *The Sign of Four*.

Vivian Vedder organises the transport of her deceased mother to Scotland with the carpenter who has to complete her mother's coffin. She boards the train alongside Lady Margaret Carstairs who is taking her diamond "The Star of Rhodesia" back to her family. Later Lestrade finds Lady Carstairs dead with nothing but a tiny spot of blood on her body, and the diamond missing. Whilst Holmes and Watson examine the luggage compartment they notice that a coffin belonging to a passenger named Vivian Vedder has a false compartment which the thief could have used to sneak onto the train. After questioning Vedder, she confesses that she was hired to bring the coffin to Edinburgh and that she knew about it being used to smuggle a person on board. Holmes reveals to Lestrade that he actually has the diamond and gives it to him for safe keeping when another murder takes place, this time the luggage guard and he too has only a small spot of blood on his body. After inspecting the body, Holmes finds a dissolvable poisoned dart and deduces that this is how Lady Carstairs was killed.

Watson's friend Duncan-Bleek is visited by a man named Sands, Bleek tells him the stolen diamond is a fake and orders Sands to attack Lestrade and steal the real gem. Once Sands has put Lestrade out of action and stolen the gem, Bleek kills him with the dart gun. The train stops just across the Scottish border and Inspector MacDonald boards. Holmes informs MacDonald that Duncan-Bleek is actually the jewel thief Sebastian Moran and pulls the emergency brake. When the lights

come up, the criminal is trapped and tangled in a coat and Inspector MacDonald takes him off the train. But instead of being enmeshed in the coat, Moran lays unconscious on the train floor. Holmes explains to a confused Watson that he knew Inspector MacDonald was a fake and an accomplice of Moran, so under cover of darkness he switched Moran for Lestrade. When Moran wakes, Holmes shows him that he still has the real diamond in his possession.

Trivia: This was to be the final Sherlock Holmes film that stared Dennis Hoey as Inspector Lestrade. The next, and last, film starring Rathbone and Bruce as Holmes and Watson *Sherlock Holmes and the Secret Code* (1946) would, instead, feature Carl Harbod as Inspector Hopkins.

Terror by Night

Testament of Sherlock Holmes
Computer game - 2012 (UK)

Writer: Frogwares
Director: Frogwares
Sherlock Holmes: Kerry Shale
Doctor Watson: David Riley

The sixth adventure game in the *Sherlock Holmes* series developed by Frogwares focuses the action on the original story of Sherlock Holmes being framed for murder. Set in 1898 Holmes solves a jewel theft only to be accused of the theft himself when the jewels turn out to be fake. After discovering the Bishop of Knightsbridge tied up and burned along with a severed finger, Holmes believes a poison was administered which throws the victim into madness. Wanting more information on the poison, Holmes heads to a prison to interview a man called Han Scheilman, the rat killer, but a fire breaks out and Scheilman manages to escape. Watson becomes furious after seeing Holmes helping him escape.

It is discovered that O'Farnely, a journalist, has written a slanderous piece on Holmes and the jewelled necklace, stating that Holmes is a fraud. Holmes vanishes only to be discovered later disguised as a woman in Whitechapel. Watson tells them his location and when the police inspector Baynes is thrown from a window, Holmes is branded a murderer and shoots himself. Watson continues the investigation and finds Holmes alive but, this time, in the sewers. They return to Baker Street after Holmes explains he needed to be thought of as dead to investigate Professor Moriarty who is poisoning the poor by adding the deadly substance to the soup-kitchen food, causing them to riot and become hysterical. He plans to cause thousands of deaths, help stage a revolution and thus place a puppet monarch on the throne. Holmes deduces that Moriarty knew he would be able to figure this out and had to disgrace him to get him out of the picture. As Moriarty dies after an attack by Han Scheilman, his last request is that Holmes raise his daughter.

Quote:
Sherlock Holmes: The animal had been hidden inside the room for several hours, calmly waiting the signal from his master...a high frequency whistle alerted the monkey that it was time to begin the procedure for which he had been trained.

They Might be Giants
Film – 1971 (USA)

Writer: James Goldman
Director: Anthony Harvey
Sherlock Holmes: George C. Scott
Doctor Watson: Joanne Woodward

This offbeat American comedy/mystery film is based on the stage play of the same name, both of which were written by James Goldman. In this film, Sherlock Holmes is actually Justin Playfair who has retreated into the persona of Holmes as a way to cope with the death of his wife. His brother, who is after his inheritance money, needs to have him certified as mad and so sends him to see the psychiatrist Doctor Mildred Watson who is excited to be presented with such a pure example of delusion. After "Holmes" discovers that this is his "Watson" the pair head out to the streets of New York in search of clues left by Moriarty. After visiting the New York Telephone exchange and a cinema sparsely populated by strange customers and starting a fight over a bag of rubbish, they end up visiting Peabody at a records and research facility. Watson confesses to Peabody that she cannot have "Holmes" sectioned and rather than being forced to sign his papers, she quits her job and decides to help "Holmes" find his Moriarty. Once they deduce the meaning of the bag of rubbish as a reference to the Bagg School for Agriculture, they head towards a dilapidated building where an elderly couple have been living since the 1930s without venturing outside.

Later Watson invites "Holmes" for dinner where it appears somebody attempts to shoot him. In a reversal of Doyle's *The Adventure of The Three Garridebs,* Watson rushes to his side and he is startled when she calls him Holmes. More determined than ever, and with the help of all of the people they have encountered so far, "Holmes" works out that Moriarty means for them to meet by the racing school. In an ending which is famed for its ambiguity, "Holmes" and Watson stand by the entrance to a tunnel as Watson pledges to stay by his side. As "Holmes" hears the approaching horse which will carry Moriarty to them, Watson panics that she can't hear them. The film ends with Watson finally hearing the hooves and the two of them looking expectantly at the face of Moriarty, but as the camera doesn't move from their faces, it is not made clear whether Moriarty is real or if Watson has just been sucked into the "Holmes" delusion.

Trivia: It has been rumoured that actress Joanne Woodward was so unhappy during the filming of this title that she almost gave up acting. Although never giving a reason for her misery, she insisted that it was not due to her co-star George C. Scott whom she described as a gentleman.

The Three Garridebs
Film – 1937 (USA)

Writer: Thomas H. Hutchinson
Director: Eustace Wyatt
Sherlock Holmes: Louis Hector
Doctor Watson: William Podmore

This show was broadcast live on November 27th, 1937 on the NBC network in America during field tests and try-outs before the actual television service started. Thus, *The Adventure of the Three Garridebs,* became the first Sherlock Holmes television adaptation to be beamed from the Radio City studio in New York into a select number of homes. As there was no way to capture live television, the broadcast has been lost; however, there do remain several articles written about the broadcast and some of its content.

The story is faithful to the Conan Doyle original and starts with stock footage of the London skyline before showing Holmes sitting in his living room at 221b Baker Street, reading a letter from a Nathan Garrideb. In the letter he asks Holmes for help in locating another person who shares his unusual surname. The letter goes on to explain that he has been approached by another man named John Garrideb who has explained that he needs to find another person with the same surname in order to unlock a fortune. However, Holmes deduces that Jonathan Garrideb is an imposter and becomes suspicious that there is some other reason why John Garrideb has approached the quirky academic, Nathan Garrideb. Upon investigation, it is revealed that John is actually a man named James Winter, *alias* Morecroft *alias* "Killer" Evans. As Nathan leaves the house to enquire on the authenticity of another holder of the Garrideb surname (found by John), Holmes and Watson investigate his home clutching their revolvers. The pair catch Winter in the act of sneaking out of the basement which holds a counterfeit money printing machine,

and, after Watson is attacked, Holmes incapacitates Winter and sends him back to prison.

Review: In an article about the broadcast The New York Times wrote, "While the televised version of "*The Three Garridebs*", as such, offers no serious challenge to the contemporary stage or screen, considering television's present state of development, the demonstration revealed how a skilful television producer may make use of the best of two mediums, how viewers may witness realism in the flesh-and-blood acting allied with the more spectacular scenic effects achieved on the screen."

Tom and Jerry Meet Sherlock Holmes
Animation – 2010 (USA)

Writer: Earl Kress
Directors: Spike Brandt & Jeff Siergey
Sherlock Holmes: Michael York
Doctor Watson: John Rhys-Davies

This straight-to-DVD adventure is a feature length animated romp around the streets of London. Three criminal cats have stolen a pink diamond which they hand over to a cloaked man on a horse. The next day Holmes is handed a letter by Tom from a singer called Miss Red who is being blackmailed. She explains that she has been instructed to deliver money at regular intervals to her blackmailers at a location a few miles from her house. When Holmes discovers that Miss Red's home is behind the Punjabi Embassy he deduces that the real motive for the blackmailer is to get Miss Red to leave her location. When the Punjab diamond is stolen by the cats from under the nose of the security guard, the police believe Miss Red is responsible and give chase through London with Tom and Jerry in tow. They end up at St. Paul's Cathedral and are let in by Jerry's brother Tuffy. After locating the criminals at *The Twisted Lip* pub they follow them to a graveyard where they find the diamond being held by a statue.

Before Jerry can capture it, the cloaked horseman returns and takes the gem. Miss Red suggests hiding out at her uncle's house but Tom and Jerry end up being shut out. Whilst on the roof, looking for a way in, the pair finds a strange weather vane containing many stolen jewels, including the Star of Punjab, and Miss Red gagged and bound in the living room. The blackmailer, Moriarty, captures them and reveals his plan to steal the Crown Jewels by harnessing the diamond's ability to intensify the sun's light and burn a hole in the Tower of London. As Holmes and Watson give chase through the streets of London to Tower Bridge, which is still being constructed. Holmes leaps from his carriage onto Moriarty's steam powered car where they fight on the roof. Unfortunately the car hurtles off the edge of the unfinished bridge and into the Thames, and it is assumed that Sherlock Holmes is dead. But when Watson stands by the edge he hears Holmes's voice and then sees him clinging onto the bridge holding a bag of jewels having saved the day once more.

Connection: The film features three nods to three familiar Sherlockian actors: There are references to a tailor in Lancashire named *Jeremy Brett*, a theatre called *The Bruce Nigel Music Hall* and a bar called *The Rathbone Inn*.

The Treasure of Alpheus T. Winterborn: Children's Mystery Theatre
Television – 1980 (USA)

Writer: Kimmer Ringwald
Director: Murray Golden
Sherlock Holmes: Keith McConnell
Doctor Watson: Laurie Main

The story was made for the television series CBS Children's Mystery Theatre which was an anthology series aimed at young children and was adapted from the book of the same name. The story is split into two very distinct sections, the story of Alpheus T. Winterborn and clips of Sherlock Holmes explaining to Doctor Watson how he would have solved the case.

At 221b Baker Street Holmes smells a mystery in the air and reads the Winterborn

Mirror looking for a potential crime. He eventually points out a story to Watson about the treasure of Alpheus T. Winterborn, announcing that they will read the story and solve the mystery. A young Anthony Monday takes tea with a librarian and they talk about the rumour, which says that Winterborn supposedly hid a large pot of treasure somewhere in the town. Monday later finds a gold coin whilst cleaning the library fresco and a secret panel reveals a note which gives clues to the whereabouts of the hidden treasure. Monday and the old librarian woman follow each of the clues; through a hall of mirrors, researching back issues of the local paper, Winterborn's headstone and, finally, to Doc Tweedy's house.

Believing their latest clue has to do with Tweedy's furniture auction, Monday heads to the auction with the librarian to buy a vanity unit. Back at Baker Street Holmes writes his clues on a chalk board and tells Watson that the problem is that people are looking too closely and hopes that Anthony Monday will take a step back to see the whole picture. Monday deduces that the treasure must be in the weather vane but he is stopped by Winterborn's nephew who believes the treasure belongs to him. Forced up onto the roof to hammer at the weather vane, Monday slips and grabs the horse sculpture for safety but it breaks and he falls just as members of the fire crew unfurl their safety net. The treasure which fell from inside the statue is declared his and the nephew is arrested. Holmes explains to Watson that the child should have found the treasure sooner but that the joy in a mystery is the road to it, not the solution.

Trivia: This episode was also released under an edited version called *The Clue According to Sherlock Holmes*.

The Trials of the Demon!
Batman: The Brave and the Bold
Television - 2009 (USA)

Writer: Todd Casey
Director: Michael Chang
Sherlock Holmes: Ian Buchanan
Doctor Watson: Jim Piddock

This Sherlockian episode is taken from the animated television show, based on the DC comics series, and was broadcast on the WB television network in America.

In Victorian England Holmes and Watson stroll down the street talking about the spate of strange murders when they hear a scream. They run towards it and find a lady lying in the road with her face wizened and drained, much like the other murder victims. An angry mob rushes to the house of Jason Blood, convinced his black magic is the cause of the killings and wanting him dead. Before they carry him away, Blood begins a ritual which is then finished by Holmes and as he pours a potion onto a chalk drawing, it lights up and Batman appears. Holmes tells him that Blood has been accused of murder and Batman rushes to find Blood, finding him tied to a pile of burning logs. After the rescue, Jason explains that he is bonded to a demon, Etrigan, but insists that neither of them is responsible for the attacks. When a woman is seen being carried to a carriage, Etrigan emerges to try and stop it but is defeated. Batman recognises the cloaked man as Craddock, the Gentleman Ghost. Craddock is collecting souls in order to make himself immortal and when Holmes discovers where he is hiding, he attacks him, ties him to a post and steals his soul sealing it inside an intricate horn.

As he opens a portal to the underworld he is followed by Etrigan and Batman where they are all confronted by a large demon who is demanding the horn of souls from Craddock. As the exchange takes place, Batman and Etrigan release the souls and vanquish the demon by exposing it to the only material which can destroy it, iron via an iron rod thrown by Batman. With the souls returned to their rightful owners, Blood sends Batman back to his own time as Craddock's ghost is seen rising from his grave, vowing to he will get his revenge on Batman.

Quote:
Sherlock Holmes: Before you depart, I must know: how did you really deduce my identity?

Batman: Everyone knows who you are. You're the world's greatest detective.

The Trials of the Demon! Batman:
The Brave and the Bold

The Triumph of Sherlock Holmes
Film- 1934 (UK)

Writers: H. Fowler Mear & Cyril Twyford
Director: Leslie S. Hiscott
Sherlock Holmes: Arthur Wontner
Doctor Watson: Ian Fleming

A very loose adaptation of *The Valley of Fear* which places Holmes and Watson in the more "contemporary" setting of the 1930s and is told, partly, in flashback.

As Holmes packs up Baker Street, ready for his retirement to Sussex, he reminisces about past cases with Watson. His lamenting that Moriarty has always slipped through his fingers annoys Watson who cannot understand why Holmes holds an innocent man in such low esteem. As Watson leaves Moriarty arrives to wish Holmes a happy retirement and informs him that if he were not retiring he would have to kill him. Later, in Moriarty's office, an American gangster asks for his help in killing an ex member of his crime organisation for a $50,000 fee. He agrees. In Sussex, Holmes tends to his bees as Watson comes to visit with a coded letter for Holmes which, when deciphered, warns of a murder that may take place at Birlstone Castle. When Lestrade sees the decoded message, he is taken aback as the owner of the castle, Mr. Douglas, was murdered the previous night, his face completely destroyed by a gunshot wound.

Against Watson's wishes, Holmes investigates the crime scene and notes objects of interest such as a single dumbbell and a half burned candle. In flashback, told by the wife, Ettie Douglas, Mr. Murdoch (who later became Mr. Douglas), a Freeman, arrives in a new town to meet McGinty who is the head of the town's Freeman chapter, known locally as The Scowrers. Already causing waves after being accused of trying to steal chapter member Ted Balding's girlfriend, Murdoch accompanies some of The Scowrers on a job to silence the editor of the paper. Murdoch makes his way up the ranks of the society, proving his bravery and his strength by terrifying the local businesses and residents. A little while later Murdoch calls for Ettie to say a Pinkerton detective, Birdy Edwards, has arrived to make arrests and so he wants to get out of the valley tonight with her. He then informs the society about the arrival of the Pinkerton and devises a plan to kill him. When Murdoch meets them all at the Pinkerton's house, he reveals that he is, in fact Birdy Edwards, and his entire time in the valley was an undercover operation to destroy The Scowrers.

Back at the castle Mrs. Douglas goes for some air and Watson sees her laughing and joking with her friend Mr. Barker just as Holmes fishes something heavy out of the castle moat. That night, Holmes catches, the supposedly dead, Mr. Douglas when he appears from a hidden part of the castle wall, revealing that the dead man was really Balding, who had come back to seek revenge for his disbanding of The Scowrers. In the struggle the gun went off and mutilated Balding's face and so Douglas thought up a plan which would play the death to his advantage. By telling the world he was dead, they would stop coming after him. Holmes informs Watson and Lestrade that Moriarty is behind the attack and they lay in wait, with Watson and Lestrade still skeptical. Moriarty then appears and calls for Balding but comes face to face with Holmes whom he attempts to strangle. Moriarty is set upon by Lestrade and Watson but he escapes and runs to the top of the castle. Whilst attempting to throw a rock, he is shot and falls to his death.

Trivia: Doctor Watson actor Ian Flemming is often credited as the same Ian Flemming who wrote the James Bond novels. A fact which even made its way onto some promotional material and film cases. But they are not the same person and they are not even related.

Unlocking Sherlock Television - 2014 (UK)

Writer: Susannah Ward
Director: Susannah Ward
Sherlock Holmes: Benedict Cumberbatch
Doctor Watson: Martin Freeman

This is a one-off television special which was broadcast on the PBS network in America (as well as being made available via BBC Worldwide) which explores the phenomenal rise in popularity of the BBC television series *Sherlock*. The television documentary includes interviews with the actors, writers, producers and directors of the show and a variety of clips from past episodes. Creators Mark Gatiss and Steven Moffat talk about their history with, and love of Sherlock Holmes and how they have tried to keep as "true" to the themes and values of Conan Doyle's original stories. The show also includes an early interview with Conan Doyle as well as clips from a variety of other Holmes adaptations including William Gillette, Basil Rathbone, Jeremy Brett and Peter Cushing. The actors and creators also talk about recreating "the fall" at Reichenbach and how the reaction of the fans, and their theories about how Holmes survived falling from St Bart's Hospital, mirrored the shock felt by the original fandom when Holmes and Moriarty fell in the actual falls in *The Final Problem* in 1893. Benedict Cumberbatch and Martin Freeman also discuss how their characters have evolved together and what parts of their own characters resemble the Holmes and Watson from Conan Doyle's stories.

Quote:

Steven Moffat: You could know a strange young man like that. A posh young man with an outrageous sense of entitlement, solving crimes with his adrenalin junkie mate.

Unlocking Sherlock

We Present Alan Wheatley as Mr. Sherlock Holmes Television – 1951 (UK)

Writer: C.A. Lejeune
Director: Uncredited
Sherlock Holmes: Alan Wheatley
Doctor Watson: Raymond Francis

This short run series of six episodes was produced by the BBC and broadcast on the BBC 1 network in the UK. These episodes were broadcast live and so no tapes or recordings of the show exist. Writer C.A. Lejeune claims that the series was created after a review of Wheatley's performance in Patrick Hamilton's *Rope* appeared in The Observer newspaper which said, "If the BBC have got any sense they will commission a series of Sherlock Holmes stories and ask Alan Wheatley to play Sherlock Holmes" and so that is exactly what they did.

Trivia: This was the only time Wheatley would play Holmes on screen (he would play him again in the Michael and Mollie Hardwick radio play, *The Man Who Was Sherlock Holmes -1963*), and he didn't much enjoy the experience, "I must say I found it the most difficult thing to speak I've ever done in the whole of my career."

A full episode list can be found in the "Television Episodes" chapter of this book.

Without a Clue
Film - 1988 (UK)

Writers: Gary Murphy & Larry Strawther
Director: Thom Eberhardt
Sherlock Holmes: Michael Caine
Doctor Watson: Ben Kingsley

This British comedy has the roles of genius and sidekick reversed as Doctor Watson is revealed to the audience as the real brains of the pair. Sherlock Holmes is actually a character actor named Reginald Kincaid who has been hired by Watson to play the part of detective in order to sell his stories to the Strand Magazine. After an argument, post case, Watson throws out "Holmes" and attempts to go it alone, unsuccessfully. Later he is visited by Lestrade and Lord Smithwick who want Holmes to help find the banknote printing plates which have been stolen from the Bank of England as well as the missing Peter Giles.

After placating "Holmes" and searching Giles' house, the pair travels to Lake Windermere where Watson reveals that Professor Moriarty is the man behind the theft of the plates and that he also knows that Watson is the brains of the duo. After meeting Lesley Giles, Watson concludes that her father has been kidnapped and that she should stay with them for safe-keeping. During their investigation at the dockyard, "Holmes" and Watson witness Moriarty importing ink, obviously to use in the press, a gun fight breaks out and Watson falls into the Thames and is feared to have drowned.

"Holmes" becomes drunk and depressed at the departure of Watson but when Lestrade goads him, he vows to solve the crime and make Watson proud. With the help of Baker Street Irregular Wiggins, Mrs. Hudson and a half printed £5 note, "Holmes" deduces that the note is a book code referencing his time in the play *The Shadow of Death* and they head to The Orpheum Theatre. Moriarty and his henchman are in the basement as Giles prints the forged bank notes when Lesley then arrives to warn them that "Holmes" has figured out their plan. Before Moriarty can shoot Giles, Watson appears explaining that he knew Lesley wasn't Giles' real daughter, as his real daughter is a transvestite man. After a swashbuckling fight between "Holmes" and Moriarty the villain tries to flee but he is killed when a gas pipe causes the theatre to explode. At the press conference outside 221b Baker Street, "Holmes" announces his retirement, but Watson steps in to ensure the pair continues to work together.

Trivia: Conan Doyle was not credited as the creators of the characters, however, at the end of the closing credits is written, "With apologies to the late Sir Arthur Conan Doyle, Creator of Sherlock Holmes and Dr. Watson"

The Woman in Green
Film - 1945 (USA)

Writer: Bertram Millhauser
Director: Roy William Neill
Sherlock Holmes: Basil Rathbone
Doctor Watson: Nigel Bruce

This is film number eleven for Rathbone and Bruce as Holmes and Watson. The police are concerned that a serial killer, who removes a victim's finger after murdering them, is still roaming free. After discussing the case with Holmes in the morgue, Inspector Gregson takes their talk to the pub and, whilst there, they comment on Sir George Fenwick leaving with a young woman, Lydia. Fenwick wakes up, disorientated, in a B&B, fully clothed and with something odd in his pocket. Rushing back to Lydia's flat he asks if she can remember anything about the previous night. He is interrupted by a strange man who produces Fenwick's cigarette case which he claims fell out of his pocket when he was "bending over something with a knife."

At 221b Baker Street a distraught Maude Fenwick tells Holmes that she found a finger buried in her garden and now her father has vanished. Holmes and Watson immediately rush to Fenwick's house but find him dead from a gunshot wound in the back. It appears he was being blackmailed and Holmes suspects Moriarty, even though he

was hanged, a suspicion which is confirmed when Moriarty arrives to threaten him.

In an empty house across the street, Watson sees the silhouette of Holmes in his chair before witnessing a man shoot him through the window. Luckily it was just a bust of Julius Caesar and when Holmes interviews the assassin he notes that he has been hypnotised leading Holmes to deduce that the murders are men who have been hypnotised and then blackmailed. Later at the Mesmer Club, a group for hypnotists, Holmes spots Lydia and he confides in her that his murder investigations are leaving him unable to sleep. She offers to cure his insomnia via hypnotism and, along with a sedative drug, puts him in a trance.

Once under, she calls for Moriarty who dictates a suicide letter for Holmes and places it in his pocket and he is then taken to the balcony where he walks, precariously, across the edge. Just as he is about to step on a loosened brick, Watson arrives with the police. Holmes then reveals that he is not actually hypnotised and Lydia is arrested. Moriarty, however, tries to run over the rooftops of London but thanks to a loose pipe, he slips and falls to his death.

Trivia: During a scene at Baker Street where Professor Moriarty confronts Sherlock Holmes, the writer has included some familiar dialogue and narrative from Conan Doyle's original story *The Final Problem*.

O Xangô de Baker Street *(The Xango from Baker Street)*
Film – 2001 (Brazil/Portugal)

Director: Miguel Faria Jr.
Writers: Marcos Bernstein, Miguel Faria Jr, Patrícia Melo & Jô Soares
Sherlock Holmes: Joaquim de Almeida
Doctor Watson: Anthony O'Donnell

Set in Rio de Janeiro in 1886 the film starts at the city municipal theatre where an actress named Sarah Bernhardt performs to rapturous applause. Later, in her dressing room, the Emperor Dom Pedro II visits to compliment her performance and lavishes her with commendations. As they talk, he tells her that a precious Stradivarius violin, given to him by Baroness Maria Luiza, has gone missing. Bernhardt suggests that the Baron contact her friend Sherlock Holmes, the greatest detective, as he would undoubtedly solve his case. When Holmes arrives he meets the Countess of Alvaré and learns the history of the violin from the Emperor. At the same time Holmes learns that a killer is at large, a sexual predator who tangles his victim's pubic hair with a violin string. The first victim has also been mutilated, her ears having been cut off as well as the violin string entangled in her pubic hair. Holmes is unsure if the killings are related to Dom Pedro's missing Stradivarius or if, indeed, Dom Pedro is the killer. Luckily for the next intended victim, Holmes is at hand with the killer strikes again.

Hearing the victim's cries he pursues the killer into the National Library but he escapes through a window. Although he didn't catch the criminal, Holmes does fall in love with the young actress Anna Candelária, whom he saved. Another victim is found butchered and murdered but by now Holmes has become preoccupied with things other than the case, including the local cannabis, cocktails and, of course, the young actress. The murderer claims the life of the Countess of Alvaré and still remains uncaught, but Holmes does not seem to be that concerned by it.

Dom Pedro II, as a consolation for his failure, allows Holmes to keep the stolen Stradivarius, which had been left by the murderer in the hotel room. He then takes Watson and the violin and heads home.

History: This Brazilian-Portuguese film is based on the debut novel of the same name by the author Jô Soares. The book is also known by the English title *Samba for Sherlock*.

O Xangô de Baker Street

Young Sherlock Holmes
Film - 1985 (USA)

Director: Barry Levinson
Writer: Chris Columbus
Sherlock Holmes: Nicholas Rowe
Doctor Watson: Alan Cox

This murder mystery story focuses on the very young Sherlock Holmes solving crimes at his boarding school with new boy, John Watson, at his side. A very young John Watson begins to move his possessions into the dorm of a new school when he meets a young Sherlock Holmes. Sherlock introduces John to his close friend, Elizabeth, and they visit Elizabeth's uncle, the retired schoolmaster and inventor Rupert T. Waxflatter, who is continuously trying to invent a flying machine. After Holmes returns from a humiliating fencing class where, once again he has been defeated by Professor Rathe, the school bully, Dudley, challenges Holmes to deduce where he has hidden a school trophy. Holmes, of course, finds it, and in retaliation Dudley frames Holmes for cheating during a test and he is expelled. When Professor Waxflatter becomes the third victim of a deadly hallucinogenic drug to die a horrible death, Holmes visits Lestrade and tries to convince him that all of the deaths are connected, but he is told that there isn't enough evidence to pursue his childish hunch. Undeterred, Holmes and Watson dig deeper and uncover an Egyptian cult which is conducting ritual killings in a strange temple.

They sneak in but are discovered and attacked with darts from a blow pipe (which, luckily, fail to hit their target) which reveal themselves as the source of the hallucinating deaths. Elizabeth has been captured and the boys formulate a plan to free her. The cult leader is revealed as Professor Rathe who tries to escape the temple with Elizabeth as a hostage. After foiling his escape by hooking a rope to Rathe's carriage, Rathe takes a gun and starts to shoot at Holmes before turning the gun on Elizabeth. The pair then fights with swords, and Holmes jabs Rathe who vanishes through a hole in the frozen Thames. For all Watson's help, Elizabeth dies from her wound and Holmes is compelled to leave school. In the last, post credit, scene of the film a man checks into a hotel under the name "Moriarty" and slowly Professor Rathe is revealed as he turns to smile at the camera.

Trivia: This was the first film to feature a CGI character. The knight who is seen emerging from a stained glass window took Industrial Light & Magic artists 4 months to create.

Young Sherlock: The Mystery of the Manor House
Television - 1982 (UK)

Director: Nicholas Ferguson
Writer: Gerald Frow
Sherlock Holmes: Guy Henry
Doctor Watson: N/A

This eight part television series was made by Granada for the ITV network in the UK and tells the story of a seventeen-year-old Sherlock Holmes as he returns home from school. Each episode starts with a title sequence of Doctor Watson rifling through some old dictation cylinders which Holmes had recorded in his retirement. The voice of Holmes explains that these stories are from his younger days and the box carries a note which reads, "To be handed to Doctor Watson and listened to after my death." Holmes recalls the time when a typhoid epidemic forced him back to the manor house of his childhood and set him on his path to being the world's only consulting detective.

Whilst home he is faced with strange and mysterious incidents, thefts, conspiracies and treason. The eight-part series each took up a half hour slot, however, the first episode was an hour long special. The show, although set some time before the Conan Doyle original stories, does try to bring in references and character names that Sherlockians will be familiar with including Moran, Moriarty and a housekeeper who is conspicuously engaged to a Mr. Hudson.

Connection: Although the series wasn't recommissioned, the tales were explored further in the book, *Young Sherlock: The Adventure of the Ferryman's Creek* which was also written by Frow.

A full episode list can be found in the "Television Episodes" chapter of this book.

Young Sherlock: Doyle no Isan
(Young Sherlock: The Legacy of Doyle)
Computer game - 1987 (Japan)

Director: Pack-In-Video
Writer: Pack-In-Video
Sherlock Holmes: N/A
Doctor Watson: N/A

This adventure game was made exclusively for the Japanese market for the MSA. Playing as Holmes and Watson you are tasked with investigating the murder of a millionaire whose daughter, Cindy, was found in incriminating circumstances near the body. Having been hired by Cindy's fiancé, Roger, the player must question witnesses, find clues and explore the 1875 London Landscape. This text-based game sees the screen split into three sections with the text at the bottom and the top split into the graphics and the commands (walk, talk, take, inventory etc). The game also allows a map of London to be brought up which shows the players their locations. Once all of the clues are found and all of the suspects are spoken to, Holmes and Watson present their evidence and free the daughter.

Connection: The game is, supposedly, based on the idea of the movie *Young Sherlock Holmes* (1985). Although the packaging and promotion all tie in with the

Barry Levinson movie, the plot of the game is completely different from the film.

Your Show Time: The Adventure of the Speckled Band
Television - 1949 (USA)

Director: Sobey Martin
Writer: Walter Doniger
Sherlock Holmes: Alan Napier
Doctor Watson: Melville Cooper

This television adaptation episode was shown as part of the American anthology drama series *Your Show Time* which broadcast on the NBC Television network on the East Coast in 1948 (and then on both the East and West Coasts by 1949). *The Speckled Band* was number ten out of a twenty-six episode series and is a faithful adaption of the original Conan Doyle story. Although given its time constraints the story zips through each plot point thanks to the narration by Shields. The young Miss Stoner turns to Holmes for help as she fears for her life after her stepfather Dr. Grimesby Roylott has forced her to sleep in her sister's old bedroom. The bedroom has been untouched since she died there under suspicious circumstances a few years ago with the words, "speckled band" on her lips. Now Miss Stoner is starting to hear the metallic tinkle sound the same as her sister did just before she died. As she leaves, Dr Roylott enters in a temper and is told to leave by Holmes. Later, Holmes and Watson visit Miss Stoner at her home, and Holmes investigates whilst poor Watson is attacked by a monkey. Holmes finds the bell pull that doesn't pull and a ventilator that leads to the stepfather's room.

Miss Stoner's fiancé arrives back from his trip and catches Holmes trying to break into the house, but Miss Stoner asks him to trust her and leave. In a deviation from the story, Holmes and Watson wait in Miss Stoner's room and when her fiancé enters angrily asking what they are up to, Holmes draws a gun and Watson knocks him unconscious and ties him to the foot of the bed. As the snake appears along the pull rope, Holmes beats it back along into Roylott's bedroom.

In another deviation, instead of coaxing the swamp adder back into the safe, Holmes shoots it dead. Miss Stoner's fiancé, still none the wiser but now freed from the bedroom, is instructed to pour everybody a glass of "soothing spirits" as the narrator, Shields, lights his Lucky Strike and ends the story.

Trivia: The show was hosted and narrated by Arthur Shields, and the series was sponsored by Lucky Strike cigarettes which would account for him smoking throughout the program.

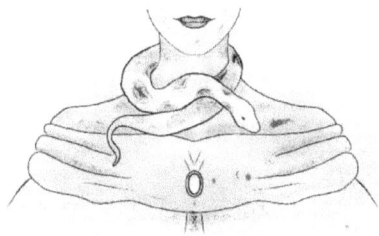

Your Show Time: The Adventure of the Speckled Band

TELEVISION EPISODES

The Adventures of Jamie Watson and Sherlock Holmes:

List of Episodes: 2014

Ask Sherlock Holmes
Hello Hannah
The Girl with the Deerstalker Hat
My Roommate's a Weirdo
The Science of Deduction
Room Tour
The Lambda Gamma Mystery
A Study in Dirt
The Ad Brought a Visitor
A Light in the Dark
Hope
How Sherlock Solved It
The Case of the Missing Case
The Watch
Mary
International Treasure
The Episode of Embarrassment
The End of the Road
The Great Lost Treasure
Sherlock Holmes Struts Her Stuff
An Ace Case
Ask Sherlock Holmes
Blanket Burrito
Intervention
The Speckled Band
Slither Slither
Myra Who?

List of Episodes: 2015

Mean Girls
Ask Sherlock Holmes

List of Episodes: 2016

The Adventure of the Empty Dorm
The Adventure of the Cardboard Box
The Adventure of the Solitary Cyclist
The Adventure of Norbury Hotel
The Adventure of the Bruce-Partington Plans
The Adventure of Abbey Granger
The Adventure of C.A.M.

The Adventures of Sherlock Holmes:

Series One Episodes:

Scandal in Bohemia
Broadcast: April 24th, 1984
Writers: John Hawkesworth, Alexander Baron
Director: Paul Annett

Sherlock Holmes is tasked with finding and extracting a scandal-inducing photograph of the King of Bohemia and the singer Irene Adler.

The Adventure of the Dancing Men
Broadcast: May 1st, 1984
Writers: John Hawkesworth, Anthony Skene
Director: John Bruce

A husband becomes suspicious of his wife and her past when drawings of stick figures start appearing at their home.

The Adventure of the Naval Treaty
Broadcast: May 8th, 1984
Writers: John Hawkesworth, Jeremy Paul
Director: Alan Grint

A mystery thief steals some important documents from a foreign office clerk who is forced to stay in bed due to "brain fever."

The Adventure of the Solitary Cyclist
Broadcast: May 15th, 1984
Writers: John Hawkesworth, Alan Plater
Director: Paul Annett

A young woman comes to Holmes to ask for help when a mysterious stranger begins to follower her during her bike rides.

The Adventure of the Crooked Man
Broadcast: May 22nd, 1984
Writers: John Hawkesworth, Alfred Shaughnessy
Director: Alan Grint

At his home, Col. Barclay is found dead and his wife is arrested for murder. However, Sherlock Holmes is not convinced they have the right person.

The Adventure of the Speckled Band
Broadcast: May 29th, 1984
Writers: John Hawkesworth, Jeremy Paul
Director: John Bruce

A young woman comes to Sherlock Holmes after becoming frightened by the behaviour of her step-father who has placed her in the bedroom where her sister died under mysterious circumstances.

The Adventure of the Blue Carbuncle
Broadcast: June 5th, 1984
Writers: John Hawkesworth, Paul Finney
Director: David Carson

A man is arrested for stealing a precious gem which is later found in the crop of a Christmas goose. Holmes and Watson investigate in order to stop an innocent man from being sent to prison.

Series Two Episodes:

The Copper Beeches
Broadcast: August 25th,1985
Writers: John Hawkesworth, Derek Marlowe
Director: Paul Annett

Sherlock Holmes comes to the aid of a young woman who is employed to take care of a young boy. But her employer's strange rules regarding her hair and dress start to take on a sinister tone.

The Adventure of the Greek Interpreter
Broadcast: September 1st, 1985
Writers: John Hawkesworth, Bill Craig
Director: Alan Grint

Mycroft Holmes asks his brother Sherlock to help investigate a gang who used the services of a Greek interpreter to translate their demands to a kidnapped man.

The Adventure of the Norwood Builder
Broadcast: September 8th, 1985
Writers: John Hawkesworth, Richard Harris
Director: Ken Grieve

John Hector McFarlane asks Sherlock Holmes for help as he is to be arrested for a murder of which he is innocent. Having been left a fortune, the man's benefactor appears to have been killed and the body burned.

The Adventure of the Resident Patient
Broadcast: September 15th, 1985
Writers: John Hawkesworth, Derek Marlowe
Director: David Carson

A doctor with a promising career is offered a practice by a benevolent stranger who is later found hanged in his bedroom.

The Red-Headed League
Broadcast: September 22nd, 1985
Writer: John Hawkesworth
Director: John Bruce

Pawnbroker Jabez Wilson becomes a member of the Red-Headed League and is paid a wage to write out the encyclopaedia. However, Sherlock Holmes suspects something entirely more ominous is at hand.

The Final Problem
Broadcast: September 29th, 1985
Writer: John Hawkesworth
Director: Alan Grint

Professor Moriarty follows Holmes and Watson all the way to Switzerland where he plans to exact his revenge on Holmes for meddling in his affairs.

The Adventures of OG Sherlock Kush:

List of Episodes: 2015

The Hidden Message
The Bloody Painting
The Invisible Cloak
The Test of Wills
The Royal Ghost
The Deadly Meeting
The Foggy Scoundrel
The Secret Twist
The Final Betrayal
The Second Assassin
The Last Resort
The Shallow Grave

List of Episodes: 2016

The Deadly Brothel
The Blood Moon
The Hangman's Folly
The Villainous Strain
The End of the Line
The Iron Bong
The Womanly Touch
The Super-Secret Twist
The Growing Threat

Baker Street:

Series Episodes:

Baker Street One:
Broadcast: January 9th, 2015

Jane Watson has dropped out of medical school and is alone with no money. She moves in to a new place with a roommate whom she thinks may be insane.

Baker Street Two:
Broadcast: January 16th, 2015

After a couple of months living with Sherlock Holmes, Watson's patience is starting to wear thin. Sherlock may be a good cook and extremely smart but her inability to sleep is causing Jane problems.

Baker Street Three:
Broadcast: January 23rd, 2015

Sherlock is on the hunt for a stolen object but Jane doesn't want to be involved. Unfortunately for the both of them, somebody is hell bent on eliminating them both from their investigation.

The Baker Street Boys:

Series One Episodes:

The Adventure of the Disappearing Dispatch Case, Part 1
Broadcast: March 8th, 1983

The gang find themselves in the middle of a political storm as a foreign office minister's case goes missing. London is now vulnerable to dangerous anarchists.

The Adventure of the Disappearing Dispatch Case, Part 2
Broadcast: March 11th, 1983

Conclusion of Part 1.

The Ghost of Julian Midwinter, Part 1
Broadcast: March 15th, 1983

Is there an air of the supernatural creeping around London? The boys need to find out if Julian Midwinter exists or if a ghost is on a crime spree. This episode was broadcast on BBC 2 due to the budget coverage on BBC 1.

The Ghost of Julian Midwinter, Part 2
Broadcast: March 18th, 1983

Conclusion of Part 1.

The Adventure of the Winged Scarab, Part 1
Broadcast: March 22nd, 1983

Wiggins becomes obsessed with a jewel, the winged scarab, and his motives and actions are questioned by the rest of the gang.

The Adventure of the Winged Scarab, Part 2
Broadcast: March 25th, 1983

Conclusion of Part 1.

The Case of the Captive Clairvoyant, Part 1 Broadcast: March 29th, 1983

A young girl is rescued from the clutches of her evil stepfather who is part of Moriarty's network. He is a mystic who is later found murdered and his stage helper, Rosie, kidnapped.

The Case of the Captive Clairvoyant, Part 2 Broadcast: April 4th, 1983

Conclusion of Part 1.

Call me Sherlock:

<u>**Series One Episodes:**</u>

A Study in Pudding
Broadcast: November 7th, 2015

A woman is found dead at her home in a suspected murder but "Sherlock Holmes" is more interested in the amount of pudding which is being stored in the woman's kitchen.

The Longest Path between Two Points
Broadcast: December 16th, 2015

When a mangled body is discovered at an alligator ranch, "Sherlock Holmes" is the only person who believes the injuries were made by a human, not a reptile.

Bad Influence
Broadcast: January 15th, 2016

"Sherlock Holmes" is given a case by "Lestrade" when physicists are found crushed to death. But this could be one case that manages to stump the world's greatest detective.

The Case-Book of Sherlock Holmes:

<u>**Series One Episodes:**</u>

The Disappearance of Lady Frances Carfax
Broadcast: February 21st, 1991
Writer: T.R. Bowen
Director: John Madden

Lady Frances Carfax goes missing from a hotel in which Doctor Watson is staying on vacation. Holmes suspects she is in immediate and mortal danger.

The Problem of Thor Bridge
Broadcast: February 28th, 1991
Writer: Jeremy Paul
Director: Michael Simpson

Maria Gibson is murdered by a shot to the head at Thor Bridge and the governess, Miss Dunbar, is arrested. Holmes uncovers the truth behind the supposed murder.

Shoscombe Old Place
Broadcast on: March 7th, 1991
Writer: Gary Hopkins
Director: Patrick Lau

The staff is concerned about the odd behaviour of Sir Robert Norberton who is cracking under the pressure of his money troubles. Sherlock Holmes and Doctor Watson discover the lengths he will go to in order to get out of debt.

The Boscombe Valley Mystery
Broadcast on: March 14th, 1991
Writer: John Hawkesworth
Director: June Howson

William McCarthy is found dead not long after he is seen having a heated argument with his son. The word "rat" could well be the key to proving his son's innocence.

The Illustrious Client
Broadcast on: March 21st, 1991
Writer: Robin Chapman
Director: Tim Sullivan

Despite their best efforts, nobody seems to be able to prevent Violet Merville from marrying the dangerous Baron Gruner. Holmes and Watson are brought in to try to dissuade her from marrying a man who is already suspected of murdering his previous wife.

The Creeping Man
Broadcast on: March 28th, 1991
Writer: Robin Chapman
Director: Tim Sullivan

A woman sees a man at her window in the middle of the night, even though her bedroom is on the second floor. Holmes must discreetly investigate Professor Presbury and his sudden erratic behaviour.

Series Two Episode:
The Master Blackmailer
Broadcast on: January 2nd, 1992
Writer: Jeremy Paul
Director: Peter Hammond

In a longer episode of the series, Sherlock Holmes attempts to prevent an inevitable scandal at the hands of the notorious blackmailer Charles Augustus Milverton.

Series Three Episodes:

The Last Vampyre
Broadcast on: January 27th, 1993
Writer: Jeremy Paul
Director: Tim Sullivan

Sherlock Holmes and John Watson are called to a village to investigate a man who is behaving like a vampire. He is the suspected link between all of the tragic and strange happenings in the village.

The Eligible Bachelor
Broadcast on: February 3rd, 1993
Writer: T.R. Bowen
Director: Peter Hammond

Doctor Watson tries to convince a sick Sherlock Holmes, who is plagued with bad dreams, to come to Vienna to visit Sigmund Freud. However, the case of a missing bride proves to be a temporary distraction.

The Diogenes Documentaries:

Series One Episodes:

The Original Baker Street Babes
Broadcast: April 5th, 2014

A look at the women who have played the roles of Sherlock Holmes and Doctor Watson.

The Dark Side of the Coin
Broadcast: July 31st, 2014

This episode focuses on Holmes's most fearful rival, Moriarty, and examines the character more closely.

From Watson with Love
Broadcast: August 9th, 2014

This episode looks at the Russian onscreen adaptations of Holmes and Watson and why they are also popular outside of Russia.

Series Two Episodes:

Around the World with Sherlock Holmes
Broadcast: April 3rd, 2015

Here the presenter explores the first international actors who have played Sherlock Holmes around the world.

The One Fixed Point
Broadcast: June 28th, 2015

This programme takes a look at the many men who have played Watson alongside William Gillette who played Holmes over 1300 times.

Series Three Episodes:

The Cowboy in a Deerstalker
Broadcast: December 19th, 2016

Asks the question, how many Oscar winning actors have played the role of Sherlock Holmes?

Beam Me Up Sherlock
Broadcast: January 14th, 2017

This episode focuses on those actors who have starred in both Sherlock Holmes adaptations and Star Trek movie adaptations.

Watson, the Envelope Please!
Broadcast: February 25th, 2017

A further examination of Oscar winning actors who have played Holmes and Watson.

Silent Doyle
Broadcast: April 16th, 2017

A study of the silent film adaptations of Sherlock Holmes between 1915-1927.

Dr. Doyle - An Author and an Actor
Broadcast: May 30th, 2017

Uncovering and examining the small part Conan Doyle played on the silver screen as an actor between 1914-1926.

Zasada Sherlock Holmes
Broadcast: October 7th, 2017

Presenting an overview of the popular and highly creative Polish adaptations of Sherlock Holmes.

Series Four Episodes:

The Baker Street Brawler
Broadcast: October 6th, 2018

The episode explores the relationship between Sherlock Holmes and the sport of wrestling

Elementary:

Series One Episodes:

Pilot
Broadcast: September 27th, 2012
Writer: Robert Doherty
Director: Michael Cuesta

Watson meets Holmes and helps him solve a case involving an ingenious serial Killer

While You Were Sleeping
Broadcast: October 4th, 2012
Writer: Robert Doherty
Director: John David Coles

Joan and Sherlock investigate the murders of a wealthy man's illegitimate children and the only witness is in a coma.

Child Predator
Broadcast: October 18th, 2012
Writer: Peter Blake
Director: Rod Holcomb

A serial killer known as The Balloon Man appears to have committed suicide, but all is not as clear cut as it seems.

The Rat Race
Broadcast: October 25th, 2012
Writer: Craig Sweeny
Director: Rosemary Rodriguez

A Wall Street banker is found dead of a heroin overdose but Sherlock suspects it wasn't self-inflicted.

Lesser Evils
Broadcast: November 1st, 2012
Writer: Liz Friedman
Director: Colin Bucksey

Sherlock accidentally discovers that somebody is killing patients who are near to death.

Flight Risk
Broadcast: November 8th, 2012
Writer: Corinne Brinkerhoff
Director: David Platt

At the scene of a plane crash Sherlock tells Joan that one of the passengers was murdered before the accident happened.

One Way to Get Off
Broadcast: November 15th, 2012
Writer: Christopher Silber
Director: Seith Mann

Sherlock assists Captain Gregson with what he thinks is a copycat killing. But when Sherlock delves into the cold case, he is frozen out.

The Long Fuse
Broadcast: November 29th, 2012
Writer: Jeffrey Paul King
Director: Andrew Bernstein

A bomb goes off four years after it was meant to and Sherlock becomes befriends a car thief

You Do It To Yourself
Broadcast: December 6th, 2002
Writer: Peter Blake
Director: Phil Abraham

Although unwell, Sherlock helps investigate the murder of a college professor who has been shot in both of his eyes.

The Leviathan
Broadcast: December 13th, 2012
Writers: Corinne Brinkerhoff & Craig Sweeny
Director: Peter Werner

Sherlock is brought in to investigate a bank vault called "The Leviathan" that is supposed to be uncrackable but has been broken into for the second time.

Dirty Laundry
Broadcast: January 3rd, 2013
Writers: Liz Friedman & Christopher Silber
Director: John David Coles

Joan and Sherlock are called to investigate the murder of a man who has been found inside an industrial washing machine.

M.
Broadcast: January 10th, 2013
Writer: Robert Doherty
Director: John Polson

Sherlock is reunited with a British serial killer known as M who is behind the murder of his lover, Irene Adler.

The Red Team
Broadcast: January 31st, 2013
Writer: Jeffrey Paul King
Director: Christine Moore

After trolling conspiracy theorists online, Sherlock finds he now has to investigate one who has been murdered.

The Deductionist
Broadcast: February 3rd, 2013
Writer: Craig Sweeny & Robert Doherty
Director: John Polson

Serial killer Martin Ennis escapes whist in hospital preparing for a kidney operation.

A Giant Gun, Filled with Drugs
Broadcast: February 7th, 2013
Writer: Corinne Brinkerhoff & Liz Friedman
Director: Guy Ferland

Sherlock is brought in to help his friend Rhys find his abducted daughter.

Details

Broadcast: February 14th, 2013
Writer: Jeffrey Paul King & Jason Tracey
Director: Sanaa Hamri

Detective Bell is shot at and recognises the shooter's car as a drug-dealer he helped put away.

Possibility Two
Broadcast: February 21st, 2013
Writer: Mark Goffman
Director: Seith Mann

Samuel Hagan is suffering from a degenerative disease and comes to Sherlock to find out if the disease was administered by a business rival.

Déjà Vu All Over Again
Broadcast: March 14th, 2013
Writer: Brian Rodenbeck
Director: Jerry Levine

Sherlock and Joan investigate the disappearance of a woman who has left behind a VHS tape for her husband.

Snow Angels
Broadcast: April 4th, 2013
Writer: Jason Tracey
Director: Andrew Bernstein

A robbery of mobile phones may just be a cover in order to steal a set of blueprints.

Dead Man's Switch
Broadcast: April 25th, 2013
Writer: Liz Friedman & Christopher Silber
Director: Larry Teng

Joan wants Sherlock to celebrate his first sober year but he is reluctant.

A Landmark Story
Broadcast: May 2nd, 2013
Writer: Corinne Brinkerhoff
Director: Peter Werner

Moran helps Sherlock catch a murderer which leads him to speak to Moriarty.

Risk Management
Broadcast: May 9th, 2013
Writer: Liz Friedman
Director: Adam Davidson

Moriarty goads Sherlock into solving an old case in return for information about his murdered girlfriend.

The Woman
Broadcast: May 16th, 2013
Writer: Robert Doherty & Craig Sweeny
Director: Seith Mann

Sherlock remembers his murdered lover Irene Adler and discovers that Moriarty is a woman.

Heroine
Broadcast: May 16th, 2013
Writer: Robert Doherty & Craig Sweeny
Director: John Polson

Sherlock is in the hospital recovering from a gunshot wound and readies himself for a showdown with Moriarty.

Series Two Episodes:

Step Nine
Broadcast: September 26th, 2013
Writer: Robert Doherty & Craig Sweeny
Director: John Polson

Sherlock and Joan travel to London to solve a case which has gotten Lestrade suspended.

Solve for 'X'
Broadcast: October 3rd, 2013
Writer: Jeffrey Paul King
Director: Jerry Levine

A murdered mathematician's walls are covered in a complicated formula which could be a key to unlock any encryption.

We Are Everyone
Broadcast: October 10th, 2013
Writer: Craig Sweeny
Director: Michael Pressman

A government operative is on the run after leaking secrets. Sherlock discovers he is part of a wider group of cyber-activists.

Poison Pen
Broadcast: October 17th, 2013
Writer: Liz Friedman
Director: Andrew Bernstein

A wealthy man is poisoned but after further investigation Sherlock finds it hard to morally expose the identity of the killer.

Ancient History
Broadcast: October 24th. 2013
Writer: Jason Tracey
Director: Sanaa Hamri

Sherlock discovers the body of a former assassin whilst at the morgue and investigates his murder.

An Unnatural Arrangement
Broadcast: October 31st, 2013
Writer: Cathryn Humphris
Director: Christine Moore

Gregson's wife shoots and kills a burglar at their home and Sherlock discovers a case of mistaken identity.

The Marchioness
Broadcast: November 7th, 2013
Writer: Christopher Hollier & Craig Sweeny
Director: Sanaa Hamri

Mycroft arrives in New York to open a restaurant and brings with him an ex-girlfriend who may not be all that she seems.

Blood is Thicker
Broadcast: November 14th, 2013
Writer: Bob Goodman
Director: John Polson

A young woman is stabbed before falling from a balcony and it is revealed that she is the mistress of a rich technology mogul.

On the Line
Broadcast: November 21st, 2013
Writer: Jason Tracey
Director: Guy Ferland

A woman stages her suicide to look like a murder and uncovers a serial killer who has gone undetected for years.

Tremors
Broadcast: December 5th, 2013
Writer: Liz Friedman
Director: Aaron Lipstadt

Bell is shot whilst protecting Sherlock from a schizophrenic man with a gun who wanders into the police station.

Internal Audit
Broadcast: December 12th, 2013
Writer: Bob Goodman
Director: Jerry Levine

Joan is refused permission to reveal her professional relationship with a woman who finds a murdered hedge fund manager.

The Diabolical Kind
Broadcast: January 2nd, 2014
Writer: Robert Doherty & Craig Sweeny
Director: Larry Teng

Sherlock discovers that Moriarty is behind the kidnaping of a child who may be Moriarty's daughter.

All in the Family
Broadcast: January 9th, 2014
Writer: Jason Tracey
Director: Andrew Bernstein

A body is discovered in a barrel by Bell and Joan identifies him as a member of the Mafia.

Dead Clade Walking
Broadcast: January 30th, 2014
Writer: Jeffrey Paul King
Director: Helen Shaver

Sherlock and Joan investigate cold cases and Joan discovers a misplaced stone in the victim's garden.

Corpse de Ballet
Broadcast: February 6th, 2014
Writer: Liz Friedman
Director: Jean de Segonzac

A ballerina is murdered and the star performer is the main suspect. Sherlock, however, needs more data.

The One-Percent Solution
Broadcast: February 27th, 2014
Writer: Craig Sweeny
Director: Guy Ferland

Sherlock suspects that Lestrade is covering something up after watching CCTV of him during a bomb investigation.

Ears to You
Broadcast: March 6th, 2014
Writer: Lauren MacKenzie & Andrew Gettens
Director: Seith Mann

A man receives two severed ears along with a ransom note nearly five years after his wife's disappearance.

The Hound of the Cancer Cells
Broadcast: March 13th, 2014
Writer: Bob Goodman
Director: Michael Slovis

A researcher dies by helium asphyxiation after testing a breathalyser invented to detect cancer.

The Many Mouths of Aaron Colville
Broadcast: April 3rd, 2014
Writer: Jason Tracey
Director: Larry Teng

Bite marks from a dead serial killer are showing up on new bodies but Sherlock doesn't think the reason is supernatural.

No Lack of Void
Broadcast: April 10th, 2014
Writer: Liz Friedman & Jeffrey Paul King
Director: Sanaa Hamri

A pickpocket dies of anthrax poisoning which could have something to do with the anti-government group Sovereign Army.

The Man with the Twisted Lip
Broadcast: April 24th, 2014
Writer: Craig Sweeny & Steve Gottfried
Director: Seith Mann

The sister of Sherlock's friend is found dead and Mycroft Holmes is back in New York.

Paint It Black
Broadcast: May 1st, 2014
Writer: Robert Hewitt Wolfe
Director: Lucy Liu

Joan is kidnaped and it is up to Mycroft and Sherlock to find her.

Art in the Blood
Broadcast: May 8th, 2014
Writer: Bob Goodman
Director: Guy Ferland

Mycroft reveals that he is working for MI6 and Sherlock is asked to investigate the murder of an undercover MI6 analyst.

The Grand Experiment
Broadcast: May 15th, 2014
Writer: Robert Doherty & Craig Sweeny
Director: John Polson

Sherlock tells Mycroft that he is being framed as a spy and sends him and Joan to a safe-house which is a library which only Sherlock can access.

Series Three Episodes:

Enough Nemesis to Go Around
Broadcast: October 30th, 2014
Writer: Robert Doherty & Craig Sweeny
Director: John Polson

Joan is running her own investigation company and Sherlock is now working with a new protégé Kitty Winter.

The Five Orange Pipz
Broadcast: November 6th, 2014
Writer: Bob Goodman
Director: Larry Teng

After children are killed by toxic beads, a spring of vengeful murders occur.

Just a Regular Irregular
Broadcast: November 13th, 2014
Writer: Robert Hewitt Wolfe
Director: Jerry Levine

Whilst participating in a math-based puzzle game a man stumbles across a dead body whose mouth is full of mothballs.

Bella
Broadcast: November 20th, 2014
Writer: Craig Sweeny
Director: Guy Ferland

Sherlock is called in when it appears that somebody has copied a state of the art Artificial Intelligence system called Bella.

Rip Off
Broadcast: November 27th, 2014
Writer: Jason Tracey
Director: John Polson

Sherlock and Kitty investigate a severed hand and a case involving smuggled diamonds.

Terra Pericolosa
Broadcast: December 4th, 2014
Writer: Bob Goodman
Director: Aaron Lipstadt

Whilst investigating a murder Sherlock discovers plans to illegally move border lines in order to open up a new casino.

The Adventure of the Nutmeg Concoction
Broadcast: December 11th. 2014
Writer: Peter Ocko
Director: Christine Moore

Sherlock and Joan investigate a complicated set of murders but the scent of nutmeg and sodium hydroxide at each crime scene becomes significant.

End of Watch
Broadcast: December 18th, 2014
Writer: Robert Hewitt Wolfe
Director: Ron Fortunato

Sherlock, Kitty and Joan investigate the murder of a police officer whose firearm has been replaced by an airgun.

The Eternity Injection
Broadcast: January 8th, 2015
Writer: Craig Sweeny
Director: Larry Teng

Joan and Sherlock uncover the existence of an illegal drug trial which causes Sherlock to struggle with is past addictions.

Seed Money
Broadcast: January 15th, 2015
Writer: Brian Rodenbeck
Director: John Polson

An old couple die together in bed and a toxic gas is believed to be to blame but a rare orchid may also play a part.

The Illustrious Client
Broadcast: January 22nd, 2015
Writer: Jason Tracey
Director: Guy Ferland

A suspect is found to be working in a brothel that kidnaps illegal immigrants. Sherlock investigates as Joan settles into her new job.

The One That Got Away
Broadcast: January 29th, 2015
Writer: Robert Doherty
Director: Seith Mann

Joan is suddenly fired from her job and so Sherlock starts to investigate the backgrounds of various kidnapped women which almost results in a dangerously sticky end.

Hemlock
Broadcast: February 5th, 2015
Writer: Arika Lisanne Mittman
Director: Christine Moore

Sherlock and Joan investigate the death of a debt collector with far too many suspects.

The Female of the Species
Broadcast: February 12th, 2015
Writer: Jeffrey Paul King
Director: Lucy Liu

Sherlock investigates a couple of missing zebras with Bell. Joan finds she is struggling with grief and wants to move back into the brownstone.

When Your Number's Up
Broadcast: February 19th, 2015
Writer: Bob Goodman
Director: Jerry Levine

A serial killer is leaving envelopes of money on the victims which leads Sherlock to investigate the world of insurance compensation.

For All You Know
Broadcast: March 5th, 2015
Writer: Peter Ocko
Director: Guy Ferland

Sherlock investigates himself when he is implicated in a murder which was committed during the height of his drug addiction.

T-Bone and the Iceman
Broadcast: March 12th, 2015
Writer: Jason Tracey
Director: Michael Slovis

A woman is found dead and mummified in a refrigeration unit which leads Joan and Sherlock to discover more frozen murder victims.

The View from Olympus
Broadcast: April 2nd, 2015
Writer: Bob Goodman
Director: Seith Mann

A case of competitive rivalry seems to have resulted in a man being murdered.

One Watson, One Holmes
Broadcast: April 9th, 2015
Writer: Robert Hewitt Wolfe
Director: John Polson

An internet activist is murdered but the case isn't interesting enough to coax Joan out of her introspective funk.

A Stitch in Time
Broadcast: April 16th, 2015
Writer: Peter Ocko
Director: Ron Fortunato

A man who makes it his business to debunk the paranormal is found murdered. Sherlock also discovers that this could be a threat to national security.

Under My Skin
Broadcast: April 23rd, 2015
Writer: Jeffrey Paul King
Director: Aaron Lipstadt

During a kidnaping two paramedics are killed and so Sherlock and Joan head the manhunt to find the murderer and the abducted woman.

The Best Way Out Is Always Through
Broadcast: April 30th, 2015
Writer: Arika Lisanne Mittman
Director: Michael Slovis

It appears that a judge has been killed by the woman he sentenced, but Sherlock thinks there is more to it.

Absconded
Broadcast: May 7th, 2015
Writer: Jason Tracey
Director: Guy Ferland

A member of Sherlock's beekeeping community dies whilst researching a deadly honey bee outbreak.

A Controlled Descent
Broadcast: May 14th, 2015
Writer: Robert Doherty
Director: John Polson

Sherlock reflects on his own addiction as a heroin addict kidnaps his friend.

Series Four Episodes:

The Past Is Parent
Broadcast: November 5th, 2015
Writer: Robert Doherty
Director: John Polson

Sherlock is determined to stay sober even though he and Joan have been fired from the police department.

Evidence of Things Not Seen
Broadcast: November 12th, 2015
Writer: Jason Tracey
Director: Ron Fortunato

Sherlock and Joan investigate a triple homicide at a research facility and Sherlock considers an offer made by his father.

Tag, You're Me
Broadcast: November 19th, 2015
Writer: Bob Goodman
Director: Christine Moore

Two men are murdered whilst impersonating each other which leads Bell and Joan to look into face recognition software.

All My Exes Live in Essex
Broadcast: November 26th, 2015

Writer: Robert Hewitt Wolfe
Director: Michael Pressman

A technician where Joan used to work goes missing and her skeleton later is found in a classroom, laid out for students.

The Game's Underfoot
Broadcast: December 10th, 2015
Writer: Arika Lisanne Mittman
Director: Alex Chapple

An archaeologist is found dead after searching for an old '80s computer game, Nottingham Knights. Apparently there is more than just garbage at the landfill site.

The Cost of Doing Business
Broadcast: December 17th, 2015
Writer: Jason Tracey
Director: Aaron Lipstadt

An apparently random mass-shooting by a sniper seems too organised to not have been targeting a specific person.

Miss Taken
Broadcast: January 7th, 2016
Writer: Tamara Jaron
Director: Guy Ferland

A retired FBI agent is found mashed to death inside a wood-chipper, Sherlock and Joan visit his last case to look for clues.

A Burden of Blood
Broadcast: January 14th, 2016
Writer: Nick Thiel
Director: Christine Moore

A woman who was two months pregnant is found suffocated to death in her car. The police suspect her lover, but Sherlock suspects somebody closer to home.

Murder Ex Machina
Broadcast: January 21st, 2016
Writer: Robert Hewitt Wolfe
Director: Guy Ferland

When a Russian oligarch is shot dead and, later, their killers are murdered, Sherlock and Joan start asking questions at a government level.

Alma Matters
Broadcast: January 28th, 2016
Writer: Bob Goodman
Director: Larry Teng

Sherlock discovers a ruthless man is using cash-strapped former students to threaten and murder those who threatened the college.

Down Where the Dead Delight
Broadcast: February 4th, 2016
Writer: Jeffrey Paul King
Director: Jerry Levine

Down in the morgue a body which hides a bomb explodes and destroys vital evidence as it does so.

A View with a Room
Broadcast: February 11th, 2016
Writer: Richard C. Okie
Director: John Polson

Sherlock infiltrates a drug-dealing gang of bikers and becomes integral in planning their next heist.

A Study in Charlotte
Broadcast: February 18th, 2016
Writer: Robert Hewitt Wolfe
Director: Guy Ferland

A lecturer and group of students are killed when they ingest mushrooms laced with a deadly synthetic toxin.

Who Is That Masked Man?
Broadcast: February 25th, 2016
Writer: Jason Tracey
Director: Larry Teng

Sherlock and Joan break into a house to investigate if his father's mistress was involved in an assassination attempt gone wrong.

Up to Heaven and Down to Hell
Broadcast: March 3rd, 2016
Writer: Tamara Jaron
Director: John Polson

A wealthy old woman falls from the penthouse of her apartment killing her and the man she lands on.

Hounded
Broadcast: March 10th, 2016
Writer: Robert Hewitt Wolfe
Director: Ron Fortunato

A young Charles Baskerville is run down by a lorry after running away from a large, glowing animal.

You've Got Me, Who's Got You?
Broadcast: March 20th , 2016
Writer: Paul Cornell
Director: Seith Mann

A man dressed as a comic book superhero is found dead, and Sherlock discovers that it was a really heroic end for the man.

Ready or Not
Broadcast: March 27th, 2016
Writer: Bob Goodman
Director: Christine Moore

A doctor goes missing as evidence comes to light that he was selling prescription drugs illegally. When the body is found, Sherlock investigates a murder rather than a suicide.

All In
Broadcast: April 10th, 2016
Writer: Kelly Wheeler
Director: Aaron Lipstadt

A high stakes poker game is targeted and robbed, but the robbery may have more to do with espionage than cash.

Art Imitates Art
Broadcast: April 10th, 2016
Writer: Arika Lisanne Mittman
Director: Ron Fortunato

A woman is shot and killed when getting into her car-share, but this may go deeper than mistaken identity.

Ain't Nothing Like the Real Thing
Broadcast: April 17th, 2016
Writer: Nick Thiel & Jeffrey Paul King
Director: Jeremy Webb

A carjack is staged to hide a hired hit but when the wife is mistakenly shot, Sherlock Holmes steps in to find the assassin.

Turn It Upside Down
Broadcast: April 24th, 2016
Writer: Bob Goodman
Director: Lucy Liu

Joan reveals the identity of a double-agent and the pair investigates a murder at a diner.

The Invisible Hand
Broadcast: May 1st, 2016
Writer: Robert Doherty & Jason Tracey
Director: Guy Ferland

Sherlock Holmes believes that somebody is running Moriarty's criminal network whist she is behind bars and comes home to find a bomb waiting for him.

A Difference in Kind
Broadcast: May 8th, 2016
Writer: Jason Tracey & Robert Doherty
Director: John Polson

Sherlock manages to disarm the bomb at his home, after some investigation he discovers that there is a connection to an Iranian diplomat.

Series Five Episodes:

Folie a Deux
Broadcast: October 2nd, 2016
Writer: Robert Doherty & Jeffrey Paul King
Director: Christine Moore

Sherlock chases a suspect after arriving at the scene of an exploded IED. The evidence points to the man being an ex con.

Worth Several Cities
Broadcast: October 16th, 2016
Writer: Robert Hewitt Wolfe
Director: Guy Ferland

Sherlock is kidnaped by a gang who want him to investigate who has murdered one of their own.

Render, and Then Seize Her
Broadcast: October 23rd, 2016
Writer: Jason Tracey
Director: Alex Chapple

Sherlock is asked to investigate a murder at a nudist retreat which leads to him chasing leads for a kidnaping case.

Henny Penny the Sky Is Falling
Broadcast: October 30th, 2016
Writer: Bob Goodman
Director: John Polson

Joan and Sherlock attempt to solve the murder of a financial advisor and get sucked into the world of asteroid research.

To Catch a Predator Predator
Broadcast: November 6th, 2016
Writer: Tamara Jaron
Director: Guy Ferland

A secret online vigilante is murdered after outing several dating website sexual predators and publically shaming them.

Ill Tidings
Broadcast: November 13th, 2016
Writer: Jeffrey Paul King
Director: Ron Fortunato

Sherlock is called in to investigate after a chef and his customers are killed when a special tasting menu is found to be laced with snake venom.

Bang Bang Shoot Chute
Broadcast: November 20th, 2016
Writer: Celeste Chan Wolfe
Director: Jerry Levine

Two extreme sports base jumpers are killed by sabotage and by shooting and Sherlock is called to find the killer.

How the Sausage Is Made
Broadcast: November 27th, 2016
Writer: Mark Hudis
Director: Michael Pressman

A man who is working on creating an artificial, cruelty-free, meat substitute is found dead after eating a poisoned sausage.

It Serves You Right to Suffer
Broadcast: December 11th, 2016
Writer: Kelly Wheeler
Director: Aidan Quinn

Sherlock and Joan work to discover who is the killer of a rival gang member found on SBK territory.

Pick Your Poison
Broadcast: December 18th, 2016
Writer: Bob Goodman
Director: Jeremy Webb

When Joan's DEA number is taken by a drug mill it leads to the discovery of two dead bodies.

Be My Guest
Broadcast: January 8th, 2017
Writer: Jason Tracey
Director: Maja Vrvilo

After investigating a murder, Sherlock stumbles upon a woman who has been held captive for years and has to track her before she is murdered.

Crowned Clown, Downtown Brown
Broadcast: January 15th, 2017
Writer: Jordan Rosenberg
Director: Michael Slovis

A plot to contaminate the New York water supply is uncovered whist Sherlock investigates the murder of a man dressed as a clown.

Over a Barrel
Broadcast: January 29th, 2017
Writer: Jeffrey Paul King
Director: Guy Ferland

The father of a crime victim holds a diner full of people for ransom in order to force Sherlock into taking his case.

Rekt in Real Life
Broadcast: February 19th, 2017
Writer: Robert Hewitt Wolfe
Director: John Polson

A former video game player dies after being attacked whilst streaming a video live online.

Wrong Side of the Road

Broadcast: March 5th, 2017
Writer: Robert Doherty & Jason Tracey
Director: Jennifer Lynch

After three years away, Sherlock's former assistant and protégé returns to warn him that somebody is killing everybody who worked on a case with them.

Fidelity
Broadcast: March 12th, 2017
Writer: Jason Tracey & Robert Doherty
Director: Christine Moore

Kitty and Sherlock find a link between a spate of murders connected to their old case and an international conspiracy.

The Ballad of Lady Frances
Broadcast: March 19th, 2017
Writer: Bob Goodman & Jordan Rosenberg
Director: Aaron Lipstadt

Joan and Sherlock are asked to solve the mystery of a shooting which was "heard" but which has no hard evidence to prove it happened.

Dead Man's Tale
Broadcast: March 26th, 2017
Writer: Tamara Jaron
Director: Alex Chapple

Joan and Sherlock hunt for treasure in New York after finding a pirate's old treasure map.

High Heat
Broadcast: April 16th, 2017
Writer: Kelly Wheeler
Director: Michael Hekmat

Sherlock is brought in to investigate the murder of a person he considers to be the worst private investigator in New York.

The Art of Sleights and Deception
Broadcast: April 23rd, 2017
Writer: Mark Hudis
Director: Ron Fortunato

When a magician dies whilst performing a dangerous stunt, Sherlock and Joan join the magic fraternity.

Fly Into a Rage, Make a Bad Landing
Broadcast: April 30th, 2017
Writer: Bob Goodman
Director: Guy Ferland

Bell's girlfriend is assaulted and then her ex-boyfriend is murdered, and Bell is having a hard time not making it personal.

Moving Targets
Broadcast: May 7th, 2017
Writer: Robert Hewitt Wolfe
Director: Lucy Liu

A police chief takes part in a reality television show and is murdered. When Sherlock delves deeper he discovers a world of corruption and bribery.

Scrambled
Director: May 14th, 2017
Writer: Jason Tracey
Director: Christine Moore

Sherlock's interaction with a mysterious woman has Joan worried as he becomes more and more erratic.

Hurt Me, Hurt You
Broadcast: May 21st, 2017
Writer: Robert Doherty & Jeffrey Paul King
Director: John Polson

As Sherlock experiences blackouts, memory loss and hallucinations he is given an MRI scan.

Series Six Episodes:

An Infinite Capacity for Taking Pains
Broadcast: April 30th, 2018
Writer: Bob Goodman
Director: Christine Moore

Sherlock is diagnosed with post-concussion syndrome and he helps Joan track down a missing partner when a sex tape is released.

Once You've Ruled Out God
Broadcast: May 7th, 2018
Writer: Robert Hewitt Wolfe
Director: Guy Ferland

Watson's father dies but she continues to work with Sherlock as they trace stolen plutonium which may be earmarked for a dirty bomb.

Pushing Buttons
Broadcast: May 14th, 2018
Writer: Jeffrey Paul King
Director: Christine Moore

A man is murdered during a history war re-enactment and Sherlock becomes intrigued by the world of antique collecting.

Our Time Is Up
Broadcast: May 21st, 2018
Writer: Liz Friedman
Director: Guy Ferland

Watson's former therapist is found murdered and after reading her notes, Watson considers motherhood.

Bits and Pieces
Broadcast: May 28th, 2018
Writer: Tamara Jaron
Director: John Polson

When Sherlock turns up with a severed head and no memory of how he acquired it, he and Joan discover the man may have been a tissue donor who was infected by accident and murdered as a cover up.

Give Me the Finger
Broadcast: June 4h, 2018
Writer: Jordan Rosenberg
Director: Jonny Lee Miller

There are worries over nuclear security when a former Japanese crime-ring member is murdered.

Sober Companions
Broadcast: June 11th, 2018
Writer: Jason Tracey
Director: Seith Mann

Even though his health is deteriorating, Sherlock insists on working to solve the case of serial killer before he strikes again.

Sand Trap
Broadcast: June 18th, 2018
Writer: Kelly Wheeler
Director: Jennifer Lynch

Sherlock returns from his recovery holiday in Vermont to find Watson has moved in a pregnant lady whose baby she wants to adopt.

Nobody Lives Forever
Broadcast: June 25th, 2018
Writer: Jeffrey Paul King
Director: Guy Ferland

A professor who is working at a research institute for immortality is murdered after winning a $5 million award. Could the murderer's motive be to save the company money?

The Adventure of the Ersatz Sobekneferu
Broadcast: July 2nd, 2018
Writer: Robert Hewitt Wolfe
Director: Lucy Liu

Sherlock's father visits to rewrite his will after Mycroft's death but Sherlock is busy investigating a murder victim who has been passed off as an Egyptian Mummy.

You've Come a Long Way, Baby
Broadcast: July 16th, 2018
Writer: Bob Goodman
Director: Guy Ferland

A lawyer is found dead the day before the tobacco company he was working for was to merge. The solution may be found in the finance records and company accounting books.

Meet Your Maker
Broadcast: July 23rd, 2018
Writer: Robert Hewitt Wolfe
Director: Ron Fortunato

Joan's sister recommends her to a friend who is looking for a missing woman. When Joan and Sherlock find the woman's apartment, they discover she has been kidnapped.

Breathe
Director: July 30th, 2018
Writer: Bob Goodman
Director: Christine Moore

A dead man who specialised in relocating people turns out to have been a contract killer.

Through the Fog
Broadcast: August 6th, 2018
Writer: Jeffrey Paul King
Director: Guy Ferland

Detective Bell is a victim of an attempted chemical attack on the police station and the entire building is forced into quarantine.

How to Get a Head
Broadcast: August 12th, 2018
Writer: Sherman Li
Director: Christine Moore

Joan and Sherlock dabble in the occult as a headless corpse is discovered in a communal garden.

Uncanny Valley of the Dolls
Broadcast: August 13th, 2018
Writer: Tamara Jaron & Kelly Wheeler
Director: Jonny Lee Miller

An engineer who is working on the construction of a teleportation device is murdered and Sherlock must decide if the killing is connected to his work or his sex life.

The Worms Crawl in, the Worms Crawl Out
Broadcast: August 20th, 2018
Writer: Jordan Rosenberg
Director: Jon Michael Hill

A zoologist who is known to be having numerous affairs is found dead but there are too many motives and too many suspects. Sherlock has to find a way to narrow it down.

The Visions of Norman P. Horowitz
Broadcast: August 27th, 2018
Writer: Jason Tracey
Director: Lucy Liu

A killer is choosing his next victims based on the premonitions of a dead man who believed he could predict the future. One of the predicted victims is Sherlock Holmes.

The Geek Interpreter
Broadcast: September 3rd, 2018
Writer: Tamara Jaron & Kelly Wheeler
Director: Christine Moore

One of the Baker Street Irregulars is the prime suspect in a woman's disappearance. Sherlock works quickly to clear his name.

Fit to Be Tied
Broadcast: September 10th, 2018
Writer: Jason Tracey
Director: Ron Fortunato

Joan discovers information which could be deadly and an old face returns during a murder investigation.

Whatever Remains, However Improbable
Broadcast: September 17th, 2018
Writer: Robert Doherty
Director: Christine Moore

Joan and Sherlock uncover the murderer of a friend and colleague, however, capturing the killers could have devastating and far-reaching consequences.

Holmes University:

Episode list:

Holmes University: The Master Blackmailer.
Broadcast: September 17th, 2013

After meeting for the first time at university, roommates Sherlock Homes and John Watson have to work together to find the mystery blackmailer.

Holmes University 2: The Longest Winter.
Broadcast: February 27th, 2014

The pair finds themselves pulled deep into a dark and disturbing case as a series of horrifying murders are committed on the university campus.

Holmes University 3: Crusade of Darkness.
Broadcast: July 29th, 2015

A serial killer is attacking young couples and as the friendship between John Watson and

Sherlock Holmes grows, Mycroft Holmes is determined to interfere in Sherlock's life.

Holmes University 4: Origins of the Fall
Broadcast: September 15th, 2016

Moriarty is hiding bombs in locations which are significant to John and Sherlock. It is up to the detective duo to stop the worst from happening.

The Mary Morstan Mysteries:

Series One Episodes:

Where's Watson
Broadcast: March 24th, 2012

Watson has gone missing and so Sherlock Holmes enlists Watson's fiancée, Mary Morstan, to help find him

Hell Hath No Fury
Broadcast: September 1st, 2012

Mary Morstan investigates the suffragette movement after it seems a few of their members will stop at nothing to get their vote, or perhaps, something more sinister.

Morstan vs. Milverton
Broadcast: December 23rd, 2012

Mrs. Cecil Forrester, Mary's ex-boss, is being blackmailed by the notorious Charles Augustus Milverton. It's up to Mary to try to prevent Forrester's secret from being revealed.

Series Two Episodes:

Rings of Change
Broadcast: April 19th, 2014

Mary's engagement ring is missing and she suspects it has been stolen by The Moriarty Club. Soon, however, she discovers that they have more serious criminal plans in mind.

The Day the Milk Ran Dry
Broadcast: June 1st, 2014

Mary Morstan and Mrs Hudson take a holiday on a farm for a week and soon discover that they may be able to leave London, but crime will follow them anywhere.

Murder Most Horace
Broadcast: August 26th, 2014

Mary Morstan has an alter ego called Horace Moustachio who gets accused of murder. Can Mary prove his/her innocence?

The Ecuador Equation
Broadcast: November 14th, 2014

The Moriarty Club releases a serum onto the black market which enhances strength and Mary needs to figure out how she can defeat those who have taken it.

The Devil's Gambit
Broadcast: April 21st, 2015

Moriarty bets a vast amount of money on Steve Dixie winning his next fight. He is sure that his simian strength serum will guarantee a win, but he has a sinister plan in case the fight is lost.

Meitantei Holmes
(Sherlock Hound):

Series one episodes:

The Four Signatures AKA He's the Famous Detective
Broadcast: November 6th, 1984

As Sherlock returns to England his ship is attacked by pirates who are looking for a passenger. Sherlock saves the day with the help of fellow passenger Doctor John Watson

The Crown of Mazalin AKA The Evil Genius, Professor Moriarty
Broadcast: November 13th, 1984

A crown on loan from the Queen goes missing and the son of an aristocrat is the main suspect. Sherlock investigates and has his first run in with Moriarty.

A Small Client AKA Little Martha's Big Mystery
Broadcast: November 20th, 1984

Sherlock Hound suspects Professor Moriarty is responsible for the counterfeit money problem in London, and a little girl who is looking for her missing father may be what he needs to prove it.

Mrs. Hudson is Taken Hostage AKA The Mrs. Hudson Kidnapping Case
Broadcast: November 27th, 1984

Professor Moriarty attempts to kidnap Mrs. Hudson, thinking that she is a way to get to Sherlock Hound, however, things do not go as smoothly as he would like.

The Adventure of the Blue Carbuncle AKA The Blue Ruby
Broadcast on: December 4th, 1984

Moriarty steals a precious gem but it gets stolen by a little girl named Polly who pickpockets him. Regardless of her age, Moriarty will stop at nothing to get the gem back

The Green Balloon AKA Solve the Mystery of the Green Balloon
Broadcast: December 11th, 1984

A mysterious green balloon lands in Sherlock Hound's garden along with a message for help from the prison on Dolphin Island.

A Sacred Image Disappears AKA The Great Chase of the Little Detectives
Broadcast: December 18th, 1984

Moriarty steals a gold statue but Sherlock Hound knows it is hidden somewhere by the docks. He must work quickly to locate it before Moriarty returns to collect it.

The Speckled Band
Broadcast: January 8th, 1985

After living in America for a number of years, a young woman returns to England but her uncle is not quite the man she remembers.

Treasure Under the Sea AKA Treasures of the Seabed
Broadcast: January 15th, 1985

A submarine has been stolen by Professor Moriarty and so the Royal Navy asks Hound and Watson to help them recover it.

The White Cliffs of Dover AKA The Air Battle Over Dover!
Broadcast: January 22nd, 1985

The new airmail service is being sabotaged and it's up to Hound, Watson and Mrs. Hudson to figure out who is doing it and why.

The Sovereign Gold Coins AKA The Targeted Giant Coin Bank
Broadcast: January 29th, 1985

When a collection of sovereign gold coins is stolen from an "un-crackable" safe, Sherlock Hound and Doctor Watson are asked to investigate by one of the richest men in London.

The Stormy Getaway AKA The Professor's Big Failure in the Storm
Broadcast: February 5th, 1985
The police have been sabotaged and so are unable to escort a large shipment of cash. Sherlock Hound and Watson are called to follow the precious cargo to ensure its safe arrival in London

The Runaway Freight Car AKA Missing Freight Car!? The Professor's Big Magic Trick
Broadcast: February 12th, 1985

Sherlock Hound is tasked with figuring out how a freight car in the middle of a passenger train disappeared on the way to London.

The Coral Lobsters AKA Gourmet! The Coral Lobsters
Broadcast: February 19th, 1985

Moriarty managed to steal an entire collection of diamond-encrusted lobster carvings after craving actual lobster for dinner. Hound and Watson must now track him down and recover the carvings.

The Golden Statue of the Great Burglar AKA Look! The Shining Thief
Broadcast: February 26th, 1985

A sculptor vanishes on the same night that a bank's entire collection of gold is stolen. Moriarty is whom Hound suspects when his likeness shows up in sketches at the sculptor's house.

The Secret of the Sacred Cross Sword AKA The Magic Castle! Holmes, Dead or Alive?"
Broadcast: March 5th, 1985

Hound and Watson are invited to the first unveiling of "The Sacred Sword of the Wizards" in decades, but when the safe containing it is broken into and the sword isn't even touched, it's up to Hound to figure out why.

The Adventure of the Thames Monster AKA The Monster of the Thames River
Broadcast: March 12th, 1985

A sea monster is reported to be attacking ships on the Thames but when a passenger goes missing in an attack and no body can be found, Hound is called to locate him and solve the mystery.

The Adventure of the Three Students AKA Blundered Operation at Loch Ness
Broadcast: March 19th, 1985

Three French art students have gone missing in London and Lestrade starts investigating stolen reproduction paintings.

The Rosetta Stone AKA The Soseki Kite Battle Over London
Broadcast: March 26th, 1985

The Rosetta Stone floats away from the British Museum and Hound investigates the various countries who claim ownership of the stone. Each one is a suspect to Hound and Watson

The White Silver Getaway AKA Chase the Airship White Silver!
Broadcast: April 2nd, 1985

Moriarty steals a shipment of gold but he can't get the gold out of London whilst Lestrade is investigating. During the case Hound and Watson investigate a robbery at a company which makes blimps.

The Disappearance of the Splendid Royal Horse AKA Buzz Buzz! The Fly Fly Mecha Operation
Broadcast: April 9th, 1985

Moriarty has competition for the cleverest thief as a new criminal arrives in London. Hound discovers that his next target could be the Queen's favourite horse.

Disturbance, The World Flight Championship AKA Grand Flight Championship of Chaos!
Broadcast: April 16th, 1985

Moriarty enters into a prestigious aeroplane race and plans to sabotage his way into first place by stealing parts from other entrants to make his plane the best. His main competition in the race, however, is Mrs. Hudson, Hound and Watson

The Secret of the Parrot AKA Game of Wits! Parrot vs Professor
Broadcast: April 23rd, 1985

Moriarty steals a parrot off a train and so Hound and Watson investigate in order to find out why the parrot is special.

The Bell of Big Ben AKA Listen! The Tribute to Moriarty
Broadcast: May 7th, 1985

Hound is asked to keep quiet about Big Ben's bell having been stolen and so he investigates in secret so the London police can save face.

The Priceless French Doll AKA Chaos! The Doll Swap Case
Broadcast: May 14th, 1985

After stealing a very big diamond, Moriarty hides it in a doll. He ends up with more than he bargained for when the doll is mistakenly sold.

The Missing Bride Affair AKA Goodbye Holmes! The Last Case
Broadcast: May 21st, 1985

A bride vanishes moments before she is to walk down the aisle and Sherlock Hound is hired to find her. However, when Hound learns about her past he is reluctant to reveal her location.

The Memoirs of Sherlock Holmes:

Series one episodes:

The Three Gables
Broadcast: March 7th, 1994
Writers: Jeremy Paul
Director: Peter Hammond

The affairs of a now dead Douglas Maberley come back to haunt his grandmother who is offered a large sum of money to sell her house, including all of her belongings to a mystery buyer.

The Dying Detective
Broadcast: March 14th, 1994
Writers: T.R. Bowen
Director: Sarah Hellings

Sherlock Holmes is called to the estate of Mrs. Adelaide Savage who fears for her husband's life. After her husband dies in suspicious circumstances, Holmes appears to contract the same deadly illness and calls for the help of Culverton Smith to cure him.

The Golden Pince-Nez
Broadcast: March 21st, 1994
Writers: Gary Hopkins
Director: Peter Hammond

Sherlock Holmes and his brother Mycroft work together to try and solve the murder of Willoughby Smith who was found dead clutching a pair of pince-nez.

The Red Circle
Broadcast: March 28th, 1994
Writers: Jeremy Paul
Director: Sarah Hellings

The strange behaviour of an elusive lodger uncovers a larger and more sinister case involving secret societies and murder.

The Mazarin Stone
Broadcast: April 4th, 1994
Writers: Gary Hopkins
Director: Peter Hammond

Sherlock Holmes is in the Highlands and so Watson and Mycroft take up the case of the missing Mazarin Stone. At the same time Watson also learns that very large reward has been offered to a professor if he can find another person with the surname Garrideb.

The Cardboard Box
Broadcast: April 11th, 1994
Writers: T.R. Bowen
Director: Sarah Hellings

Having been employed to investigate the case of a missing sister, Sherlock Holmes is brought in again when a grisly gift of a box containing two human ears turns up at the house of his client.

Miss Sherlock:
Series One Episodes

The First Case
Broadcast: April 27th, 2018
Writers: Amane Marumo, Yôsuke Masaike & Jun'ichi Mori
Director: Jun'ichi Mori

Wato joins consulting detective Sherlock to investigate the case of the mysteriously exploding stomach

Sachiko's Mustache
Broadcast: May 4th, 2018
Writers: Amane Marumo, Mami Oikawa & Jun'ichi Mori
Director: Jun'ichi Mori

The owner of an expensive painting asks Sherlock for help when a vandal draws a moustache on it.

Lily of the Valley
Broadcast: May 11th, 2018
Writers: Nobuaki Kotani, Mami Oikawa & Jun'ichi Mori
Director: Jun'ichi Mori

Reiko Haitani's identity is stolen by somebody who needs to break into the pharmaceutical lab, and a man is tortured into revealing details of his "anti-fear" drug.

The Wakasugi Family
Broadcast: May 18th, 2018
Writers: Nobuaki Kotani, Yôsuke Masaike & Jun'ichi Mori
Director: Yûsuke Taki

Sherlock is needed to help solve the horrific mystery of a mother who appears to be sucking her daughter's blood.

The Missing Bride
Broadcast: May 25th, 2018
Writers: Nobuaki Kotani, Amane Marumo, Yôsuke Masaike & Jun'ichi Mori
Director: Yûsuke Taki

Wato is suffering from PTSD but still helps Sherlock solve the puzzle of the bride who vanished after her wedding ceremony.

Stella Maris
Broadcast: June 1st, 2018
Writers: Nobuaki Kotani, Amane Marumo, Yôsuke Masaike & Jun'ichi Mori
Director: Yûsuke Taki

An ear is sent in the post to Yuichi Takayama and Sherlock also investigates the truth behind Stella Maris

Stolen Virus
Broadcast: June 8th, 2018
Writers: Amane Marumo, Mami Oikawa & Jun'ichi Mori
Director: Takashi Matsuo

Sherlock is on the run from the police and must also stop a deadly virus from infecting and potentially wiping out all of Tokyo.

The Dock
Broadcast: June 8th, 2018
Writers: Nobuaki Kotani, Amane Marumo,

Mami Oikawa & Jun'ichi Mori
Director: Yûsuke Taki

Wato seeks some help after the death of Toru, and Sherlock tries to stop the plans for a new nuclear bomb from falling into the wrong hands.

No Place like Holmes:

Series One Episodes

Moving Forward
Broadcast: May 8th, 2010

When on the trail for the Hound of the Baskervilles once more, a strange occurrence catapults Holmes and Watson into the future, changing their lives forever.

Old Habits Die Hard
Broadcast: June 6th, 2010

Adjusting to life in a new century, Holmes finds a new home, housekeeper and case with Watson.

The Dubious Spiritualist
Broadcast: September 26th, 2010

A woman is tricked into giving a con artist her antique watch and so she comes to visit Holmes with her sister to see if he can retrieve it. But the more he investigates the more he learns about his client and himself.

Holmes in Time for Christmas
Broadcast: December 18th, 2010

Holmes sits in his chair and tells Watson one of the stories from his Great Hiatus which involves his brother, Irene Adler and some Christmas themed killings.

Series Two Episodes

The Two Fold Bond
Broadcast: March 3rd, 2011

When Miss Isabelle Kensington's fiance goes missing she employs Holmes to investigate. But all is not what it appears on the surface.

The Absent Phantom
Broadcast: May 26th, 2011

A man suspects that he is being haunted by his dead wife who moves objects and attacks him during the night. He calls for Holmes and Watson to investigate but the explanation isn't as spooky as it seems.

The Creature in the Rye
Broadcast: October 1st, 2011

Holmes recounts another tale from his Hiatus Years to Watson, this time it involves his brother, a strange beast and a kidnaped minister's daughter.

Hats Off Mr Holmes
Broadcast: December 22nd, 2011

All Sherlock Holmes wants for Christmas is an interesting case to solve. He gets his wish when a blood-stained hat comes into his possession.

Series Three Episodes

Red Rising
Broadcast: July 21st, 2012

Miss Blake has had enough of stuffed shirts, and wants a change. However, everybody soon realises that a change of scenery is the least of their problems.

Reign Will Fall
Broadcast: November 3rd, 2012

The "Red-Headed League," a gang of vicious criminals, tries to uncover Sherlock's past. Meanwhile a new case takes Holmes and Watson back to school

Dialysis Murder
Broadcast: March 31st, 2013

When Daniel Moonshine Digweed is released from jail after serving time for attacking a lab technician, the same day the technician is found murdered, Digweed is the obvious suspect, but Sherlock Holmes isn't so sure.

Series Four Episodes

Dawn of the Red
Broadcast: August 26th, 2013

The "Red-Headed League" criminal gang finally gets a breakthrough in finding out about Sherlock Holmes's past. All they have to do is infiltrate Miss Constance's former workplace "The Bruce Stock Academy."

Once Upon a Time
Broadcast: October 27th, 2013

Madeline Chambers stumbles across the diaries of Professor Moriarty and reads an entry from 1889 where Holmes attempts to solve a Rumplestiltskin-inspired crime.

Heat of the Moment
Broadcast: December 24th, 2013

A military building is broken into by two Russian spies who manage to steal war plans. For the safety of the country, Holmes and Watson are tasked with their return.

A Study in Secrets
Broadcast: February 22nd, 2014

The "Red-Headed League" gang returns and the members' attention is caught by a house filled with treasures. Unfortunately for them, however, Sherlock Holmes has been hired to ensure they are kept safe.

Series Five Episodes

The Sign of Things to Come
Broadcast: September 30th, 2015

Holmes and Watson go on a treasure hunt after it is discovered that Jonathan Small might not have thrown the Agra treasure into the Thames.

Truth or Date
Broadcast: October 31st, 2015

Miss Blake drags Sherlock to a speed-dating evening and, as if that isn't bad enough, he confides in Miss Madeline Chambers about his secret past even though he is not sure how she may use the knowledge against him.

Ashes to Assets
Broadcast: November 28th, 2015

When the urn containing her father's ashes is stolen, Faith Endicott turns to Holmes and Watson for help. As they investigate they discover that this is not an isolated incident.

Dough or Die
Broadcast: December 17th, 2015

Food poisoning keeps recurring in a small bakery but no evidence of virus or bacteria can be found. When Holmes investigates, what he uncovers means he is forced to be judge, jury and executioner.

Series Six Episodes

The Walls Have Eyes
Broadcast: December 30th, 2016

When money goes missing from the vault of an aristocrat, Holmes is called in to investigate. As he does so, Agent Pinkerton and PC Burke try to dig for dirt in Holmes' secret past.

The Penultimate Problem
Broadcast: January 30th, 2017

Agent Pinkerton and PC Burke are convinced that Sherlock Holmes was brought to present-day Britain in a time machine and they gather their closest allies in order to force his hand to confess.

Quid Pro Qu
Broadcast: February 28th, 2017

After a big falling out, Holmes and Watson's friendship is in tatters, and Madeline has been kidnaped. Sherlock Holmes has to decide what lengths he will go to in order to set everything right.

Series Seven Episodes

The Surrey Vampire
Broadcast: February 28th, 2018

Sherlock Holmes is brought in to investigate when three men are found murdered with all of the blood drained from their bodies. Is it a vampire or somebody closer to home?

The Hesitant Highwayman
Broadcast: March 22nd, 2018

Three highway robberies occur in an hour. Sherlock Holmes and Inspector Lestrade investigate and wonder if there is more going on than simple robbery.

Holmes is Where the Heart is
Broadcast: April 6th, 2018

Holmes may be getting his facts muddled up with his feelings as he starts to despise Miss Blake's new boyfriend. After trying to convince her that the boyfriend is not what he seems, Sherlock has to examine himself as well as his "case."

Priklyucheniya Sherloka Khomsa i doktora Vatsona (The Adventures of Sherlock Holmes and Dr Watson):

Episode List:

King of Blackmailers
Broadcast: 1980

At the Diogenes Club, Mycroft Holmes asks Sherlock to help Lady Eva Blackwell who is being blackmailed by the evil Charles Augustus Milverton.

Mortal Fight
Broadcast: 1980

The criminal underclass, and in particular Professor Moriarty, are angry at Sherlock Holmes for removing one of their lucrative sources of income (Milverton's blackmail money). A battle to the death ensues at the Reichenbach falls between Moriarty and Holmes.

The Hunt for the Tiger
Broadcast: 1980

Dr. Watson is the executor of Sherlock Holmes' will and final note goodbye. But when a lord is murdered under suspicious circumstances, Holmes triumphantly returns.

The Real Adventures of Sherlock Jones and Proctor Watson:

Series One Episodes:

Double Duped
Broadcast: January 4th, 1987
Writer: Paul D. Marks
Director: Leo Eaton

Sherlock Jones and Proctor Watson use their skills to help prove that Bryan and Teddy are not involved in buying or selling illegal video tapes.

The Great Hot Dog Caper
Broadcast: January 11th, 1987
Writer: Paul D. Marks
Director: Leo Eaton

Teddy and Bryan ask for Sherlock's help when exotic bird eggs start to vanish from the zoo.

Too Many 100s
Broadcast: January 18th, 1987
Writer: Paul D. Marks
Director: Leo Eaton

Bryan and Teddy have been accused of cheating in class so Sherlock Jones and

Proctor Watson use the latest technology to catch the real cheaters.

The Case of the Dog Gone Wrong
Broadcast: January 25th, 1987
Writer: Paul D. Marks
Director: Leo Eaton

When the neighbourhood dogs start to go missing Sherlock and Bryan start looking for clues. The investigation takes on a more personal note when Proctor also vanishes.

Hard Luck Harold
Broadcast: January 25th, 1987
Writer: Paul D. Marks
Director: Leo Eaton

The most unlucky boy thinks his luck has changed when he finds a wallet full of money. Bryan and Teddy need to investigate a missing Civil War statue and start to wonder if the two things are linked.

The Case of the Wanetka Giant
Broadcast: February 8th, 1987
Writer: Paul D. Marks
Director: Leo Eaton

Tensions run high between Sherlock, Proctor and Bryan and it's all to do with a strange 11-foot petrified giant that may be buried in the outskirts of town.

The Case of Lynn's Dangerous Admirer
Broadcast: February 22nd, 1987
Writer: Paul D. Marks
Director: Leo Eaton

Bryan's sister, Lynn, starts receiving some scary and mysterious phone calls. Could it be that Bryan's practical joking has gone too far?

The Case of the Wilted Witness
Broadcast: March 1st, 1987
Writer: Paul D. Marks
Director: Leo Eaton

There is a criminal causing trouble at school who has been nicknamed The School Locker Bandit. Could the plants provide Sherlock and Bryan with the answers they are looking for?

The Case of the Unfair Science Fair
Broadcast: March 1st, 1987

Writer: Paul D. Marks
Director: Leo Eaton

Teddy is accused of sabotaging the school science fair projects so Sherlock and Bryan use their computer to re-enact the events which lead to the projects being destroyed.

Return of Sherlock Holmes:

Series One Episodes:

The Empty House
Broadcast: July 9th, 1986
Writer: John Hawkesworth
Director: Leo Eaton

Believed to be dead, Sherlock Holmes surprises Doctor Watson with his return. He now needs to solve the murder of Ronald Adair and prevent his own murder at the hands of Sebastian Moran, Moriarty's second-in-command.

The Abbey Grange
Broadcast: July 16th, 1986
Writers: John Hawkesworth
 & T.R. Bowen
Director: Peter Hammond

When a bruised and battered wife is found bound next to the body of her dead husband, it poses more questions than it answers. Holmes finds the answer in the empty wine glasses.

The Second Stain
Broadcast: July 23rd, 1986
Writer: John Hawkesworth
Director: John Bruce

The Prime Minister asks Holmes to help locate some politically delicate documents. But when a blood stain on a rug at the scene of a murder doesn't match the stain on the floor, Holmes suspects the thief is closer than they may think.

The Musgrave Ritual
Broadcast: July 30th, 1986
Writers: John Hawkesworth
& Jeremy Paul
Director: David Carson

A piece of paper detailing a ritual passed down through generations may hold the answer to the disappearance of a maid and a butler. Holmes must figure out the puzzle which should lead to the solution.

The Man with the Twisted Lip
Broadcast: August 6th, 1986
Writers: John Hawkesworth
& Alan Plater
Director: Patrick Lau

A woman believes that her husband has been kidnapped and murdered above an opium den. However, the filthy bigger who has been locked up as a suspect may hold the key to finding the husband.

The Priory School
Broadcast: August 13th, 1986
Writers: John Hawkesworth
& T.R. Bowen
Director: John Madden
The young son of a powerful duke vanishes, believed kidnaped, from his school. Holmes uncovers a plot steeped in family secrecy.

The Six Napoleons
Broadcast: August 20th, 1986
Writers: John Hawkesworth
& John Kane
Director: David Carson

Lestrade informs Holmes that there have been a string of crimes all involving smashed busts of Napoleon. When a murder takes place, Holmes rushes to find the last bust as well as the murderer.

Feature Special:

The Sign of Four
Broadcast: December 29th, 1987
Writer: John Hawkesworth
Director: David Carson

A young woman receives a precious pearl every year and has now received a note which indicates she may be entitled to more. A murder brings to light a terrible past of theft, deception and the terrible fate of the young woman's lost father.

Series Two Episodes:

The Devil's Foot
Broadcast: April 6th, 1988
Writers: John Hawkesworth
& Gary Hopkins
Director: Ken Hannam

Whilst Sherlock Holmes recovers with Doctor Watson in Cornwall, he is drawn into the mysterious death of a woman and the sudden madness of her brothers in the village. When the last brother dies in similar circumstances Holmes must investigate, regardless of Watson's disapproval.

Silver Blaze
Broadcast: April 13th, 1988
Writer: John Hawkesworth
Director: Brian Mills
Holmes and Watson are brought in to investigate a murder and the disappearance of the prized race horse Silver Blaze. The solution is the curious incident of the dog in the night-time.

Wisteria Lodge
Broadcast: April 20th, 1988
Writers: John Hawkesworth
& Jeremy Paul
Director: Peter Hammond

A man is arrested for the murder of a Spanish cartographer who went missing, along with his servants, from a rented house. What Holmes discovers is a litany of political violence, kidnap and more murder.

The Bruce-Partington Plans
Broadcast: April 27th, 1988
Writer: John Hawkesworth
Director: John Gorrie

Sherlock's brother Mycroft enlists his help to locate the missing plans which are vital in the construction of a new submarine. A body on the rail tracks leads to a deeper and more complicated discovery involving espionage.

Feature Special:

The Hound of the Baskervilles
Broadcast: August 31st, 1988
Writer: John Hawkesworth
& T.R. Bowen
Director: Brian Mills

When the last heir to the Baskerville fortune is threatened by the same curse which has befallen his predecessors. Holmes and Watson travel to Dartmoor to solve the mystery of the monstrous hound.

Sherlock:

Series One Episodes:

A Study in Pink
Broadcast: July 25th, 2010
Writers: Steven Moffat & Mark Gatiss
Director: Paul McGuigan

After returning from the war, Doctor John Watson is introduced to Sherlock Holmes and assists him in trying to catch a fiendish serial killer who is making his murders look like suicides.

The Blind Banker
Broadcast: August 1st, 2010
Writers: Steven Moffat, Mark Gatiss
& Steve Thompson
Director: Euros Lyn

Mysterious symbols are being found at murder scenes, most in impossible locations. Holmes and Watson have to figure out the code to catch and stop the Chinese crime syndicate.

The Great Game
Broadcast: August 1st, 2010
Writers: Steven Moffat & Mark Gatiss
Director: Paul McGuigan

Moriarty is setting Sherlock timed tasks with deadly consequences but Mycroft would rather his brother solve the mystery of the body on the train tracks.

Series Two Episodes:

A Scandal in Belgravia
Broadcast: January 1st, 2012
Writers: Steven Moffat & Mark Gatiss
Director: Paul McGuigan

The Woman, Irene Adler, has some compromising pictures of a member of the Royal family. Sherlock needs to find the phone with the pictures and stop her from making a dent in the British budget.

The Hounds of Baskerville
Broadcast: January 8th, 2012
Writers: Steven Moffat & Mark Gatiss
Director: Paul McGuigan

Sherlock and John travel to Dartmoor in order to help a young man who is being terrorised by the memory of a hound who killed his father. After spending time at the Baskerville Research Station, more wrongdoing is uncovered.

The Reichenbach Fall
Broadcast: January 15th, 2012
Writers: Steven Moffat, Steve Thompson & Mark Gatiss
Director: Toby Haynes

Jim Moriarty hatches a plan to seek revenge on Sherlock Holmes and destroy his reputation. The only solution is for Sherlock to jump off the roof of St. Bart's hospital.

Series Three Episodes:

Many Happy Returns
Broadcast: December 24th, 2013
Writers: Steven Moffat & Mark Gatiss
Director: Not credited

This is a mini-episode lasting only 7 minutes. Anderson tries to convince Lestrade that Sherlock Holmes is alive and well and solving crimes around the world. Lestrade visits John with a box of Sherlock's belongings including a video Sherlock made for John's Birthday.

The Empty Hearse
Broadcast: January 1st, 2014
Writers: Steven Moffat & Mark Gatiss
Director: Jeremy Lovering

Sherlock Holmes is called back to London by Mycroft to help prevent a terrorist attack. After the violent shock of seeing his friend back from the dead, Doctor Watson helps investigate and locate the terrorist bomb.

The Sign of Three
Broadcast: January 5th, 2014
Writers: Steven Moffat, Steve Thompson & Mark Gatiss
Director: Colm McCarthy

A murder is going to be committed during John and Mary's wedding and it's up to Sherlock to figure out the intended victim.

His Last Vow
Broadcast: January 12th, 2014
Writers: Steven Moffat & Mark Gatiss
Director: Nick Hurran

Media tycoon and blackmailer, Charles Augustus Magnussen, sets his sights on John's wife, Mary, a former assassin who has already shot Sherlock in the chest. Sherlock and John visit his home which leads to Sherlock taking drastic action to solve the problem.

Feature Special:

The Abominable Bride
Broadcast: January 1st, 2016
Writers: Steven Moffat & Mark Gatiss
Director: Douglas Mackinnon

Doctor Watson meets Sherlock Holmes once more in the 1890s to solve the case of a mysterious bride ghost who is on a killing spree. The episode turns out to be in the mind of a drug-addled Holmes, who has been sent away by Mycroft.

Series four episodes:

The Six Thatchers
Broadcast: January 1st, 2017

Writers: Steven Moffat & Mark Gatiss
Director: Rachel Talalay

A criminal is destroying the busts of Margaret Thatcher but when Sherlock finds the culprit he uncovers an AGRA hard drive rather than a pearl. The perpetrator of the crime attempts to kill Holmes but he is saved by Mary who pays the ultimate price for her actions.

The Lying Detective
Broadcast: January 8th, 2017
Writers: Steven Moffat & Mark Gatiss
Director: Nick Hurran

In a drug-fuelled haze Sherlock Holmes goes up against media darling Culverton Smith. John Watson has to put aside his feelings of betrayal and save Holmes from Smith who is, in reality, a serial killer.

The Final Problem
Broadcast: January 15th, 2017
Writers: Steven Moffat & Mark Gatiss
Director: Benjamin Caron
The discovery of another Holmes sibling, Eurus, unleashes dark secrets. Kept in a secure prison, Eurus puts into place her devious plan to destroy her family and their friends.

Sherlock Holmes 1954 – 55:

Series One Episodes
The Case of the Cunningham Heritage
Broadcast: October 18th, 1954
Writer: Sheldon Reynolds
Director: Jack Gage

Doctor Watson first meets Sherlock Holmes and assists him in proving the innocence of a young woman accused of murder.

The Case of Lady Bery
Broadcast: October 25th, 1954

Writer: Sheldon Reynolds
Director: Jack Gage

Lady Beryl confesses to a murder but Holmes is not convinced she is telling the truth. He and Watson set out to reveal the identity of the real killer

The Case of the Pennsylvania Gun
Broadcast: November 1st, 1954
Writer: Sheldon Reynolds
Director: Sheldon Reynolds
A locked castle murder sees Holmes and Watson travelling to Sussex to solve the mystery.

The Case of the Texas Cowgirl
Broadcast: November 8th, 1954
Writers: Charles Early & Joseph Early
Director: Steve Previn
A man is found dead in the hotel room of a rodeo cowgirl, she turns to Holmes and Watson to find the killer.

The Case of the Belligerent Ghost
Broadcast: November 15th, 1954
Writer: Charles Early
Director: Sheldon Reynolds

When Doctor Watson is convinced he has been attacked by the ghost of Albert Higgins, Holmes finds a connection between that and a forged painting at Pembroke Museum.

The Case of the Shy Ballerina
Broadcast: November 22nd, 1954
Writers: Sheldon Reynolds & Charles Early
Director: Sheldon Reynolds

A case of mistaken identity and murder as Watson's hat is found at a crime scene. To further arouse suspicion, Watson is also wearing the coat of a murdered man.

The Case of the Winthrop Legend
Broadcast: November 29th 1954
Writer: Harold Jack Bloom & Sheldon Reynolds
Director: Jack Gage

Winthrop family legend states that any family member who finds five coins is doomed to die. Holmes and Watson separate fact from fiction

The Case of the Blind Man's Bluff
Broadcast: December 6th, 1954
Writers: Sheldon Reynolds & Lou Morheim
Director: Sheldon Reynolds

After a chicken's foot is found at two separate murders, Lestrade employs the help of Sherlock Holmes to find the perpetrator.

The Case of Harry Crocker
Broadcast: December 13th, 1954
Writers: Sheldon Reynolds & Lou Morheim
Director: Sheldon Reynolds

When escape artist Harry Crocker is accused of murdering a chorus girl, Holmes and Watson's attention falls on a jealous man.

The Mother Hubbard Case
Broadcast: December 20th, 1954
Writer: Lou Morheim
Director: Jack Gage

A murderer uses a young girl to lure his victims into an empty house which is discovered by Holmes after taking on the case of Margaret Martini's vanished fiancé

The Case of the Red-Headed League
Broadcast: December 27th, 1954
Writer: Lou Morheim
Director: Sheldon Reynolds
A shopkeeper comes to Holmes after the League of Red-Headed Men' is suddenly dissolved.

The Case of the Shoeless Engineer
Broadcast: January 3rd, 1955
Writer: Harold Jack Bloom
Director: Steve Previn

An injured man carrying an unconscious lady disturbs Holmes and Watson's day in the country. Back in London he tells of how he has escaped some deadly dangerous clutches

The Case of the Split Ticket
Broadcast: January 10th, 1955
Writer: Lou Morheim
Director: Steve Previn

Holmes is asked to find the man who possesses the last piece of a sweepstake ticket but, instead, Holmes suspects fraud.

The Case of the French Interpreter
Broadcast: January 17th, 1955
Writer: Lou Morheim
Director: Steve Previn

A French interpreter calls on Watson to fetch Holmes after he was employed by dangerous kidnapers. The identity of the man needs to be found before it's too late.

The Case of the Singing Violin
Broadcast: January 24th, 1955
Writer: Kay Krausse
Director: Steve Previn

Guy Durham sends his step-daughter insane by playing ghostly violin music in order to take her fortune. Holmes solves the puzzle before she is murdered like her poor fiancée, James Winant.

The Case of the Greystone Inscription
Broadcast: January 31st, 1955
Writers: Gertrude Fass & George Fass
Director: Steve Previn

Holmes and Watson are called to Greystone Castle when a woman's fiancée goes missing. All of this leads to the discovery of treachery and King Richard II's possessions.

The Case of the Laughing Mummy
Broadcast: February 7th, 1955
Writer: Charles Early
Director: Sheldon Reynolds

Strange laughter is coming from an ancient Egyptian mummy at a manor house but Holmes finds the cause is more devilish murder than spectre at the Manor.

The Case of the Thistle Killer
Broadcast: February 14th, 1955
Writers: Charles Early & Joseph Early
Director: Steve Previn

Lestrade is instructed to employ the help of Holmes and Watson after three thistles are found next to murder victims.

The Case of the Vanished Detective
Broadcast: February 21st, 1955
Writers: Charles Early & Joseph Early
Director: Steve Previn

Watson is worried about the safety of Sherlock Holmes who has gone missing. He is, in fact, working undercover as a shopkeeper in order to catch an escaped convict.

The Case of the Careless Suffragette
Broadcast: February 28th, 1955
Writers: Charles Early & Joseph Early
Director: Steve Previn

A suffragette works with an anarchist who acquires a bomb shaped like a croquet ball. When the bomb explodes prematurely, Holmes must find the real murderer.

The Case of the Reluctant Carpenter
Broadcast: March 7th, 1955
Writers: Sidney Morse & Sheldon Reynolds
Director: Steve Previn

An extortionist has planted a bomb somewhere in London. Using deduction and forensic evidence, Holmes learns the site of the next bombing and rushes to find it before it detonates.

The Case of the Deadly Prophecy
Broadcast: March 14th, 1955
Writers: Gertrude Fass & George Fass
Director: Sheldon Reynolds

Holmes and Watson visit a school where a young boy has started sleepwalking. The mystery starts when he writes the names of faculty members on the church steps and they are later found dead.

The Case of the Christmas Pudding
Broadcast: April 4th, 1955
Writers: Gertrude Fass & George Fass
Director: Steve Previn

Before his execution, John Norton swears he will have his revenge on Holmes. When Norton escapes, thanks to what is hidden inside a Christmas pudding, Holmes goes after his accomplice.

The Night Train Riddle
Broadcast: April 11th, 1955
Writer: Lou Morheim
Director: Steve Previn

When a boy goes missing on a train after arguing with his father, Holmes and Watson investigate which leads to a rather unfortunate outcome.

The Case of the Violent Suitor
Broadcast: April 18th, 1955
Writer: Lou Morheim
Director: Steve Previn

An advice columnist, Alex Doogle, advises a young woman to break up with her violent fiancée but when he is attacked, he turns to Holmes and Watson for help

The Case of the Baker Street Nursemaids
Broadcast: April 25th, 1955
Writers: Sheldon Reynolds & Joseph Victor
Director: Sheldon Reynolds

A baby is left on the doorstep of 221b Baker Street by a woman who fears it will be kidnaped like her husband. When Watson is attacked the real motive of the kidnaping, acquiring U-Boat plans, is uncovered.

The Case of the Perfect Husband
Broadcast: May 2nd, 1955
Writer: Hamilton Keener
Director: Steve Previn

A rich art collector threatens to kill his wife at 9 p.m. on their first wedding anniversary. Holmes devises a plan to catch the killer before her time runs out.

The Case of the Jolly Hangman
Broadcast: May 9th, 1955
Writers: Charles Early & Joseph Early
Director: Steve Previn

A travelling salesman is found hanging in his hotel room but his widow believes there is more to it than suicide. Holmes and Watson start their investigation in which they suspect there has been a covered-up murder.

The Case of the Impostor Mystery
Broadcast: May 16th, 1955
Writer: Lou Morheim
Director: Steve Previn

When Holmes leaves London an imposter poses as the Great Detective and causes havoc. Holmes and Watson go undercover to catch him.

The Case of the Eiffel Tower
Broadcast: May 23rd, 1955
Writer: Roger Emerson Garris
Director: Steve Previn

Lestrade finds a mysterious code in the clothing of a murdered man and employs Holmes to solve the riddle which leads them to Paris.

The Case of the Exhumed Client
Broadcast: May 30th, 1955
Writers: Charles Early & Joseph Early
Director: Steve Previn

Holmes and Watson investigate the murder of Sir Charles who put in his will that his death should be investigated by Holmes. After arsenic is found in the Sir Charles's body Holmes must eliminate the large number of people who wanted him dead.

The Case of the Impromptu Performance
Broadcast: June 6th, 1955
Writer: Lou Morheim
Director: Steve Previn

A man is to be executed in the morning and uses his last request to ask Sherlock Holmes to prove his innocence.

The Case of the Baker Street Bachelors
Broadcast: June 20th, 1955
Writers: Roger Emerson Garris & Joseph Victor
Director: Steve Previn

Holmes and Watson join a lonely-hearts club in order to investigate the blackmailing of a political figure however, Holmes himself is incarcerated.

The Case of the Royal Murder
Broadcast: May 27th, 1955
Writers: Charles Early & Joseph Early
Director: Steve Previn

Holmes and Watson are invited to spend a weekend at an estate in the Balkans as a reward for solving a case. During their stay a prince is murdered and the host is the prime suspect. Holmes and Watson must expose the culprit and avert a war.

The Case of the Haunted Gainsborough
Broadcast: July 4th, 1955
Writers: Charles Early & Joseph Early
Director: Steve Previn

Mr. McGregor asks for the help of Holmes and Watson as a mysterious ghost appears before him. This could be connected to the fact that he will lose his family home if he does not make a mortgage payment by midnight.

The Case of the Neurotic Detective
Broadcast: July 11th, 1955
Writer: Lou Morheim
Director: Steve Previn

Watson starts to believe that Holmes may be a criminal mastermind after he links him to a number of thefts in London.

The Case of the Unlucky Gambler
Broadcast: July 18th, 1955
Writer: Lou Morheim
Director: Steve Previn

A young boy asks for Holmes to help find his missing father who turns out to be a gambler on the run from his creditors.

The Case of the Diamond Tooth
Broadcast: September 19th, 1955
Writer: Lou Morheim
Director: Steve Previn

Watson finds a diamond tooth but the body of a murdered man is found close by and Lestrade asks him to find the killer.

The Case of the Tyrant's Daughter
Broadcast: October 17th, 1955
Writer: Roger Emerson Garris
Director: Steve Previn

A chemist is accused of murdering his fiancée's stepfather who disapproves of their relationship. Holmes believes he is innocent and sets out to prove the fact.

Sherlock Holmes 1964 – 68:

Series one episodes:

The Speckled Band
Broadcast: May 18th, 1964
Writer: Giles Cooper
Director: Robin Midgley

Miss Stoner asks Sherlock Holmes for help as she fears that her guardian Grimesby Roylott may be trying to harm her the way she suspects he harmed her sister.

The Illustrious Client
Broadcast: February 20th, 1965
Writer: Giles Cooper
Director: Peter Sasdy

Violet Merville is to be married to the sinister Baron Gruner and cannot be persuaded that she is in mortal danger. It is up to Holmes and Watson to find a way to persuade her.

The Devil's Foot
Broadcast: February 27th, 1965
Writer: Giles Cooper
Director: Max Varnel

Whilst in Cornwall Holmes and Watson learn of the mysterious death of Brenda Tregennis and the madness of her two brothers. Their investigation turns up an unexpected revenge plot and a near-death experience for the both of them.

The Copper Beeches
Broadcast: March 6th, 1965
Writers: Anthony Read & Vincent Tilsley
Director: Gareth Davies

Violet Hunter is employed by Mr. Rucastle as a governess but is suspicious after her new employer asks her to do a variety of odd tasks, including sitting in a window wearing a blue dress.

The Red-Headed League
Broadcast: March 13th, 1965
Writer: Anthony Read
Director: Peter Duguid
Red-headed shopkeeper Jabez Wilson visits Holmes to investigate the disbanding of the Red-Headed League. When Holmes discovers the location of Wilson's shop, all becomes clear.

The Abbey Grange
Broadcast: March 20th, 1965
Writer: Clifford Witting
Director: Peter Cregeen

Holmes is asked to investigate the death of Sir Eustace Brackenstall who is believed to have been murdered by a gang of thieves. However, Holmes believes that explanation to be far too convenient and endeavours to uncover the painful truth.

The Six Napoleons
Broadcast: March 27th, 1965
Writer: Giles Cooper
Director: Gareth Davies

Somebody is smashing up busts of Napoleon Bonaparte and whilst Watson believes it to be the work of a monomaniac, Holmes suspects the reason is far more sinister.

The Man with the Twisted Lip
Broadcast: April 3rd, 1965
Writers: Anthony Read & Jan Read
Director: Eric Tayler

Mrs. St. Clair comes to Holmes believing she witnessed her husband being murdered in an opium den. Holmes turns his attention to the beggar, Hugh Boone, who may hold the key to solving the mystery.

The Beryl Coronet
Broadcast: April 10th, 1965
Writers: Nicholas Palmer & Anthony Read
Director: Max Varnel

A notable customer has left a beryl-encrusted coronet as security against a large loan. But when the banker believes that his son has attempted to steal it, he calls in Sherlock Holmes who suspects the blame should be placed elsewhere.

The Bruce-Partington Plans
Broadcast: April 17th, 1965
Writer: Giles Cooper
Director: Shaun Sutton

Mycroft Holmes brings in his brother Sherlock to solve the mystery of a dead government official found on the railway track with secret submarine plans in his pocket. How did he get there and where was he going?

Charles Augustus Milverton
Broadcast: April 24th, 1965
Writers: Anthony Read & Clifford Witting
Director: Philip Dudley

Lady Eva Blackwell asks Sherlock Holmes to try to negotiate with the famous blackmailer Charles Augustus Milverton on her behalf. But when Holmes and Watson break into his house to find the letters, things take an unexpected and deadly turn.

The Retired Colourman
Broadcast: May 1st, 1965
Writers: Anthony Read & Jan Read
Director: Michael Hayes

Josiah Amberley employs Holmes to find his wife whom he has accused of stealing his money and running away with a lover. Watson is sent on a wild goose chase whilst Holmes searches the house and uncovers a far more sinister plot.

The Disappearance of Lady Frances Carfax
Broadcast: May 8th, 1965
Writer: Vincent Tilsley
Director: Shaun Sutton

Lady Frances Carfax goes missing whilst travelling and suspicion falls on a missionary holy man who is, in reality, a jewel thief and criminal. Holmes must rush to her rescue before a terrible fate befalls her.

Series two episodes:

The Second Stain
Broadcast: September 9th, 1968
Writer: Jennifer Stuart
Director: Henri Safran

The Prime Minister visits Sherlock Holmes to investigate the case of the politician's wife, the blackmailer and a witnessed murder. All becomes clear after the bloodstain on the rug isn't in the same position as the one on the floor.

The Dancing Men
Broadcast: September 16th, 1968
Writers: Michael Hardwick & Mollie Hardwick
Director: William Sterling

Hilton Cubitt employs Sherlock Holmes to investigate a number of stick figure drawings which are having an adverse effect on his wife. Holmes must figure out the code before it claims its first victim.

A Study in Scarlet
Broadcast: September 23rd, 1968
Writer: Hugh Leonard
Director: Henri Safran

After finding the word "Rache" written on the wall in blood, Lestrade calls in Sherlock Holmes and Doctor Watson to solve the mystery of the murder.

The Hound of the Baskervilles Parts 1 & 2
Broadcast: September 30th & October 7th, 1968
Writer: Hugh Leonard
Director: Graham Evans

Holmes and Watson must protect the new Lord Baskerville from the family curse, a gigantic hound set to murder him on the moors. All is not what it seems when it comes to the Stapletons

The Boscombe Valley Mystery
Broadcast: October 14th, 1968
Writer: Bruce Stewart
Director: Viktors Ritelis

Bill McCarthy is found bludgeoned to death after an argument with his son. However, Holmes discovers that the identity of the true murderer is closer than the police may think.

The Greek Interpreter
Broadcast: October 21st, 1968
Writer: John Gould
Director: David Saire

Mr. Melas is employed by a man called Latimer as a translator, but he needs the help of Sherlock Holmes when he discovers that a man is being held against his will.

The Naval Treaty
Broadcast: October 28th, 1968
Writer: John Gould
Director: Antony Kearey

An important naval treaty is stolen from the desk of a government employee, and friend of Watson, late at night. After the man spends weeks in his sick bed, Holmes devises a plan to catch the thief red-handed.

Thor Bridge
Broadcast: November 4th, 1968
Writer: Harry Moore
Director: Antony Kearey

Neil Gibson comes to Holmes and Watson to ask them to prove the innocence of his governess after his wife was found shot dead clutching a note which reveals they met just before she died. What transpires is both sinister and devilishly clever.

The Musgrave Ritual
Broadcast: November 11th, 1968
Writer: Harry Moore
Director: Antony Kearey

When his butler vanishes, Reginald Musgrave calls in Holmes to figure out what he was doing with family documents pertaining to a family ritual. Holmes must decipher the ritual to figure out the location of the butler as well as something which is historically significant.

Black Peter
Broadcast: November 18th, 1968
Writer: Richard Harris
Director: Antony Kearey

Inspector Hopkins is stuck investigating the murder of the aggressive drunkard Peter Carey who has been killed with a harpoon. The arrested man claims he is too weak to have carried out the attack, so Holmes and Watson investigate further.

Wisteria Lodge
Broadcast: November 25th, 1968
Writer: Alexander Baron
Director: Roger Jenkins

Mr. John Scott Eccles stays overnight at Wisteria Lodge but awakens in an empty house. Later he is accused of murder and Holmes and Watson uncover a story of historical intrigue and political deception.

Shoscombe Old Place
Broadcast: December 2nd, 1968
Writer: Donald Tosh
Director: Bill Bain

John Mason asks Holmes to help him figure out the strange goings on at Shoshcombe Old Place including human remains in the furnace and a dog who has suddenly turned on its owner. All is certainly not what it seems.

The Solitary Cyclist
Broadcast: December 9th, 1968
Writer: Stanley Miller
Director: Viktors Ritelis

Violet Smith is being followed during her long bicycle rides and asks Sherlock Holmes and Doctor Watson to investigate. They must act quickly as the kind Mr. Carruthers may not be what he appears and Miss Smith's life may be in danger.

The Sign of Four
Broadcast: December 16th, 1968
Writers: Michael Hardwick & Mollie Hardwick
Director: William Sterling

Sherlock Holmes is employed by Mary Morstan to figure out who is sending her precious pearls and why. What Holmes uncovers about the death of her father adds fuel to those who are pursuing her.

The Blue Carbuncle
Broadcast: December 23rd, 1968
Writer: Stanley Miller
Director: Bill Bain

Sherlock Holmes turns down Lady Morcar's request to find her missing blue Carbuncle, but when the stone turns up in the crop of a Christmas goose, Sherlock Holmes becomes intrigued.

sHERlock Holmes

Episodes

The Adventure of Mo Money Mo Problems

An old friend of Watson's comes to her for some advice about the behaviour of her cranky landlord.

The Adventure of the Devil's Dance

During a family get-together the fun is interrupted by a murder, can Holmes and Watson investigate the circumstances surrounding the odd nature of the crime and catch the culprit?

The Adventure of Charlotte Agnes Milverton

Holmes is asked to appeal to New England's most prolific blackmailer but will it end the way Holmes thinks it will?

The Adventure of the Dreamlover

One of Watson's online friends contacts her and asks for Sherlock's help to find her missing love.

Sherlock Holmes in the 22nd Century:

<u>Series One Episodes:</u>

The Fall and Rise of Sherlock Holmes
Broadcast: September 18th, 1999
Writer: Phil Harnage

Based on the story *The Adventure of the Final Problem*, Moriarty is back from his cave tomb in Switzerland and Beth Lestrade needs to find a way to defeat the Napoleon of Crime. She needs Sherlock Holmes.

The Crime Machine
Broadcast: September 25th, 1999
Writer: Martha Moran
Directors: Robert Brousseau & Scott Heming

Based on *The Valley of Fear,* Martin Fenwick is causing a crime wave by turning innocent citizens into criminals. Holmes calls on his new network of Baker Street Irregulars for help.

The Hound of the Baskervilles
Broadcast: October 2nd, 1999
Writer: Martha Moran
Directors: Robert Brousseau & Scott Heming

Three visitors from the moon are attacked by a phantom hound and Holmes learns of Moriarty's plan to take over the moon and the Earth.

The Adventure of the Empty House
Broadcast: October 9th, 1999
Writer: Marv Wolfman
Directors: Robert Brousseau & Scott Heming

When Holmes and Moriarty fall into the laserwave sanitation grid they appear to just vanish into thin air. Watson and Lestrade must figure out where the pair are actually located before they are lost forever.

The Crooked Man
Broadcast: October 16th, 1999
Writers: Terence Taylor & Eleanor Burian-Mohr

Directors: Robert Brousseau & Scott Heming
Mrs. Barkley is unconscious and her husband has vanished after they are heard arguing. Holmes suspects that there is a third party who may hold all of the answers but he has to find him before it's too late.

The Adventure of the Deranged Detective
Broadcast: October 23rd, 1999
Writer: Henry Gilroy

Based on *The Adventure of the Dying Detective*, Lestrade goes on an angry rampage having been infected by nanobots. When a Chinese puzzle box shows up at 221b Baker Street, Holmes begins to develop similar symptoms. Or does he?

The Adventure of the Sussex Vampire
Broadcast: October 30th, 1999
Writer: Phil Harnage

Based on *The Adventure of the Sussex Vampire*, people are losing data after a computer vampire attacks London's computer grids. As the Irregulars and Holmes work to uncover its identity, Moriarty plans to find another partner in crime.

The Scales of Justice
Broadcast: November 6th, 1999
Writer: Ken Pontac

Based on *The Adventure of the Speckled Band*, an animal-rights movement has been blamed for stealing from GeneTech, but Holmes discovers that the solution to the puzzle is not so simple.

The Resident Patient
Broadcast: November 13th, 1999
Writer: Robert Askin

Professor Moriarty gets his hands on a new machine which changes people's DNA, and he uses it to make criminals undetectable. Holmes, Watson and Lestrade need to get it back into safe hands before it becomes impossible to identify London's criminal fraternity.

The Sign of Four
Broadcast: November 20th, 1999
Writer: Phil Harnage

Mary Morstan is summoned to the moon by a man who used to work with her father. It's been twenty years since the moonquake killed him so Holmes and Watson accompany her to find out what the former business partner wants.

The Adventure of the Dancing Men
Broadcast: November 27th, 1999
Writers: Terence Taylor & Eleanor Burian-Mohr

A dancing-man code is sent in an email and Holmes needs to crack it before things turn sinister. The Baker Street Irregulars come to see Holmes because they want to become more involved with the cases.

The Musgrave Ritual
Broadcast: December 4th, 1999
Writer: Robert Askin

The Musgrave sword is stolen from the British Museum, and Moriarty thinks he has deciphered the ritual which will lead him to the meteor where the sword came from. He needs to be stopped before he can take advantage of the sword's power.

The Adventure of the Blue Carbuncle
Broadcast: December 11th, 1999
Writer: Seth Kearsley
The number one Christmas toy is a blue carbuncle but there is much more to it than a children's play thing.

Silver Blaze
Broadcast: January 31st, 2000
Writer: Robert Askin

The racing spacecraft Silver Blaze is stolen just before it is due to compete, and probably win, the Asteroid Belt Grand Prix.

There is an array of different suspects with Holmes, Watson and Lestrade all convinced they have the culprit.

The Five Orange Pips
Broadcast: February 7th, 2000
Writer: Greg Johnson

A modern day Luddite who has rejected modern technology is poisoned and sends his son to find Sherlock Holmes to help him. However, being anti-technology he refuses to interact with the android Watson.

The Red-Headed League
Broadcast: February 14th, 2000
Writer: Martha Moran

The owner of the "Fish 'n' Virtual Reality Chips" café, Carter Wilson, is invited to become a member of the Red-Headed League. When Sherlock Holmes uncovers a plan to steal some art from the nearby National Art Gallery, the reason for the league becomes clearer.

The Man with the Twisted Lip
Broadcast: February 21st, 2000
Writer: Greg Johnson

Although a funeral took place for her husband one month before, Mrs. Lois St. Clair contacts Holmes and Watson to help find him, convinced he is still alive. The trail stops with a beggar who has a disfigured lip.

Series Two Episodes:

The Secret Safe
Broadcast: March 31st, 2000
Writers: Reed Shelly & Bruce Shelly

Based on *His Last Bow,* Ten Downing Street is broken into and an African doll is taken. The doll is a mere decoy, Holmes and Watson are really on the lookout for plans to the security systems.

The Adventure of the Second Stain
Broadcast: April 21st, 2000
Writer: Reed Shelly & Bruce Shelly

Lord Bollinger calls for the help of Sherlock Holmes after it appears some sensitive information has been taken from Mark Trenton's safe. However, it seems the key to solving the crime lays with Trenton's wife.

The Adventure of the Engineer's Thumb
Broadcast: April 21st, 2000
Writer: Ken Pontac

Moriarty's crime associate, Fenwick, plans to get his hands on blood generators which two arguing scientists are working on separately. Holmes and Watson need to stop him before he gets his hands on either of them.

The Gloria Scott
Broadcast: May 12th, 2000
Writer: Woody Creek

Victor Trevor calls on his friend, Sherlock Holmes, to decipher a cryptic message sent to his father. Holmes uncovers some unsavoury details about the father's involvement in a lunar prison hijack more than 20 years ago.

The Adventure of the Six Napoleons
Broadcast: May 19th, 2000
Writer: Martha Moran

The last of the Napoleon Excelsior ships is having its decorative crystals stolen. Sherlock Holmes realises that the thief may be after one crystal in particular which is more valuable than all of them combined.

The Adventure of the Creeping Man
Broadcast: May 26th, 2000
Writer: Martha Moran

Lestrade's friend Alice is getting married to the father of another school friend, Edith. But Alice seeks the help of Holmes and Lestrade because she is convinced she is being followed by a large gorilla. Edith, however, is convinced that Alice is just after her inheritance.

The Adventure of the Beryl Board
Broadcast: June 23rd, 2000
Writers: Eleanor Burian-Mohr &Terence Taylor

The Beryl Board, a new kind of processor, has been invented by 12-year-old Helphin-Payne. Holmes is called in when the processor is stolen from his business partner's high security home. He suspects his own son but Holmes has his suspicious elsewhere.

The Adventure of the Mazarin Chip
Broadcast: June 30th, 2000
Writer: Gildart Jackson

The Mazarin Chip, which is a voice-activated virtual reality microchip, has been stolen by Moriarty and Fenwick. The pair plan to kidnap the Prime Minister of England and crash the stock market from the comfort of their secret hideout.

A Case of Identity
Broadcast: July 21st, 2000
Writer: Robert Askin

Lestrade is ordered to partner with the new cop, Constable Abner Angel. But Holmes and Lestrade believe that his strange behaviour may be linked to the identity of the jewel thief Linus Beaumont.

Sherlock Holmes and Doctor Watson:

Series One Episodes:

A Motive for Murder
Writer: Robin Bishop & Harold Jack Bloom
Director: Freddie Francis

Successful businessman George Markham has been murdered and Holmes has been asked to investigate. Suspicion lands on the niece, Andrea, and her half-brother, Peter, who stand to gain the most from the murder

The Case of the Speckled Band
Writer: Robin Bishop & Harold Jack Bloom
Director: Freddie Francis & Sheldon Reynolds

Lady Langley asks Sherlock Holmes to accompany her to Bavaria as she feels apprehensive about her stepfather. Her sister died under suspicious circumstances after crying out about a "spotted ribbon" and if something were to happen to her, he would inherit her fortune.

Murder on a Midsummer's Eve
Writer: Robin Bishop & Michael Allen Bloom
Director: Sheldon Reynolds

Lady Warminster comes to Holmes to ask for help after her husband has been accused of murdering his associate, Albert Neale, and has now gone missing. But all is not what it seems and when Holmes exhumes the coffin of Neale, things take another unexpected turn.

Four Minus Four Is One
Writer: Robin Bishop
Director: Sheldon Reynolds

After discovering the mummy of a pharaoh, members of the research team start getting murdered and suspicion falls on the last surviving member of the team, Professor Taunton. However, there may be another person in the picture who is not quite all that he seems to be.

The Case of the Perfect Crime
Writer: Joe Morheim
Director: Roy Stevens

Holmes rejects the plea from Lestrade to help him solve a string of impossible crimes, including the theft of some of the Crown Jewels. After finding a diamond necklace in a teapot, Doctor Watson and Lestrade follow Holmes believing him to be the master criminal

The Case of Harry Rigby
Writer: Ray Allen & Sheldon Reynolds
Director: Val Guest

After the release of criminal Harry Rigby, who was in jail for bank robbery, members of his former gang start to get murdered. Police suspect Harry is murdering his accomplices in order to take their share of the stolen cash. Rigby has a solid alibi and so Holmes turns his attention to a more unexpected figure.

The Case of the Blind Man's Bluff
Writer: Robin Bishop & Joe Morheim
Director: Peter Sasdy

Murders with similar patterns appear in various locations, all leaving behind a chicken's foot tied in black ribbon. Holmes recognises the symbol as the Trinidad code for imminent death but when Holmes questions Dr Jones at the naval hospital, it brings up more questions than it answers about his past on the ship, The Gloria North.

A Case of High Security
Writer: Robin Bishop
Director: Roy Ward Baker

Lestrade rushes to find Sherlock Holmes as a terrorist threatens to blow up a government building within the hour. But Holmes sees that there is more than a possible explosion at stake.

The Case of Harry Crocker
Writer: Robin Bishop & Harold Jack Bloom
Director: Freddie Francis

Illusionist and escapologist Harry Crocker is accused of murdering a young dancer and all attempts to contain him fail due to his skill at escapology. Holmes offers his help in return for being taught an escapology trick which leads to the real murderer being identified.

The Case of the Deadly Prophecy
Writer: George Fass & Gertrude Fass
Director: Freddie Francis

A young sleepwalking child writes the names of faculty members onto the steps of a church and, in turn, they end up dead. When Sherlock Holmes is called in to investigate, his name appears on the steps but he suspects the threat is coming from the headmaster rather than a supernatural source.

The Case of the Baker Street Nursemaids
Writer: Joseph Victor
Director: Val Guest

When a baby arrives on the steps of 221b Baker Street, Holmes, Lestrade and Watson watch over it. The child belongs to a kidnaped inventor and when Watson is caught off guard, it is taken from under their noses. Holmes puts into action his plan to catch the kidnapper and prevent him from taking important government submarine blueprints.

The Case of the Purloined Letter
Writer: George Fowler & Sheldon Reynolds
Director: Val Guest

When a scandalous letter is stolen from Lord Brompton, Sherlock Holmes is called in to retrieve it before it falls into the wrong hands and jeopardizes the safety of the country.

The Case of the Travelling Killer
Writer: George Fowler
Director: Val Guest

Similar murders have occurred in Amsterdam, New York and Paris, all destinations of a travelling circus. When a trapeze artists dies by falling from her trapeze, Holmes and Watson turn their attention to the circus owner for answers.

The Case of the Sitting Target
Writer: Sheldon Reynolds
Director: Aurelio Crugnola

A testifying witness is shot and killed on the same day as the criminal he testified against, Peter Channing, is released from jail. As more witnesses are murdered. Holmes invites Channing to Baker Street where he learns of his revenge ploy. Holmes, however, is not so easily intimidated.

The Case of the Final Curtain
Writer: Joe Morhaim
Director: Val Guest

Edward Brighton, an actor and director, uses his last request to call for Sherlock Holmes to prove his innocence before he is sent to his death in the morning. Holmes investigates and discovers that perhaps something as simple as a pouch of tobacco could save a man's life.

The Case of the Three Uncles
Writer: Joe Morhaim
Director: Val Guest

When three uncles inherit the family business after Meredith Stanhope's parents die, two are murdered leading to suspicions that the remaining uncle, a serial gambler, has killed them for a greater share of the business. Holmes, however, uses Meredith's fiancé to flush out the real criminal.

The Case of the Body in the Case
Writer: Tudor Gates
Director: Roy Ward Baker

Lady Helen Fairfax comes to Sherlock Holmes for help after her fiancé is accused of committing a murder when the body of a woman is found in his luggage. The key to the murder could be held by the art dealer, Hugo Verne, in a crime which is far from an open-and-shut case.

The Case of the Deadly Tower
Writer: Joe Morhaim
Director: Roy Ward Baker

After Lord Tarlton is found murdered, Sherlock Holmes receives a letter asking him to investigate. Holmes and Watson travel to Tarlton Castle where Holmes finds himself on the receiving end of a murder attempt.

The Case of Smith & Smythe
Writer: Joe Morhaim
Director: Roy Ward Baker

The family of Jane Smith and John Smythe own businesses which are in direct competition with each other. When the warring families get out of hand, Sherlock Holmes needs to step in to resolve the issues, if only for the sake of Jane and John's impending marriage.

The Case of the Luckless Gambler
Writer: Joe Morhaim
Director: Roy Ward Baker

A young boy asks for Holmes to help find his missing father who has been reported as dead. When Holmes digs a little deeper he discovers that the man may actually be a gambler on the run from his creditors

The Case of the Shrunken Heads
Writer: Tudor Gates
Director: Val Guest

A shrunken head is sent along with a ransom note to the family of a kidnaped boy. The family agrees to pay the ransom but it seems that the kidnapper has died under suspicious circumstances and the money has vanished. Sherlock Holmes looks a little closer to home to find the real perpetrator of the crime.

The Case of Magruder's Murder
Writer: Joe Morhaim
Director: Val Guest

When police make a call of suicide, Sherlock Holmes is contacted asking to help prove that the death was actually murder. When Holmes and Watson investigate, they discover a mess of intrigue, con men and fake identities all of which leads to the capture of Sherlock Holmes who needs to make his escape before a treacherous deal is made.

The Case of the Other Ghost
Writer: Tudor Gates & Julian Fellowes
Director: Val Guest

Holmes and Watson are summoned to Kindersley House to investigate a murder. But when the client is also murdered, it is up to Holmes to figure out who is next, prevent the crime and catch the criminal.

The Case of the Close-Knit Family
Writer: Andrea Reynolds
Director: Sheldon Reynolds

Whilst Holmes and Watson stay at a hotel, due to their rooms in Baker Street being renovated, they hear of a spate of thefts. Holmes has more important matters to deal with and so Watson attempts to solve the case, however, it isn't until Holmes steps in, of course, that the matter is put to rest.

Sherlock Yack - Zoo-Détective (Sherlock Yack: Zoo-Detective):

List of Episodes:
May 4th, 2011 - December 22nd, 2012.

Qui a fracassé le kangourou?
(Who Broke the Kangaroo's Hand?)
Qui a assommé le singe hurleur?
(Who Knocked Out the Howler Monkey?)
Qui a carotté l'otarie?
(Who Robbed the Seal?)
Qui a taggué l'oiseau de paradis?
(Who Tagged the Bird of Paradise?)
Qui a repeint l'autruche?
(Who Painted the Ostrich?)
Qui a bouché la trompe de l'éléphant?
(Who Plugged Up the Elephant's Trunk?)
Qui a intoxiqué le guépard?
(Who Poisoned the Cheetah?)
Qui a écrabouillé le panda?
(Who Crushed the Panda?)
Qui a parasité le porc-épic?
(Who Bugged the Porcupine?)
Qui a pané le piranha?
(Who Wants to Fry the Piranha?)
Qui a fait éternuer le ara?
(Who Made the Parrot Sneeze?)
Qui a vandalisé le vampire?
(Who Vandalized the Vampire Bat?)
Qui a cassé la voix de la grue?
(Who Broke the Crane's Voice?)
Qui a aveuglé la girafe?
(Who Blinded the Giraffe?)
Qui a toiletté le phacochère?
(Who Cleaned Up the Warthog?)
Qui a englué l'orang-outang?
(Who Glued Up the Orangutan?)

Qui a braqué le boa?
(Who Mugged the Boa?)
Qui a harcelé le Yack?
(Who Harassed the Yak?)
Qui a saboté la machine de Mme Fennec?
(Who Sabotaged Mrs. Fennec's Machine?)
Qui a barboté le babouin?
(Who Robbed the Baboon?)
Qui a assommé le Yack?
(Who Knocked Out the Yack?)
Qui a cambriolé le Tapir?
(Who Robbed the Tapir?)
Qui a carambolé la tortue?
(Who Dented the Turtle?)
Qui a dézèbré le zèbre?
(Who Unstriped the Zebra?)
Qui a fait mourir de rire le grizzly?
(Who Choked Up the Grizzly with Laughter?)
Qui a dépouillé le héron?
(Who Stripped the Heron?)
Qui a noué la pieuvre?
(Who Knotted Up the Octopus?)
Qui a fait chanter le mainate?
(Who Blackmailed the Myna?)
Qui a taillé la roue du paon?
(Who Trimmed the Peacock?)
Qui a fait mousser Mme Hippo?
(Who Soaped Up Mrs. Hippo?)
Qui a ridiculisé le lion?
(Who Ridiculed the Lion?)
Qui a graffité hermine?
(Who graffitied Hermione?)
Qui a ensablé le gorille?
(Who Stuck the Gorilla in the Sand?)
Qui a détroussé la grue?
(Who Robbed the Crane?)
Qui a fait pleurer le croco?
(Who Made the Crocodile Cry?)
Qui a trompé l'éléphant?
(Who Trunked the Elephant?)
Qui a peinturluré la moufette?
(Who Painted Up the Skunk?)
Qui a ligoté le castor?
(Who Tied Up the Beaver?)
Qui a fait dérailler les cochons d'inde?
(Who Derailed the Guinea Pigs?)
Qui a refroidit le piranha?
(Who Cooled Off the Piranha?)
Qui a congelé Mme Pingouin?
(Who Froze Up Mrs. Penguin?)
Qui a entarté le zébu?
(Who Smeared the Zebu?)
Qui a berné monsieur Hippo?
(Who Fooled the Hippopotamus?)

Qui a fait péter la cigogne?
(Who Made the Stork Fart?)
Qui a visé le tigre?
(Who Targeted the Tiger?)

We Present Alan Wheatley as Mr Sherlock Holmes Television:

Series Episodes:

The Empty House
Broadcast: October 20th, 1951

In the midst of an investigation into the suspicious death of Ronald Adair, Doctor Watson comes face to face, once more, with Sherlock Holmes who is seemingly back from the dead.

A Scandal in Bohemia
Broadcast: October 27th, 1951

The King of Bohemia comes to Sherlock Holmes and John Watson to ask for help in the matter of a scandalous past love with the singer, Irene Adler, which could create problems during his upcoming marriage.

The Dying Detective
Broadcast: November 3rd, 1951

The sinister Culverton Smith is the only man who can save Sherlock Holmes from a deadly tropical disease. Unfortunately, Smith might just be the man who infected Holmes in the first place.

The Reigate Squires
Broadcast: November 17th, 1951

As Holmes attempts to take a break due to exhaustion, a series of strange burglaries and a murder seem keen to keep him busy.

The Red-Headed League
Broadcast: November 24th, 1951

Pawnbroker, Jabez Wilson, is welcomed into an exclusive club for gentleman who have red hair. But when his instructions to write out the encyclopedia suddenly stop, he turns to Sherlock Holmes for help.

The Second Stain
Broadcast: December 1st, 1951

A top-secret document goes missing and Holmes is tasked with finding it; however, a curious blood stain at the house of an infamous spy may hold a bigger clue to the document's whereabouts.

Young Sherlock: The Mystery of the Manor House:

Series One Episodes

The Young Master
Broadcast: October 31st, 1982

Young Sherlock arrives home from boarding school after an epidemic of typhoid. He returns, however, to find that his parents are gone, his house has been sold and he must live with his puritanical aunt and gluttonous uncle. Natty Dan, a tramp and storyteller, is found dead after leaving the new owners of the manor house and Sherlock is intrigued by the strange paw prints outside the place where his body was found.

The Gypsy Calls Again
Broadcast: November 7th, 1982

Sherlock tries to decipher the strange message left on the wall by Natty Dan before he died. A boy called Newbugs identifies the earlier animal tracks as being from a black Labrador and an invitation to the manor house reveals that the young Jason Moran is studying under a Professor Moriarty.

The Riddle of the Dummies
Broadcast: November 14th, 1982

A number of shop dummies have been brought to the manor house by Gypsies and are being used in some curious charade. A man on horseback arrives late at night and the occupants are at pains to keep it quiet. Sherlock spies a dinner party with dummies that he can't quite deduce.

A Singular Thorn
Broadcast: November 21st, 1982

Holmes starts to piece together what he knows about the new occupants at the manor house. The former officer in the Indian army, a female music hall actress impersonating Mrs. Turnbull, Jason Moran and a dog which has been trained to walk on three legs so it can carry a poisoned rose thorn. Could any of this have to do with the Munshi sent to test the fake Mrs. Turnbull on languages and classical music?

The Woman in Black
Broadcast: November 28th, 1982

John Whitney (a doctor and Sherlock's close friend) and Sherlock sneak into the tunnels that run underneath the old manor house. Once above the library, they break in to try to find some clues to the mystery. What they find is a blow pipe, an empty room with an inaccurate clock, a calendar and a room full of shop dummies set up on a the floor plan of a train.

The Glasscutter's Hand
Broadcast: December 5th, 1982

John and Sherlock watch the occupants of the manor house from their hiding place behind some theatre props. They can hardly believe their eyes as a look-alike of Queen Victoria comes out and they uncover a plot to abduct the real Queen. Their cover is blown by a friendly dog and, having been drugged, they awake in hospital nearly a week later. Or do they?

7. The Unexpected Visitors
Broadcast: December 12th, 1982

Having deduced that their hospital room was a fake and that they are still inside the manor house, Sherlock and John carry out a brave escape. Unfortunately they find themselves in a booby-trapped, airtight room which is slowly filling with deadly gas. With Newbugs out cold and a strange explosion at his aunt's house, who will be around to rescue them?

8. The Eye of the Peacock
Broadcast: December 19th, 1982

Having deduced the motive for the crime was to steal a jewel worn by Queen Victoria which belonged to the Maharaja now living in exile in Britain, Sherlock brings his adventurous school holiday to a close. But who is Moriarty and will their paths cross again?

THE CHRONOLOGY OF HOLMES & WATSON

(F) Film
(T) Television broadcast
(A) Animation/stop-motion/Puppet
(I) Internet
(C) Computer game

1900 – 1910

Sherlock Holmes Baffled
(F) – 1900 (USA)
Sherlock Holmes Uncredited

The Adventures of Sherlock Holmes AKA Held for a Ransom
(F) – 1905 (USA)
Sherlock Holmes played by Gilbert M. Anderson, Dr. Watson played by H. Kyrle Bellew

Miss Sherlock
(F) – 1907 (Finland)
Sherlock Holmes played by P. M. Arnoldy

Un Rivale di Sherlock Holmes AKA Le Rival de Sherlock Holmes AKA Rival Sherlock Holmes
(F) – 1907 (Italy)
Sherlock Holmes Uncredited

Det hemmelige Dokument AKA Sherlock Holmes im Gaskjelderen AKA Sherlock Holmes III
(F) – 1908 (Denmark)
Sherlock Holmes played by Einar Zangenberg

Ein Meisterstück von Sherlock Holmes AKA A masterpiece by Sherlock Holmes
(F) – 1908 (Germany)
Sherlock Holmes Uncredited

A Fool for Luck
(F) – 1908 (USA)
Sherlock Holmes Uncredited

Miss Sherlock
(F) – 1908 (USA)
Sherlock Holmes played by Florence Turner

Raffles Flugt Fra Fængslet AKA Sherlock Holmes II
(F) – 1908 (Denmark)
Sherlock Holmes played by Viggo Larsen

Sherlock Hochmes
(F) - 1908 (Hungary)
Sherlock Holmes played by Baumann Károly

Sherlock Holmes in the Great Murder Mystery
(F) - 1908 (USA)
Sherlock Holmes Uncredited

Sherlock Holmes i Livsfare AKA Sherlock Holmes I
(F) – 1908 (Denmark)
Sherlock Holmes played by Viggo Larsen

Amateur-Detektiv als Nacheiferer Sherlock Holmes AKA Amateur detective Disguised as Sherlock Holmes
(F) – 1909 (Germany)
Sherlock Holmes Uncredited

Den Grå Dame AKA Af Sherlock Holmes Oplevelser IV AKA Sherlock Holmes Experiences IV
(F) – 1909 (Denmark)
Sherlock Holmes played by Viggo Larsen

Detective Barock Holmes and His Hound
(F) – 1909 (France)
Sherlock Holmes Uncredited

Droske 519 AKA Cab 519
(F) – 1909 (Denmark)
Sherlock Holmes played by Viggo Larsen

The Exploits of Three-Fingered Kate
(F) – 1909 (UK)
Sherlock Holmes played by Charles Calvert as Sheerluck Finch

Il piccolo Sherlock Holmes AKA The Little Sherlock Holmes
(F) – 1909 (Italy)
Sherlock Holmes Uncredited

The Latest Triumph of Sherlock Holmes
(F) – 1909 (France)
Sherlock Holmes Uncredited

Sangerindens Diamanter AKA The Singer's Diamonds
(F) – 1909 (Denmark)
Sherlock Holmes played by Viggo Larsen

A Squeedunk Sherlock Holmes
(F) – 1909 (USA)
Sherlock Holmes Uncredited

Three-Fingered Kate: Her Second Victim, the Art Dealer
(F) – 1909 (UK)
Sherlock Holmes played by Charles Calvert as Sheerluck Finch

Arsène Lupin contra Sherlock Holmes AKA Arsène Lupin against Sherlock Holmes
(F) – 1910
Sherlock Holmes played by Viggo Larsen

Der blaue Diamant AKA The Blue Diamond
(F) – 1910 (Germany)
Sherlock Holmes played by Viggo Larsen

Die falschen Rembrandts AKA The Wrong Rembrandts
(F) – 1910 (Germany) Sherlock Holmes played by Viggo Larsen

Die Flucht AKA The Escape
(F) - 1910 (Germany)
Sherlock Holmes played by Viggo Larsen

Hemlock Hoax, the Detective
(F) – 1910 (USA)
Sherlock Holmes Uncredited

Meisterstück von Sherlock Holmes AKA Masterpiece by Sherlock Holmes
(F) – 1910 (Germany)
Sherlock Holmes Uncredited

Sangerindens Diamanter AKA The Singer's Diamonds
(F) – 1910 (Denmark) Sherlock Holmes played by Viggo Larsen

Sherlock Holmes i Bondefangerklør AKA Den Stjaalne Tegnebog AKA The Farmer's Cave
(F) – 1910 (Denmark) Sherlock Holmes played by Otto Lagoni

Three-Fingered Kate: Her Victim the Banker
(F) – 1910 (UK)
Sherlock Holmes played by Charles Calvert as Sheerluck Finch

Three-Fingered Kate: The Episode of the Sacred Elephants
(F) – 1910 (UK)
Sherlock Holmes played by Charles Calvert as Sheerluck Finch

1911 – 1920

The $500 Reward
(F) – 1911 (USA)
Sherlock Holmes Uncredited

Arsène Lupins Ende AKA Arsène Lupins Tod
(F) - 1911 (Germany)
Sherlock Holmes played by Viggo Larsen

Les Aventures de Sherlock Holmes AKA The Adventures of Sherlock Holmes
(F) – 1911 (France)
Sherlock Holmes played by Henri Gouget

A Case for Sherlock Holmes
(F) – 1911 (UK)
Sherlock Holmes Uncredited

Caught with the Goods
(F) – 1911 (USA)
Sherlock Holmes Uncredited

Den Forklædte Guvernante AKA Den Forklædte Barnepige AKA The Disguised Nanny
(F) – 1911 (Denmark)
Sherlock Holmes played by Otto Lagoni

Den Sorte Hætte AKA The Black Hood
(F) – 1911 (Denmark)
Sherlock Holmes played by Lauritz Olsen

Den sorte hand AKA Mordet i Bakerstreet AKA Medlam af den Sorte Hånd AKA The Black Hand
(F) – 1911 (Denmark)
Sherlock Holmes played by Otto Lagoni

A Desperate Lover
(F) – 1911 (USA)
Sherlock Holmes Uncredited

Ein Fall für Sherlock Holmes AKA A Case for Sherlock Holmes
(F) – 1911 (Germany)
Sherlock Holmes Uncredited

Fritzchen als Sherlock Holmes AKA Fritzchen as Sherlock
(F) – 1911 (France/Germany)
Sherlock Holmes played by Fritz Abélard as Fritz

Hotelrotterne AKA Hotelmysterierne AKA Sherlock Holmes' Sidste Bedrifter AKA Sherlock Holmes' Last Business
(F) - 1911 (Denmark)
Sherlock Holmes played by Einar Zangenberg

Little Sherlock Holmes
(F) – 1911 (France)
Sherlock Holmes Uncredited

Sherlock Holmes contra Professor Moriarty AKA Der Erbe von Bloomrod AKA The heir of Bloomrod
(F) - 1911 (Germany)
Sherlock Holmes played by Viggo Larsen

Millionobligationen AKA Milliontestamentet AKA Den Stjålne Millionobligation AKA The Stolen Million Bond
(F) -1911 (Denmark)
Sherlock Holmes played by Alwin Neuss

A Neat Trick
(F) -1911 (France)
Sherlock Holmes Uncredited

Sherlock Holmes, Jr.
(F) - 1911 (USA)
Sherlock Holmes played by Helen Anderson as Sherlock Holmes Jr.

Their First Divorce Case
(F) – 1911 (USA)
Sherlock Holmes Uncredited

Tom, Sherlock Holmes gelehriger Schüler AKA Tom, Sherlock Holmes' Docile Student
(F) – 1911 (Germany)
Sherlock Holmes Uncredited

Trailing the Counterfeiters
(F) -1911 (USA)
Sherlock Holmes Uncredited

At It Again
(F) - 1912 (USA)
Sherlock Holmes Uncredited

Baby Sherlock
(F) – 1912 (USA)
Sherlock Holmes Uncredited

A Bear Escape
(F) – 1912 (USA) Sherlock Holmes Uncredited

The Beryl Coronet
(F) – 1912 (France/UK)
Sherlock Holmes played by Georges Tréville
Dr. Watson played by Mr. Moyse

A Canine Sherlock Holmes
(F) – 1912 (UK)
Sherlock Holmes Uncredited

Charlie Colms and the Dancer's Necklace
(F) – 1912 (France)
Sherlock Holmes Uncredited

Charlie Colms and the Knave of Spades
(F) – 1912 (France)
Sherlock Holmes Uncredited

The Copper Beeches
(F) – 1912 (France/UK)
Sherlock Holmes played by Georges Tréville
Dr. Watson played by Mr.Moyse

Cousins of Sherlock Holmes AKA Cousins of Sherlocko
(F) – 1912 (USA)
Sherlock Holmes Uncredited

The Dandies Club
(F) – 1912 (France)
Sherlock Holmes Uncredited

Dupin and the Stolen Necklace
(F) – 1912 (UK)
Sherlock Holmes Uncredited

The Flag of Distress
(F) - 1912 (USA)
Sherlock Holmes played by Hayward. S.
"Red" Mack

The Hypnotic Detective
(F) - 1912 (USA)
Sherlock Holmes played by Charles Clary as
Professor Locksley

The Kid and the Sleuth
(F) -1912 (USA)
Sherlock Holmes Uncredited

A Midget Sherlock Holmes
(F) – 1912 (France)
Sherlock Holmes Uncredited

Mr. Whoops, the Detective
(F) – 1912 (USA)
Sherlock Holmes Uncredited

The Musgrave Ritual
(F) – 1912 (France/UK)
Sherlock Holmes played by Georges Tréville
Dr. Watson played by Mr. Moyse

The Mystery of Boscombe Vale
(F) – 1912 (France/UK)
Sherlock Holmes played by Georges Tréville
Dr. Watson played by Mr. Moyse

The Pipe
(F) – 1912 (USA)
Sherlock Holmes Uncredited

The Reigate Squires
(F) – 1912 (France/UK)
Sherlock Holmes played by Georges Tréville
Dr. Watson played by Mr. Moyse

The Right Clue
(F) – 1912 (USA)
Sherlock Holmes Uncredited

The Robbery at the Railroad Station
(F) – 1912 (USA)
Sherlock Holmes Uncredited

**Schlau, Schlauer, am Schlauesten AKA
Smart, Clever, the Smartest**
(F) – 1912 (France/Germany)
Sherlock Holmes Uncredited

**Sherlok Holmes und seine Arbeit AKA
Sherlock Holmes and his Work**
(F) – 1912 (Germany)
Sherlock Holmes Uncredited

Silver Blaze
(F) – 1912 (France/UK)
Sherlock Holmes played by Georges Tréville
Dr. Watson played by Mr. Moyse

The Speckled Band
(F) – 1912 (France/UK)
Sherlock Holmes played by Georges Tréville
Dr. Watson played by Mr. Moyse

The Stolen Papers
(F) – 1912 (France/UK)
Sherlock Holmes played by Georges Tréville
Dr. Watson played by Mr. Moyse

Surelock Jones, Detective
(F) – 1912 (USA)
Sherlock Holmes Uncredited

Their First Kidnapping Case
(F) – 1912 (USA)
Sherlock Holmes Uncredited

**Three-Fingered Kate: The Case of the
Chemical Fumes**
(F) – 1912 (UK)
Sherlock Holmes played by Charles Calvert
as Sheerluck Finch

**Three-Fingered Kate: The Pseudo-
Quartette**
(F) – 1912 (UK)
Sherlock Holmes played by Charles Calvert
as Sheerluck Finch

Three-Fingered Kate: The Wedding Presents
(F) – 1912 (UK)
Sherlock Holmes played by Charles Calvert as Sheerluck Finch

The Amateur Sleuth
(F) - 1913 (UK)
Sherlock Holmes Uncredited

Burstup Holmes AKA Burstup Homes, Detective
(F) -1913 (USA)
Sherlock Holmes played by Fraunie Fraunholz as Burstup Homes

Burstup Homes' Murder Case
(F) -1913 (USA)
Sherlock Holmes played by Fraunie Fraunholz as Burstup Homes

The Case of the Missing Girl
(F) – 1913 (USA)
Sherlock Holmes played by Fraunie Fraunholz as Burstup Homes

Fricot als Sherlock Holmes Konkurrent AKA Fricot Competes with Sherlock Holmes
(F) – 1913 (Italy)
Sherlock Holmes Uncredited

Griffard's Claw
(F) – 1913 (Italy)
Sherlock Holmes Uncredited

Homlock Shermes
(F) – 1913 (USA)
Sherlock Holmes Uncredited

The Mystery of the Lost Cat
(F) – 1913 (USA)
Sherlock Holmes played by Fraunie Fraunholz as Burstup Homes

One on Tooty
(F) – 1913 (France)
Sherlock Holmes Uncredited

Piu forte che Sherlock Holmes AKA Stronger Than Sherlock Holmes
(F) – 1913 (Italy)
Sherlock Holmes Uncredited

The Sherlock Holmes Girl
(F) – 1913 (USA)
Sherlock Holmes played by Bliss Milford as Sally

Sherlock Holmes Solves the Sign of Four
(F) – 1913 (USA)
Sherlock Holmes played by Harry Benham
Dr. Watson played by Charles Gunn

The Sleuths at the Floral Parade
(F) – 1913 (USA)
Sherlock Holmes Uncredited

The Sleuths' Last Stand
(F) – 1913 (USA)
Sherlock Holmes Uncredited

The Stolen Purse
(F) – 1913 (USA)
Sherlock Holmes Uncredited

Their First Execution
(F) – 1913 (USA)
Sherlock Holmes Uncredited

The Tongue Mark
(F) – 1913 (USA)
Sherlock Holmes played by Fred Mace as Sureshock Holmes

Tweedledum and the Necklace
(F) – 1913 (Italy)
Sherlock Holmes Uncredited

A Would-Be Detective
(F) – 1913 (USA)
Sherlock Holmes Uncredited

Another Tale
(A) – 1914 (USA)
Sherlock Holmes Uncredited

Der Hund von Baskerville AKA The Hound of the Baskervilles
(F) – 1914 (Germany)
Sherlock Holmes played by Alwin Neuß

Der Hund von Baskerville I AKA Das einsame Haus AKA Das Unheimliche Haus AKA The Hound of the Baskerville
(F) – 1914 (Germany)
Sherlock Holmes played by Alwin Neuss

En rædsom Nat AKA A Horrible Nat
(F) – 1914 (Denmark)
Sherlock Holmes Uncredited

The Foreign Spies
(F) – 1914 (UK)
Sherlock Holmes played by Arthur Finn

Gontran émule de Sherlock Holmes AKA Gontran emulates Sherlock Holmes
(F) – 1914 (France)
Sherlock Holmes played by René Gréhan as Gontran

Harry's Waterloo
(F) – 1914 (USA)
Sherlock Holmes Uncredited

Karlchens Traum als Sherlok Holmes AKA Karl's dream of Sherlok Holmes
(F) – 1914 (Germany)
Sherlock Holmes Uncredited

Piu forte che Sherlock Holmes II AKA Stronger than Sherlock Holmes
(F) – 1914 (Italy)
Sherlock Holmes Uncredited

Sherlock Bonehead
(F) - 1914 (USA)
Sherlock Holmes played by Lloyd Hamilton as Sherlock Bonehead

The Sherlock Boob
(F) – 1914 (USA)
Sherlock Holmes Uncredited

Sherlock Holmes Contra Dr Mors AKA Detektiv Braun AKA Sherlock Holmes vs. Dr Mors
(F) – 1914 (Germany)
Sherlock Holmes played by Ferdinand Bonn

Sherlock Holmes roulé par Rigadin AKA Sherlock Holmes rolled by Rigadin
(F) – 1914 (France)
Sherlock Holmes played by André Simon

Shorty and Sherlock Holmes
(F) – 1914 (USA)
Sherlock Holmes Uncredited

Some Hero
(F) – 1914 (USA)
Sherlock Holmes played by Charles De Forrest as Sherlock Doyle

A Study in Scarlet
(F) - 1914 (UK)
Sherlock Holmes played by James Bragington

A Study in Scarlet
(F) – 1914 (USA)
Sherlock Holmes played by Francis Ford
Dr. Watson played by Jack Francis

The Tale of a Chicken
(F) – 1914 (USA)
Sherlock Holmes played by Maha Raja as Sherlock Jackson Holmes

The Crimson Sabre
(F) – 1915 (USA)
Sherlock Holmes played by Hector Dion

The Crogmere Ruby
(F) – 1915 (USA)
Sherlock Holmes played by Hector Dion

Das dunkle Schloß AKA The Dark Castle
(F) – 1915 (Germany)
Sherlock Holmes played by Eugen Burg

Der Floh von Baskerville AKA The Flea of Baskerville
(F) – 1915 (Germany)
Sherlock Holmes Uncredited

Der Hund von Baskerville III AKA Das unheimliche Zimmer AKA Das geheimnisvolle Zimmer AKA The Mysterious Room
(F) – 1915 (Germany)
Sherlock Holmes played by Alwin Neuss

Der Hund von Baskerville IV AKA Der Geheimnisvolle Hund AKA The Mysterious Dog
(F) – 1915 (Germany)
Sherlock Holmes played by Alwin Neuss

**Die Sage vom Hund von Baskerville
AKA Wie entstand der Hund von
Baskerville AKA The Origin of the
Baskerville Hound**
(F) – 1915 (Germany)
Sherlock Holmes played by Alwin Neuss

**Ein Schrei in der Nacht AKA A Scream in
the Night**
(F) – 1915 (Germany)
Sherlock Holmes played by Alwin Neuss

The Great Detective
(F) – 1915 (USA)
Sherlock Holmes Uncredited

**Kri Kri Contro Sherlock Holmes AKA Kri
Kri vs. Sherlock Holmes**
(F) – 1915 (Italy)
Sherlock Holmes Uncredited

Sherlock Boob, Detective
(F) – 1915 (USA)
Sherlock Holmes Uncredited

A Study in Skarlit
(F) – 1915 (UK)
Sherlock Holmes played by Fred Evans as
Sherlokz Homz

William Voss, der Milliondieb AKA
William Voss, the Millionth Person
(F) – 1915 (Germany)
Sherlock Holmes played by Theodor Burgarth

Adventures of Mr. Nobody Holmes
(A) – 1916 (USA)
Sherlock Holmes Uncredited

Der Wärwolf AKA The Warwolf
(F) - 1916 (Germany)
Sherlock Holmes Uncredited

Die Hand AKA The Hand
(F) - 1916 (Germany)
Sherlock Holmes Uncredited

The Mystery of the Leaping Fish
(F) – 1916 (USA)
Sherlock Holmes played by Douglas
Fairbanks as Coke Ennyday

Sherlock Holmes
(F) – 1916 (USA)
Sherlock Holmes played by William Gillette
Dr. Watson played by Edward Fielding

**Sherlock Holmes auf Urlaub AKA
Mensch, leih' mir Deine AKA Sherlock
Holmes on Vacation**
(F) – 1916 (Germany)
Sherlock Holmes played by Alwin Neuss /Carl
Schönfeld

A Society Sherlock
(F) – 1916 (USA)
Sherlock Holmes Uncredited

The Valley of Fear
(F) – 1916 (UK)
Sherlock Holmes played by H. A. Saintsbury
Dr. Watson played by Arthur M. Cullin

A Villainous Villain
(F) – 1916 (USA)
Sherlock Holmes played by Hughie Mack as
Sherlock Oomph

The Waif
(F) - 1916 (UK)
Sherlock Holmes Uncredited

Der Erdstrommotor AKA The Motor
(F) - 1917 (Germany)
Sherlock Holmes played by Hugo Flink

Die Kassette AKA The Castle
(F) – 1917 (Germany)
Sherlock Holmes played by Hugo Flink

**John Barrens und seine Geliebte AKA
John Barrens and His Lover**
(F) – 1917 (Germany)
Sherlock Holmes played by Kurt Brenkendorff

**Memoiren des Satans, Die. I: Doktor
Mors AKA The Memories of Satan**
(F) – 1917 (Germany)
Sherlock Holmes played by Ferdinand Bonn

A Modern Sherlock
(F) – 1917 (USA)
Sherlock Holmes played by Eddie Sutherland

Sherlock Holmes Nächtliche Begegnung AKA Sherlock Holmes Nightly Encounter
(F) – 1917 (Germany)
Sherlock Holmes Uncredited

The Whispered Name
(F) – 1917 (USA)
Sherlock Holmes played by T.D. Crittenden as Holmes

A Black Sherlock Holmes
(F) – 1918 (USA)
Sherlock Holmes played by Sam Robinson as Knick Garter Dr. Watson played by Rudolph Tatum as Rheuma Tism

Brockhaus, Band dreizehn AKA Brockhaus, Volume Thirteen
(F) – 1918 (Germany)
Sherlock Holmes played by Ferdinand Bonn

Das Schicksal der Renate Jongk AKA The fate of Renate Jongk
(F) – 1918 (Germany)
Sherlock Holmes played by Ferdinand Bonn

Den firbenede Sherlock Holmes AKA Ras og Lux som Detektiver AKA Ras and Lux are Detectives
(F) – 1918 (Denmark)
Sherlock Holmes Uncredited

Der Schlangenring AKA The Snake Ring
(F) - 1918 (Germany) Sherlock Holmes played by Ferdinand Bonn

Die Dose des Kardinals AKA The cardinal's box
(F) – 1918 (Germany)
Sherlock Holmes played by Ferdinand Bonn

Die Giftplombe AKA The poison seal
(F) – 1918 (Germany)
Sherlock Holmes played by Ferdinand Bonn

Die Indische Spinne AKA The Indian spider
(F) – 1918 (Germany)
Sherlock Holmes played by Hugo Flink

Little Miss Sherlock
(F) – 1918 (USA)
Sherlock Holmes played by Zoe Rae as Little Miss Sherlock

Midnight Trail
(F) – 1918 (USA)
Sherlock Holmes Uncredited

Rotterdam - Amsterdam
(F) – 1918 (Germany)
Sherlock Holmes played by Viggo Larsen

Sherlock Ambrose
(F) – 1918 (USA)
Sherlock Holmes played by Mack Swain as Sherlock Ambrose

Was Er im Spiegel Sah AKA What He Saw in the Mirror
(F) – 1918 (Germany)
Sherlock Holmes played by Ferdinand Bonn

X Y Z
(F) – 1918 (Germany)
Sherlock Holmes Uncredited

An den Herrn Ersten Staatsanwalt AKA To the First Attorney
(F) – 1919 (Germany)
Sherlock Holmes played by Ferdinand Bonn

Das Haus ohne Fenster AKA The House Without Windows
(F) – 1920 (Germany)
Sherlock Holmes Uncredited

Der Hund von Baskerville V AKA Doktor Macdonald's Sanatorium AKA MacDonald's Sanatorium
(F) – 1920 (Germany)
Sherlock Holmes played by Erich Kaiser-Titz

Der Mord im Spendid Hotel AKA Murder at the Splendid Hotel
(F) – 1919 (Germany)
Sherlock Holmes played by Kurt Brenkendorff

Drei Tage Tot AKA Three Days Dead
(F) – 1919 (Germany)
Sherlock Holmes Uncredited

Echte Perlen AKA Real Pearls
(F) – 1919 (Germany)
Sherlock Holmes played by Ferdinand Bonn

Sherlock Hawkshaw and Company
(A) – 1920 (USA)
Sherlock Holmes Uncredited

1921 – 1930

The Adventures of Sherlock Holmes
(F) – 1921 (UK)
Sherlock Holmes played by Eille Norwood Dr. Watson played by Hubert Willis

Das Detektivduel AKA Harry Hill contra Sherlock Holmes AKA Harry Hill vs. Sherlock Holmes
(F) – 1921 (Germany)
Sherlock Holmes Uncredited

Saetta piu forte di Sherlock Holmes AKA Lightening Stronger than Sherlock Holmes
(F) – 1921 (Italy)
Sherlock Holmes Uncredited

Sherlock Brown
(F) – 1921 (USA)
Sherlock Holmes played by Bert Lytell as William "Sherlock" Brown

Camillo Emulo di Sherlock Holmes AKA Camillo Emulo and Sherlock Holmes
(F) – 1922 (Italy)
Sherlock Holmes Uncredited

The Jazz Hounds
(F) -1922 (USA)
Sherlock Holmes played by Lawrence Chenault

Sherlock Holmes
(F) – 1922 (USA)
Sherlock Holmes played by John Barrymore
Dr. Watson played by Roland Young

Sherlock Holmes AKA Moriarty
(F) – 1922 (USA)
Sherlock Holmes played by John Barrymore
Dr. Watson played by Roland Young

Únos bankéře Fuxe
(F) – 1923 (Czech)
Sherlock Holmes played by Eman Fiala as Sherlock Holmes II

The Mysterious Mystery!
(F) – 1924 (USA)
Sherlock Holmes played by Mickey Daniels
Dr. Watson Joe Cobb

Sherlock, Jr
(F) – 1924 (USA)
Sherlock Holmes played by Buster Keaton as Sherlock, Jr.

Sherlock Sleuth
(F) – 1925 (USA)
Sherlock Holmes Uncredited

The Sleuth
(F) – 1925 (USA)
Sherlock Holmes played by Stan Laurel as Webster Dingle

Alice's Mysterious Mystery
(F) – 1926 (USA)
Sherlock Holmes played by Margie Gay as Alice

Slick Sleuths
(A) -1926 (USA)
Sherlock Holmes Uncredited

Do Detectives Think?
(F) - 1927 (USA)
Sherlock Holmes played by Oliver Hardy as Sherlock Pinkham

Sure-Locked Homes
(A) – 1928 (USA)
Sherlock Holmes Uncredited

Der Hund von Baskerville AKA The Hound of the Baskervilles
(F) – 1929 (Germany)
Sherlock Holmes played by Carlyle Blackwell
Dr. Watson played by Geroges Seroff

The Return of Sherlock Holmes
(F) – 1929 (USA)
Sherlock Holmes played by Clive Brook Dr. Watson played by H. Reeves-Smith

Herlock Sholmes in Be-a-Live-Crook, or Anna Went Wrong
(A) – 1930 (UK)
Sherlock Holmes Uncredited

Murder Will Out AKA A Tapestry of Detective Mysteries
(F) – 1930 (USA)
Sherlock Holmes played by Clive Brook

1931 – 1940

Fu er mo si zhen tan an AKA Fu and the Detective
(F) – 1931 (China)
Sherlock Holmes Uncredited

The Hound of the Baskervilles
(F) – 1931 (UK)
Sherlock Holmes played by Robert Rendel
Dr. Watson played by Frederick Lloyd

The Speckled Band
(F) – 1931 (UK)
Sherlock Holmes played by Raymond Massey
Dr. Watson played by Athole Stewart

The Sleeping Cardinal
(F) - 1931 (UK)
Sherlock Holmes played by Arthur Wontner
Dr. Watson played by Ian Fleming

Conan Doyle's Master Detective Sherlock Holmes AKA Sherlock Holmes
(F) -1932 (USA)
Sherlock Holmes played by Clive Brook Dr. Watson played by Reginald Owen

Lelíček ve službách Sherlocka Holmese AKA Lelíček helps of Sherlock Holmes
(F) – 1932 (Czech)
Sherlock Holmes played by Martin Frič

The Missing Rembrandt
(F) – 1932 (UK)
Sherlock Holmes played by Arthur Wontner
Dr. Watson played by Ian Fleming

Sherlock Holmes
(F) – 1932 (USA)
Sherlock Holmes played by Clive Brook Dr. Watson played by Reginald Owen

The Sign of Four: Sherlock Holmes' Greatest Case
(F) – 1932 (UK)
Sherlock Holmes played by Arthur Wontner
Dr. Watson played by Ian Hunter

Lost in Limehouse
(F) - 1933 (USA)
Sherlock Holmes played by Olaf Hytten Dr. Watson played by Charles McNaughton

The Radio Murder Mystery
(F) – 1933 (USA)
Sherlock Holmes played by Richard Gordon
Dr. Watson played by Leigh Lovel

A Study in Scarlet
(F) – 1933 (USA)
Sherlock Holmes played by Reginald Owen
Dr. Watson Watson played by Warburton Gamble

The Triumph of Sherlock Holmes
(F) – 1935 (UK)
Sherlock Holmes played by Arthur Wontner
Dr. Watson played by Ian Fleming

Silver Blaze
(F) – 1936 (UK)
Sherlock Holmes played by Arthur Wontner
Dr. Watson played by Ian Fleming

Der Hund von Baskerville AKA The Hound of the Baskervilles
(F) – 1937 (Germany)
Sherlock Holmes played by Bruno Güttner
Dr. Watson played by Fritz Odemar

Der Mann, der Sherlock Holmes war AKA The man who was Sherlock Holmes
(F) – 1937 (Germany)
Sherlock Holmes played by Hans Albers as Morris Flint, Dr. Watson played by Heinz Rühmann as Mackay McPherson

Die graue Dame AKA The Gray Lady
(F) – 1937 (Germany)
Sherlock Holmes played by Hermann Speelmans as Jimmy Ward

The Three Garridebs
(F) – 1937 (USA)
Sherlock Holmes played by Louis Hector Dr.
Watson played by William Podmore

The Adventures of Sherlock Holmes
(F) – 1939
Sherlock Holmes played Basil Rathbone,
Dr. Watson played by Nigel Bruce

Charlie McCarthy, Detective
(F) – 1939 (USA)
Sherlock Holmes played by Edgar Bergen
voicing the ventriloquist puppet Charlie
McCarthy

The Hound of the Baskervilles
(F) - 1939 (USA)
Sherlock Holmes played by Basil Rathbone,
Dr. Watson played by Nigel Bruce

Midnight Shadow
(F) – 1939 (USA)
Sherlock Holmes played by Richard Bates as
Junior Lingley

1941 – 1950

Sherlock Holmes and the Secret Weapon
(F) – 1942 (USA)
Sherlock Holmes played by Basil Rathbone,
Dr. Watson played by Nigel Bruce

Sherlock Holmes and the Voice of Terror
(F) – 1942 (USA)
Sherlock Holmes played by Basil Rathbone,
Dr. Watson played by Nigel Bruce

Crazy House
(F) – 1943 (USA)
Sherlock Holmes played by Basil Rathbone,
Dr. Watson played by Nigel Bruce

Sherlock Holmes Faces Death
(F) – 1943 (USA)
Sherlock Holmes played by Basil Rathbone,
Dr. Watson played by Nigel Bruce

Sherlock Holmes in Washington
(F) – 1943 (USA)
Sherlock Holmes played by Basil Rathbone,
Dr. Watson played by Nigel Bruce

The Spider Woman
(F) – 1943 (USA)
Sherlock Holmes played by Basil Rathbone,
Dr. Watson played by Nigel Bruce

The Case of the Screaming Bishop
(A) – 1944 (USA)
Sherlock Holmes played by John McLeish,
Dr. Watson played by Harry E. Lang

The Scarlet Claw
(F) – 1944 (USA)
Sherlock Holmes played by Basil Rathbone,
Dr. Watson played by Nigel Bruce

The Pearl of Death
(F) – 1944 (USA)
Sherlock Holmes played by Basil Rathbone,
Dr. Watson played by Nigel Bruce

The House of Fear
(F) – 1945 (USA)
Sherlock Holmes played by Basil Rathbone,
Dr. Watson played by Nigel Bruce

Pursuit to Algiers
(F) – 1945 (USA)
Sherlock Holmes played by Basil Rathbone,
Dr. Watson played by Nigel Bruce

The Woman in Green
(F) – 1945 (USA)
Sherlock Holmes played by Basil Rathbone
Dr. Watson played by Nigel Bruce

Dressed to Kill AKA Sherlock Holmes and the Secret Code
(F) – 1946 (USA)
Sherlock Holmes played by Basil Rathbone
Dr. Watson played by Nigel Bruce

The Great Piggy Bank Robbery
(A) – 1946 (USA)
Sherlock Holmes played by Mel Blanc

Terror by Night
(F) – 1946 (USA)
Sherlock Holmes played by Basil Rathbone,
Dr. Watson played by Nigel Bruce

Arsenio Lupin
(F) – 1947 (Mexico)
Sherlock Holmes played by José Baviera

Howdy Doody
(T) – 1947- 1954 (USA)
Sherlock Holmes played by Dayton Allen (1947-49) & Allen Swift (1949-54) as the Inspector John J. Fadoozle puppet.

Shivering Sherlocks
(F) – 1948 (USA)
Sherlock Holmes played Larry Fine

Sherlock Holmes in the Mystery of the Sen Sen Murder
(T) – 1949 (USA)
Sherlock Holmes played by Milton Berle Dr. Watson played by Victor Moore

Your Showtime: The Adventure of the Speckled Band
(T) – 1949 (USA)
Sherlock Holmes played by Alan Napier Dr. Watson played by Melville Cooper

The Colgate Comedy Hour with Jerry Lewis
(T) – 1950 (USA)
Sherlock Holmes played by Jerry Lewis as Sherlock Fink

1951 – 1960

The Adventure of the Mazarin Stone
(T) - 1951 (UK)
Sherlock Holmes played by Andrew Osborn, Dr. Watson played by Philip King

The Man who Disappeared
(T) – 1951 (USA/UK)
Sherlock Holmes played by John Longden, Dr. Watson played by Campbell Singer

We Present Alan Wheatley as Mr. Sherlock Holmes in...
(T) - 1951 (UK)
Sherlock Holmes played by Alan Wheatley, Dr. Watson played by Raymond Francis

The Adventure of the Black Baronet
(T) - 1953 (USA)
Sherlock Holmes played by Basil Rathbone, Dr. Watson played by Martyn Green

The Haunted House
(T) – 1953 (USA)
Sherlock Holmes played by Paul Frees voicing Professor Lightskull, Dr. Watson played by Daws Butler voicing Doc Twiddle

Private Eye Popeye
(A) - 1954 (USA)
Sherlock Holmes played by Jack Mercer as Popeye dressed as Sherlock Holmes

Red Skelton Show
(T) - 1954 (USA)
Sherlock Holmes played by Red Skelton

Sherlock Holmes
(T) – 1954-1955
(USA) Sherlock Holmes played by Ronald Howard, Dr. Watson played by H. Marion Crawford

Sherlock Holmes liegt im Sterben AKA Sherlock Holmes is Dying
(T) – 1954 (Germany)
Sherlock Holmes played by Ernst Fritz Fürbringer, Dr. Watson played by Harald Mannl

Der Hund von Baskerville AKA The Hound of the Baskervilles
(T) – 1955 (Germany)
Sherlock Holmes played by Yeardly Smith, Dr. Watson played by Arnulf Schröder

The Sting of Death
(T) – 1955 (USA)
Sherlock Holmes played by Boris Karloff as Mr. Mycroft Holmes and Sherlock Holmes

Deduce, You say
(A) – 1956 (USA)
Sherlock Holmes played by Mel Blanc as Dorlock Holmes Dr. Watson played by Mel Blanc as Porky Watkins

Dolina strachu AKA The Valley of Fear
(T) – 1958 (Poland)
Sherlock Holmes played by Tadeusz Białoszczyński Dr. Watson played by Stanisław Libner

The Hound of the Baskervilles
(F) – 1959 (UK)
Sherlock Holmes played by Peter Cushing Dr. Watson played by André Morell

Box Top Robbery
(A) – 1960 (USA)
Sherlock Holmes played by Paul Frees as
Boris Badenov/ Hemlock Soames Dr. Watson
played by June Foray as Natasha Fatale/ Dr.
Watkins

1961 – 1970

Red Hot Riding Hoods
(A) – 1961 (USA)
Sherlock Holmes played by Jerry Hausner as
Hemlock Holmes

77 Sunset Strip: Baker Street Caper
(T) – 1962 (USA)
Sherlock Holmes played by Louis Quinn as
Roscoe

Rocky and Bullwinkle & Friends
(T) – 1962 (USA)
Sherlock Holmes played by Daws Butler

**Sherlock Holmes und das Halsband des
Todes AKA Sherlock Holmes and the
Deadly Necklace**
(F) – 1962 (Germany)
Sherlock Holmes played by Christopher Lee,
Dr. Watson played by Thorley Walters

The Gumby Show: Scrooge Loose
(A) – 1963 (USA)
Sherlock Holmes played by Dallas McKennon
as Gumby, Dr. Watson played by Mike
Labonte as Pokey

**The Jack Benny Program: The Murder
of Clayton Worthington**
(T) – 1963 (USA)
Sherlock Holmes played by Jack Benny

Burke's Law: Who Killed Supersleuth?
(T) – 1964 (USA)
Sherlock Holmes played by Carl Reiner as
Inspector House of Scotland

Mr. Magoo, Man of Mystery
(A) – 1964 (USA)
Sherlock Holmes played by Paul Frees Dr.
Watson played by Jim Backus as Mr. Magoo

The Addams Family
(T) – 1965 (USA)
Sherlock Holmes played by John Astin as
Gomez Addams

The Double-Barrelled Detective Story
(T) – 1965 (USA)
Sherlock Holmes played by Jerome Raphael

Sherlock Holmes
(T) – 1965 (UK)
Sherlock Holmes played by Douglas Wilmer,
Dr. Watson played by Nigel Stock

A Study in Terror
(F) – 1965 (UK)
Sherlock Holmes played by John Neville,
Dr. Watson played by Donald Houston

Cool McCool: The Odd Boxes Caper
(A) – 1966 (USA)
Sherlock Holmes Uncredited as Sherlock
Klotz

The Dean Martin Variety Show
(T) – 1966 (USA)
Sherlock Holmes played by Bill Cosby

Gilligan's Island: Up At Bat
(T) – 1966 (USA)
Sherlock Holmes played by Russell Johnson
as the Professor, Dr. Watson played by Alan
Hale Jr. as the Skipper

**Het Avontuur van de drie studenten
AKA The Adventure of the Three
Students**
(T) – 1966 (Belgium)
Sherlock Holmes Uncredited

The Monkees: Monkee See, Monkee Die
(T) – 1966 & 1967 (USA)
Sherlock Holmes played by Micky Dolenz Dr.
Watson played by Davy Jones

**Nápady ctenáre detektivek AKA Ideas
for Detective-Story Readers**
(F) – 1966 (Czechoslovakia)
Sherlock Holmes played by Frantisek Husák
Dr. Watson played by Jirí Bruder

Shirley Holmes
(T) – 1966 (Belgium)
Sherlock Holmes played by Paula Sleyp as
Shirley

Une Aventure de Sherlock Holmes AKA The Adventures of Sherlock Holmes
(T) – 1967 (France)
Sherlock Holmes played by Jacques François, Dr. Watson played by Jaques Alric

In the Footsteps of Sherlock Holmes
(D) – 1968 (UK)
Various depictions of Sherlock Holmes and John Watson

Iz rasskazov o Sherloke Kholmse AKA The Stories of Sherlock Holmes
(T) – 1968 (Russia)
Sherlock Holmes played by Nikolai Volkov, Dr. Watson played by Lev Krugily

Pervyy sluchay doktora Vatsona AKA The First Case of Doctor Watson
(T) – 1968 (Russia)
Sherlock Holmes played by Nikolai Volkov, Dr. Watson played by Vyacheslav Garin

The Prisoner: The Girl Who Was Death
(T) – 1968 (UK)
Sherlock Holmes played by Patrick McGoohan

Sherlock Holmes
(T) – 1964 – 1968 (UK)
Sherlock Holmes played by Douglas Wilmer and Peter Cushing, Dr. Watson played by Nigel Stock

Sherlock Holmes
(T) – 1968 (Italy)
Sherlock Holmes played by Nando Gazzolo, Dr. Watson played by Gianni Bonagura

La Valle della Paura AKA The Valley of Fear
(T) – 1968 (Italy)
Sherlock Holmes played by Nando Gazzolo, Dr. Watson played by Gianni Bonagura

The Best House in London
(F) – 1969 (UK)
Sherlock Holmes played by Peter Jeffrey, Dr. Watson played by Thorley Walters

High Jinks
(T) – 1969 (UK)
Sherlock Holmes played by Ray Alan, Dr. Watson played by Derek Dene

It's Tommy Cooper
(T) - 1970 (UK)
Sherlock Holmes played by Tommy Cooper

Ministry i Syshchiki AKA Ministers and Detectives
(T) – 1969 (Russia)
Sherlock Holmes played by Vasily Lanovoy

La risa española: Los 38 asesinatos y medio del Castillo Hull AKA The 38 and a Half Murders of Castle Hull
(T) – 1969 (Spain)
Sherlock Holmes played by Valeriano Andrés

Tich & Quackers
(A) – 1969 (UK)
Sherlock Holmes played by Ray Alan voicing Holmes sock puppet

Sesame Street
(A) – 1970 – 1972 (USA)
Sherlock Holmes played by Jerry Nelson as the puppet Sherlock Hemlock

Private Life of Sherlock Holmes
(F) - 1970 (USA)
Sherlock Holmes played by Robert Stephens, Dr. Watson played by Colin Blakely

O tlustém pradedeckovi AKA The Fat Prey
(F) – 1970 (Czechoslovakia)
Sherlock Holmes played by Jirí Holý

1971 – 1980

Arsène Lupin contre Herlock Sholmes: Le Diamant bleu AKA The Blue Diamond
(T) – 1971 (France)
Sherlock Holmes played by Henri Virlojeux as Herlock Sholmes, Dr. Watson played Marcel Dudicourt as Dr. Wilson

Dave Allen at Large
(T) – 1971 (UK)
Sherlock Holmes played by Dave Allen, Dr. Watson played by Michael Sharvell- Martin

Morcambe & Wise Show: The Return of Sherlock Holmes
(T) – 1971 (UK)
Sherlock Holmes played by Eric Morcambe & Ernie Wise

Sobaka Baskerviley AKA The Dog of Baskerville
(T) – 1971 (Russia)
Sherlock Holmes played by Nikolai Volkov, Dr. Watson played by Lev Krugily

They Might be Giants
(F) – 1971 (USA)
Sherlock Holmes played by George C. Scott, Dr. Watson Joanne Woodward

Touha Sherlocka Holmese AKA The Desire of Sherlock Holmes
(F) – 1971 (Czechoslovakia)
Sherlock Holmes played by Radovan Lukavský, Dr. Watson played by Václav Voska

La aventura de los bailarines AKA The Adventure of the Dancers
(T) – 1972 (Spain)
Sherlock Holmes played by Vicente Vega

The Carol Burnett Show: A Salute to Movie Detectives
(T) – 1973 (USA)
Sherlock Holmes played by Anthony Newley, Dr. Watson played by Harvey Korman

Goober and the Ghost Chasers: Is Sherlock Holme?
(A) – 1973 (USA)
Sherlock Holmes Uncredited as Detective Sergeant Roger Sherlock

The Hound of the Baskervilles
(T) – 1972 (USA)
Sherlock Holmes played by Stewart Granger Dr. Watson played by Bernard Fox

The New Scooby-Doo Moviess: Guess Who's Knott Coming to Dinner
(A) – 1972 (USA)
Sherlock Holmes Uncredited

Vot moya derevnya AKA The Village
(T) – 1972 (Russia)
Sherlock Holmes played by Juris Strenga

Elementary, My Dear Watson - The Strange Case of the Dead Solicitors: Comedy Playhouse Television
(T) – 1973 (UK)
Sherlock Holmes played by John Cleese Dr. Watson played by Willie Rushton

NBC Follies
(T) – 1973 (USA)
Sherlock Holmes played by Sammie Davis Jr. as Sherlock Jones

Rowan and Martin's Laugh-In
(T) – 1973 (USA)
Sherlock Holmes played by Dennis Allen, Dr. Watson played by Ernest Borgnine

Le chien des Baskerville AKA The Hound of the Baskervilles
(T) – 1974 (France)
Sherlock Holmes played by Raymond Gérôme, Dr. Watson played by André Haber

Das Zeichen der Vier AKA The Sign of Four
(T) – 1974 (Germany)
Sherlock Holmes played by Rolf Becker, Dr. Watson played by Roger Lumont

It's a Mystery, Charlie Brown
(A) – 1974 (USA)
Sherlock Holmes played by Snoopy, Dr. Watson played by Woodstock

Dr. Watson and the Dark Water Hall Mystery Television
(T) – 1974 (UK)
Dr. Watson played by Edward Fox

Michael Bentine's Potty Time: Sherlock Holmes
(A) – 1974 (UK)
Sherlock Holmes played by Michael Bentine as a Sherlock Potty, Michael Bentine as Dr. Watson as Watson Potty

Murder in Northumberland
(F) – 1974 (UK)
Sherlock Holmes played by Keith McConnell, Dr. Watson played by Anthony Searle

Yeshche raz o Sherlok Kholms
(T) – 1974 (Russia)
Sherlock Holmes played by Sergey Yursky, Dr. Watson played by Mikhail Danilov

The Adventure of Sherlock Holmes' Smarter Brother
(F) – 1975 (USA)
Sherlock Holmes played by Douglas Wilmer, Dr. Watson Thorley Walters

The Adventures of Shirley Holmes
(F) – 1975 (USA)
Sherlock Holmes Uncredited

The American Adventures of Surelick Holmes
(F) – 1975 (USA)
Sherlock Holmes played by David L. Chandler as Surelick Holms, Dr. Watson played by Frank Massey

De dwaze Lotgevallen van Sherlock Jones AKA The Silly Fate of Sherlock Jones
(F) – 1975 (Netherlands)
Sherlock Holmes played by Piet Bambergen as Sherlock Jones

Dawson's Electric Cinema
(T) – 1975 (UK)
Sherlock Holmes played by Les Dawson

The Interior Motive
(F) - 1976 (USA)
Sherlock Holmes played by Leonard Nimoy, Dr. Watson played by Burt Blackwell

The Mumbly Cartoon Show: Sherlock's Badder Brudder
(A) – 1976 (USA)
Sherlock Holmes Uncredited

The Muppet Show: Sherlock Holmes and the Case of the Disappearing Clues
(A) – 1976 (USA)
Sherlock Holmes played by Jim Henson as 'Rowlf' Sherlock Holmes, John Lovelady as Baskerville the Hound/Watson

Sherlick Holmes
(F) – 1976 (USA)
Sherlock Holmes played by Harry Reems as Sherlick Holmes, Dr. Watson played by Zebedy Colt

Sherlock Holmes in New York
(T) – 1976 (USA)
Sherlock Holmes played by Roger Moore, Dr. Watson played by Patrick Macnee

The Seven-Per-Cent Solution
(F) – 1976 (USA)
Sherlock Holmes played by Nicol Williamson, Dr. Watson played by Robert Duvall

Return of the World's Greatest Detective
(T) – 1976 (USA)
Sherlock Holmes played by Larry Hagman, Dr. Watson played by Jenny O'Hara

The Adventures of Steel Rod Holmes
(F) – 1977 (USA)
Sherlock Holmes played by Scott Allen Nollen, Dr. Watson played by Troy Jacobsen

The Case of the Missing Bird
(T) – 1977 (USA)
Sherlock Holmes played by John C. Eskridge, Dr. Watson played by Nick Tael

Silver Blaze: The Sunday Drama
(T) – 1977 (Canada/UK/USA)
Sherlock Holmes played by Christopher Plummer, Dr. Watson played by Thorley Walters

The Strange Case of the End of Civilization as We Know It
(T) – 1977 (UK)
Sherlock Holmes played by John Cleese, Dr. Watson played by Arthur Lowe

Murder by Decree
(F) – 1978 (Canada/UK)
Sherlock Holmes played by Christopher Plummer, Dr. Watson played by James Mason

My Dear Uncle Sherlock: ABC Weekend Specials
(T) – 1977 (USA)
Sherlock Holmes performed by Royal Dano, Dr. Watson played by Robbie Rist

The Hound of the Baskervilles
(F) – 1978 (UK) Sherlock Holmes played by Peter Cook Dr. Watson played by Dudley Moore

Sherlock Holmes and Moriarty's Secret Weapon
(F) – 1978 (USA)
Sherlock Holmes played by Jeff Nelson, Dr. Watson played by Charles Kline

SNL: The Case of the Scarlet Membrane
(T) – 1978 (USA)
Sherlock Holmes played by Michael Palin, Dr. Watson played by Dan Ackroyd

I sogni del signor Rossi AKA Mr. Rossi's dreams
(A) – 1978 (Italy)
Sherlock Holmes played by Giuseppe Rinaldi as Mr. Rossi

3-2-1: The Victorian Era
(T) – 1979 (UK)
Sherlock Holmes played by Chris Emmett

The Case of the Fantastical Passbook
(F) – 1979 (UK)
Sherlock Holmes played by Jeremy Young, Dr. Watson played by Robert Dorning

End of Part One: The Adventures of Sherlock Holmes
(T) – 1979 (UK)
Sherlock Holmes played by Dudley Stevens, David Simeon and Denise Coffey; Dr. Watson played by Dudley Stevens & David Simeon

Goluboy karbunkul AKA The Blue Carbuncle
(T) – 1979 (Russia)
Sherlock Holmes played by Algimantas Masiulis, Dr. Watson played by Ernst Romanov

The Treasure of Alpheus T. Winterborn: Children's Mystery Theatre
(T) – 1980 (USA)
Sherlock Holmes played by Keith McConnell, Dr. Watson played by Laurie Main

Scooby-Doo and Scrappy: The Night Ghoul of Wonderworld
(A) – 1979 (USA)
Sherlock Holmes Uncredited

Sherlok Kholms i doktor Vatson AKA Sherlock Homles and Doctor Watson: The Acquaintance
(T) – 1979 (Russia)
Sherlock Holmes played by Vasiliy Livanov Dr. Watson played by Vitali Solomin

Goluboy karbunkul AKA The Blue Carbuncle
(T) – 1980 (Russia)
Sherlock Holmes played by Algimantas Masiulis Dr. Watson played by Ernst Romanov

Priklyucheniya Sherloka Khomsa i doktora Vatsona AKA The Adventures of Sherlock Holmes and Dr Watson
(T) – 1980 (Russia)
Sherlock Holmes played by Vasiliy Livanov Dr. Watson played by Vitali Solomin

Sherlock Holmes and Doctor Watson
(T) – 1980 (Poland/UK)
Sherlock Holmes played by Geoffrey Whitehead, Dr. Watson played by Donald Pickering

1981 – 1990

The Private Eyes
(F) – 1980 (USA)
Sherlock Holmes played by Don Knotts as Inspector Winship, Dr. Watson played by Tim Conway as Dr. Tart

Sherlok Kholms i doktor Vatson: Znakomstvo AKA Sherlock Holmes and Doctor Watson
(T) – 1980 (Russia)
Sherlock Holmes played by Vasilij Livanov, Dr. Watson played by Vitalij Solomin

Give Me a Hand - Something's Afoot: The Fonz and the Happy Days Gang
(A) – 1981 (USA)
Sherlock Holmes Uncredited

Lupin tai Holmes AKA Lupin vs. Holmes
(A) – 1981 (Japan)
Sherlock Holmes played by Shingo Yamashiro, Dr. Watson played by Osami Nabe

The Mystery of the Willing Victims
(F) – 1981 (USA)
Sherlock Holmes played by Jeff Smith as Surelock Homes, Dr. Watson played by Jim Deuter as John Watson III

Standing Room Only: Sherlock Holme, The Strange Case of Alice Faulkner
(T) – 1981 (USA)
Sherlock Holmes played by Frank Langella, Dr. Watson played by Richard Woods

Body Dimensions AKA Les Mensurations
(A) – 1982 (Canada)
Sherlock Holmes Uncredited

The Hound of the Baskervilles
(T) – 1982 (UK)
Sherlock Holmes played by Tom Baker,
Dr. Watson played by Terence Rigby

The Jeffersons: Death Smiles on a Dry Cleaner
(T) - 1982 (USA)
Sherlock Holmes played by Sherman
Hemsley as George Jefferson

The Kenny Everett Television Show
(T) – 1982 (UK)
Sherlock Holmes played by Kenny Everett,
Dr. Watson played by Michael Sharvell-Martin

Fantasy Island: Save Sherlock Holmes
(T) – 1982 (USA)
Sherlock Holmes played by Peter Lawford,
Dr. Watson played by Donald O'Conner as a
security guard

Sherlock Holmes
(T) – 1982 (France)
Sherlock Holmes played by Paul Guers Dr.
Watson played by Philippe Laudenbach

Young Sherlock: The Mystery of the Manor House
(T) – 1982 (UK)
Sherlock Holmes played by Guy Henry

Alvin and the Chipmunks: The Cruise
(A) – 1983 (USA)
Sherlock Holmes played by Ross Bagdasarian
as Simon Dr. Watson played by Janice
Karman as Theodore

The Baker Street Boys
(T) – 1983 (UK)
Sherlock Holmes played by Roger Ostime,
Dr. Watson played by Hubert Rees

The Hound of the Baskervilles
(T) – 1983 (UK)
Sherlock Holmes played by Ian Richardson,
Dr. Watson played by Donald Churchill

Sherlock Holmes Baskerville Curse
(A) – 1983 (Australia)
Sherlock Holmes played by Peter O'Toole,
Dr. Watson played by Earle Cross

Sir Arthur Conan Doyle's The Sign of Four
(T) – 1983 (UK)
Sherlock Holmes played by Ian Richardson,
Dr. Watson played by David Healy

The Adventures of Sherlock Holmes
(T) – 1984-1985
Sherlock Holmes played by Jeremy Brett,
Dr. Watson played by David Burke

Muppet Babies: The Case of the Missing Chicken
(A) – 1984 (USA)
Sherlock Holmes played by Russi Taylor as
Baby Gonzo

Magnum, P.I: Holmes is Where the Heart Is
(T) – 1984 (USA)
Sherlock Holmes played by Patrick Macnee
as David Worth, Dr. Watson played by John
Hillerman as Higgins/Watson

Elementary Steel. Remington Steele
(T) – 1984 (USA)
Sherlock Holmes played by Peter Evans,
Dr. Watson played by William Griffis

The Case of Marcel Duchamp
(D) - 1984 (UK)
Sherlock Holmes played by Guy Rolfe,
Dr. Watson played by Raymond Francis

Sherlock Doo: The New Scooby-Doo Mysteries
(A) – 1984 (USA)
Sherlock Holmes Uncredited

Sherlock
(C) –1984 (UK)
Sherlock Holmes Uncredited

Sherlock Holmes Another Bow
(C) – 1984 (UK)
Sherlock Holmes Uncredited

Meitantei Holmes AKA Sherlock Hound
(T) – 1984-85 (Italy/Japan)
Sherlock Holmes played by Taichirô
Hirokawa, Dr. Watson played by Lewis
Arquette

The Masks of Death
(T) – 1984 (UK)
Sherlock Holmes played by Peter Cushing,
Dr. Watson played by John Mills

Dot and the Koala
(A) – 1985 (Australia)
Sherlock Holmes played by Keith Scott as
Sherlock Bones, Dr. Watson played by Keith
Scott

**Mi es Sherlokom Kholmsom AKA Me
and Sherlock Holmes**
(A) – 1985 (Russia)
Sherlock Holmes played by Vasilij Livanov

The Many Faces of Sherlock Holmes
(D) - 1985 (USA)
Various depictions of Holmes and Watson

Young Sherlock Holmes
(F) – 1985 (USA)
Sherlock Holmes played by Nicholas Rowe,
Dr. Watson played by Alan Cox

The Great Mouse Detective
(F) – 1986 (USA)
Sherlock Holmes played by Barrie Ingham as
Basil of Baker Street, Dr. Watson played by
Val Bettin as Doctor David Q. Dawson

**Henry's Cat: The Case of the Pilfered
Pearls**
(A) – 1986 (UK)
Sherlock Holmes played by Bob Godfrey as
Henry's Cat, Dr. Watson played by Bob
Godfrey as Chris Rabbit

Pound Puppies: In Pups We Trust
(A) – 1986 (USA)
Sherlock Holmes played by Pat Fraley as
Sherlock Bones

Fame: Holmes Sweet Holmes
(T) – 1986 (USA)
Sherlock Holmes played by Carlo Imperato
as Danny Amatullo, Dr. Watson played by
Billy Hufsey as Chris Donlon

The Case of Sherlock Holmes
(D) – 1987 (UK)
Various depictions of Holmes and Watson

Duck Tales: Dr. Jekyll & Mr. McDuck
(A) – 1987 (USA)
Sherlock Holmes played by Clive Revill as
Shedlock Jones

The Loss of a Personal Friend
(T) – 1987 (UK)
Sherlock Holmes played by Peter Harding,
Dr. Watson played by Ian Price

Murder on the Bluebell Line: QED
(D) - 1987 (UK)
Sherlock Holmes played by Hugh Fraser,
Dr. Watson played by Ronald Fraser

**The Real Adventures of Sherlock Jones
and Proctor Watson**
(T) – 1987 (USA)
Sherlock Holmes played by Mark Ritts,
Dr. Watson played by Michael Costello

The Return of Sherlock Holmes
(T) – 1987 (USA)
Sherlock Holmes played by Michael
Pennington, Dr. Watson played by Margaret
Colin as Jane Watson

**Young Sherlock: Doyle no Isan AKA
Young Sherlock: The Legacy of Doyle**
(C) – 1987 (Japan)
Sherlock Holmes Uncredited

**BraveStarr: Sherlock Holmes in the
23rd Century**
(A) – 1988 (USA)
Sherlock Holmes played by Pat Fraley Dr.
Watson played by Peter Cullen

**Elementary, My Dear Simon. Alvin and
the Chipmunks**
(A) – 1988   (USA)
Sherlock Holmes played by Ross
Bagdasarian, Jr. Dr. Watson played by
Janice Karman

Testimony
(F) – 1988 (UK)
Sherlock Holmes played by Rodney Litchfield

Time Exposures
(T) – 1988 (Canada)
Sherlock Holmes played by Philip Linfield

Without a Clue
(F) – 1988 (UK)
Sherlock Holmes played by Michael Caine,
Dr. Watson played by Ben Kingsley

Babar: The Missing Crown Affair
(A) – 1989 (Canada)
Sherlock Holmes played by Jacques Ferrière,
as Zéphyr (French version); Sherlock Holmes
played by Jeff Pustil as Zephir (English
version)

**Chip 'n Dale Rescue Rangers: Pound of
the Baskervilles**
(A) – 1989 (USA)
Sherlock Holmes played by Tress MacNeille
as Sureluck Jones

**Elementary, My Dear Worty. Worzel
Gummidge Down under**
(T) - 1989 (UK)
Sherlock Holmes played by Jon Pertwee,
Dr. Watson played by Ian Mune

**Elementary My Dear Winston. The Real
Ghostbusters**
(A) - 1989 (USA)
Sherlock Holmes played by Maurice
LaMarche, Dr. Watson played by Frank
Welker

**My Dear Watson: Alfred Hitchcock
Presents...**
(T) – 1989 (USA)
Sherlock Holmes played by Brian Bedford,
Dr. Watson played by Patrick Monckton

**Le Retour d'Arsène Lupin AKA The
Return of Arsene Lupine**
(T) – 1989 (France)
Sherlock Holmes played by Rade Serbedzija
as Herlock Sholmès, Dr. Watson played by
Branko Cvejic

On the Scent of the Baskerville Hound
(D) – 1989 (UK)
Various depictions of Holmes and Watson

**Opening Night at Rodney's Place: The
Adventures of Sherlock Holmes**
(T) – 1989 (USA)
Sherlock Holmes played by Rodney
Dangerfield, Dr. Watson played by Chuck
McCann

The Super Mario Bros. Show
(A) – 1989 (Canada/USA)
Sherlock Holmes played by Lou Albano

**The Adventures of Barratt Holmes: The
Case of the Phantom Police Killer**
(T) – 1990 (UK)
Sherlock Holmes played by Russ Abbot as
Barratt Holmes, Dr. Watson played by Jeffrey
Holland as Dr Wimpy

Beetlejuice: A-Ha!
(A) – 1990 (USA)
Sherlock Holmes played by Stephen
Ouimette as Sherlock Homely

**Elementary, My Dear What-Not. T.Bag
and the Pearls of Wisdom**
(T) – 1990 (UK)
Sherlock Holmes played by Georgina Hale,
Dr. Watson played by John Hasler

Hands of a Murderer
(T) – 1990 (USA/UK)
Sherlock Holmes played by Edward
Woodward, Dr. Watson played by John
Hillerman

Sherlock Holmes Leading Lady
(T) – 1991 (Belgium/ France/ Italy/
Luxembourg/ UK/ USA)
Sherlock Holmes played by Christopher Lee,
Dr. Watson played by Patrick Macnee

**Tales of the Rodent Sherlock Holmes:
Wilson the Notorious Canary Trainer**
(A) – 1990 (UK)
Sherlock Holmes played by Guyu as Roland
the Rat, Dr. Watson played by David Claridge
as Kevin the Gerbil

1991 – 2000

Brave Tales of Real Rabbits
(A) – 1991 (USA)
Sherlock Holmes played by Charlie Adler as Brainey Domes

The Case-Book of Sherlock Holmes
(T) – 1991-1993 (UK)
Sherlock Holmes played by Jeremy Brett,
Dr. Watson played by Edward Hardwicke

The Consulting Detective Mystery: Father Dowling Investigates
(T) – 1991 (USA)
Sherlock Holmes played by Rupert Frazer

The Crucifer of Blood
(T) – 1991 (USA)
Sherlock Holmes played by Charlton Heston,
Dr. Watson played by Richard Johnson

Elementary, My Dear Pan. Peter Pan and the Pirates
(A) – 1991 (USA/Japan)
Sherlock Holmes played by Jason Marsden,
Dr. Watson played by Jack Lynch

Elementary, Dear Data. Star Trek: The Next Generation
(T) – 1991 (USA)
Sherlock Holmes played by Brent Spiner,
Dr. Watson played by LeVar Burton

Jim Henson's Mother Goose Stories: Mother Hubbard
(A) - 1991 (USA)
Sherlock Holmes played by Mak Wilson as Sherlock Hubbard

Life Goes on: Lighter Than Air
(T) –-1991 (USA)
Sherlock Holmes played by Chris Burke as Corky, Dr. Watson played by Ann Orsi as Zoe

Sherlock Holmes: Consulting Detective
(C) -1991 (USA)
Sherlock Holmes played by Peter Farley,
Dr. Watson played by Warren Green

Sherlock Holmes en Caracas AKA Sherlock Holmes in Caracas
(F) – 1991 (Venezuela)
Sherlock Holmes played by Juan Manuel Montesinos, Dr. Watson played by Gilbert Dacournan

SNL: Sherlock Holmes's Surprise Party
(T) – 1991 (USA)
Sherlock Holmes played by Jeremy Irons,
Dr. Watson played by Phil Hartman

Elementary, My Dear Turtle. Teenage Mutant Ninja Turtles
(A) – 1992 (USA)
Sherlock Holmes played by Peter Renaday,
Dr. Watson played by Pat Fraley

Incident at Victoria Falls
(T) – 1992 (UK, Belgium, Italy & Luxembourg)
Sherlock Holmes played by Christopher Lee,
Dr. Watson played by Patrick Macnee

Mathnet: The Case of the Mystery Weekend
(T) – 1992 (USA)
Sherlock Holmes played by Joe Howard as George Frankley, Dr. Watson played by Toni di Buono as Pat Tuesday

The Other Side
(T) – 1992 (UK)
Sherlock Holmes played by Richard E. Grant

Raw Toonage: Sheerluck Bonkers
(A) -1992 (USA)
Sherlock Holmes played by Jim Cummings as Sheerluck Bonkers, Dr. Watson played by Jeff Bennett as Dr.Jitters

Science Fiction: Sherlock Holmes and the Case of the Missing Link
(T) – 1992 (UK)
Sherlock Holmes played by Reece Dinsdale
Dr. Watson played by Gerald Horan

Sherlock Goof: Goof Troop
(A) - 1992 (USA)
Sherlock Holmes played by Bill Farmer,
Dr. Watson played by Frank Welker

Sherlock Holmes: Consulting Detective Vol. II
(C) -1992 (USA)
Sherlock Holmes played by Peter Farley,
Dr. Watson played by Warren Green

Sherlock Holmes und die Sieben Zwerge AKA Sherlock Holmes and the Seven Dwarfs
(T) – 1992 (Germany)
Sherlock Holmes played by Alfred Müller as Hans Holms

The Adventures of Sherlock Howser: Doogie Howser M.D
(T) – 1993 (USA)
Sherlock Holmes played by Neil Patrick Harris, Dr. Watson played by Max Casella

The Hound of London
(F) – 1993 (Luxemburg/Canada)
Sherlock Holmes played by Patrick Macnee,
Dr. Watson played by John Scott-Paget

Pomoc, za kopcem je obr AKA There is a Fig Behind the Hill
(T) -1993 (Czechoslovakia)
Sherlock Holmes played by Radoslav Brzobohatý

Šplhající Profesor AKA The Climbing Professor
(T) -1993 (Czechoslovakia)
Sherlock Holmes played by Viktor Preiss,
Dr. Watson played by Josef Somr

The All New Alexei Sayle Show
(T) – 1994 (UK)
Sherlock Holmes played by Peter Capaldi,
Dr. Watson played by Alexei Sayle

Freddie Starr
(T) - 1994 (UK)
Sherlock Holmes played by Freddie Starr,
Dr. Watson played by Brian Murphy

Fu er mo si yu zhong guo nu xia AKA Sherlock Holmes and the Chinese heroine AKA Sherlock Holmes in China
(F) – 1994 (China)
Sherlock Holmes played by Fan Ai Li Dr. Watson played by Zhongquan Xu

The Memoirs of Sherlock Holmes
(T) – 1994 (UK)
Sherlock Holmes played by Jeremy Brett,
Dr. Watson played by Edward Hardwicke

Sherlock Holmes Returns AKA 1994 Baker Street
(T) –1993 (USA)
Sherlock Holmes played by Anthony Higgins

Sherlock: Undercover Dog
(F) – 1994 (USA)
Sherlock Holmes played by Huey the dog as Sherlock Bones

Animaniacs : Deduces Wild
(A) – 1995 (USA)
Sherlock Holmes played by Jeff Bennett,
Dr. Watson played by Jeff Bennett

Les Nouveaux Exploits d'Arsène Lupin AKA The new Adventures of Arsène Lupin
(T) -1995 (France)
Sherlock Holmes played by Joseph Sartchadjev as Herlock Sholmès, Dr. Watson played by Valentin Ganey

Sherlock Homie - The Case of Isabella the Maneater
(F) -1995 (USA)
Sherlock Holmes played by Sean Michaels as Sherlock Homie, Dr. Watson played by Julian St. Jox as Dr. Whatsup

Sherlock Holmes: The Great Detective
(D) – 1995 (USA)
Various depictions of Holmes and Watson

Wishbone : The Slobbery Hound
(T) – 1995 (USA) Sherlock Holmes played by Larry Brantley as Wishbone

In the Footsteps of Sherlock Holmes
(D) - 1996 (USA)
Various depictions of Holmes and Watson

Maurice Sendak's Little Bear: Little Sherlock Bear
(A) - 1996 (USA)
Sherlock Holmes played by Kristin Fairlie as Little Bear

Muppets Tonight
(A) - 1996 (USA)
Sherlock Holmes played by Bill Barretta

Oscar y Sherlock
(T) - 1996 (Spain)
Sherlock Holmes played by Francisco Basilo

Sherlock Holmes: The Case of the Temporal Nexus
(T) – 1996 (USA)
Sherlock Holmes played by Patrick Macnee

The Adventures of Shirley Holmes
(T) – 1997 (Canada)
Sherlock Holmes played by Meredith Henderson as Shirley Holmes

Animal Crackers: Sherlock Dodo
(A) – 1997 (Canada)
Sherlock Holmes played by Teddy Lee Dillon as Dodo

Sliders: Murder Most Foul
(T) – 1997 (USA)
Sherlock Holmes played by John Rhys-Davies as Maximillian Arturo

Pipe Dream Continues: An Irregular Look at Sherlock Holmes in Minnesota
(D) – 1998 (USA)
Sherlock Holmes played by James D. Wallace, Dr. Watson played by Terry O'Sullivan

The Hound of the Baskervilles
(T) – 2000 (Canada)
Sherlock Holmes played by Matt Frewer, Dr. Watson played by Kenneth Welsh

Vospominaniya o Sherloke Kholmse AKA The Memoirs of Sherlock Holmes
(T) - 2000 (Russia)
Sherlock Holmes played by Vasilij Livanov, Dr. Watson played by Vitalij Solomin

2001 – 2010

Les Dalton Contre Sherlock Holmes. Les Nouvelles Aventures de Lucky Luke AKA Lucky Luke vs. Sherlock Holmes: The New Adventures of Lucky Luke
(A) – 2001 (France/Canada)
Sherlock Holmes played by Eric Legrand

O Xangô de Baker Street AKA The Xango from Baker Street AKA A Samba for Sherlock
(F) – 2001 (Brazil/Portugal)
Sherlock Holmes played by Joaquim de Almeida, Dr. Watson played by Anthony O'Donnell

The Royal Scandal
(T) – 2001 (Canada/USA)
Sherlock Holmes played by Matt Frewer, Dr. Watson played by Kenneth Welsh

Sherlock Holmes in the 22nd Century
(A) – 1991–2001 (USA/UK)
Sherlock Holmes played by Jason Gray-Stanford, Dr. Watson played by John Payne

Sherlock Holmes à Trouville
(F) – 2001 (France)
Sherlock Holmes played by Hervé Gauem, Dr. Watson played by Jean-Pierre Lazzerini

Sign of Four
(T) - 2001 (Canada)
Sherlock Holmes played by Matt Frewer, Dr. Watson played by Kenneth Welsh

The Secret of Harlot Hill
(F) – 2001 (USA)
Sherlock Holmes played by Tyce Bune, Dr. Watson played by Gina Ryder as Dr. Emma Watson

The Case of the Whitechapel Vampire
(F) - 2002 (Canada)
Sherlock Holmes played by Matt Frewer, Dr. Watson played by Kenneth Welsh

The Hound of the Baskervilles
(T) – 2002 (UK)
Sherlock Holmes played by Richard
Roxburgh, Dr. Watson played by Ian Hart

**Sherlock Holmes: Mystery of the
Mummy**
(C) – 2002 (Ireland/Ukraine)
Holmes and Watson are uncredited

Tracey McBean: Sherlock Tracey
(A) – 2002 (Australia)
Sherlock Holmes played by Roslyn Oades as
Tracey McBean

**Elementary, My Dear Watson: An
Interview with Edward Hardwicke**
(D) – 2003 (UK/USA)
Sherlock Holmes played by Jeremy Brett,
Dr. Watson played by Edward Hardwicke

Sherlock Holmes: The True Story
(D) – 2003 (Canada)
Various depictions of Holmes and Watson

**The Late Shift, Comedy Inc. -
Disappearing Twin**
(T) – 2004 (Australia)
Sherlock Holmes played by Gabriel Andrews

**Sherlock Holmes and the Case of the
Silk Stocking**
(T) – 2004 (UK)
Rupert Everett Dr. Watson played by Ian
Hart

**Sherlock Holmes: The Case of the Silver
Earring**
(C) – 2004 (Ukraine/Ireland)
Sherlock Holmes played by Guy Harris,
Dr. Watson played by David Riley

Sherlock Chuckle: Chuckle Vision
(T) – 2004 (UK)
Sherlock Holmes played by Paul Chuckle,
Dr. Watson played by Barry Chuckle

**The Simpsons: Treehouse of Horror XV
- Four Beheadings and a Funeral**
(A) - 2004 (USA)
Sherlock Holmes played by Yeardly Smith as
Eliza Simpson, Dr. Watson played by Nancy
Cartwright as Dr. Bartley

**CSI: Crime Scene Investigation: Who
Shot Sherlock?**
(T) – 2005 (USA)
Sherlock Holmes played by Ted Rooney as
Dennis Kingsley, Dr. Watson played by Rod
McLachlan as Nelson Oakes

**The Shortest Casebook of Sherlock
Holmes**
(F) – 2005 (UK)   Sherlock Holmes played by
David Hayman, Dr. Watson played by Dave
Anderson

**The Strange Case of Sherlock Holmes &
Arthur Conan Doyle**
(T) – 2005 (UK)
Sherlock Holmes played by Tim McInnerny

**El Último Caso del Detective Prado AKA
The Last Case of Detective Prado**
(T) – 2005 (Puerto Rico)
Sherlock Holmes played by Eugenio
Monclova

**Veggie Tales: Sheerluck Holmes and
the Golden Ruler**
(A) – 2005 (USA)
Sherlock Holmes played by Mike Nawrocki as
Larry the Cucumber, Dr. Watson played by
Phil Vischer as Bob the Tomato

**Yibijstvo lorda Yoterbruka AKA The
Lord of Yoterbruka**
(A) – 2005 (Russia)
Sherlock Holmes played by Alexei Koltan,
Dr. Watson played by Alexei Koltan

God Rocks! BibleToons: Seek and Find
(A) – 2006 (Canada)
Sherlock Holmes played by Jordan Elgie as
Sherlock Splint, Dr. Watson played by Tyler
Seidenberg as Dr. Carb

Sherlock Holmes: The Awakened
(C) – 2006 (Ukraine/Ireland)
Sherlock Holmes played by Rick Simmonds,
Dr. Watson played by David Riley

**That Mitchell and Webb Look: Holmes
and Watson**
(T) – 2006 (UK)
Sherlock Holmes played by David Mitchell &
Robert Webb, Dr. Watson played by David
Mitchell & Robert Webb

Elementary My Dear Viewer
(D) – 2007 (UK)
Various depictions of Holmes and Watson

The Shackles of Sherlock
(D) – 2007 (UK)
Various depictions of Holmes and Watson

Sherlock Holmes Vs. Arsène Lupin AKA Sherlock Holmes: Nemesis
(C) – 2007 (Ireland/ Ukraine)
Sherlock Holmes played by Rick Simmonds,
Dr. Watson played by David Riley

Sherlock Holmes and the Baker Street Irregulars
(T) – 2007 (UK)
Sherlock Holmes played by Jonathan Pryce,
Dr. Watson played by Bill Paterson

Pinky Dinky Doo
(A) – 2008 (UK)
Sherlock Holmes played by India Ennenga as
Sherlock Pinky

Sherlock Holmes Kung Fu
(I) – 2008 (USA)
Sherlock Holmes played by Dillon Francis

The Trials of the Demon! Batman: The Brave and the Bold
(T) – 2009 (USA)
Sherlock Holmes played by Ian Buchanan,
Dr. Watson played by Jim Piddock

Bert and Ernie's Great Adventures: Ernlock Holmes
(A) - 2009 (USA/ Italy)
Sherlock Holmes played by Steve Whitmire
as Ernlock Holmes, Dr. Watson played by
Eric Jacobson as Bert

Sherlock Holmes
(F) – 2009 (USA)
Sherlock Holmes played by Robert Downey
Jr. Dr. Watson played by Jude Law

Sherlock Holmes Vs. Jack the Ripper
(C) – 2009 (Ireland/ Ukraine)
Sherlock Holmes played by Rick Simmonds,
Dr. Watson played by David Riley

The Armstrong & Miller Show
(T) - 2010 (UK)
Sherlock Holmes played by Alexander
Armstrong, Dr. Watson played by Ben Miller

Important Things with Demetri Martin: Sherlock Holmes, Victorian Bachelor
(T) – 2010 (USA)
Sherlock Holmes played by Demetri Martin,
Dr. Watson played by H. Jon Benjamin

La dernière enquête de Sherlock Holmes AKA The Last Survey of Sherlock Holmes
(F) – 2010 (Switzerland)
Sherlock Holmes played by Vincent Aubert,
Dr. Watson played by Michel Moulin

No Place like Holmes
(I) – 2010 (USA)
Sherlock Holmes played by Ross K. Foad,
Dr. Watson played by Mike Archer

Sherlock
(T) – 2010 (UK)
Sherlock Holmes played by Benedict
Cumberbatch Dr. Watson played by Martin
Freeman

Sir Arthur Conan Doyle's Sherlock Holmes AKA Sherlock Holmes
(F) – 2010 (USA)
Sherlock Holmes played by Ben Syder, Dr.
Watson played by Gareth David-Lloyd

Tom and Jerry Meet Sherlock Holmes
(A) - 2010 (USA)
Sherlock Holmes played by Michael York,
Dr. Watson played by John Rhys-Davies

2011 – Present

Bartitsu: The Lost Martial Art of Sherlock Holmes
(D) – 2011 (USA)
Various depictions of Holmes and Watson

The Charing Cross Caper
(I) – 2011 (UK)
Sherlock Holmes played by Steve Bowditch,
Dr. Watson played by Paul Norcross

Sherlock Holmes Game of Shadows
(F) – 2011 (USA)
Sherlock Holmes played by Robert Downey Jr. Dr. Watson played by Jude Law

Sherlock Holmes' London: The Investigation
(D) – 2011 (UK)
Various depictions of Holmes and Watson

Sherlock Holmes nevében AKA In the Name of Sherlock Holmes
(F) – 2011 (Hungary)
Sherlock Holmes played by Szénási Kristóf, Dr. Watson played by Ungvár Ádám

Sherlock Holmes and the Shadow Watchers
(F) – 2011 (Canada)
Sherlock Holmes played by Anthony D. P. Mann, Dr. Watson played by Terry Wade

Sherlock Holmes: Wherever he Goes the Mistery Follows the Pipe
(F) – 2011 (USA)
Sherlock Holmes played by Kevin Glaser, Dr. Watson played by Charles Simon

Sherlock Yack, Zoo-Détective
(A) – 2011 (France)
Sherlock Holmes played by Martial Le Minoux as Sherlock Yack, Dr. Watson played by Céline Melloul

Doctor Who: The Snowmen
(T) – 2012 (UK)
Sherlock Holmes played by Matt Smith as The Doctor

Elementary
(T) – 2012 – Present (USA)
Sherlock Holmes played by Jonny Lee Miller, Dr. Watson played by Lucy Liu

Epic Rap Battles of History: Batman vs. Sherlock Holmes
(I) – 2012 (USA)
Sherlock Holmes played by Zach Sherwin, Dr. Watson played by Kyle Mooney

Gravity Falls: Headhunters
(A) – 2012 (USA)
Sherlock Holmes played by John Oliver as a Sherlock Holmes wax figure

Holmes and Watson: College Years
(I) – 2012 (USA)
Sherlock Holmes played Aaron Butler, Dr. Watson played by David Craig

Holmes & Watson: Madrid Days
(F) – 2012 (Spain)
Sherlock Holmes played by Gary Piquer, Dr. Watson played by José Luis García Pérez

King Bachelor's Pad: Sherlock Homeboy
(T) – 2012 (USA)
Sherlock Holmes played by Andrew Bachelor

The Mary Morstan Mysteries
(I) – 2012-2015 (USA)
Sherlock Holmes played by Ross K. Foad, Dr. Watson played by Mike Archer

Sherlock Holmes and the Case of the Mysterious Vampire
(I) – 2012 (UK/USA)
Sherlock Holmes played by Andy Due, Dr. Watson played by Dustin Tylman

Sherlock Blue's Clues: College Humor Originals
(I) – 2012 (USA)
Sherlock Holmes played by Thomas Middleditch

Sherlock Bones
(F) – 2012 (UK)
Sherlock Holmes played by Mark Sloan as Sherlock Bones, Dr. Watson played by Lucy Love as Hotson

Sherlock Holmes Nevében AKA On Behalf of Sherlock Holmes
(T) – 2012 (Hungary)
Sherlock Holmes played by Szénási Kristóf Dr. Watson played by Ungvár Ádám

The Real Sherlock Holmes
(D) – 2012 (Canada)
Various depictions of Holmes and Watson

Testament of Sherlock Holmes
(C) – 2012 (UK)
Sherlock Holmes played by Kerry Shale, Dr. Watson played by David Riley

You Don't Know Jack
(T) – 2012 (USA)
Sherlock Holmes played by Tariq Leslie

The Case Of Violet Smith
(I) – 2013 (UK)
Sherlock Holmes played Nathan Carter,
Dr. Watson played by Lewis Wheelhouse

The Doctor's Case
(F) – 2013 (Canada)
Sherlock Holmes played by Kristopher
Bowman, Dr. Watson played by Kristian
Bruun

Disguise
(I) 2013 (UK)
Sherlock Holmes played by Vauxhall
Jermaine, Dr. Watson played by Alexander
Clarke

Family Tree: Country Life
(T) – 2013 (UK/USA)
Sherlock Holmes played by Jake Harders,
Dr. Watson played by Ashley Walters

Holmes University
(I) – 2013-2016 (USA)
Sherlock Holmes played by Ben Lord & Justin
Maldonado, Dr. Watson played by Chris
Rodriguez

How Sherlock Changed the World
(D) – 2013 (USA)
Sherlock Holmes played by Edward
Cartwright Dr. Watson played by Geraint Hill

**Murdoch Mysteries: The Return of
Sherlock**
(T) – 2013 (Canada)
Sherlock Holmes played by Andrew Gower as
David Kingsley

**Pete Holmes Show: Sherlock Holmes
Sucks at Deduction**
(T) – 2013 (USA)
Sherlock Holmes played by Pete Holmes,
Dr. Watson played by Matthew J. McCarthy

**Return of Sherlock Holmes: Murdoch
Mysteries**
(T) – 2013 (Canada)
Sherlock Holmes played by Andrew Gower as
David Kingsley

**Sherlock Holmes and the Case of his
Missing Girlfriend**
(I) – 2013 (USA)
Sherlock Holmes played by Nick Cloud,
Dr. Watson played by Dorian Cunningham

**Sherlock Homes: Detective of the
Barrio**
(F) – 2013 (USA)
Sherlock Holmes played by Shaun Fletcher as
Sherlock Homes, Dr. Watson played by
Patrick L. Peterson as Johnny 'Juan' Watson

**Sherlock Holmes and The Stolen
Emerald**
(F) – 2013 (UK)
Sherlock Holmes played Edward Daw,
Dr. Watson played by David King

**The Adventures of Jamie Watson and
Sherlock Holmes**
(I) – 2014-2016
Sherlock Holmes played by Shannen
Michaelsen, Dr. Watson played by Sara-
Renee Weatherby

The Diogenes Documentaries
(I) – 2014-2017 (UK)
Various depictions of Holmes and Watson

Famiy Guy: Secondhand Spoke
(A) – 2014 (USA)
Sherlock Holmes played by Seth MacFarlane,
Dr. Watson played by Cary Elwes

**Sharokku Houmuzu AKA Sherlock
Holmes**
(A) – 2014 (Japan)
Sherlock Holmes played by Kōichi Yamadera
Dr. Watson played by Wataru Takagi

**Sherlock Holmes Crimes and
Punishments**
(C) – 2014 (Ukraine/Ireland)
Sherlock Holmes played by Kerry Shale,
Dr. Watson played by Nick Brimble

**Sherlock Holmes I Ludzie Jutra AKA
Sherlock Holmes and People of
Tomorrow**
(F) – 2014 (Poland)
Sherlock Holmes played by Tomasz
Gwincinski

Sherlock: L'Enquête AKA Sherlock: Behind the Scenes
(D) – 2014 (France))
Sherlock Holmes played by Benedict Cumberbatch, Dr. Watson played by Martin Freeman

Sherlock Holmes Variety Hour
(I) – 2014 (USA)
Sherlock Holmes played Quaid Atkinson, Dr. Watson played by Caden Clegg

Unlocking Sherlock
(D) – 2014 (UK)
Sherlock Holmes played by Benedict Cumberbatch, Dr. Watson played by Martin Freeman

Baker Street
(I) – 2015 (Canada)
Sherlock Holmes played Hannah Drew, Dr. Watson played by Karen Slater as Jane Watson

Call me Sherlock
(I) – 2015-2016 (USA)
Sherlock Holmes played by Travis Ammons, Dr. Watson played by Tom Long

Herlock
(I) – 2015 (USA)
Sherlock Holmes played by Gia Mora, Dr. Watson played by Alana Jordan

Mr. Holmes
(F) – 2015 (UK/USA)
Sherlock Holmes played by Ian McKellen, Dr. Watson played by Colin Starkey

The Adventures of OG Sherlock Kush
(A) – 2015-2016
Sherlock Holmes played by Peter Serafinowicz, Dr. Watson played by Rich Fulcher

Houdini and Doyle
(T) – 2016 (Canada/UK)
Sherlock Holmes played by Mark Caven

Mysteries at the Castle
(T) – 2014-2016 (USA)
Sherlock Holmes played by Billy Freda

sHERlock Holmes
(I) – 2016 (USA)
Sherlock Holmes played by Helen Davies, Dr. Watson played by Lisa Bunker

Sherlock Holmes: The Devil's Daughter
(C) – 2016 (Ukraine/Ireland)
Sherlock Holmes played by Alex Jordan, Dr. Watson played by Andrew Wincott

The Unpublished Sherlock Holmes
(F) – 2016 (USA)
Sherlock Holmes played by David Engel, Dr. Watson played by James F. Trumm

Puppet Holmes
(I) – 2017 (USA)
Sherlock Holmes played by Carter Delaat, Dr. Watson played by Joey Matthews

Sherlock Holmes Contre Conan Doyle AKA Sherlock Holmes Against Conan Doyle
(D) – 2017 (France)
Various depictions of Holmes and Watson

Holmes & Watson
(F) - 2018 (USA)
Sherlock Holmes played by Will Ferrell, Dr. Watson played by John C. Reilly

Miss Sherlock
(T) – 2018 (Japan)
Sherlock Holmes played by Yûko Takeuchi, Dr. Watson played by Shihori Kanjiya

Sherlock Gnomes
(A) —2018 (US/USA)
Sherlock Holmes played by Johnny Depp, Dr. Watson played by Chiwetel Ejiofor

Search for a Holmes

Search for a Watson